I0762166

Omega:
An Icon Story

Riley Tune

Omega: An Icon Story 1st Edition

Cover Design by GoOnwrite.com

Edited by Carol Tietsworth

I can't thank you enough for buying this book! If, after reading, you find that you enjoyed it, please leave a review on the site from which it was purchased or any other book review site. I'd love to hear what you think. Also, if you would like to keep in touch with me, just use the following info.

If you want to learn more about me, visit my personal website:

www.rileytune.weebly.com

If you're curious about my approach to writing, if you are interested in writing, or just want to connect, subscribe to my YouTube:

www.youtube.com/onewordatatime

For my all- around random thoughts, follow my twitter:

www.twitter.com/rileytuneauthor

To the people that were embracing my imagination before I found writing as an outlet.
To the people that were reading my stories before they were even half good.
To the people that still continue to believe even when I don't.

Thank you.

TABLE OF CONTENTS

TABLE OF CONTENTS

PROLOGUE

If only a year's passing could make one forget about the serial killing maniac that targeted people with powers, that would certainly make things easier. Sadly, things like that you couldn't forget. You lived with it forever and tried to make the best of it. And the friends that were lost, and the lives that were changed seem to haunt you every day.

Such was the case with Hunter Monroe. The memories were there and so was the pain, but he refused to let them control his life. Maybe he succumbed to them the first month or so, but not now. Now, he wore the mask of a young man with everything together.

Slowly, he walked down the quiet halls of the location that was once the Imperial Lords' base, and couldn't help but smile as he thought back to his days at Purgatory academy. This smile wasn't out of love for the school that taught him how to use his powers and handle situations that a hero would face in the world. Far from it.

His time at Purgatory wasn't exactly what one would consider good. Verbal clashes with teachers, legendary fights, and mediocre grades don't really add to what one would call a good experience. No, the smile was because after all this time he currently found himself dressed in a uniform, heading to train with his fellow heroes. It was comforting to him that with everything that had changed, a small portion of his life had stayed the same.

This, along with a few other factors, had Hunter feeling pretty good inside. He was appreciated by the hero community, which for him was a first- time experience. He had a girlfriend that loved him, millions in the bank, and in a month his Paragon, his bad boy-themed toy line would be released nationwide. According to preorders, he was one of the most popular heroes in the world right now.

Yes, life was pretty good for him, and for some reason, he felt bad about it. He had wondered if he actually didn't deserve this good fortune, or if karma would catch up to him, and balance things out with enough bad to compensate for all his wins. "What in Atlas' name is wrong with you?" He asked himself under his breath. "That is a very good question, young lord," a voice said as Prism, the base's holographic assistant sprang into life.

Prism had a variety of preselected uniforms that made him look like a real-life butler. This current uniform even came with a bow tie and his ever-present white gloves.

"Don't," Hunter began, but then stopped. He was going to tell Prism not to call him that, but now it was acceptable. Once the Imperial Lords was disbanded, Prism still referred to the heroes in the base as *young lords.* Something that Hunter and the rest of the inhabitants reprimanded him about constantly. Now, the title was acceptable since the government ordered them to be rebranded, and established.

"Sorry," Hunter said as he walked through the hologram and up the hall. "This New Lords title we have now is taking some getting used to." "No doubt, I'm sure." Prism responded. "It is my belief that you are smarter than you look, and will eventually get used to it."

Hunter took in a deep breath and exhaled. While plenty had changed for him in the last year, Prism being a smartass wasn't one of them. "Hey Paragon," a voice called to him from down the hall. "After almost a year, you still can't say my name without laughing some?" Hunter asked. "And you say you love me. You know, I expected more effort from you," he said with a slight shake of the head.

"I do love you," Danielle said as she walked up to him and kissed him gently on the cheek. "I'm a rebel, boo. I do what I want. Weren't you the one that called me your little villain?" Hunter glanced at Prism, and saw the hologram flicker for a moment and then reappear with wide eyes. For a hologram, his shocked expression was very realistic.

"That was in private last night and my exact words were that you can be my villain in the sheets, hero in the streets. You know that's my motto," he replied, as he motioned to move by her. "Maybe you should work on a name for yourself. Then you'll stop laughing at mine."

Danielle shrugged in response.

"I'll see you in training, young lords," Prism said he flickered away one final time. Danielle laughed. "Leave it to you, to make a hologram feel uncomfortable." She said as she removed the rubber band from her wrist and began to pull her long black hair back. "I do what I can," he said as he paused at another door on the hall and tapped his knuckles on the frame.

"Yeah yeah, I'm ready," a voice came from inside the room. Perkins stepped out and looked at Hunter and Danielle. They were wearing the same training outfit as she was. Black shirt, gray shorts, black sneakers. All courtesy of one of the New Lords most recent sponsors.

Before she could say another word, a loud beeping sound came from inside her room.

Hunter leaned around her and tried to get a view inside. He wasn't surprised to find that Perkins' room was a mess. She had a love for not cleaning her personal space.

"What's that?" he asked as he craned his neck. "Something that likely isn't your business, Paragon." As she said his name, Danielle tried to conceal the laughter in her voice. "It's coming from her room, so it's her business."

"You're going to respect my name, you hear me, woman?" Hunter replied back through a laugh of his own. "I have the highest toy preorders in the last five years, I'll have you know. I'm even being courted by several cereal companies. So, suck it."

Danielle smiled at him and raised an eyebrow. "Remember, a hero in the streets. A hero in the streets," Hunter said as he turned back to look in Perkins' room. She had walked back inside and was holding something in her hand.

Hunter really couldn't see it from behind her. All he could see was her spiky blond- haired head moving around. "It's my multibox from back home," Perkins said. Her multibox was one of the two inventions she had on her when she arrived from Mo'eizus, the dimension of the Spellborn, a year ago.

This same box allowed her, for a brief time, to produce a pale green force field similar to the one Hunter could manifest. Before she told them it came from the box, many of the New Lords members thought it was her power.

"So, you fixed it?" Hunter asked. "Because I thought Danielle busted it during a training session." "Sorry again about that," Danielle said as she slapped Hunter in the back of the head while she walked by him to look over Perkins' shoulder.

"It was busted," she said as she reached for her goggles and looked through them at the multibox. Her goggles were the other invention that she brought with her. She twirled the multibox in her hand, looking at it from top to bottom. It was about the size as a deck of playing cards. Made out of shiny black metal, with a few buttons on top, and a dial on the side. "As far as I know, it should still be busted."

She twirled the box in her hands once more. "I'll look at it after training is over," she said. "It's not going to like, blow up the base or anything, is it?" A male voice came from behind them. As they turned, they saw the dark-haired Asian youth standing in the door.

Dressed like the rest of them, he sported a tight black shirt and gray workout shorts. "You're such a hero, Kevin. The mighty Power Prince, worried about a little box going boom," Hunter said in a mocking tone.

"Dude, I just don't want the base looking like the White House from Independence Day after the aliens attacked," he replied. Danielle exhaled. "Eventually, you're going to run out of tv and movie references for life situations."

He ignored her remarks. Danielle had only known Kevin a year, and she knew what she just said was far from true. The boy had a revolving knowledge on television and film that could be considered to be borderline scary to most people.

"Well, I am second in command around these halls. If anybody should know about a bomb it should be me, right?" Power Prince said as he placed a hand on Hunter's shoulder and sent a small charge through it. Hunter grunted as he felt a slight shock. "You realize we train in about five minutes, right?" Power Prince said. "You may want to keep your smartassness down to a minimum."

"That's like asking a model to not look good in designer clothes," Hunter replied as he moved in closer to whisper in the ear of Perkins. "It's not going to explode though is it?" Perkins shook her head. "I mean it shouldn't." "That's not comforting at all," Danielle said as she swiftly left the room, and stood behind Power Prince who was now out in the hall. "It would be a fresh dose of excitement though. I'm all for a big explosion, as long as I'm not at the center of it," she said, as Power Prince suddenly realized he had become her human shield.

"It looks like somebody is trying to reach me from back home, but until the box is repaired, I can't know for sure." As she spoke, she slipped off her shoes, and firmly placed her goggles around her eyes.

Then she placed the multibox on a desk in her room and pulled several long metal tools from the drawer. "Tell Flex I'm not coming to practice. It's unlikely a serious issue, but I want to make sure, so I can't put it off."

Power Prince cleared his throat. "Last time I missed practice, he drilled me with the responsibility talk, and I'm a full member." "Hey, screw you," Hunter replied. "Interns matter." Power Prince laughed. "Sure, buddy. Sure."

"I'm guessing he will cut her some slack," Danielle said. "Boyfriends are funny like that, aren't they," Perkins replied from a hunched over position at her desk. "Alright, now kick rocks guys. I can't focus with you standing there talking and fricking around."

"Dicking," Hunter replied as he walked out of the room. "Dicking around. I'll teach you the ways of a foul mouth if it's the last thing I do." Perkins didn't reply. Hunter glanced at Power Prince, and Danielle shrugged her shoulders and headed down the hall. The boys both followed her and left Perkins alone in her room.

In moments, they found Flex standing in the center of the training room. He actually wore a white shirt so tight that his muscles could be seen, and some blue sweatpants. Hunter looked down at himself and pointed to his outfit. "Why aren't you dressed like the rest of the team?" Flex shrugged. "Perks of being the leader I suppose," Flex said as his eyes moved from one of them to the other. "Where's Perkins?"

Danielle started jogging in place to warm up as Power Prince began to stretch. "She had some stuff to do, so she's staying behind," Flex frowned, and then looked at Power Prince. "You just let her skip? Come on Kevin, you're my number two." "Something he won't shut up about," Danielle chimed in. Kevin spread his feet and assumed a boxer potion as his fist began to glow with pink energy.

As he tossed practice punches, he glanced to Flex. "Dude, you know as well as I do, she isn't going to just drop a project. Maybe lover boy can convince her, but I can't." Flex paused for a few moments as he considered his options.

Perkins was like a dog with a bone when a project came up. Despite her determination, she really wasn't a tech whiz. She was just above average in that department. Flex knew he couldn't tell her that, though. If she skipped training, it must have been important.

He sighed "Just start the warmup, and then drills." Flex said as he walked, waited for the doors to open, and then proceeded to go speak one on one with his better half.

Flex cautiously made his way to Perkins' room to sort everything out. He felt that for some reason he had misunderstood. Surely, she wasn't going to miss practice. They had only been an item for a few months, but her dedication to things of importance was one of the reasons why he had fallen for and chosen her to be the one. This made him even more curious about what was keeping her away.

He was so determined to figure out what was going on that he didn't even question why Hunter was following him at a distance. In the back of his head, Flex could only assume Hunter thought he was being stealthy. It wasn't important now, but talking to Perkins was. Still, he made a mental note to add stealth training to his interns' weekly requirements.

When Flex arrived in her room, Perkins was still hunched over her desk and entranced by her multibox. Several pieces were sprawled on the desk, along with some wire, extra tools, and oddly, a stick of gum. "Got a minute?" Flex asked as he entered to room. "What's up?" Perkins asked without even looking up.

"Funny, that was going to be my next question for you. The team says you're skipping practice today." Flex paused for a moment. It was hard being both leader and lover. He was trying to make sure he handled the situation correctly. "So, what's up?" he asked.

Perkins shook her head and turned around at her desk. Flex looked into her vivid green eyes and almost ditched trying to be a leader all together for the more enjoyable role of lover. "I'm not sure, but I think somebody is trying to get a message to me." As she spoke, she held up her multibox. "I just can't figure out how to fix it." Flex felt his heart skip a beat. "Are you leaving?"

As soon as the words left him, he felt like he didn't conceal his fear well at all. He cursed at himself inside. Catching planes out the sky, saving kids, walking through a steady stream of bullets, that was easy for Flex. Being a boyfriend was still taking some getting used to. "Of course, I'm not leaving," Perkins replied. "At least I don't think so. I don't know." Then she looked up at Flex and twisted her lips.

"Aw, you're worried." Flex cleared his throat. "I, I." Perkins stepped to him and wrapped her arms around him. "It's something about having one of the strongest men on the planet stammering over the thought of you leaving him that makes a girl feel good inside." Flex smiled, and in return wrapped his arms around her.

As he did so he could feel the soft curves that were hidden under her baggy clothes.

"It makes me wish we slept together sooner than we did," Perkins said as she looked up at him. "But I'm glad we took our time. I wanted your first time to be special, and on your terms." Flex stiffened.

Perkins grimaced as she looked into the bulging eyes of her boyfriend. "What's wrong?" Flex began to breathe heavily as he turned to look at the open door to her room. He took in a deep breath. "Heard all that, huh?" Flex said as he looked at the door. Silence filled the air.

"What are you?" Perkins began, but Flex silenced her as he held up a finger. "I know you're there, Hunter," he said. On cue, Hunter stepped around the corner and was red in the face. "Wow. All this time I assumed Ken Doll over here was living it up." Hunter said through laughter. "All that strength, and fame. Those envied good looks. I just knew you were knocking some top-shelf boots. Come to find out, you're as innocent as a baby in a bank robbery."

Flex rolled his eyes and looked to Perkins. "Take as much time as you need." He kissed her on the cheek, turned to Hunter and jerked his head in the direction up the hall from which they came.

Perkins stood there for a moment until their footsteps were out of earshot and then put her attention back on her multibox. She had to figure it out, or she really would likely have to leave. It could have been anything, and she couldn't just stay, and not know.

She hadn't felt this type of focus in months. Since her time being here, she always kind of just went with the flow, and things worked out. Her multibox going off wasn't part of the flow, though. She tried to be casual about it in front of the others to avoid questions, but she was more worried that something was going on back in her home dimension. Considering that the only people that knew of this method to contact her were members of a rebel group, she had a strong feeling that whatever was going on, wasn't a social call.

CHAPTER 1:
TRAINING DAY

Hunter shifted his weight from side to side as he stood in a single line with Kevin, and Danielle. "Hey! You sure you don't want to join us?" Hunter said, as he turned his head and shouted to his adopted sister. Jen had recently made it to the base but wasn't dressed for training. Then again, she didn't usually train with the team anyway. She felt her talents were more of a gentle slash from a knife than the devastating blow from a hammer.

"Nope, I'm keeping my invisible ass over here and eating some sushi," Jen said as she pulled some food out from her bag. "You get me any?" Hunter asked. Jen didn't even respond, she just shook her head and kept unloading her bag.

"Bitch," Hunter mumbled under his breath as he eyed the sushi. He loved sushi. He loved it more when it was fried, covered in spicy mayo, and dunked in sauce. In reply, Jen casually gave him the middle finger and kept pulling out her food.

She loved her brother, but she only had the power of invisibility and the power to turn things intangible. Over the last year of her internship, she had learned that there were a time and place for powers like hers, and going toe to toe with a person that could lift trucks, withstand bombs, or create energy wasn't the time.

She also embraced that hand to hand wasn't her strong area, even though during her entire school career she told herself it would improve. As a result, she had invested the last year learning the art of swordplay from various teachers around town. To many of their surprise she was a natural. Combined with her powers, Jen had found a way to even the playing field, and often joked she would be an assassin for hire if being a hero didn't work out.

"I thought you just ate," Danielle said. Jen looked at her as she held a sushi roll in her hand. "Okay?" Danielle shook her head and cracked a smile. "Never mind." Jen closed her eyes and moaned as she proceeded to pop the portion of sushi in her mouth. "Oh, it's so good, too," she said in a mocking tone. Hunter refused to look. He wouldn't give her the satisfaction.

Not only that, but he refused to give his sister a reason to use the katana that rested near the wall. Jen had decided to name the weapon Big Whopper. It was a custom- made blade of her own design. Big Whopper had a handle made out of a carbon fiber alloy that was wrapped in red leather, a blade just over two feet in length, and Jen's Icon name etched into the steel.

"Alright, here's the agenda for the day," Flex said as he descended from the sky. "First and foremost, Perkins will not be joining us today in practice." Kevin and Danielle looked at each other, brows raised. This was a surprise to them. Flex usually got his way when it came to training, so for Perkins to get a slide was rather unexpected. Especially because of fixing a piece of equipment.

Kevin leaned into Hunter, "Dude. You followed him, how did the argument go. Was there yelling? Name calling?" Hunter thought for a moment. A year ago, he would have blurted out what he heard in an instant. Also, a year ago he and Flex were mortal enemies that had fought on two different occasions. Now, though, he respected Flex and his privacy. So, he shook his head. "Nope. They talked some and then Flex left her to it. Girlfriend perks. You know how it goes."

Kevin nodded his head as he turned back to Flex. He actually didn't know how it went at all. It had been so long since he had a girlfriend that he couldn't even recall how his last relationship ended. At that moment, Kevin made a decision to himself to eventually, find a woman. Everybody but him had a better half to relax and share with. Even Jen, and from what he gathered she had a history of being, well, friendly with various people.

Kevin had just decided to make sure his life as Power Prince didn't control his life. He had to make time for Kevin, too.

"First line of business, we practice." Flex continued. "We have gotten much better over the last year, but if we want to be taken seriously, we have to keep going." "Taken seriously?" Jen asked between mouths of food. "We took down Infinity. That nutbag had like," she swallowed some food loudly. "Twenty plus powers. If that's not serious, then I don't know what is."

Flex went to open his mouth, but Hunter raised a hand as if he was in school. "I got this one," he said to Flex as he walked out of formation and stood by his sister. Hunter felt it was his duty as a brother to embarrass, poke fun, and insult his sister at almost any given time, and damn if this wasn't the time. Especially after she refused to give him some sushi.

"Jen, dear sweet Jen, *we* didn't do anything. If I remember correctly, you were tied up with bands of energy when I arrived. We got you free, and then the rest of the fight you pretty much turned invisible and stayed out of the way." Jen shook her head. "Oh no. Don't paint me like I'm a victim." "But you *were* the victim," Kevin added in.

Jen flipped her middle finger to him and he promptly turned back around. "Let's not forget, I kept our ace in the hole concealed until he arrived, and put him in place to neutralize big bad Infinity. I played just as big a part as you two." "Meh, did you though?" Hunter asked as he shrugged his shoulders and began to laugh.

"I hate you," Jen said as she placed her last chunk of sushi in her mouth. Hunter, in turn, did a slight bow, "then my work here is done." He then turned around and went back to stand in line beside Kevin, completely missing the gesture that Jen gave him behind his back.

"Moving on," Flex said as he looked at them all. "Prism!" He called out. A few seconds went by, and then the holographic butler appeared beside Jen, causing her to jump. "Yes, young lord?" "Hang around, and keep time for us," Flex said as the flickering hologram did a slight bow. "Keep an eye on Perkins too, in case she needs anything."

"I have already chatted with her, sir. I'm standing in her room now, on standby." Prism was almost a god of the New Lords' base. He could be anywhere and everywhere within its walls, and network. He could clone himself to be in multiple places at once, hear all, see all, and insult all that was in the base or anywhere connected to the base's network.

Many of the New Lords' members had never seen a computer system as advanced as Prism, and even though they didn't admit it, he was a valuable member of the team that was almost a friend to them. He may have insulted them, but he also told them the unwanted unvarnished truth. Traits that some of the best friends have.

"Training will be about two hours or so," Flex continued. "For Atlas' sake. Two hours." Hunter said as he exhaled. "Training will be about three hours," Flex said in response. Kevin took in a deep breath and glared at Hunter, who in response cleared his throat and took a step closer to Danielle.

"Once training is over, Hunter and I are on the list to go to Vincula. Shouldn't take long, but still, it has to be done. After that, Power Prince and I have to head to DC." Kevin gave Flex a slight nod at this. "Why double P? I'd like to go, I've never been to DC," Danielle said. In response, Flex shook his head.

"Has to be me and Kevin. We are the only members here that aren't technically interns. We were full, active members on the Imperial Lords, and have several victories under our belts. We have a better chance of swaying them."

Hunter didn't want to admit it, but Flex was right. Two decorated heroes that had saved a few hundred lives, would have better luck with the suits of I.C.E. The branch of government commonly referred to as Icon

Character Enforcement, had been up their asses for a while now, and Hunter was happy they finally were meeting with Flex and Power Prince.

"If this goes well, we should be given some breathing room." Flex continued.

"Breathing room?" Jen asked as she pulled out her phone. Hunter was the first to respond, but this time he didn't poke fun at her. He was, surprisingly, serious. "You know how it was in the old days. It was damn near the wild, wild west for heroes. The government used to give us a good amount of freedom. They monitored supergroups and made sure schools like Purgatory Academy stayed licensed and able to adequately train Icons. They passed laws here and there for us, and for the people we protected, but in the grand scheme of things they quietly let us do what we wanted as long as we stopped the villains, and didn't cause too much property damage."

"All that changed with Infinity," Flex said. "The world hadn't seen a being with power like his. Not even during the Battle of Ages. So, the people of I.C.E. feel it needs to be more hands-on and prepared. Special fighting teams, closer audits on sponsors, even new ranking systems are all being developed. Power Prince and I, are merely tokens of the Icon community. We show up, shake hands, smile, whatever they want."

Power Prince didn't like the term token, and it had nothing to do with his Asian heritage. He mostly didn't like being a pawn in a political game, but he knew it served a larger purpose so he went along. "Dude, your cousin really fucked things up for us over here," he whispered to Hunter.

Unknown to Power Prince, Hunter was actually thinking along the same lines. Infinity, the ultra-powerful being from a year ago, like Hunter, had belonged to an other-dimensional race of magic wielders called Spellborn. He was also a murderer with daddy issues. Daddy issues that finally came to a boiling point, and as a result left more people than Hunter could count, dead.

Despite his actions, Hunter still understood how Infinity had arrived at that point. He was traded away as a bargaining chip, in a war that was created by their fathers. Hunter had forgiven most of the people involved and had to use most of the last year to accept that while his friends were Icons, humans born with special gifts, he was a hybrid.

Half Icon, half Spellborn. Deep inside him were slithers of magic, and not just a mutation. It was the reason he had four powers, while most only had one, two, or three. Those same powers were once the source of his arrogance, but he was learning to better that side of himself.

"Alright," Flex said as he stepped closer to them and removed his shirt. Hunter grimaced. Not because Flex was built like a Greek god, but because he kept taking his shirt off in front of his girlfriend. Danielle loved him, but Flex was Flex. Any girl would look, and while Hunter wasn't out of shape, he surely wasn't built like Flex. for that matter, neither was Kevin.

"Keep your shirt on pretty boy," Hunter said as he slowly lifted from the ground and allowed energy to flow to his eyes. "Nobody here needs to see you shirtless," Hunter said. While Jen didn't reply, inside her head she was thinking *speak for yourself.*

Flex shifted and turned to Danielle. "Alright, oh lady of darkness, let's see whatcha got." Danielle took a fighting stance, and tendrils of dark energy crept around her arms. She knew her energy couldn't damage the living tank that was Flex, but she damn sure was going to give it all she had. Plus, in her mind, she felt she was a better hand- to- hand fighter than Flex.

This wasn't entirely untrue. Powerful types like Flex usually relied on their powers more than their natural skills. Hunter had the same issue, and Power Prince had been training them both in boxing. "Bring it on pretty boy," she replied as Flex leaped through the air with a fist drawn back.

"Wait," Hunter said as he watched them fight. He usually trained with Flex. Before he could realize that their leader had decided to switch things up for the day, a fist of glowing pink energy hit him square in the jaw, sending him to the ground and rolling comically.

Hunter could feel the energy travel through his body and it hurt. Touching his jaw, he looked up to see Power Prince bouncing on the balls of his feet, with both fists glowing. The boy was virtually a living battery with unlimited generating abilities on a supreme scale. He was also a damn good boxer.

"Dude, how many times do I have to tell you? Keep your guard up" Kevin said as he kept moving. Hunter stood up and called a pale blue force field to life. "Don't mistake luck for talent," he said as he rose into the sky. Power Prince looked up and laughed. "Don't run now," he said as he grunted some, and using his hands of energy, propelled himself into the air.

He wasn't actually flying. His powers didn't allow that, but he was able to jump and hover there for a few moments before he fell. Hunter was ready for him though, and as soon as Power Prince was in the air, Hunter's eyes turned blue as he released energy from them and hit Power Prince in the chest, sending him down to the ground.

"Paragon one. Power Prince, one cheap shot." Hunter said. Just at that moment Flex screamed out "Switch." and as Hunter hovered in the air, he felt the crushing arm powered by the unmatched strength of Flex, wrap around his neck.

The more Hunter moved, the more pressure Flex seemed to apply around his neck. The two of them moved rapidly through the air as Hunter tried to shake Flex off, but his efforts yielded no results. "Do something, Paragon," Flex said as he continued to squeeze. Hunter could tell he meant business.

Flex didn't use true names often unless he was being really serious. It was almost like when a mother used a child's entire name to get the point across of how serious she was. Hunter used his hands to try to remove Flex's arm, but he couldn't.

As he floated there helplessly, he could see Danielle and Power Prince going at it. Fists of pink electricity swung and Danielle shifted into her shadow form, making Power Prince stumble. Before he could regain his footing, a blast of ebony energy hit his back and sent him flying.

It was a good shot. A good lasting shot, seeing as Power Prince didn't have regeneration or any sort of defense powers.

Changing his course of action, Hunter delivered several quick blows to Flex's body with his elbow. Flex didn't move at first, but after a few more strikes, his grip loosened some. With air flowing to him normally now, Hunter opened his hand and created a force field around Flex's head.

He looked almost like a spaceman or a scuba diver as he watched the force field get smaller and smaller. He released one arm from around Hunter and used it to punch at the bubble around him. It slowly began to crack, but that was all the time Hunter needed. He quickly slammed his elbow into Flex one more time, while at the same using his control over the force field, sent it rocketing in an opposite direction.

Once free in the air, Hunter turned and flew directly towards Flex, like a black-haired bullet. Hunter drew his fist, and at the same time released his Impact Blast from his eyes. To his surprise, Flex dodged the attack and flew directly to him.

In a fluid motion from years of practice, Flex caught Hunter's raised fist with ease, grabbed it, and at the same time sent a blow of his own to Hunter's face. Hunter had maybe a split second of time to form his force field to take as much of the damage from the attack before it was too late.

His force field cracked as the punch from Flex sent him to the ground. Flex landed on the ground and stood over top of him. "Damn. I was hoping to break it this time." Hunter coughed as he rolled over on the ground and slowly stood up.

Flex nodded his head, and screamed out "Switch!"

Danielle walked over to Hunter. Sweat from her match with Power Prince rolled down her face, and even as she spoke, she was breathing heavy. "Looks like I finally get some time with the mighty Paragon," she said as she formed two floating orbs of dark pulsing energy.

"Now don't go easy on me." Hunter in response wrapped a force field around her and lifted it in the air. "Oh, I won't. I know you like it rough." "Gross," Jen shouted from the sideline as she twirled Big Whopper in her hand.

CHAPTER 2:
NERF AND SPARKS

Over the next two or three hours, Perkins sat quietly in her room, only speaking out to curse or talk to herself as she tried to figure out just what was going on with her multibox. She had only a basic knowledge of how the box worked, though.

If she was home, she could have had Cord, Cayden, or any of the upper level technical people on her team look the device over, troubleshoot it, and likely fix the problem in no time. Sadly, she wasn't back home in her dimension, and for the first time in a long time, she wished she was. They didn't need her, though. Impervious was there, and the life of a rebel was far from a life she could live nonstop. Another person of royal blood was there, and she hoped more than anything, that he had made things right since she had been gone.

Her extended vacation with the New Lords had turned into a life she thoroughly enjoyed. Her finding comfort, and passion from Flex, was an added bonus. A bonus she had no intention of leaving anytime soon.

She sighed as she reached for a different tool. Her thoughts were consuming her again, and now wasn't the time for that. Now was the time for focus, razor-sharp precision, and perhaps a little luck.

She could hear screams, grunts, and loud bangs echoing from down the long hall. Her head jerked up as her eyes darted. "Everything okay there?" She asked Prism.

The hologram standing in her room flickered some, and then casually responded. "Yes, young lord. It appears that master Flex is fighting the entire team at once. As of now, it is three against one, and he is having a time at it. Master Hunter is proving to be quite the obstacle." She nodded her head, and then looked back down to her multibox, and touched it with the end of her tool.

An impressive spark jumped from the box, causing her to drop everything and shake her hand. "Nerf," she said as she stood from the table and placed a finger in her mouth. Prism didn't react this time, but the first time he heard this swear from her world he, and the rest of the team, were confused, to say the least.

"Shall I alert the others?" Prism asked. Perkins shook her head. "No. Let them do whatever they are doing training- wise." She said as she ruffled through her drawers. Each drawer she opened she tossed the contents inside out on the floor and finally found a large pair of thick gloves.

"Now we're talking, she said as she slid one of the large gloves on her hand and crossed the room. Only a few minutes had passed before another spark came, and this one was so intense that it knocked her out of her chair and down onto the floor.

Prism looked down at her. Perkins slowly stood up and adjusted her goggles. "Not going to ask me if I'm okay?" Perkins said. "If you were okay, which you seem to be, then there was no need to ask."

Perkins spun around in her chair. "And if I wasn't okay?" "Well then, young lord, there wasn't much a hologram could do, now was it." Perkins nodded. "Valid point."

Over the next few minutes, Perkins had easily disassembled several remote controls, a keyboard, and the single serve coffee machine from Power Prince's room that he used when he binge watched his shows late into the night. In the place of said coffee machine, she left a note with the words *see Perkins* scribbled across it.

When this was all over, she had made a mental note to replace the machine with the latest model. For now, she needed the parts. That wasn't exactly true. She didn't know which parts she needed. She had ideas and theories, but for the most part, it was just her taking random shots in the dark. So, when something actually happened with the multibox, she found it as a surprise.

Perkins was pissed and was ready to call it quits when a light flashed on the small box and static came through. The static filled the room for a while and then, to her surprise, a series of words followed. Perkins turned to Prism.

"You heard that, right? The stress isn't making me crazy?" "Quite the contrary, young lord. An inaudible noise is radiating from that box." Prism said as he looked at the box on the desk in front of him.

Perkins exhaled several breaths and slowly picked up her instrument. Her hand was shaking as she tried to adjust some of the wires in hopes of clearing up the message. Her next move turned the semi-audible series of words and static into pure static. Prism made a sound of one that was clearing their throat. "I know. I know. I'll get it." Perkins grunted as her eyes narrowed.

If she wasn't anything else, she was determined. Now that she had heard something, Perkins was practically a detective on a hot case and refused to give it up. She turned her tool slowly in a counter direction, and as the moments of silence and desperation passed, the static faded some, and for a second, she heard a word. A single word came from a familiar voice, and it was enough to make Perkin's stiffen, as her fears were confirmed and her mind began to race.

When she realized that the message was on a loop, she knew she must fix the multibox as soon as possible. Prism noticed the change in her posture. "Does that word hold meaning to you, young lord?" Prism asked. Perkins slowly nodded her head as she adjusted herself in her desk to work.

The loop replayed over again, as the word came through, just clear enough to hear over the static. "I see," Prism said. "So exactly what, or who is this?" Prism paused as the loop played again and waited for the only word they could make out. "This Omega?" Perkins closed her eyes and, even though Prism didn't see it, clenched her fist for a second. "Pray to Atlas you don't have to ever find out," Perkins said as she continued working.

CHAPTER 3:
LIES WITH GOOD INTENTIONS

Aside from its occupant's heavy breathing, the training room was oddly quiet now. The loud grunts, bangs, screams, and sound of powers being used had faded away. "You know what?" Hunter said to the room between breaths.

Nobody answered, but he took their silence as a sign that they were listening to him anyway. "Voids don't have this much fun when they train," he said as he continued to rest on the cool floor with his arms stretched out. "You did it again," Danielle said as she kicked Hunter's foot with her own.

She would have likely slapped him or even punched his shoulder had she been standing up and near him. Instead she too, just like Flex and Power Prince, remained sprawled on the floor of the training facility, drenched in sweat. Three hours of super training took it out of a person.

"Did what?" Hunter asked as he playfully kicked her back. For the next few seconds, they both engaged in a foot kicking session beside each other. As they continued to kick each other Hunter wondered would they ever flirt like a normal couple. Cliché nicknames, hand holding and stuff like that.

"Said Void, dude," Power Prince said from his position on the floor. Hunter didn't respond as his eyes darted around in his head while he repeated his previous statement to himself. "Did I?" he finally asked. "Yep," Power Prince responded. "Sure did," Jen said from the across the room. Hunter grunted gently. "You're as forgetful as that fish from Finding Nemo," Power Prince said.

Hunter didn't mean to say it, but it was so hard to break the habit he had spent most of his life doing. He didn't even mean it in a disrespectful way. Humans were devoid of power, and as such were voids. To him, it was no different than calling a tall person tall, or a smart person smart. It was what they were. No way around that.

Yet, he still hadn't liked that he said it, and in truth, he had gotten better with using the word. Many people had. It had been around so long that for the older generation it was just a normal part of their vocabulary. "Sorry," Hunter finally said. "Keep working on it," Flex said as he propped himself up from the floor. "You don't want to use the word at the wrong time, or when the cameras are rolling. The general public will get the wrong idea of you, and that's a fight we don't want to have. Understood, Paragon?"

Flex said the last part in a mocking tone and cracked a faint hint of a smile.

"Yes, dad," Hunter said as Jen laughed slightly while she looked through her phone. Hunter had a sneaking feeling she would have given him a fist bump if he was closer to her. Flex ignored his comment, a talent he had developed well over the last year, and stood up on his feet and stretched.

Power Prince watched him rise and rolled his eyes. He wanted to lie on the ground some more and gather himself. While Power Prince had a background in boxing and was pretty well conditioned, he didn't bounce back as well as Flex did. Few people did, now that he thought about it.

Flex had the powers of flight, near invulnerability, and strength on a supreme scale that wasn't matched, and as far as Power Prince knew, those were his only powers. Flex didn't have four powers like Hunter, for that matter nobody did, but Power Prince was beginning to wonder if Flex's strength extended to his endurance as well. Against his personal wishes, Power Prince wiped the sweat from his brow, and slowly stood up beside Flex.

He took his role as second in command seriously, even if their numbers were small. "Speaking of fights," Flex said as he covertly took a step away from Power Prince, "as per usual we will all review footage from today's training, and look for ways to improve."

Flex glanced at Prism who was standing beside Jen. "Prism, email us all a copy of today's training please." The hologram seemed to freeze for a few seconds. "Done, sir." Prism replied. Flex gave the hologram a slight nod.

"Bullet points, though. We're all doing better, and improving. The time spent with Power Prince working on basic striking, and boxing principles is evident in our training. So be proud of that, but we all still have areas to improve in." Hunter, still on the ground, rolled over and pushed himself up to face Power Prince and Flex.

He was mentally preparing for the other shoe to drop. He had known, trained with, and followed Flex long enough to know when he was trying to ease into things, and this was that time.

Hunter looked down at Danielle and extended his hand. "I think I'm good to stay down here for a few more minutes," she replied through closed eyes. "Danielle is doing great, but her body language is giving away her attacks before they happen."

Danielle's eyes popped open as she jerked Hunter's hand so hard to get up that she almost pulled him down to the ground instead. "Are you serious?" she asked Flex. It was a question but it was more hurled at him with surprise. "I am. Especially when you are about to use your powers. You draw your arm back rather far before releasing your energy." This time she didn't say anything, but her jaw clenched visibly, and her breathing became unusually loud.

"Don't get upset. We all have stuff to work on." Flex continued. "So, relax," Hunter said as he placed his arm around Danielle, which she quickly removed. He jokingly continued to try to embrace her. "We all can't be as good as Paragon." Flex cleared his throat.

"Uh, Paragon, you may want to take the jokes down a bit." Hunter turned to Flex. "What's that supposed to mean?" Flex tightened his lips. He wanted to select his words carefully and try not to come off as some hardnose teacher.

"Well I know we're all friends here, but we're also all Icons. We're capable of taking a punch. Even your girlfriend. No more holding back punches or powers. Come at her as hard as you do Power Prince and me."

"Let's not forget the black eye he gave me in training a few weeks ago," Jen added. Hunter pointed a finger at her. "You know that was an accident." "All I know is that my girlfriend had to use a lot of makeup to cover it," Jen replied. Hunter went to open his mouth but a hand was placed on his shoulder that turned him around.

"You've been going easy on me?" Danielle asked. Hunter stuttered as he tried to find words to explain. "Save it for later," Flex said. "Power Prince has a tendency to try to learn and use his powers in different ways when a good old electric punch will get the job done, and I'm overconfident with my strength. We all have things to work on. It comes with the territory, nobody is perfect, or any other common motivational phrase you want to use. We have gotten better and will continue to do so. End of story."

Danielle laughed. "It's easy to be overconfident when no other Icon is stronger than you," Flex smirked. "We don't know that. There are a lot of Icons out there that fly under the radar or have home training. For Atlas' sake, there may be an Icon stronger than me right now working secretly for the government. In any case, I can't always expect to be the strongest. So, as I said, we all have things to work on."

Flex checked the time. "Otherwise, good session today. Same time tomorrow." Hunter exhaled some. He was fearful that Flex was going to make them all return later tonight for a second session of training.

After the Imperial Lords fell, that was his way of training. Two times a day for two hours each. It was brutal, it was intense and possibly went against some work labor laws. Yet, to a certain degree, it was needed. It helped every one of them find something to focus on in an uncertain time. It also showed the world that they were actively still there, training and prepping for a time when they were needed.

"I'm going to shower and change then we need to get moving," Flex said as he looked at Hunter. "Guess I should do the same," Hunter replied. "I still don't know why that bitch requested to see you?" Jen said as she walked over to them. "No offense, Flex," she said as she glanced at their leader who was walking away.

He didn't reply, though. He just kept right on walking. "Apparently she feels that she needs to talk to me or something. Who knows how she is thinking now? Either way, I'll go. For all I know she wants to apologize," Hunter replied.

"She killed Detach, tried to kill you, and pretty much sided with a nut job," Power Prince said. "That's a damn good amount of apologizing." Hunter shrugged and removed his shirt. He couldn't see it, but Danielle bit her lip a little as she watched him undress. "Need some help there?" She asked. "You were upset with me a moment ago. Don't try to sneak back to my good side because you caught a glimpse of all this," Hunter said as he extended his arms and exposed his body.

Over the last year of training, he had put on a little muscle. His arms were more defined, his chest was a little thicker, and even faint hints of abs were becoming visible on his stomach. If he stood next to Flex shirtless, he would still look like a malnourished child, but he was still happy with his progress.

Danielle didn't reply, instead, she rolled her eyes and motioned for him to leave with the flick of her hand. "Guess I should shower and change, too," Hunter said as he walked towards the entrance door.

"Wait for me, dude," Power Prince said as he darted to catch up with Hunter. "I'm gonna brew some coffee, and unwind with a few episodes of Breaking Bad before I clean up," he said. He had no idea of the surprise he had waiting for him in his room from Perkins.

"Just us girls then I suppose," Danielle said as she wrapped her arm around Jen. "What should we do?" Jen frowned and removed Danielle's arm from around her, and took several steps back. "You should take a lesson from them and go shower. You smell worse than a restaurant dumpster."

Danielle grimaced. "A restaurant, you know what, it doesn't even matter. Fine," she said as she threw her hands up. "I'm going to shower."

Forty-five minutes later, Flex and Hunter were standing in front of the main entrance to their base. Hunter took in Flex's appearance and instantly felt like he had misread the dress code for the trip. Flex was dressed rather nicely to be heading to a maximum- security prison for some of the most notorious Icons around. He had on one of his nicer button-up shirts that were tucked into his black slacks, and perhaps the shiniest shoes Hunter had seen in a long time.

Then Hunter looked down at himself. Blue jeans, graphic shirt, and some white canvas shoes. A part of him wanted to go back and change, but then Hunter realized that of all the people in the world that had opinions of him, both good and bad, that the opinions of the prison residents meant the least to him.

Jen and Power Prince came through the glass doors of the base and stood outside with them. "What's this?" Flex asked Power Prince as he took the chunk of paper out of his hand, and read it. "I found this beside the cannibalized remains of my coffee maker," Power Prince replied. "I'll talk to her about it," Flex said as he gave the paper back to him.

Power Prince shook his head. "Oh no dude, it's all good. I already talked to her, and told her the replacement model I want. I'm getting a major upgrade." Power Prince paused for a second. "But, since Perkins doesn't have a job, and most of the money she spends comes from the New Lords account, I guess you'll be cutting the check."

"In that case, get me one too," Hunter said casually. "You're the rich one here." Flex replied. "Touché," Hunter said back. He didn't like to consider himself rich, even though he was.

His father was an infamous villain known as Blue Rush, and Blue Rush was very good at being bad. So good in fact, that the others usually teased him about his fortune. "We'll be back in a few hours or so. If you need anything just radio us." Flex said as he tapped his ear, and turned his head slightly to show the black earbud inside it.

"Why aren't you guys in uniform?" Jen asked. "Any Icon visiting a prisoner in a non-traditional capacity has to wear street clothes," Flex said as he adjusted his pants and then looked down at himself.

"What's considered traditional then?" Power Prince asked. "Interrogation type stuff," Hunter said. "This is more of a family visit, so low key it is."

"For Atlas' sake, it took you long enough," Jen said. Hunter raised his brow in confusion. Before he could speak, Jen pushed him out the way to greet the girl walking towards the base front entrance. She was short, curvy, with caramel skin and a short buzz cut. Flex turned his head as Power Prince leaned over. Jen grabbed the girl by her waist and kissed her on the lips to the point that the rest of the people watching became uncomfortable.

"Now it's a party," Danielle said as she came out the door. "You don't kiss me like that," she said to Hunter as she wrapped her arms around his waist. "Oh, I do. Just in private," he replied. As they watched, the kiss was still going on. Flex cleared his throat. The kissing continued.

"Jen," Hunter said in a slightly raised voice. Hearing her name seemed to bring her back to reality, as she casually dabbed at the corner of her mouth with her fingers. "Hi Sasha," Danielle said.

Sasha waved to them all. Sasha and Jen had been together for some time now. Deep down, Hunter felt like he couldn't have chosen a better partner for his sister. Not only was Sasha cool, but she was also a member of Up Up and Away. They were A supergroup composed of members that had to have a flight- based power to get in. They were well liked, had connections, and some truly powerful members filled their ranks. All in all, good people for Jen to be around.

"We've got to move," Flex said to Hunter as he rose off the ground a few feet in the air. Hunter followed his lead and began to hover as well. "Keep them in line," Flex said over his shoulder as he looked down on them. "I got it." Power Prince said with a thumbs up. Flex grimaced. "I was talking to Sasha. The mature one of the group." Power Prince shifted fingers from the thumb to the middle.

"Kevin knows I have his back," Sasha replied. She, unlike the rest of the group, only called Power Prince by his birth name. She felt the bouncing around from one name to another was confusing so she picked one, and stuck to it.

As Hunter and Flex continued to gather altitude, the remaining members of the team, along with Sasha went back inside the base. "I still think we should have told them the truth," Hunter said to Flex as they moved through the air, and cut through the dome that surrounded the Diamond district part of the city. "You know it's bad when I'm the voice of reason right?" Hunter asked.

Flex didn't speak at first. Instead, he just continued to propel himself through the sky. "It's for their own good. If they knew the truth, they would ask more questions than we have answers. Trust me. I'm doing it for all their sakes." "Then why in Atlas did you tell me? I would have been fine with being oblivious."

Flex laughed. "Of that, I have no doubt. Despite that, you're the one who caught her. I love Zeva, she's my sister and nothing will change that, but she has demons inside of her." Hunter didn't speak but he did agree.

He thought back to the look he saw on Zeva's face almost a year ago when she used her ice powers to murder a member of the Imperial Lords. She had a blank slate of a face. No remorse. No hesitation. And most of all no regrets. "How close had she come?" Hunter asked. "This time? Too close," Flex replied. "This time?" Hunter said as he slowed down flying. "How many times has she tried to escape?" "Seven." Flex replied. "Seven, and that's including the most recent one.

"The Commander didn't go into details, but something about this time was different. He said I needed to come, and that you had been requested." Hunter took in a deep breath but decided to say nothing. Instead, he looked at the world around him as the continued to move through the sky.

From where they were, if he looked behind him, he could see the opposing domes of light and darkness covering the city. Those same domes grew smaller and smaller as they both moved away from it. In seconds they would be in an area where they would only be able to see water in all directions. "This entire thing is giving me the creeps." Hunter began before Flex cut him off.

"Creeps? Not you, Paragon," Flex said in return. "Mock me all you want, but something isn't right, and placing ourselves in a trap, which this feels like, doesn't help our situation anymore." "I can agree with you there, unfortunately, we're here," Flex said as he stopped flying and hovered over the open water.

"Really?" Hunter said as he looked around. He had never been to Vincula before. All they knew were legends, but so far, they seemed true. At any rate, they had made it to the prison in record time, but time often went by fast when supreme flight was added to the mix.

"Pretty sure," Flex said as he pulled out his phone and made a single call. "I've been coming here a few times now, and this looks like the spot." A grunt came from Hunter's mouth. From where he hovered it all looked the same.

Just miles and miles of water on all sides. Flex continued on his phone. Hunter could only see him. He couldn't understand what he was saying on the phone, but moments later a large lift exploded from the surface of the water. "Looks like I was right," Flex said as he put his phone up.

Hunter watched with a gaped mouth as the platform slowly emerged from under the water's surface. That was a secret entrance if he ever saw one. "Welp, here we go," Flex said as he descended on to the platform.

CHAPTER 4:
VINCULA

"Oh, for Atlas' sake, get your ass down here, please," Flex said as he looked up. Flex had already landed on the once-submerged platform, but Hunter hadn't as yet. He was still hovering in the air several feet above.

He didn't know why but the sudden appearance of the platform was off-putting to him. Where had it come from? Who controlled it? How many more were around them? All questions that had floated to the top of Hunter's mind as easily as the platform to the top of the water.

While Flex waited, he tried to control himself in front of Hunter, but deep down he was nervous. He always was nervous when he came here. Not because of the villains, some of which he had helped put here, but because now his sister was one of them. He hated seeing her like that and hated that he couldn't do anything to help her. To save her. No, that time had passed.

"Fine," Hunter said as he slowly descended to the platform and landed in a small puddle. "I know I'm new and all, but," Hunter said as he looked around the platform. "Where do we go from here?" He looked around once more and still didn't see anything.

The platform they landed on was a large black square, composed of what seemed to be a dark blue metal, and not black as Hunter had thought moments ago. What it was missing, however, was a door. There was nothing. No door, no hatch, no anything. Hunter would have even settled for a window, but as far as he could see, there was no way into the prison from here.

"Oh, I got it," Hunter said as he laughed and snapped his fingers. "They pick us up from here?" Flex shook his head. "Nope. This is it," he said as he pointed ahead of them. Hunter followed his finger with his eyes and saw that seemingly from out of nowhere, a door appeared. A single, heavy-duty door, with a massive frame, was now standing where there was previously nothing but open space.

"Invisibility?" Hunter asked. "Cloaking of some sort, from what I can tell." Flex replied. "They aren't overly giving with the way their security works around here." Hunter grimaced. "Why not? You likely put some of their guests here." Hunter gave an exaggerated wink when he said the word guest.

"True. But that was before the Imperial Lords became taboo, and my sister joined their ranks." Hunter didn't respond, he simply just nodded in agreement. He knew Flex was right, and that even after all this time, Flex was still hurting about it. Hunter looked for words to say to fill the void of silence that danced around them, but before he could, the door in front of them opened.

Flex took in a deep breath and exhaled. "Just act natural. Like it's your first time being here," he said to Hunter. Hunter eyed him but didn't turn his head and under his breath responded. "This *is* my first time being here." "Right. Forgot." Flex said quickly. Hunter turned up his face slightly as he continued looking forward.

He felt like being in this place was cracking that invulnerable shell that Flex always wore. Like being here to see Zeva was making him act almost, normal. For at least now, Hunter felt, his supremely strong, invulnerable leader, was now simply an older brother, waiting to see the sister who was never going to be coming home.

As the door finally opened, a white light beamed through as a figure stepped out. Hunter couldn't make the person out at first. All he could see was a silhouette standing before them. As the figure moved closer, he came into being.

"Commander Lopez, nice to see you again," Flex said as the man walked closer. As the silhouette became a man, Hunter was surprised at his appearance. When he heard *Commander,* he naturally assumed the man would look like the Commanders of jails he had seen on television. Old men, out of shape and wore suits that were off the rack. This wasn't the case for Commander Lopez.

The first thing that made Hunter's brow raise was how the Commander was dressed. He had on a suit, but it was definitely not off the rack. Instead, the dark black suit fit him only the way a tailored one could. His large hat tilted down some, but it didn't block his chiseled jaw or stubbled face hair. Lastly, and this is what really surprised Hunter, the man had a revolver in a holster around his waist.

The same holster had several silver bullets that lined the belt. Hunter tried to find a different word for it, but there was no way around it. For lack of a better word, Commander Lopez looked like a very well dressed, cowboy.

The Commander made it into touching distance and removed his hat before shaking Flex's hand. "A pleasure as always," he said. He had a gentle voice, one that didn't overly match his cowboy appearance.

His hand shifted from Flex to Hunter. "Hunter Monroe in the flesh, I presume. Or should I call you Paragon?" Hunter shook the man's hand in return. "Either works, I'm not picky." Commander Lopez smiled and flashed what appeared to be nearly perfect teeth, as he placed his hat back on.

"If I'm being honest son, I thought we'd always meet under different circumstances." Flex cleared his throat. "I know, I said I wouldn't mention it," Commander Lopez said to Flex. "But it's my duty as a man to admit when I was wrong." The Commander turned back to Hunter. "I had written you off."

"Say what?" Hunter asked. "Written you off. Like many, I considered you a stain on Icon history. Villain dad, hero mom. I also heard of how you had a temper. Hell, even you two went at it a couple times," The Commander said as he looked at them both.

"All in the past now." Flex replied quickly. "He just got tired of me kicking his ass," Hunter added in. "Figured it's easier. You know how the saying goes." Commander Lopez laughed some as he nodded. "If you can't beat em, join em."

Flex exhaled. "Alright. Alright. Well, jokes aside. I was wrong. I get so used to seeing the worst our kind has to offer, that I assumed you were no better." "Water under the bridge," Hunter replied. Then he thought about what the Commander has said. *Worst of our kind.* It was safe to assume that he was an Icon too.

Hunter realized that did make sense. In his head, he felt having a normal human in charge would make things difficult. "Enough of the small talk," Commander Lopez said, as he turned around and motioned for them to follow him. Flex immediately began to walk, but it took Hunter half a second to follow.

"C'mon now." Commander Lopez shouted from inside the door. Once they all were inside, the door slammed closed so fast that it made Hunter jump a little. He didn't jump because of the door, he jumped because once the door closed, it cut them off from outside, and as a result, left the three of them in a very small space.

Hunter hated small areas. It was one of the reasons he always made his personal force field so large. He swallowed as he tried to remain calm before his claustrophobia could set in. He had been working on this issue over the last year. Purposefully putting himself in small spaces just to see how long he could keep his cool. The results weren't great.

His heart seemed to be pounding in his chest now, as he wiped sweat from his brow. A keypad appeared and then the Commander went to press his finger against a number but paused. "You boys mind?" He asked them.

Hunter looked at Flex who had already turned around to face away from the keypad.

Clearly, his time before had made him aware of the protocol. "Sure, just get us out of here," Hunter said. "He's not a fan of tight spaces," Flex said from a mouth that Hunter couldn't even see now. He followed Flex's lead and turned away from Commander Lopez as he felt a tremor run across his body. As soon as he turned, he heard several beeps, as Commander Lopez touched no less than ten keys.

Instantly a door appeared in front of Hunter and Flex where, only seconds ago, a blank wall had stood. Hunter darted out and took in a deep breath. Once he had himself together, he turned and looked at Commander Lopez and Flex only to see that the door they had just entered through was no longer there. Only a slab of the wall remained. "Excuse me," Commander Lopez said as he moved, followed by Flex and exited into the hall, and began walking. "Commander, what was so different about this time? You mentioned that Z, I mean Zeva, tried to escape again, but this time was different." Flex took off at a little sprint as he tried to catch up.

Hunter glanced back at the lift, door, closet, type thing and shivered. He hadn't seen anything like it before, and coming from a base as well-funded as theirs, that was saying a lot. As he followed Flex and the Commander, his surroundings were not what he expected. He was expecting lasers, security guards, and holding rooms. Instead, it looked like he was inside of a high-end hotel. Paintings were on the walls, the floor was soft cream- colored carpet, elegant lights hung from above, and it even smelled like somewhere, somebody was baking.

It took him a few seconds to catch up to Flex and Commander Lopez. "Well," Commander Lopez replied as he came to another door. "She killed somebody. She then used the body as a way to divert security to one part of the prison, so she and her colleagues could try to escape from another part." "Colleagues?" Hunter asked.

"Oh, trust me, I'll get to that part," Commander Lopez said as he finally came to another door. This door had a keypad as well. Several beeps later, it opened and all three of them went inside. This hallway was more what Hunter had been expecting. Inside several guards stood, dressed in white and purple body armor. Each nodded to the Commander as he walked by, and led Flex and Hunter around a corner. "She killed again?" Flex said faintly. Hunter looked at him and was surprised at how weak his voice sounded.

He decided it may have been better for him to take the lead for the moment. Commander Lopez arrived at another door, one that looked more like a garage door than anything else. This time, the guard at the door entered a key sequence and placed his hand on the pad. The large door opened, and the Commander walked inside. "Almost there now," he said as the door shut behind them and the floor began to drop.

On the door in front of them, Hunter saw large numbers ticking until it stopped on the number fifteen. "Fifteen floors down!" Commander Lopez said as the doors opened to reveal a golf cart and a long passageway. It seemed like more of a tunnel than a hall.

Hunter was becoming more and more impressed with how large this place was. He was also confused on just how Zeva had had the nerve to assume she could even escape. That thought brought a question to the surface for him. Since Flex seemed to be trapped in his own thoughts, Hunter went with it.

"You said she and her colleagues killed another inmate?" "Prisoner," Commander Lopez responded. "We don't call them inmates. We call them prisoners. We want them all to know they have nowhere to go. Nowhere to run. They belong to us. They are prisoners." Hunter shook his head.

"Okay Prisoners. They killed one. How did it happen? I mean surely you have some sort of security measures in a place like this." "Indeed, we do," Commander Lopez said as he undid his suit jacket and sat behind the wheel of the golf cart. He gave Hunter and Flex a look and jerked his head some to signal them inside. They followed his directions and both sat side by side on the seat behind him.

"All of this you're seeing is just the outer levels." Commander Lopez said as he started driving the cart. The long tunnel lights began to zoom by them as the cart moved at speeds that it shouldn't have been able too. "The upper levels are where we have rooms for the guards and other workers that live on site. You see the first fifteen floors are mainly a compound for staff. Homes, medical facilities, gyms, restaurants, even a movie theater. All a perk of working with the worst the Icon community has to offer. So, we like to keep our staff happy." Hunter nodded as the Commander kept speaking.

He couldn't help but notice that Flex seemed to be in his own world as he watched the tunnel pass them by. Hunter assumed it was because he had heard all this before. He had been here enough to know how things worked.

"Majority of our staff are Icons that, while having powers that are impressive, didn't have what it took to make the cut in the big time. No fancy sponsors, toy lines, movie deals, or legendary accolades." "But," Hunter said, but before he could finish, Commander Lopez took a sharp turn on the cart that almost made him fall out. As Hunter regained control he continued with his question.

"That's cool and all, but that doesn't answer the security question." He said to Commander Lopez. The Commander adjusted his hat. "It plays into it, though. Beyond the first fourteen floors, is where the prisoners are held. Floors ten through fourteen are constructed to be a maze. The path changes daily, and guards are given the new path on an as needed basis." "And the rest of the floors?" Hunter asked.

"Each floor thereafter is monitored by a state- of- the- art security system, the walls are reinforced with ten inches of steel, which itself is diamond plated. Even our dear Flex couldn't punch through it, in theory." The Commander meant for this to be a joke. He glanced back towards Flex with a slight smile but was met with a saddened face and distant eyes.

The Commander cleared his throat. "Lastly, we have four powerful Icons on staff at all time. I'm talking battle- tested, heavy hitters. Two always have a powerset around reducing powers." Hearing this made Hunter think about a thug named Eric he had a fight with last year. Eric was able to render an Icon powerless for three minutes. To this day, those were the longest three minutes Hunter had ever experienced. "And the other two are usually bad asses in some form or fashion.

They are on break right now, seeing as how you two are on site. We haven't had any issues before this in three years, so I trust your services will not be needed. That combined with the bracelets, pretty much keeps everybody in line." The Commander continued.

"Bracelets?" Hunter asked.

The Commander nodded his head as he allowed the cart to slow. "Yes, sir. The bracelets keep all of our prisoners completely powered down. Which is why when prisoner Greene used an ice shard eight inches long to kill another prisoner, we were confused." For the first time since he learned she killed, Flex finally seemed like he was listening.

The Commander stepped out of the cart and motioned for Flex and Hunter to follow. They walked by several guards that were roaming the halls before they followed Commander Lopez through a stained wooden door. Before walking in, Hunter realized that this was the only door made of wood that he had seen since he had been in the prison. It was actually the only wooden anything among the metal and steel that was Vincula.

Then, he saw the inside of the Commander's office. It had a rustic feel to it. Flex walked in and sat down, ignoring everything that had caused Hunter to stop in his tracks. He had seen all of this before. It was old news to him, but to Hunter, he was just realizing how wrong he was about Commander Lopez. He had assumed, because of the hat, revolver, and bullet- lined belt, that Commander Lopez wanted to be a cowboy. Now, seeing the office, he realized that Commander Lopez wanted to be, and considered himself, a sheriff of the wild west.

The entire office was created to look like the inside of a wooden building. Several rifles were resting on mounts on the wall. A large grandfather clock stood beside what appeared to be a holding cell in the back of the office, and one wall was covered in papers that resembled wanted posters. If Hunter had any doubts about his sheriff theory, what Commander Lopez did next washed that away.

Commander Lopez stood behind a large wooden desk and motioned for them to sit down. Then he removed the golden star badge from the desk and pinned it to the outer part of his suit jacket. Hunter found it funny that the Commander acted as if this was a normal office.

"Commander this is all well and good but I need to see Z. To make sense of all this before any decisions are made." Flex said as he stood. Hunter looked at him from his seat and wondered if he should stand up too. "Calm down." Commander Lopez said. "I haven't made any decisions yet. Nor have I made any calls to the powers that be."

Flex took a deep breath and finally sat down. He knew what usually came next when a prisoner killed another. There would be no trial. No questions. No remains. Just a call to I.C.E and then an empty cell. It would be as if his sister had never been there. He couldn't let that happen to her, even if she deserved it. Flex rested his face in his hands for a second as he thought about the conversation he was going to have to have with his parents later on about all of this.

"Naturally, we want to know how she was able to use her abilities. I know you come from purestock, but still, it shouldn't have been possible. That combined with the throne she sits on here has made the other prisoners begin to rebel." The Commander paused as he placed two folders on the table.

"Throne?" Hunter asked as Flex eyed the folders. "While she is young, Ms. Greene is the only Icon here that has the title of Lord Killer." Hunter raised a brow. "It's a title created by the prisoners here. It's what many of them inspire to be. Reserved for any that would be able to kill an Imperial

Lord. Up until Ms. Greene, it was just that, a title. Nobody had done it before, but now that she has, she has a bit of a rep. A rep that comes with followers, flunkies, and even lieutenants." Flex adjusted in his chair.

"So, Z is a top dog in here is what you're saying?" "*The* top dog," the Commander replied. "I just want you to know that the person you are coming to see today, isn't the person you've been visiting." Flex couldn't help but think that the person he had been visiting wasn't the sister he had known. She wasn't the girl that grew up looking up to him, as he helped her control her darker side. She wasn't the same girl that loved rap music and working out.

Then he thought, maybe she never was any of that. That could have been the pills keeping her demons hidden from the world. Now that she didn't have them, her true self was finally coming out. "Why me, though?" Hunter asked. His question ripped Flex from his own memories.

"We don't know," The Commander said. "She just requested for both of you. Normally we don't bend to a prisoner's will. Heck, their request means less to me than a hobo's spit. I only gave in to her, because." "You want us to figure out how she did it," Flex said at last. "Bingo," the Commander replied. "We already interviewed her lieutenants. They naturally aren't talking. No surprise there."

The Commander finally opened the folders on the table. He pointed to the first file as Hunter and Flex looked to it. "Betsy Baker. Better known as Betty Boom Boom." The picture of a young girl looked back at them. Hunter was surprised a prisoner could look so tamed in a mugshot. Not only that, but she looked so young. Her round face and short hair looked almost comical to him.

"She looks like a kid from the Disney channel," Hunter replied. "She's not, though," Flex said as he read the file. "Betty, or triple B as she is called throughout the prison," the Commander said, "can create baseball- sized explosive balls of energy. The ball is always the same size, but she can manipulate how big the explosion is. She killed around twenty people in seven states before she was captured." Hunter didn't feel impressed.

He was shocked at the crimes, sure. He hadn't expected such a face to belong to such a killer. But her power wasn't that impressive. Then again, unimpressive powers, while they couldn't make you a hero of legend, could easily make you a villain that the normal community would fear.

"And this one?" Hunter asked as he opened and looked at the second folder. The face looking back at him was that of a young boy with spiked black hair, and a smirk on his face. Hunter was confused, as he expected another female to be the second lieutenant. He looked to the Commander.

"You have men and women prisoners together?" The Commander shook his head. "Normally no. Reggie, or Regina I should say, identifies as female. She is a special case." Hunter passed the file to Flex, who muttered the words "not this one too," under his breath. Hunter looked at Flex who was reading the file more than expected.

"What is it?" Hunter asked as he leaned over trying to look inside the file. "What's his, I mean her, power?" Commander Lopez answered the question. "Regina goes by the name Slingshot and is able to teleport. It's limited to a five-mile radius, but still, you can hide in a lot of places with that type of radius."

"How did they all end up together?" Flex asked. "Or was this all by chance?" "Kitchen detail," Commander Lopez said as he took the folders from Flex and placed them in a drawer. "All of them were assigned to serve in the kitchen, and their little ragtag team was born, all with your sister as the head. Now was she just looking for friends, or was she specifically looking for Icons you put here? I truly don't know." The Commander said as he stood.

Hunter turned to Flex, who in return nodded to him." "You just had to be the best at your job, huh," Hunter said as they followed Commander Lopez to the door. The Commander grabbed the doorknob and then paused. "Remember, keep it simple, and try to see if she will reveal how she did it." Flex nodded. "Got it," Hunter replied.

From this moment on, Hunter would be Paragon. No more jokes, or funny remarks. All business. He knew when it was time to be a jerk and to be a hero. "I'll let you see Ms. Greene, and triple B first," The Commander said. "Regina is on lockdown for touching one of the male guards again. Fifth time this month." "Sure. I'd rather see Z first anyway." Flex said as he looked to Hunter.

Hunter gave a slight nod. He figured it was better to just let Flex led the way, and he would follow. He was the more experienced leader, and with the extra measures in place, what was the worst that could happen?

CHAPTER 5:
ESCAPE

Hunter felt out of place as he followed the Commander and Flex down another hall. This hall, like the many they passed to get here, was lined with cells. He didn't know why but Hunter was expecting to see cells fashioned like the ones he had seen on crime shows. Room with doors that were locked by a control panel somewhere in the facility.

It never came to mind that such traditional cells wouldn't be used in Vincula. "Here we are," Commander Lopez said as he walked over to a large window in the wall. It stretched from the ceiling to the floor and was easily eight feet wide. The window was frosted over, but Hunter could still see a figure moving behind it.

Commander Lopez tapped a single blue button on the wall, and instantly the frosted window became transparent. Hunter's eyes looked around the room. It was very clean, compared to some of the other cells they had passed to get there. There was a bed on each side and a small section in the back where a toilet and sink were. Both were behind a waist-high divider of frosted glass. It gave privacy, but not total privacy.

Each corner of the of the ceiling had a moving camera. Combined with the camera in the middle of the cell, there shouldn't have been any blind spots. Hunter's training had taught him one thing about cameras. They rarely messed up or missed anything. The person monitoring them, was another story.

In the opposite corner of the room was a small metal desk attached to the wall with several books neatly stacked on top of it. The bed to the left of the room had a person on it, sitting cross-legged, dressed in a gray jumpsuit, and reading a book. Hunter could tell by the youthful face, that this was Betty Boom Boom. Then finally his eyes turned to the other person standing in the room.

He couldn't see her face, because her back was facing them. Hunter still recognized her instantly, even though she wasn't looking his way. That athletic frame and dark hair belonged to a woman he had become friends with only the year before.

She turned around, and Hunter could hear Flex inhale some as she walked to the window. Her mouth moved but no words came out, and as they did, Betty looked up from her book to wave at them slightly. "Oh, sorry about that," Commander Lopez said as he tapped another button from the side.

"I told you they would come." Hunter jerked some as the words sprung into existence from the unseen speaker around the window. "Hey, big brother," Zeva said as she placed both arms on the glass and leaned in. She too, like the rest of the prisoners, had on a gray jumpsuit.

Her head shifted from Flex to Hunter. As she locked eyes with him, Hunter felt like he had never seen this person before. He squinted at her, and she didn't waver in her glare.

He could see her face. He knew it was Zeva, but something about her was off. She didn't look like the girl he had once bickered with in school and became partnered with in the Imperial Lords. It was as if the life that was behind her eyes had long gone, leaving a shell of a person he didn't even know. "Well, if it isn't the half- breed," Zeva said as she looked at him. Hunter smirked some to hide the fact that her words had cut him.

She had never called him anything of the sort before. Hunter had been called half- breed, mistake, abomination, and many other things by the Icon community, but never by Zeva. She was always nice to him in that regard. "Sticks and stones, Zeva. Sticks and stones. Words will never hurt me," Hunter finished as he leaned on the glass in return and gave a kissing motion towards her.

"As you can see, without her pills for an extended amount of time, can only make my sister more sinister." "It's all good," Hunter replied. "I'd be that way too, if I had to live the rest of my life in a fishbowl." She laughed at him. A laugh that caught Hunter off guard.

In honesty, he felt the entire prison was throwing him off his game. He felt bad thinking that had he made the wrong decision a year ago, he could have ended up one of Vincula finest residents. "So, Lord Killer, huh?" Hunter asked. "That's different." "Well we all can't go by Paragon, now can we?" she shot back in a hiss.

"Why did you want to see us Z?" Flex asked. The cold eyes of his sister turned to him again. He didn't know what it was, but something was different, and Flex could feel it, even if he couldn't identify it. He had seen his sister a lot over the year, and she wasn't nearly as chatty and direct as she was now. She would talk to him, but not much.

Now here she was, talking to them both and even smiling. Flex felt an uneasy pain in his stomach. "I wanted to see the look on your face." As she said the words, Hunter and the Commander, had missed what just happened but Flex didn't. As she spoke, a slight string of mist came from her mouth. "Cut the crap Z." Flex replied. "How were you able to use your powers?"

Flex looked at the bracelet on her arm and noticed that it wasn't the same one he normally saw on her. "I see they fitted you with an upgrade." She shrugged. "They figured my bracelet malfunctioned. So, I got a new one." She took in a deep breath. "Yay me."

"Was it a malfunction?" Flex asked. "Just like my brother," Zeva said. "Directly to the point. No questions of how I'm doing or anything." A small patch of ice slowly spread on the bottom of the glass, unknown to everyone. Then Betty Boom Boom stood up from her bed as the book she was reading dropped to the floor. Betty waved to Hunter and smiled while licking her lips some.

Hunter inadvertently stiffened and took a step back from the glass. The last thing he wanted was a fan that was truly a villain.

"But I'll tell you," Zeva said as she took a few steps away from the glass. "Regina is to thank for it all. That girl has a magic mouth apparently." Hunter flinched at the words. "Regina got you your powers back?" Flex said as he looked to the Commander. "Impossible," Commander Lopez said as his hand fell to his gun. "Not her alone." Hunter's head jerked as the words came from Betty Boom Boom.

"Hey, Paragon," Betty said as she looked towards Hunter again. "The things I'd do to you if I had you to myself." Hunter cleared his throat loudly as he glanced to Commander Lopez. "She's something of a fan of yours. Many of the residents are actually," he replied. "Girls got taste. Creepy, but facts are facts," Hunter said.

Her voice matched her youthful face and came out as almost a squeak. Zeva snarled at Betty as she turned to her. "Sorry Z," Betty said as she took a step back from Zeva. Hunter didn't like it, but for some reason, he was surprised at how quick Betty Boom Boom apologized. Zeva was powerful, but Betty had more than triple the body count on her file, yet she all but cowered in fear before Zeva.

Flex had flinched for an entirely other reason. Betty had called her Z. That was his nickname for her. Only his. He had seen his sister correct others in the past for trying to use it. "Nobody ever stops to think why the transgender inmate," "Prisoner," Commander Lopez called back. Zeva rolled her eyes and continued. "Would be touching guards. Especially the male ones. Narrow-minded ways of thinking make one blind to the obvious."

"I don't follow," Flex said out loud. "Neither do I," Commander Lopez voiced from the other side of him. Hunter didn't follow but his mind was racing trying to connect the dots. As he did so he happened to glance down, and finally saw the ice on the glass that was slowly spreading. "I wonder what would happen if a prisoner and a guard started hooking up. Screwing each other on the low. Not only that, but the guard was in love with the prisoner."

Zeva tapped her finger on her chin and rolled her eyes in a mock fashion of thinking. "And the only way they could have alone time was if the guard was on lockdown detail, and the prisoner kept getting sent back?" Zeva said.

"The guard." Hunter finally said as he turned and saw Flex's jaw clench. "Excuse me," Commander Lopez said as he failed to see what was unfolding in front of him. "Keep up, Commander. Your guard is crooked." Hunter said as he stepped back from the glass. At that very moment, several guards on the hall fell down to the ground.

"I love kitchen duty. These people will eat anything, even if it's served to them by an inmate that with the right material, could slip something right in their food. You can kill a crap ton of people, yet a few months of good behavior and they trust you with their food. Normally guards eat their own food, but some like to eat ours just to taunt us." This time the words came from Betty Boom Boom. Zeva rolled her eyes and stretched out her hand.

In a fluid motion, a sword of ice materialized there, and with one slash it tore through the neck of Betty Boom Boom. Her head fell to the ground and rolled around before Zeva kicked it at the glass. The smile on her face made Hunter feel sick, as she shook her shoe a few times to get the blood off.

"What's going on?" a female voice asked. It made Hunter, and Commander Lopez turn in surprise, while Flex kept an eye on Zeva. His mouth gaped open as he looked at the head on the ground just behind the glass. "Z." was all he could say in a low voice as shock consumed him.

A prisoner had stepped from out of her cell. Her glass window had retracted into the floor. At that moment, several other prisoners stepped out. Lights began to flash and alarms sounded off in the prison. Flex turned for a moment to look at the scene that was unfolding in the hall. Then he quickly looked back into Zeva's cell.

Where she stood alone, she was now accompanied by another person. A person with spiky black hair, and a strong face despite the womanly features. "Let's go, Regina." "What happened to Betty?" The feminine voice came back from Regina.

"Bitch wouldn't shut up," Zeva said as Regina placed a hand on her shoulder. "Z!" Flex said as he punched the glass to the cell. It shattered under his strength like an ice cube under a sledgehammer. "We'll have our rematch, half breed," Zeva said as she glared at Hunter.

Then with those words, she and Regina vanished. "We have to go after them," Flex said as he turned to Commander Lopez. "Son, I think we have bigger problems than that right now." Flex and Hunter stood beside each other as they witnessed several other prisoners down the hallway.

"You know I was impressed by this place when we first got here. Now, not so much." Hunter said as he created a force field around him, making sure to keep it larger than normal for breathing room. "Don't worry about them. All the Icons here are chipped. We'll find them," Commander Lopez said as he reached to his belt and removed several bullets one by one. As his hand touched each bullet, he began saying something under his breath. It sounded almost like a prayer.

He spun each bullet into place, and then pulled the hammer on the revolver. "I didn't know she was chipped," Flex said to the Commander. "This isn't the time to have a discussion about it," Hunter said as he looked behind them. Other prisoners were stepping from their quarters, and into the hallway.

Hunter rose from the ground and moved to face the prisoners on the other end of the hall, while Flex stood with Commander Lopez. "Everybody back in their cells. Don't make us do this the hard way," Commander Lopez said as suddenly three different replicas of himself appeared beside him.

For a moment Hunter thought the Commander could create copies of himself. The same power wielded by Detach, the Imperial Lord that Zeva had murdered. Then he saw one of the copies flicker for a second. An idea began to form about the Commander's power.

"Last warning." The Commander said out loud. "Non-lethal force if you can help it," the Commander said over his shoulder. Flex nodded. "I don't do non-lethal. I do survival." Hunter shot back. "Fair enough," Commander Lopez said.

Hunter was surprised to see some of the prisoners on his end, actually listened and casually returned to their cells. Despite that, he noticed that the prisoners that remained in the hall, with fists balled and teeth showing were much larger in number. "I believe they are more interested in me," Flex said as he looked around.

"I know at least three of them I put in here personally. I recognize the faces." " For Atlas' sake," Hunter swore. He had become friends with Flex, but now they were looking at a lot of pain for his good deeds. As soon as the thought was in his head, he pushed it away.

That was the sort of mindset a villain would have, and those days and thinking that way were behind him now. "I think we are much happier out here with you, Commander." A mohawked female said as she stepped through the crowd. "Atlas as my witness, Ava," the Commander started, but Ava just kept walking. As she took her next steps, she transformed into a large muscle- bound woman.

This new form she took on stood around seven feet tall and had muscles that put Flex's to shame. Each new step she took made the ground shake. Several other prisoners began to flex their powers as they realized that somehow, their abilities were back in full effect. Some hovered in the air, while others took fighting stances. One that was facing Hunter even pulled a large hammer from out of thin air that began to glow red.

Hunter didn't waste time. In seconds he created force fields around the prisoners facing him, and with the control over his force fields, sent them rushing back down the hall. Once they were far enough away, he released them, but their momentum slung them into a wall. This gave him some time to think, or so he thought, as his attention shifted to what was unfolding behind him.

In that second, Hunter watched the Commander run up the side of a wall, and up to the ceiling. The other versions of himself that the Commander had created did the same in opposite directions. They were all easily ten feet in the air, and despite being upside down, none of them fell to the ground.

"Illusion casting, and limited gravity manipulation," Hunter said to himself as he watched. Hunter eyed them all as they ran around each other, and he lost track of which one was the original Commander.

Each version of the commander made a dash towards their target. They all seemed to move as one, and even their hats fell to the ground at the same time. Ava swung at the first one and ripped through it as it faded away. Her massive fist whistled through the air again as the next version of the commander faded away.

The final two commanders split up and ran in two different directions. The hulking form of Ava looked from side to side. She finally set her sights on the commander to her left, and the figure smiled, then faded away. Her eyes went wide as she turned to look at the other Commander, but it was too late. While upside down on the ceiling, he aimed his revolver, and a crack exploded through the air.

CHAPTER 6:
ROYAL RUMBLE

Ava stumbled, but she didn't fall. Commander Lopez knew she wouldn't. It would take more than a single bullet to put an Icon like Ava down. He was their commander, not their executioner. He didn't want to kill them, he could if he wanted to, but only if he was pushed to that point.

He took in a deep breath as Ava pushed herself up from the knee she had taken, a red spot was now in the middle of her head where the bullet had made the impact. Commander Lopez smiled as he created an illusion around himself that left him invisible. Ava shook her head like a dog being annoyed by a fly. "No more tricks!" she shouted as she slammed her massive fist to the ground.

As she did so, the Commander, caught off guard, fell back into visibility, but instead of falling, he rolled slightly in the air as if he was on a string, and fired three more shots toward Ava. All finding their mark, and pushing her back, while making her angrier at the same time.

"You ready to quit Ava?" The brute of a woman replied by cracking her neck. "It's going to be a long day," Commander Lopez said to himself as a pissed- off Ava charged at him.

Before her fist could crash down, it was caught in the air with by a single hand. Flex now hovered in front of Commander Lopez as with one hand he held Ava's attacking fist, and his other hand formed a fist of his own. Ava smiled down at him, as her massive- size compared to Flex gave her a false sense of superiority. It was short- lived as Flex delivered a punch to Ava's face that broke her jaw and her pride. "Easy, big boy." Commander Lopez said to Flex. "She can take it," Flex replied as he flew towards Ava.

On the other end of the hall, Hunter wasn't having as much luck as Flex. His attackers had returned, and the prisoner that wielded the glowing hammer was swinging it with precision. She was joined by two other prisoners, one that could transform into a demonic- looking monster, and the other that could hurl small bolts of electricity. Hunter called forth a force field around himself.

The strain was heavy on his body as attacks landed from clawed hands, glowing weapons, and jolts of electricity. "Come out and play, Paragon." the demonic- looking monster said as she continued to slash at the force field. Hunter couldn't help but notice that while she was in demonic form, the prisoner still had the appearance of a curvy woman in spite of her gray jumpsuit.

"Stupid ass name," the prisoner with the glowing hammer muttered between her attacks.

Hunter was tired of playing defense and was tired of people taking shots at his name. He had to be smart about his point of attack, though. He couldn't unleash his impact blast. Not at full power, at least. The damage to the prison could cause more problems than it solved. From inside his force field, he looked to Flex and Commander Lopez.

Both had their hands full. Flex was trading blows with Ava. A fight that he could have won easily if he was allowed to fight at full power, but the request by the commander, mixed with the rapid healing that Ava seemed to have, was causing a problem. Lopez was easily fighting the weaker of their attackers as he fired shots at limbs instead of lethal locations.

One by one, the weaker of their attackers yelled out in pain as they fell to the ground. He was an excellent shot too. Not one of his bullets missed their target, as he twirled and spun around the hall. It didn't happen often, but Hunter was impressed. He didn't know if the commander's aim and agility was a power he wielded, or simply just years of practice, but it was getting the job done.

At that moment, as his force field took another blow from his attackers, Hunter wondered where the Icons were that reduced their prisoner's powers. He began to see the downside of having such a large facility and concluded that was why help hadn't arrived yet. "Young Lords," a voice came through to both Hunter and Flex.

"Not now, Prism," Hunter said. "Busy." There was silence for a moment before a response came back. "I wanted to alert you of an issue with Perkins," Prism said in reply. "Is she okay?" Flex said as he dodged a punch from Ava while lifting her up into the air and slamming her back to the ground. "Yes, but." "Then it can wait," Flex replied.

"As you wish," Prism replied, and then silence filled the coms once more. "Screw it. I'll just pay for damages." Hunter said as he dropped his force field while allowing his vision to turn blue. "Hunter," Commander Lopez screamed from down the hall.

His pleas fell on deaf ears as the demonic prisoner was first to fall as the Impact Blast struck her full in the face. As she flew back, a scream came from her than transformed from heavy and raspy to soft and feminine as she fell to the ground.

A curvy woman with blond hair and neck tattoos now lay unconscious on the ground, where the demonic figure once was. "Ah," Hunter screamed in pain as he fell to the ground and twitched. His eyes closed with pain as he felt the energy surge through his body. Those electric bursts packed a punch, but so did he.

With his hand stretched, Hunter wrapped a force field around the prisoner with the hammer once more, as he flew to the prisoner that controlled electricity. For a few minutes, he was able to maneuver in the air as bolt after bolt of electricity was hurled at him, but the confines of the hall weren't great for flying. That was Likely why the prisoner that Commander Lopez faced that was in the air, went down so fast.

It took a lot to focus on the prisoner in front of him because Hunter winced every time the hammer wielder attacked the force field she was in. That was the downside of having such a power. His force fields were an extension of himself. While they made Hunter very durable, he could still feel some of the force applied to them, and this lady was packing force by the ton in her swings.

Hunter released several short bursts of energy from his eyes, and the electric- hurling prisoner moved at speeds faster than a normal human could, but definitely not at super speeds. She dodged all the blasts, and the energy from his eyes continued up the hall, where it collided with several walls, monitors, and doors, leaving massive holes in its wake.

A blast also clipped Commander Lopez.

"Son of a," Commander Lopez could be heard screaming from down the hall. Later, when this was over Hunter felt that maybe he should work with Lopez one day on his own aiming skills. When Hunter finally came in close on the prisoner, she created two things of electricity in her hands again, only this time she didn't throw them at him.

Instead, she wielded them like stun batons in her hands. Before she could swing them, however, another bang cracked in the air, and Hunter's attacker screamed as a hole ripped from her leg. He glanced down the hall and saw Commander Lopez still standing with his gun aimed. Hunter nodded at him, as he sent a punch into the prisoner's stomach.

He didn't pack the strength in his blows like Flex, nobody did, but the prisoner folded over just the same as she curled up in a ball and wrapped her hands around her now bleeding leg. "One more," Hunter said as he turned to face his captive inside his force field.

What he saw, wasn't what he was expecting. The hammer- wielding prisoner held her hammer in front of her and it disappeared. Seconds later, she pulled a long sword out of the air. Much like the hammer it had a glow to it, but this time it was blue.

As she slashed at the force field, Hunter could feel sharp pings of pain take over. The prisoner's sword cut through his force field easier than he could have ever imagined. This was one of the rare occasions that he had seen this happen, and Hunter found himself being happy that he found out this way, and not in a way that involved him being stabbed when he expected the force field to be a protective barrier.

The prisoner charged towards Hunter, as from behind him, several shots rang through the air from Commander Lopez. The prisoner ducked, leaped, and spun around as she dodged them all. "Damn," Hunter said to himself as he prepared to fire his Impact Blast. She had skills, that was for sure. Before he could, the well-dressed form of Flex flew by him and drew back a fist.

Moments later, the prisoner was unconscious on the ground. Commander Lopez limped over to Hunter. "Damage to the prison aside-You'll be getting a bill for that by the way. Nicely done." "Seeing as how her knife cut through my force field like hot piss through snow, I'm glad Flex stepped in." At that same moment, doors around them opened and guards flowed in, along with two men dressed in long red trench coats.

"Better late than never I suppose," Hunter said as he pointed to all the bodies around them. "A little help a few seconds ago would have gone a long way." "Apply new bracelets to all of the prisoners, then take them to medical, only after the bracelets have been applied and confirmed to be in working order." Commander Lopez said as he placed his gun back in the holster.

Hunter eyed his belt and realized only about three bullets were left. "I doubt you'll find him, but get guard Hamell. He should be on lockdown duty." One of the men in the red trench coat walked forward while stepping over the unconscious body of the prisoner that could take a demonic form.

He had a deep voice and a pointy nose that seemed to look down as he spoke. "Hamell's body was found before the alarms went off. It was actually why they went off. We didn't know of the fighting here until later," he said to Commander Lopez. "Well I hope he's ready to join the prisoners he seems so fond of," Commander Lopez replied. The man in the trench coat shifted his posture some.

"Guard Hamell is dead, sir. Throat slashed. We can only assume Regina," the man was cut off as Commander Lopez, waved a hand and turned away from him. "Atlas as my witness, we will find them." Commander Lopez said out loud. Flex moved to speak but was cut off by the voice in his ear.

"Young Lords," Prism came back once more. Hunter responded this time. "Prism, I like you. I really do. In fact, I've grown fond of you over the last year, but your timing today is horrible. Can you just spit it out please?" "Certainly. It's about Ms. Perkins."

Flex stopped talking to the guard, and the other man in the red trench coat. "What's up, Prism?" He asked. "She has requested for you both to return at once. It's about the message from her multibox." There was a long pause of silence from Prism. Hearing the normally quick-witted program, have a lack of words was off-putting to Hunter.

For a second, he thought they lost connection. "Prism. You there?" Hunter asked. "Yes. Please return to base at once. It isn't good."

CHAPTER 7:
LONG DISTANCE MESSAGE

Perkins looked at the hologram flickering before her as she waited for a reply. She knew Prism was usually very prompt. He made jokes and insults at other's expense, but none could deny the hologram's efficiency. "Well?" she asked. "They are on their way-" "Good," she said as she cut the hologram off and paced around the room a few more times. Suddenly she stopped, rubbed her chin, and then picked up the multibox from the table gently.

It was a mess. The smooth outer layer was dented now, and various wires, portions of tape, and even glue could be seen holding parts in place. Mess or not, she had gotten it to work. She had heard the message all the way and it was worse than what she had expected. With care, she placed the box back down on the table.

She couldn't risk damaging it. She needed it to serve a purpose two more times. "Get the others, too," Perkins said over her shoulder as she opened her closet, and moved all of her clothes aside to reveal a secondary door. Once the second door was opened, she was faced with no fewer than fifteen different styles of weapons. All guns and all selected carefully by her over the last year.

"My babies," she said under her breath as she debated on what to do with them. One of the best things about this world for Perkins was the selection of weaponry. It was far superior to that in her dimension. Her world had weapons, just not such a wide selection. This world had guns, knives, cannons, and blasters for every occasion. For Perkins it was nothing short of heaven.

Surely, she couldn't bring them all. If not all, then she would have to settle for her favorites. Her first favorite was a long slender rifle. It had a great range and massive power, but it was slow. She let her fingers dance on the polished frame of the weapon before she moved on. She then moved over to a plasma cannon she had acquired a few months back. It was perfect, custom made and only reacted to her handprint.

The downside was that it required a massive amount of energy to charge, and once charged it only had a few shots in it. Now those shots could take down a few tanks at once, but they were still limited. She had loved that gun so much that she used some of the Imperial Lords' contacts, and with the help of Power Prince, arranged for some smaller versions to be created.

She smiled to herself as her eyes fell to two smaller guns directly below the plasma cannon. They were identical and even favored their older brother plasma cannon. Each big enough just for her hand, she could maneuver with them with ease, they had good stopping power, a self-healing cooling system, and when fully charged could produce several hundred thousand rounds of bolt energy each. There was even a bolt setting on the blasters. Depending on the size of the target, she could adjust how much power each round had. Stopping a person, or cracking a mountain, the blasters could get it done.

She gripped the pistols in each hand, and as soon as she did, they glowed and hummed to life with her touch. The indicator on the upper part of the handle displayed the number thirty-eight. "Thirty-eight percent," she said to herself as her eyes moved in her head with each calculation. "You rang?" Power Prince said in a long drawl as he stepped in the room with a smile.

He looked at Perkins, and then back to Jen and Sasha beside him. "Really?" They all looked at him with blank expressions on their face. "Lurch. Addams Family?" The silence continued to fill the room. "Uncultured. The lot of you," he said as he leaned on the door frame. Jen grimaced as she shoved her way pass Power Prince. "What's up?"

Perkins looked at them. "Where's Danielle?" "Sleep. She refused to get up and called me something I won't repeat, when I insisted that she did," Prism replied. Perkins took in a deep breath and clasped the pistols in her hands together before she looked back to Jen. "I'll explain when the boys get here." She tossed each gun in her hand to Power Prince who caught them with ease. Had they been any normal guns, the room at large would have flinched, but these could only work if Perkins were holding them or programmed them on auto so anybody could use them. "Charge them for me. One hundred percent, all the way." Power Prince looked at her, and then the guns in his hand. "Okay," he said with confusion in his voice.

His hands glowed with his pink energy, as the low hum of sparks echoed in the room, and then faded away. He placed the twin pistols side by side and gave them back to Perkins. She held them in her hands and checked the indicator again. "Good," she said as she placed them in the back of her pants.

"You're welcome." Power Prince said as he returned to his stance, while his eyes darted back to Jen and Sasha. He was trying to look casual, but Perkins' actions were beginning to bother him. His time as an Imperial Lord had allowed him to see several people in their natural habitat, and the actions that came with them. He was starting to see that Perkins was acting like a person on the run.

The secrets. The rapid movement, and broken sentences. It was as if her mind was firing too fast for her mouth to keep up. Power Prince tried to think positive. It wasn't like she had packed her bags or anything.

"You okay?" Jen asked as she slouched over to try to lock eyes with Perkins. Her efforts were useless as Perkins was too busy pulling two large duffle bags out from her closet. Power Prince took in a deep breath. "And there go the bags," he said under his breath. Sasha looked to him with her brows raised. He just shook his head. "Nothing."

"I need help with this table and I need the bags brought out to the entrance lobby," Perkins said as she stood beside the table and looked at them.

None of them moved, instead they all shared glances at each other. "Today," Perkins shouted. Power Prince shrugged, stepped over the bags, and grabbed the opposite end of the table. Jen and Sasha each grabbed a bag, and struggled under their weight, as they moved into the hall.

"Oh, thank Atlas," Jen said as she dropped her bag at the feet of Flex. "Just in time." "What's going on?" Flex asked. He and Hunter both stood in the hall, breathing heavily as they looked at Perkins and Power Prince coming out of the room carrying a table with nothing but the multibox on it. "I'll explain when we get to the main lobby," Perkins said as she and Power Prince shuffled by them.

Sasha dropped her bag to the floor with a loud thud. "Thanks," she said as she looked at Flex and followed Jen up the hall. Flex glanced at Hunter, who in return looked up the hall. "Well, to the main lobby I suppose." He took a few steps. "Don't forget the bags." At that very moment, Flex grabbed each bag with ease and followed the rest of them.

Once in the lobby, Flex dropped the bags to the ground and looked at Perkins as she stood beside the table. "For Atlas' sake, can somebody please fill us in?" He looked at Power Prince, expecting his second in command to fill him in on the details. Instead, he received a shoulder shrug.

"Just listen to this," Perkins said as she leaned over on the table and gently pressed a button on the side of her multibox, and a clear, deep voice filled the room.

Perkins. I don't know if you'll get this. But I nerfed everything up, and I need help. They're dead. All of them. I lost everybody on a mission. Only me, Cayden, and a few others, and I do mean few, are left of Bravado. The Curse of Varo is much worse than we thought before you left, and then Impervious.

The voice from the multibox took a long deep sigh, and let out a brief faint laugh that sounded muffled.

By the Great Beast, I'm calling him that now too. Impervious has gone missing. He decided to take the fight to them. To end it all, but he hasn't returned, and I fear that somehow even he has lost. We are losing this fight, and Omega grows in strength. If you get this, and I know that's a big if, I could use some help. Cord out.

The message stopped and Perkins turned to look at them all. The entire time the message was being played, she never halted from looking at the multibox. "That's Cord." "We heard that much," Hunter said with folded arms. "He's a friend. We founded Bravado together. Well, us and a few other people." Flex stepped closer to her and looked her in the eye. "You're going back aren't you?" he asked. Hunter had never heard this tone on Flex before.

He had heard Flex be cocky, smug, and even cautious. But in all the times he had fought alongside Flex, he had never heard what he was hearing now. Was it fear or uncertainty?

For the first time, Flex wasn't his normal confident self. He was grasping at anything to keep himself in control. Very few among them noticed the signs. The crack in the voice, the shaky hands. Hunter did, though.

"I am. I have to," Perkins replied. "Prism, you little shit," Danielle said as she stumbled into the room. She had on some dark blue sweats and a green shirt that were the same color as her sneakers. She raised her hand as tendrils of darkness formed. "Whoa. Whoa." Hunter said as he grabbed Danielle by the arm. "Relax."

"Don't tell me to relax. I was sleeping perfectly fine until some Cord guy started speaking at max volume in my room." She pointed to the hologram. I know it was you that filtered that audio in there." They all looked a Prism, who flickered some and then with a slight bow flickered away completely.

"I'm going to upload a virus to him if it's the last thing I do," Danielle said. "Like Independence Day," Power Prince casually said. Sasha laughed. "I get that reference." Power Prince grinned at her. "Wish you were here earlier when I made another reference to it," he said with a smirk.

"Could you all just," Flex said in a loud voice as he neglected to even finish the request. Still, his order was granted, as the room became quiet again. Even the fist bump that Power Prince extended to Sasha was barely heard.

"I'm coming with you." Perkins smiled and kissed Flex on the lips. "I figured you would." She stepped beside him and faced the others. "You heard the message, and I know you have questions. So, do I, but I can't figure things out in this dimension. I do know that he said most of our team has been wiped out, and the Curse of Varo is worse than we thought."

"Yeah, Curse of Varo sounds real welcoming," Hunter said as he glared at Flex. Perkins went to one bag and opened it and began pulling some clothes out. "It's more so a sickness, not curse. Not how the term is used by her anyway. I believe plague, is the word associated with it here," Perkins said as she tossed some dirty blue pants, a brown shirt with holes in it, and a large pair of gloves to Flex. "Change."

Flex looked at the clothes and even sniffed at the shirt. It smelled old. Like it had been sitting in a damp area for a long time. He couldn't help but wonder where she had gotten the rags that she called clothes from. He didn't ask questions, though.

Instead, he slowly began to undress. "Turn around pretty boy," Hunter said. We don't want to see you change." He pointed a finger to Danielle. "No jokes." "I'm going to need more help than Flex." Perkins continued. "I can tell you more once we arrive, but any volunteers?" As she asked, she looked directly at Hunter, who in return pointed to himself with a surprised look on his face. "Did you miss the comment I just made about the Curse of Varo thing? The plague."

Perkins gave a grin to him that made Hunter worry. He didn't trust that grin and almost created a forcefield out of habit for protection. "It is your homeworld, after all. Your heritage, and all that." Hunter thought about what she had said. He truly had no intentions of going to Mo'eizus at all. Home dimension or not, a place where they once sent elite members out to conquer uncharted dimensions, wasn't high on his list of places to visit. "He's in," Flex said as he tossed a bunch of smelly clothes to Hunter.

Hunter looked at the clothes and tossed them back. "Don't speak for me, Ken Doll," he said as the clothes hit Flex directly in the chest. The odor from them could be easily smelled. Flex dropped and picked the clothes up, and then walked them over to Hunter and, with perhaps too much force, slammed the clothes into Hunter's stomach.

"The intern is coming. Part of the internship." Hunter looked to him, and for a second would have been happy to fight the leader again. Instead, he kept his anger in check and began to slip out of his sneakers, and into the clothes provided to him.

"Well if Paragon is going, then so am I," Danielle said out loud. "Atlas knows I get so bored with this hero stuff around here; a good other dimension rescue mission is just what I need. So, what's in the stinky bag for me?" she said as she walked over and began to rummage through. "Count me in," Power Prince said.

In seconds Jen and Sasha had agreed to follow them to the new world as well. "No," Flex said sternly. Power Prince grimaced. "Why not." "I need you, and Jen here. Remember we have to meet with the I.C.E, and I need a ranking member there. Jen will just have to be support. We need to get on their good side, and from under their radar. If this meeting goes well it will open more doors for the New Lords. Maybe even get us the green light to have new members audition to join."

Power Prince nodded his head as he took a deep breath. Inside, he knew Flex was right. He usually was, but damned if he didn't want to go with him on this otherworldly rescue. Now he was, more or less, stuck babysitting Jen, and sweet-talking the politicians. No excitement in that at all. For the first time, he found himself agreeing with Danielle about the boredom around them.

Flex looked at Power Prince, Jen, and Sasha. "Another thing. There was an issue on our visit today to see Z." Hunter snorted as he and Danielle stood side by side in their new outfits. "That's one way of putting it. The other way is calling it an utter shit show."

"How much of a shit show?" Power Prince asked. "She organized the killing of a guard, a total of two inmates, and escaped with an accomplice." Jen let out a slow whistle. "That does sound like a shit show." Power Prince added. "I need you to work with some local Icons, and see what you can do to help catch her, but keep in mind Z is very dangerous, and very powerful."

Power Prince smiled as a few crackles of energy ran from his hands, and up his arms. "So am I." He hated to admit it, but Zeva may have just given his dull day some new life. He was ready to welcome the fight. As a full member of the Imperial Lords, Power Prince had danced with the devil a few times and somehow made it out alive. He glanced at Jen.

She wasn't the direct approach type like him, but he had seen her use Big Whopper on several occasions with deadly precision. Still, as the leader, he had to make sure his team was as safe as possible first. While Flex was gone, this was how he had to think about situations. He had others to care about, now.

Flex turned to Sasha. "Maybe some Up Up and Away members can help." Sasha pulled out her phone. "I'll check and see." "Thanks," Jen said as she kissed her on the cheek before Sasha walked away. Perkins stepped beside the table. "We really need to get going," she said as she pressed another button on the multibox.

Sparks danced on it for a moment before she stepped back and a large swirling green portal came into existence. Hunter felt his throat go dry. He had seen this portal several times in his life, and he never got used to it. These same portals were the heralds of invaders from his childhood. Invaders that eventually killed his parents. Now, here he was, dashing off to save some of their kind. His kind.

The portal continued to swirl and grew louder. "We don't have long before it shuts. Just remember, once inside no powers. Let the flow control you. Don't even try to fly," she said as she touched a few wires on the multibox. Flex nodded to them all as he stood with Perkins, Hunter, and Danielle. Power Prince gave him a slight salute. "Let's go save the world I guess," Hunter said as he watched Perkins leap into the portal.

CHAPTER 8:
THE CURSE OF VARO

Once Perkins was inside the Portal, Flex turned and looked at Danielle, and then to Hunter. "Don't let me leap into this thing, only to come out on the other side seeing that you decided to stay here." Hunter snorted some. "I wouldn't dream of it," he replied.

In reality, he would dream about it. He had actually been thinking just that before Flex started speaking. He could have let Flex go inside, then just stop Danielle from taking the leap. This line of thinking went out the window as Danielle, all too eager for some action, yelled out "kamikaze," and dove into the massive green portal head first, as if it were a swimming pool.

"Atlas," Hunter said under his breath as he exhaled. Would it have killed her to slow down and think about what she was literally diving head first into? Flex fought the urge to laugh as Hunter stood beside him. "Good luck with Z," Flex said to Power Prince. He had to shout over the ever-growing noise that the portal created.

"Handle the government pricks, handle insane killer hot sister." Power Prince said as he gave a thumbs up that didn't match his stern face, and forced smile. "You just go on and hop in your Stargate portal thingy. We've got this." Flex nodded and realized he would miss Power Prince with his tv and movie references, while he was away.

They had known each other some time now. Even though they interned under different teams, both of them knew of each other back then. Flex smirked some as he thought about how young and dumb, they had seemed just a few years ago. Now, here they were. Full- fledged heroes with reputations. After glancing at his team once more, Flex jumped into the portal. His departure didn't have the grace of the people who entered before him. While Danielle's entrance looked cool, his was more embarrassing. It was as if the portal had sucked him in, and a slight scream slipped from his lips on the way in.

Hunter leaned into the portal and took a deep breath. He didn't know why he did it, he just did. For some reason, it felt like the thing to do. He did the same thing with new food he had never tried before. As if the smell would be the final factor in deciding to eat or not. "It smells funny," he said out loud.

He had smelled the odor before but couldn't place it. Jen ran up to him. "Hey, stop dragging your feet. It's making you look like a punk." Hunter looked at his sister. "You think I'm scared?" Jen didn't answer but her casual shoulder shrug told all that she was thinking. "I'm not scared of this," Hunter said as he waved his hand up and down in front of the portal. "I'm worried about the world on the other side. My world. What if..."

A backhanded slap to the stomach forced him to stop talking. "Screw all that. Hunter Monroe, no, Paragon isn't afraid of shit. You took on an Icon serial killer for Atlas' sake. A quick trip to another dimension is cake." Jen said as she extended her fist to him. "Now my dear sweet, dope of a brother, go and kick this new world in the nuts. Oh, and bring me some food back if you can." Hunter smirked and bumped her fist with his own and then slapped on her ball cap.

"It's always about food for you," he said with a laugh. "But I guess you're right," Hunter said as he looked at the swirling mass before him. "Per usual," Jen said as she adjusted her ball cap on her head, and began to slowly walk away. "Think Power Prince is scared to run the show?" Hunter asked her in a slight yell. "Oh, he's scared shitless," Jen replied with a smile. "I can hear you, you know," Power Prince shouted.

Hunter nodded to Power Prince once more, and then pointed a finger to Sasha, "keep her out of trouble." he said as he jerked his head towards Jen. Then, with those last words, he swallowed back the fear that had finally crept into his body and jumped.

Much as he had seen with Flex, the portal seemed to pull him inside as he took his leap. It would have likely done the same thing with Danielle if she hadn't run in with such force. Once inside Hunter felt as if something larger than himself was holding him. An unseen body of power that kept him falling through the tunnel of green around him. The smell was becoming stronger now, too.

"Eggs," Hunter said as his plummet continued. He had finally pinpointed the smell that was coming to mind with the portal. It was eggs. Boiled eggs, with a hint of sulfur. "I may as well be falling through a fart tunnel," he said out loud as he continued to fall through the portal.

As he made his descent, he fought the urge to touch the green cloud-like walls that surrounded him. Walls that he could have sworn were further away from him than now when he initially came inside the portal.

Hunter tried to look down beyond his feet to see if he could make out Flex, or maybe even Danielle, but he couldn't see any of his team. He figured Perkins was likely on the other side waiting for them now since she entered first. He took a few deep breaths as he glanced to his surroundings again. Now he was certain that the walls of the portal were closer.

Was it shrinking? Hunter looked up above to see just how far he had come from the opening, but couldn't see anything. In his mind the portal was more of a long tube, so he was expecting to see an opening up above him. Then he realized what he had feared. The portal wasn't shrinking, it was closing.

The portal was closing and getting smaller by the second. He fought the urge to panic and instead tried to take a few slow breaths. "You're alright. You're alright. The walls are not a problem. Space is not a problem," Hunter muttered to himself.

His training while trying to improve his fear of tight places usually revolved around staying calm, and talking himself away from the edge of flipping out from being crushed to death by such tight spaces.

"Space is not a problem. The walls are not a problem. You're not going to be crushed by some otherworldly wall and left alone to die in time and space." The last few words muttered were all it took for Hunter. He was no longer on the ledge now. Instead had jumped off the ledge and landed in a pool of claustrophobia and couldn't get out.

Forgetting what Perkins had said before they entered, Hunter reverted to his default setting and created a massive force field around himself to try and stop the walls from closing. His force fields were strong, durable, and rarely let him down. In his heart, he knew it would work. He knew he'd be saved by them just as he had been a million times before.

It didn't work. In fact, the walls of the portal passed directly through his force field as if it wasn't even there. He swore to himself but didn't waste time being shocked. Instead, he released a few short bursts of energy from his eyes. Much like his force field, his Impact Blast did nothing but pass through the walls and fade away.

The portal began to thunder now. The loud sound washed over him as the walls around him, still closing in, began to crackle with light. It was like watching lighting dance in a cloud. Hunter could feel his breathing in his chest now, as the portal began to violently shake.

He could have been imagining things but he felt like he heard a voice over the rumbles of the portal screaming out *who fucked up?* Hunter looked down beyond his feet once more, and this time instead of seeing an endless tunnel of green, he saw a light. "End of the line," he said with a smile as he thought this entire ordeal was about to end.

In those moments of positive thinking, the walls closed in on him as he began to be violently slammed from side to side. He waved his arms and screamed as his worst fears were coming true. He was going to be dead in this damned green, fart- smelling tunnel. Alone and afraid. His body bounced more as he could feel the pressure squeezing on him, and then it was over.

The light consumed him as he bounced off the ground in comic fashion. Pain flooded his body as he began to groan, but before he could a hand was slapped over his mouth. It wasn't a strong hand, and he could tell that if he wanted to, he could move it with ease. The hand wasn't what concerned him. It was the bulging bright green eyes of Perkins, with a finger to her mouth that concerned him.

As he waited on the ground with Perkins kneeling near him to cover his mouth, he could feel sand or dirt under his hands. The ground, wherever he was, was soft to touch. He now knew why his impact on the ground wasn't as painful as it could have been.

Then, for a moment he felt something. At least he thought he felt something. No, it couldn't be. He didn't want to over-imagine things, but Hunter could have sworn he felt the ground shake.

Despite the clear sign from Perkins, he still tried to speak, and as a result, Perkins applied more pressure to his mouth as her eyes glared at him. Hunter finally got the hint and looked around and could see the rest of his friends in a low position, too.

None of them were standing, and there was the sensation of the ground moving again. It was faint, but he knew he felt it. "Okay," Perkins said in a low voice as she removed her hand and looked around. "I think we're clear." "Did anybody else feel the ground shake?" Hunter asked as he struggled to get to his feet.

He glanced at the ground around him and it all appeared to be sand. As if somebody had dropped him in the desert. "I did a little," Flex said. Danielle simply shook her head but looked to Perkins for an answer all the same.

Perkins took in a deep breath but continued to look around. "That's the least of our problems at the moment," she said as she touched her back to make sure her twin blasters were still there. They were and for a second, she felt a little relief. A slight hint of comfort in the cluster of a mess she had landed in. Perkins nodded quickly. "They're gone." "Who?" Danielle asked as she began to look around. She had a hard time at hiding the excitement in her voice.

Deep down she thought a fight would be good. It was also night time wherever they were in this new world, and this only added to her eagerness. Danielle was an Icon the people of her world called a Two-Fold. Her powers would get amplified under certain conditions, and for her, that condition was night time. For as long as there was darkness around her, her energy blasts were amplified and could perform feats that weren't available to her during the day. She could also hold her shadow form longer.

"The Warden's Circle," Perkins said. Hunter noticed two things. Firstly, he noticed that when Perkins spoke, she still did so in a whisper. He also noticed that while Danielle shared his expression of being confused at Perkins' words, Flex didn't. Instead, he clenched his jaw and balled his fists.

Hunter had seen this before. He knew when Flex went into hero mode. "Can you fill us in on what a Warden's patch is?" Hunter said. "Circle," Perkins replied. "Warden's Circle. I will, but we need to get somewhere safe first."

"This isn't safe?" Danielle asked. "So, I'm going to go out on a limb and say this isn't where you had set for us to land?" She had arrived at the correct conclusions before her male colleagues. "No. All of that power going off on the inside of the portal threw us off course." Perkins eyed Hunter as she said these words.

"Sure. Blame me. Sorry if I lost my cool because the damn thing was closing on me. For Atlas' sake, I was almost crushed." Perkins shook her head. "Sorry. That's my fault. I'm not a tech guru. I wasn't able to repair the multibox to the levels needed to keep it open long enough."

"None of that matters now," Flex said in a low stern voice as he assumed control of the conversation. "You weren't the one almost crushed," Hunter tossed back at him. Flex ignored his remarks. "We need to get to your people. Are we even in the East Section?" Hunter grimaced. Despite being on the homeworld of his father, a place where he may still be considered royalty, Hunter knew nothing of Mo'eizus.

Not only did he know nothing, he never had an inkling of trying to learn of his world. Not really. Not once did he ask Perkins about anything. Clearly, as her new lover, Perkins had opened up to Flex about her world. Looking around though, Hunter felt that he still hadn't missed much. This world looked like something out of a dystopian movie.

There was sand for as far as Hunter could see. Which wasn't very far. The wind blowing was agitating the sand making it hard to see and the heat was almost unbearable. He couldn't understand why there seemed to be so many empty buildings around them. Or at least what Hunter assumed were empty.

"I think so," Perkins said. "Definitely the East Section. We just have to find our way to the Bravado base." This portion did make sense to Hunter and Danielle. Perkins had told them about her group when she arrived a year ago. She and several others made up the rebel group of Bravado, but she never went into deep detail about why. She always just said they served the people. Hunter always meant to ask, but after a while, he just didn't care anymore.

Perkins began to walk slowly, and Flex followed her. "Stay with me. It's late, and the Warden's Circle will be back shortly." Hunter motioned for Danielle to move in front of him, as he brought up the rear. Even from the back, and with the sand blowing around them, Hunter could see the spiky blond hair of Perkins ahead of them.

He also noticed that she had lowered her goggles. Now it finally made sense to them all why she had them. This sand was messing with their vision, and they had to squint and dip their heads to see. Well, not all of them. Flex seemed utterly unbothered by the sand. One of the perks of being invulnerable to damage.

Perkins suddenly stopped and pulled her weapons from behind her. As she gripped her twin blasters, they came to life and emitted a faint blue glow that could be seen a few feet away. Hunter and Danielle made their way to stand beside her and Flex.

They all had been in enough fights to know something was up and had caused Perkins to pull her weapons out. Hunter and Flex both began to float in the air, as Danielle summoned her newly enhanced dark tendrils that were larger than that of those summoned back in the New Lords' base.

"No powers." Perkins hissed. "No flashy ones anyway. Only use physical- based powers. Anything else will make you stand out, and Wardens can track it." Hunter took a breath as he dipped his head to avoid sand. Whatever these Wardens were, he was beginning to not like them.

Perkins pointed her pistols directly ahead of them. Slowly, a dark silhouette began to emerge from the sands. "How in Atlas' name did you even see him?" Danielle asked. "It's my spell," Perkins replied . Danielle made a frown with her face that had nothing to do with the sand pelting across it.

"Her what?" Danielle asked. Perkins didn't respond. "We don't want trouble," Perkins said as the figure hidden by the storming sands became larger. As it moved towards them, Hunter began to see that it wasn't actually walking. Not in a normal way at any rate. It was more so, stumbling. Falling down, getting back up, moving from side to side. Like a drunk person.

Perkins noticed this too. "Please no. Nerf no," she said as she swore. Before Flex could ask a question, the figure emerged from the hidden veil of the sands. Hunter's face, along with the rest of his team, turned in disgust.

What lumbered towards them was a man. He was dressed in ragged clothes, much like the style Perkins had forced on them before they left. He had brown hair and a brown thick beard. Both were missing patches of hair, though.

As if on cue, portions of the hair just fell to the ground as the man moved closer. A dark, tar-like substance ran from his eyes, nose, ears, and mouth, and his eyes were yellow. “What’s, wrong with him?” Flex said slowly as he positioned himself between the man and the pistols of Perkins. “He’s in the final stages of the Curse of Varo,” Perkins said with a shaky voice.

Hunter remembered that Perkins had told them the curse was more so a disease or plague, and not a literal curse, but clearly, the name had stuck. She never went into more detail on the subject. As he looked at the man, Hunter could see why. “Usually the rage has consumed them by now, though.” As the words left her mouth Perkins flinched as the man screamed and leapt towards them.

Spirals of black sludge poured from the man’s mouth as his scream sounded like it had a gurgle to it. Two things happened at once. Hunter called upon a force field, and as the pale blue orb of energy surrounded him, Danielle, and Perkins, Flex grabbed the attacking man by the throat. He then flew several feet in the air and flung him back down to the sand below. The man was thrown by Flex with such force that the whirling sands around them dispersed as he passed.

Hunter, still inside his force field with the girls, made it grow even larger so they could have room to move. Perkins, guns still drawn, looked at the man. He was still breathing, but barely. Then it came to her, but it was too late. They had used their powers. The flight alone wouldn’t have been bad, but the force field that was still around them may as well had been a beacon. “Hunter, the force field,” Perkins said loudly. “They can sense power.”

Hunter didn’t ask questions. He had trained enough in his time to know when to shut up and go with the flow of things. He could tell from the tone she used, this was the time. Instead, he canceled the force field. As soon as he did, he let out a scream and dropped to the ground. One by one they all fell in agony. "What is," Danielle tried to get the words out but instead began to scream as her question faded away.

Hunter couldn't move. The pain had consumed his entire body. It was as if something was exploding below the surface of his skin and was savagely looking for a way out. Then, as suddenly as it started, it stopped. With it, so did their screams.

Breathing hard, Flex was the first to stand. "What was that?," he asked through broken breaths as he pulled Perkins up. "Warden," Perkins said through heavy breathing. "Pain Conduit," she continued as she looked around frantically, and then her entire being became consumed with fear as she looked up and saw him standing on a slight sand hill a few feet away.

"It's too late," Perkins said as she pulled her blasters from the sand. "The Warden's Circle is here." As she said these words, Hunter looked in the direction that Perkins had her twin blasters pointed. He could barely even see anything, and then it happened.

The sand itself seemed to come alive. The swirling sands and the sand-covered ground began to part with force, as if two large unseen hands had separated them. At the end of this newly formed path was a tall slender, something.

Hunter didn't want to call it a man, though. It had a man's figure, but none of the features. Before he could fully figure out what he was looking at, another figure appeared. This figure was almost as tall, but flaunted the curves of a woman. With this figure, the pain came again, and as his pain seemed to multiply, he fell to his knees. The last thing he saw was Flex charging forward, as the energy bolts from Perkins' blaster covered the area.

CHAPTER 9:
WARDEN'S CIRCLE

That was the good thing about Flex being so durable. As he moved through the air several energy bolts from Perkins' blasters collided with and bounced off his skin. He didn't even bat an eye as it happened. For that matter, neither did Perkins.

Flex balled his fist tight as he moved towards the man standing on the hill of sand. As he got closer, he realized what he was looking at only had the form of a man. He could see that the creature was dressed in a black suit that appeared to be made out of leather and that instead of skin, the creature was metallic.

The face had no eyes, nose, or mouth. Just a rounded head composed of metal that reflected its surroundings. "You picked the wrong team to ambush," Flex said as he drew back a fist. He hadn't yet noticed that Perkins had stopped shooting and that the bolts of energy were no long surrounding him.

As Flex threw his punch, he lifted off the ground at the same time, using his own momentum from flying to put some extra force behind a punch that could already destroy a mountain. He was close now, so close that he could even see the second figure. A figure that clearly was female in some sort of armor.

As far as he knew, she was the enemy, female or not. He had known plenty of Icons back in his own dimension that were killed or severely hurt because they underestimated, or went easy on a villain just because of their gender. A mistake he never made. Having a sister as powerful and deranged as Zeva made sure of that.

Flex screamed as he sent a punch flying, but the scream wasn't of his own power. Something had exploded in him with enough force to send the flying hero crashing to the ground. Flex rolled around and gripped at his own head, clawing at the sides of his ears as if he was trying to dig down to remove the pain.

On the other end of the fight, Hunter had gathered himself and was helping Danielle and Perkins to their feet. "Shit's hitting the fan, Perkins," he said as he waited for her response. This phrase was one that he had coined in training. Each member of the team knew to use it if something serious was going on, and that they needed explanations and plans fast. Flex's only rule for the phrase was that it was to be used only in severe cases.

"Warden's Circle," Perkins replied as she removed her goggles. Her vivid green eyes had a glow to them that neither Danielle or Hunter had ever seen before over the last year. "They came to play, too," Danielle said as black energy consumed her arms all the way up to her shoulder. Hunter's eyes turned blue. "So, did we," he said as he lifted in the air.

"We can't take them head on with the Pain Conduit still there. Her ability allows her to target pain receptors in the brain to control as she wishes. We're only talking and standing now because it's usually hard to use on multiple targets for a long period of time." Perkins looked at Flex, still on the ground in agony.

"All of her power is focused on Flex now, and for an Icon that isn't used to feeling pain...," Perkins stopped talking suddenly. "Where are the other two?" Danielle looked at Perkins' eyes wide, and before Hunter could reply, another slender figure fell from the sky with a sword longer than a broomstick. Hunter, Perkins, and Danielle scattered as the sword came inches away from slicing through Hunter.

"Shit," Hunter screamed as he rolled on the ground, looked up and released the energy he had in his eyes. The sword-wielding man did several backflips and landed on the ground in a perfectly balanced form.

From where Hunter was positioned on the ground, he had a good view of their newest attacker. While he was thin, he wasn't as thin as the creature in black had been. Thick plates of body armor covered his skin, and a helmet with visor hid his face. The sword in his hand was so large that a person with enhanced strength would have to use two hands to wield it, yet the attacker twirled the sword in one hand with ease.

As the sword twirled, it sliced through the air with a hissing sound. Each movement seemed to be more fluid than the last, and combined with how easily he dodged Hunter's attack, suggested a form of enhanced reflexes. Hunter wouldn't have believed it possible to maneuver with such grace while holding a weapon of that size and being covered in protective gear.

Before he could go on the attack, a larger male in the same armor stepped out of the nothingness holding a gun that Perkins would envy and began to unleash rounds of red energy. Despite being dressed in the same armor this attacker with the gun was massive in size. His height and width dwarfed their other attackers, and the gun he used was the size of a small human.

Instinct took over, and with both hands held up, Hunter created a force field around the three of them. "We have to take out the girl," Perkins said. "She hasn't relaxed her power on Flex, so she must know how strong he is." "What about thing one and thing two?" Danielle asked as she looked at the red energy bouncing off of the force field.

"I'll handle them, You two stop the girl," Hunter said as his eyes flashed blue, and he began to rise from the ground and hover in the air. He tried to keep the thoughts of possible failure out of his mind. Danielle looked at him, flexing his powers and she bit her lip. "Atlas, you're so hot right now," and she finished her words off by smacking him on the butt. "Say the word, boo," she said as her darkness faded away from her arms. "That bitch is mine," Danielle said with a grin that seemed out of place in their current situation.

"Be careful," Hunter said as he floated above them. Neither girl said anything. Perkins aimed her blasters, and Danielle nodded. "Three," Hunter said as more and more bolts of red energy peppered his force field.

"Two." The sword- carrying attacker leaped and attacked the force field now with such power that it made Hunter grit his teeth.

When the attacker saw no damage had been done by his sword, he looked at the force field and touched it with his fingers. This bothered Hunter. Their attacker was taking time to learn. Under normal circumstances Hunter would applaud the man with the sword, but now it made him seem all the more menacing. The man also seemed utterly immune to the red energy being blasted by his larger colleague. "One," Hunter screamed as he retracted his force field from Perkins and Danielle.

As soon as the force field was no longer on them, Perkins unleashed fire, causing the swordsman, and his partner to separate some as they avoided being hit. Perkins, still laying down fire, ran behind Danielle, and if she could see the maniacal smile on Danielle's face, she would have likely been equally afraid.

Leading the charge, Danielle felt an energy and power flow through her as her Two-Fold enhanced darkness consumed her. Her vision around her turned to black and white as her shadow form took over. She was moving directly toward Flex in a speed that she didn't realize she possessed. Behind her, she could hear Perkins scream as several bolts of energy from her blaster passed through the shadow form of Danielle and rocketed towards the Pain Conduit.

"Man, that's cool," Danielle said under her breath. To the running and gunning Perkins behind her, her words sounded more like a deep grunt. She had never heard Danielle speak in her shadow form before. As Danielle got closer, the girl standing over Flex shifted, and raised her hand up to Danielle. Perkins screamed as pain consumed her, and the blasts of energy stopped, but Danielle felt fine. She realized her shadow form was immune to the pain attack and didn't miss a step.

As she got closer, the Pain Conduit stepped back and looked at the metallic man standing just above her. The creature gave a slight node of the head. Before anything else could happen, Danielle's shadow arm passed directly through the conduit. Having body armor was great, but to a shadow it meant nothing.

Danielle had to time it right, and before she even extended her arm, she could feel her form beginning to change. Once her shadow arm was inside the Pain Conduit, she forced her body to return to normal, as she did so a small grunt came from the armor-clad woman who now found a solid arm rearranging her insides.

Danielle couldn't see the Pain Conduit's face behind that mask, but she could hear the sounds as the mask looked down at its own body. Her arms grabbed at Danielle's arm inside her, but weakly. "Pain's a bitch isn't it," Danielle said as darkness consumed her eyes, and tendrils began to form around her free arm. She opened her hand and a wave of dark energy exploded from her palm and collided with the Pain Conduit.

Perkins, down on one knee beside Flex looked on as a part of Danielle rose to the surface that she had never seen before. But as the Pain Conduit began to rip apart under the weight of Danielle's dark energy, Perkins saw the power that Danielle truly had, but had never used. She was always so nice, and playful. Teasing Hunter about his name, while at the same time flirting with him to the point that it made others uncomfortable.

Even in training, Perkins couldn't remember seeing Danielle with such power. Perkins grinned some, as the fear she had felt for a moment fade away. "Total badass," Perkins said as she tried to pull Flex to his feet.

"That's my girl," Hunter said to himself from across the battlefield. From the safety of his force field, he could see the events happening over by Flex, and was impressed. He hadn't really seen Danielle in such form. He assumed it was the extra boost she had gotten from using her powers in full form at night.

When they would practice, or even go out on missions, it was usually in the Diamond District, the part of the city where light and daytime was eternal. When they did venture into the Ebony District, problems were usually solved by Flex or Power Prince so fast that Danielle didn't get a chance to shine. "Well, no more pulling punches in practice," Hunter said as the swordsman attacked him again.

Hunter had done his part of the plan. He kept the other two busy while the girls had all the fun. Flex was slowly coming around, but Hunter couldn't shake the feeling that they weren't out of the fire yet. That thing on the hill still hadn't moved. It just watched, and Hunter had seen enough movies to know that when the boss is observant, it's never good.

"First things first," Hunter said as he went on the offensive. He rocketed into the air about eight feet and stretched his hand out. A force field surrounded the swordsman. As he flew around, bolt after bolt of red energy covered the night's sky as the larger of the two continued to fire. Hunter allowed his vision to turn blue and sent back a blast of his own energy.

As the dark area turned blue with the passing of Hunter's Impact Blast, the larger male's gun exploded when Hunter's attack found its mark. From the sky above, Hunter's eyes had gotten large. His aim had gotten better, but not that much better. He had been aiming for the man's armored torso, but blasting his gun away worked too. It looked more hero- like, as well.

As the gun exploded, Hunter followed it up with a balled fist delivered to the torso he was originally aiming for. While his punch found its mark, it didn't have the desired effect. Hunter had enhanced strength, but it paled in comparison to the likes of Flex. The large man stood, unflinching, as he looked down at Hunter. "Oh, for Atlas' sake," Hunter said as the larger man's arms came crashing down, and collided with the newly- formed force field.

Instantly, Hunter opened a small hole in the force field and unleashed another blast of energy from his eyes, this time it was so much that shadows danced on the ground as the area turned blue. A hole the size of a shoe box tore through the frame of the hulking man. As his body fell, Hunter turned to look at the swordsman still trapped in his force field. "Just me and you, blade boy," Hunter said as he felt a slumping in his stomach once he realized that the man had created several large cracks in his force field.

He had spoken too soon, as he heard a sound like metal being dragged across more metal. The sound was loud and caused each of them to look at the man that was slowly walking down from the hill top. He or it didn't walk like a normal person as expected. It had a slow, purposeful stride to itself. Arms clasped behind the back and radiating with all the confidence in the world. Had this metal figure had a face, Hunter felt like it would be smirking.

As the creature moved closer, Flex stood tall. The effects of the Pain Conduit were gone. Hunter, ignoring the hostage of his force field flew over to join the rest of his team. "We need to go," Perkins said quickly. "For what?" Danielle said. "Four against one, I personally like our odds," she continued. "I agree," Flex chimed in.

As his words left his mouth, the Warden's arms relaxed from being behind its back, and a haze field rippled from him. As it did so, the sand, heat, and wind seemed to come alive as it all danced within the field. "It's not just him," Perkins said. "All the Wardens are connected he could have another Warden's Circle on the way already."

They all didn't know it but they were thinking the same thing. Another Warden's Circle meant another Warden and another Pain Conduit. Even Flex wasn't ready to feel that again. Hunter glanced to Flex. Hunter never ran from a fight, but he understood that sometimes one had to retreat to only come back stronger. The version of him from a year ago wouldn't have thought things through so logically.

Hunter grunted as he felt a slight pain. He knew that pain and turned to look at the swordsman in his force field. To his surprise, the massive sword was now in a different form. Instead of being massive it was rather thin. It was also extended beyond the force field. Apparently, this new version of the weapon was able to pierce the force field. "Son of a," Hunter said formed another force field around the damaged one.

To the side of them Perkins dropped to one knee as she coughed uncontrollably. The newly dancing sand around them was covering her body now as it tried to find a way inside of her. Each member of the team noticed the same thing happening to them as the sand surrounded then and began to turn bright orange. The sand covered their skin and began to sizzle. Even Flex, to his surprise, felt pain from this heated sand.

Twice in one day he had felt pain. He was beginning to dislike this Warden's Circle more and more. As the metal man walked towards then, hands still behind its back, the sands' glow intensified as the area became so hot that specks of sand on the ground turned to glass- like pellets. "Execute black pearl," Flex shouted as he backed up. Hunter nodded from inside the force field he created for them as Danielle summoned her powers. They knew what this meant, and had done the move several times in practice. Black Pearl was a way for them to combine their powers.

Danielle unleashed waves of dark energy, that seemed to have no effect, on the Warden, but did halt his advance towards them. As she did so, Hunter began to form a force field around the creature. In seconds, the force field Hunter had created was engulfed with thick swirling black tendrils and pulsing dark energy. They couldn't see the Warden inside of his new prison, and could only hope it couldn't see them. "I don't know how long that will hold him," Perkins said. "Then we better move," Flex replied. "Lead the way."

Perkins wasted no time and dashed through the sand, followed by Danielle, Flex, and a very tired Hunter. He had used a lot of energy creating so many force fields at once, and needed a good rest or a large plate of food to replenish.

In the lead, Perkins moved as fast as she could. Never looking back to make sure her friends were with her, and never loosening the grip on her blasters. She didn't slow down until she came to what looked like a tall pillar that stretched so far into the sky that the top couldn't be seen.

“Inside. This will give us some time.” Perkins said as she opened a door at the bottom of the pillar. “What is that noise?” Danielle asked as her hand motioned to block her ear. Flex and Hunter, while they had said nothing, had heard the sound too. A strong rhythmic humming that seemed to be radiating from the pillar. “Inside,” was the only reply Perkins said. No more questions came, as they rushed into the darkness of the pillar. Once inside, Perkins shut the door and dropped to her knees panting. As soon as the door was shut, a single light came on.

It emitted only a thin beam of light, but it was enough so that they could see a few feet around themselves. Flex moved to comfort Perkins and placed a hand on her shoulder as he helped her to her feet. “We should be okay in here for a little bit. Maybe until daylight.” Perkins said. She was speaking to them all, but only Flex had her attention now.

Hunter was the first one to notice that, while her words were comforting, they weren’t exactly correct. Had Perkins been looking in the same direction as he was, she would have likely seen it first. “We can’t win from losing,” Hunter said as he tried to draw attention to the fact that they were not alone inside the pillar.

CHAPTER 10:
HELLO ABEL

Flex was the first of their group to notice Hunter's shift in posture. His leadership skills kicked in, and his eyes began to scan the room. He still couldn't see anything in the darkness, but for that matter, Hunter truly couldn't either. He knew he had heard something, though.

Hunter hadn't been on Mo'eizus long, but he had learned enough in life to trust his instincts, and instantly called a large force field into life. He stepped back and looked at it. The force field was a swirling, pale blue wall of protection, and once it was in place, Hunter instantly felt better. "By the great beast," Perkins said as she walked to stand beside Hunter. "Kill the force field," she said quickly.

"Say what now?" Hunter asked as he looked at her with a frown on his face. "No flashy powers," Perkins said. Her words were low, but just loud enough so Danielle and Flex could hear her. "We don't want the attention or the Wardens." Hunter had a quick flashback of their recent clash. In a blink of an eye he remembered the pain, seeing his force field get damaged and the feeling of that heated sand burning his skin. Then he let out a long sigh, and the force field faded away.

Perkins leaned and looked into the darkness, and as she did so her bright green eyes seemed a little brighter for a moment and then faded away. "Perkins. Is that you?" Hunter jumped some as the raspy voice came from the darkness. "Here we go," Hunter said to himself as he balled a fist. Warden's be damned, if he needed to, he was prepared to use every power he had, to face whatever was in the darkness.

He trusted Perkins and her insight, but Hunter had no dreams of being ambushed or murdered inside some creepy, old, vibrating pillar.

"Really. Somebody is already hiding in here?" Danielle said as she shifted to look into the darkness. "Not hiding," the voice came back from the darkness. "Hiding is for cowards and vermin. We are planning."

The words made Flex clench his jaw. "How many of you are there?" he asked loudly, as he stepped to the front of the group, sticking out his chest in a way that only a person with invulnerability could. Hunter, not to be outdone, moved and stood directly beside their leader. Flex looked at him through the side of his eye. "Really?" he said under his breath. "It is my planet after all. May as well, get the best view in the house."

Hunter planted his feet firmly, "and you know how I love to put on a show," he continued. "Wait for my signal," Flex said. "If I don't give the word, then no powers." Hunter groaned. "Sure." He hated it, but he had no intentions of disobeying Flex. He was the team leader and Hunter respected that, so, for now, he would follow his lead.

"Hello, Abel," Perkins said through a sigh. "Why don't you come forward into the light?" As the words left her mouth, the sound of footsteps moving began to fill the room. Slowly three men and a woman came into view. As Hunter looked at them all, his mind was flooded by hillbilly jokes. They were all dressed fairly similar to how Perkins had made the team dress. They all also had on goggles, and for some reason, they all were very dirty.

Hunter didn't notice it at first glance, but now he could clearly see that all four of them looked like they had been working for years without a single shower. "Hey there," one man said. He was the tallest of the group. He had wide shoulders, a round stomach, and short dingy hair. "Why don't you come get close to a real man?" he continued.

"Sorry big boy, but I'm spoken for," Danielle said quickly. "She's with me," Hunter said as Perkins raised a hand to stop him. "Good," the large man said. "You can keep her, too. I was talking to him." The man jerked his head towards Flex. "Nerf, he is cute," the woman of the group said. To Hunter's surprise, the other two men nodded their heads in agreement.

He furrowed his brow and smirked to Flex who took in a deep breath. "Entire new dimension, and yet your Ken Doll powers never fail you." "Not the time, Paragon," Flex said through gritted teeth. The sound of his name, made Hunter focus as he gave a slight nod. He couldn't help but joke. It was his way to keep calm in the situation, seeing as how he couldn't use his powers.

"He's with me," Perkins said to the group at large. "What are you doing here, Abel?" The large man spoke again. "As I said. I'm planning." "Fine. Plan away." Perkins continued. "We don't want any trouble, we're just." Abel laughed loudly, and as his laughter filled the pillar, Hunter got a funny feeling in his stomach.

He was already trying to ignore the fact the once roomy pillar was slowly starting to feel crowded, and now these randoms were here. "Nerf, Perkins," Abel said. "You're in here the same reason as us. You don't want to bump into the Wardens. That's also why you turned off your little box that your group loves so much."

"Box?" Perkins replied. "That created the force field." This time another person spoke. It was a pear- shaped man standing to the side of Abel. His words made him receive a stern look, followed by a fast punch to the face. The sound of Abel's hand hitting the man echoed around the pillar and made the odd- shaped man stumble. "Speak over me again, see what happens. You get one warning, Martel. One!" Abel shouted.

The man called Martel silently nodded as his hand covered the spot where he had just been punched. "As I was saying," Abel said calmly as he adjusted his clothes while spinning on the spot to face Perkins again. "We saw the force field from the multibox." Perkins darted her eyes some and then realized what they were talking about. They thought that Hunter's power was actually her using the force field on her multibox. "Oh," she replied. Abel tapped a single finger to his head. "I'm always watching. You should know this, Perkins." Abel moved a little closer to them, but this time his team didn't advance. "You see we are here because we planned on it.

Moving from pillar to pillar. Shadow to shadow. This was actually our last stop before we made it to the cage."

Perkins' eyes bulged for a second as recognition washed over her face. The look was gone in an instant, but Flex had seen it. He wanted to ask her what the cage was, but figured now wasn't the best time. No instead he allowed her to keep the lead on their conversation with Abel. "You're going to the cage," Perkins replied. It was more of a slow statement, instead of questions.

"But this isn't the route to get there," she said as she looked at Abel, and then his team. "You're sneaking in." Abel clapped slightly. "You always were smart enough to get by, Perkins." Flex glared at the man. He was pretty sure that was an insult to his better half, and if she gave him the go-ahead, he would toss this Abel directly through the pillar and into the next one.

"You see Perkins, I had a bit of unfortunate luck. I owe a lot of funds to a lot of people. Funds I don't have." Abel turned and walked into the darkness then came back holding a chunk of what looked like bread. He took a bite, and then passed it to the female. She in return took a bite and passed it on. "We were going to just run in, take their goods and then make our way to the North section."

Abel rubbed his chin and looked Flex over again. He licked his lips slowly, and Flex grimaced. "He really wants a piece of you," Danielle whispered. Flex ignored her. "I have a better plan now. One that doesn't involve my guys and I going to that nerfing cold North Section." Perkins twisted her head slightly.

"What plan?" she asked. "Well, you know the cage. Fighters are a priority, but slaves are almost as important, and now I seem to have four to use for trade. Just enough to settle my debts I'd think."

Before any of them could react to what Abel had said, he began to whistle. As his tones filled the air, Perkins opened her mouth to alert the others, but it was too late. Her voice was nowhere to be found and her body began to go limp. In seconds several thuds could be heard as bodies hit the floor. Perkins watched her friends fall into a deep sleep on the ground, as darkness began to consume her vision.

Danielle was the first to wake up. She was still groggy, but as she looked around her, everybody was passed out. Not only were they passed out, but like herself, they were standing against a wall with their hands shackled above them. She hadn't been doing this hero thing long, but she had learned enough to keep a level head in uncertain situations.

From what she could see, it was only herself and her team in the small room that was, without doubt, a cell. Everything from the dirt floor and shackles, to the barred- like door that locked them in. She gave a slight tug to the shackles. Nothing happened, of course. She didn't have strength like that of Flex or Hunter, but what she did have was her shadow ability.

As soon as she made the decision to transform and break free, she thought better of it. Perkins had said no flashy powers, and until she woke up, Danielle thought it was better to stick to that plan. "Okay, first things first," she said as she used her foot to kick Hunter. He was the closest hanging person to her.

She grunted as she performed a kick that should have done the job, and freed him from his slumber, but it didn't. She rolled her eyes as she swung her hips once more to kick him, this time with more force. He didn't wake up but he was coming to. "That's it, boo. Come to momma."

She smiled for a second as Hunter's head began moving slowly as he groaned. Danielle twisted and delivered another kick for good measure. This time a yelp of pain was the response she received. "About time," she said. Hunter's head finally looked around. "Where?" he said as he searched around the room and realized he was pretty much a prisoner.

"Where are we?" Hunter asked. "Don't know, boo. At least we're together, though," Danielle said. Hunter looked at her. "Your displays of affection, even in situations like these, are why you're so easy to love."

Danielle wanted to laugh at what Hunter had just said. A laugh that was so intense that her body began to shake as she held it in. Hunter grimaced.

"We need to work on your response to compliments," Hunter said. "I love you, but that was pretty mean to laugh at me like that. You cut me deep, woman." "For Atlas' sake," Danielle said as she rolled her eyes, and laughed at him. "I mean us. All four of us are together. We're lucky they didn't separate us." Hunter jerked his head and looked towards the cell door.

"You heard that right?" he asked Danielle. The loud noise that sounded like no less than one hundred different voices were cheering echoed into the room. "Yeah. Been going on since I woke up," Danielle said. "No idea why, but they are out there, and we are in here. That's all that matters for now."

"Where is here is the question," Hunter said as he took the cell in once more. It was clearly man-made. The dirt floor and roof with holes in it was a good indication of that. The shackles seemed to be the only thing about their cell that was created to be sufficient. From what Hunter could see, even the bars on their cell door were created from some thick, cream-colored wood.

He didn't know how things were done on this world, but surely a door made out of the same metal as their shackles would have been a better option. "We're in the cage." Her sudden voice made Hunter and Danielle's head jerk towards her. As Perkins lifted her head, she gave a slight smile to them. "Worst rescue mission ever," then she paused as she shifted some.

"Nerf. He took my blasters," Perkins said. "We've got bigger issues than that," Hunter replied. "It doesn't happen often, but I agree with Hunter," Flex said as his head looked around. He actually had been up a few seconds after Danielle but kept up the ruse to access the situation entirely. His training was so drilled into his mind that Flex naturally assumed people would be listening and monitoring them. That was of course before he had seen their archaic prison.

"Nice of you to join us, last pretty boy," Hunter said. Flex didn't correct him. I assume we are keeping up the no flashy powers order?" Flex asked. "So, no shadow form, force fields, or Impact Blast." "For now," Perkins replied. "I think I know why we are here though," She paused. "I never knew Abel could fall so far."

"Tell me about Abel," Flex said. "Not the time to be a jealous boyfriend," Hunter replied. "I'm just gathering information before I act, intern," Hunter grunted as he positioned his weight to get comfortable.

"Back when we founded Bravado, Abel wanted to join," Perkins said. "At the time it was just Cord, me and a few others." She inhaled some as her hands twitched in her shackles. "With his spell, we figured he could be a good addition to the-" "Am I the only one that doesn't know what in Atlas' name a spell is?" Danielle asked the room.

"Yes," Flex replied at the same time that Hunter replied "No." "It's like, well no it's not like that at all," Perkins said to herself more so than Danielle. "You know how we are born with our powers, and studies pretty much tell us that it's because of small differences in our genetic makeup that leads to large results?" Flex asked. "I follow so far," Danielle replied.

"Well if I understand what Perkins has told me over these few months, in this dimension their explanation for powers revolves around magic," Flex continued. "Or what your dimension calls a soul," Perkins chimed in. "Short version is that here, we are all born with a slither of magic in us called a spell. Hence why our people are called Spellborn. Some of us are lucky enough to manifest that spell into minor abilities."

Perkins paused to look at Danielle and Hunter who were hanging on to her every word. Danielle's face remained passive as she listened. Hunter's was different. He had almost a glare on his face. Inside his head, he was battling with being angry and disappointed. Angry that in all this time Perkins hadn't told him this, and disappointed with himself for not bothering to ask her about his own heritage.

Last year Impervious had told him that magic was real when he first told him about the Spellborn people. Hunter exhaled some as he closed his eyes for a minute. *You don't even know who you truly are*, he thought to himself.

"So, like when my eyes glow and allow me to see in the dark, that's me using my spell. Same for Abel. His whistle can knock people out." Perkins continued. "The flip side to this is those with elite blood." She let her gaze fall to Hunter. "Impervious, his brother, Hunter, and many others. Their spells manifest in fantastically strong ways. There is no middle ground for the elites, though. They either get a ton of power or none at all."

Hunter felt he had enough. The mention of his father, even in passing, was enough to make him want the subject changed. "History lesson aside, get to the point about Abel," Hunter replied. His words came out stronger than he intended and made it seem like he was barking an order to Perkins. An action that earned him a strong glare from Flex, and a swift kick from Danielle.

"We eventually realized he wasn't interested in liberating the people at all, and peacefully parted ways," Perkins replied. Danielle shook her hands and clattered her shackles together. "I think he missed the peaceful part." "The lady makes a valid point," Hunter said.

"And this cage place?" Flex asked. "It's a fighting arena. Funds are wagered, and fights take place. until a champion of the cage is…" her words faded out as her head jerked up. "I know how we are getting out without alerting the Wardens to our location. They likely know of your abilities since our fight with the Warden earlier. "Good because I was starting to think it was time to stop playing nice. These shackles are itchy," Danielle said.

"Do you trust me?" Perkins asked as she looked at Flex. "Oh boy," Hunter groaned. "I've seen movies. When a woman asks her man that question, she is about to do something borderline crazy."

Flex ignored Hunter's remarks and nodded to Perkins. "I do." She smiled. "Then follow my lead, and you two keep your mouths shut." "Zipped tight," Hunter replied. "We just have to bide our time until the Warden patrols are done on this area," Perkins added.

Without warning, she began to scream at the top of her lungs. "Abel! Abel!" her screams of his name were stretched out and went on for a few more minutes before Abel and the female from his team showed up.

"Perkins!" Abel hissed as he came to the cell door. "It's hard to quietly get my team in position with your screaming my name, and alerting people I'm here. If I can't sell you lot as slaves, it's back to the original plan of a snatch and grab." "Well, I figured you'd want to hear what I had to say," Perkins replied. Abel looked at her as he exhaled and leaned on the bars. "And what exactly is that?" Abel asked.

"You don't have to sell us, or rob anybody. I know how you can win all the funds back you lost, and more." "How?" the woman with Abel asked. Abel glared at her, and she retracted back some. She took an additional two steps away from her leader as images of her friend being punched flashed in her mind.

"How," Abel repeated. "By representing the next champion of the cage." Abel snickered some. Hunter grimaced and held in his laughter at a man with Abel's size letting out such a feminine sound.

"Are you saying you want to fight?" Abel asked between laughs. "You're good, but not that good, and your spell isn't gonna help you in the cage. Not with the likes of Cyn or the current Champion." Perkins shook her head. "Not me, him." She thrust her head towards Flex who remained calm and locked eyes with Abel.

Abel smiled and leaned in a little more as he licked his lips. "Him?" Perkins nodded. "I'd hate to see that face messed up. What's his spell?" "Strength," Perkins replied. "Strong muscles. Strong skin," she replied as she looked at Flex. "Show em." With her words, Flex snapped the metal shackles with less effort than a man snapping a toothpick.

Next, he removed the shackles from his wrist, balled them up, and casually flicked it across the room with enough force that left a hole in the wall. Abel's eyes grew wide as he rubbed his chin. "How can I trust you? If he's as strong as you say, what's to stop him from turning on me, and doing his own thing?" Abel asked.

Hunter looked at Perkins. He didn't like Abel or even know him well, but he clearly was smarter than he looked. In some instances, at any rate. "We need your connections and a small part of the profit. You know it's hard living in Omega's shadow." Hunter narrowed his gaze as he remembered the distress message that Perkins played for them. Omega was mentioned there, too. Clearly, there was more that Perkins hadn't told them.

Abel paused for a few minutes, and then leaned over to his female partner and whispered in her ear. She nodded and then ran off. "She's going to tell them we have a new fighter. He's going to have to beat a few guys to pay off what I owe, and then we can discuss giving you a fee for bringing him to me." Perkins snorted. "You were going to sell us, Abel. Don't make it as I sought you out with the opportunity."

Abel shrugged. "What's your name?" he asked, as he eyed Flex. As he wiped dirt from his hand, he casually replied. "Ryan." For a moment Hunter and Danielle looked at each other. They both knew that Ryan was Flex's real name, but hadn't heard it used in a long time. "Take your shirt off, Ryan," Abel said as he opened the cell door. "We got work to do." Flex took a few steps forward and then looked over his shoulder to Perkins. She gave him a slight nod as he removed his shirt and left the cell.

Abel shut the door behind Flex and locked it once more. Before they could leave, the man called Martel came into view. "What are you doing out of position?" Abel asked as he snarled at his underling. Martel took a step back. "Orena told me you had a fighter, and to come and check if you wanted the rest of them watched just in case something went wrong."

Abel sucked his teeth and thought about it. It was a good idea, a damned good idea, and he knew it. What bothered Abel was that he hadn't come up with it. Orena did. Not only did she come up with it, but she voiced it to one of his team. He exhaled some.

She was smart. Smart enough to run her own team if she wanted to, but also smart enough to be able to steal one just as easy. He made a mental note to do something about her, once they were finished here. Oddly enough, at the exact same moment, Flex was thinking how easily he could solve this entire situation.

In a matter of seconds, he could handle the two men before him, and his team could be free and heading to their original destination. As he made the decision to do just that, he balled his fist and shifted his shoulders slightly. Before he could act, a loud clearing of a throat came from inside the cell. Flex glanced inside and saw Perkins shake her head and silently mouth the words *no.*

Flex, against his own experience and judgment, decided to trust the woman that he had fallen for. He relaxed and remained silent beside Abel, who had casually put his arm around his shoulder. "Just keep an eye on them, especially Perkins. She's," Abel paused as he looked for the right words. "Unpredictable."

"You got it," Martel said as he sat down on the dirt ground in front of the cell door. Abel gave Perkins a slight wave, and then walked out of view with Flex. "So now what?" Hunter asked under his breath. "We just wait for Flex to figure out something?" Perkins didn't answer at first. She took a few minutes to run over some plans in her head. "All he has to do is win," Perkins finally said. "So, we really are just going to let all this unfold for a friend of yours?" Danielle asked.

Abel is no friend of mine," Perkins shot back. "We just need to kill time, and not draw attention to us. The Warden's rotations will be ending as the day comes. Then we leave without bringing attention to ourselves." "Still, some heads will have to get cracked in the process," Perkins said as she shot a smile to Danielle.

"Hey Martel," Perkins shouted. "Shut up," Martel replied. "I just want to know who the champion is," Perkins continued. "My boy is the real deal, so don't want you putting funds on the wrong guy." "It's Manis," Martel said casually as he sat on the ground. "I think my money is fine where it is."

The smile faded from Perkin's face, as for the first time, she was afraid for Flex.

CHAPTER 11:
THE ARENA

Flex walked alongside Abel down the makeshift hall. He noticed that, just as with their cell, this hallway seemed to have been poorly constructed. There was no floor, just a dirt ground below their feet that was equal parts trash just as much as dirt. Then there were the walls which, much like the ceiling, was composed out of different materials and had holes in it so large that outside could easily be seen.

Flex kept calm as, from an unseen location, he heard the loud cheers of a roaring crowd. He glanced over to Abel who kept up the pace with him. If Flex slowed down, so did Abel. He noticed the same for if he picked up speed. Flex felt like the man didn't trust him, and was too cautious to fall behind or walk too fast. No matter the speed Flex walked, Abel, matched it with little sign of effort. Despite his dingy appearance and attitude, Abel seemed like a smart man. It was likely the reason he was the man barking the orders in his group, and why he was able to attack them with no worry of retaliation.

"Well," Flex said passively as they walked. "Well, what?" Abel responded. Flex moved his mouth to answer but the new passage they were walking through, had left him breathless. Not only was he left breathless, but he had to stop moving altogether. The makeshift walls around them had a large portion missing. Through it, Flex saw something outside resting in the sand.

He narrowed his eyes, surely he wasn't seeing what he thought he was seeing. After a few seconds, he realized that it was indeed what it appeared to be. It was a skull. He couldn't tell what sort of animal it was but it was a skull nonetheless, and a colossal one at that.

Cream- colored and broken, the skull had to belong to an animal larger than Flex could even imagine. He stepped closer to the hole, and Abel moved to restrain him but thought better of it. Flex stuck his head out into the night outside of the hall, and as the heat and sand swirled around him, he marveled at the creature that had been forgotten by time.

Had the skull been in one piece it would have been the size of a large house. “By the Great Beast,” Flex said under his breath to himself. A few seconds went by before he released the breath, he didn’t realize he was holding, as he finally got an idea of what this term meant. Not only that, but he suddenly had the feeling that the wood used as bars on their cell door, wasn’t actually wood at all. “Bone,” Flex said to himself as he continued to look on in awe at the skull.

“What?” Abel said as he looked at Flex from behind him. Abel didn’t show it, but he was ready to whistle as loud as he could should Flex try to run, or even worse, use this as an elaborate way to cause Abel to drop his guard. Flex shook his head and returned to the center of the hall. “I need to know how this cage stuff works.”

Abel continued to walk up the hall. “We’re almost there, so here is the quick version. You fight three guys. All of them are pretty tough, usually. Some even have spells like mine or yours.” Flex listened and had no intentions of correcting Abel or his assumptions of Flex having a spell. Perkins had told some things to Flex in their time together, and the mindset of the Spellborn people was a topic casually mentioned.

Many of them didn’t remember the old days of the elite families. The days where the Spellborn would go from dimension to dimension and wage war. He wasn’t totally sure, but from what he understood, the passage of time was faster on Mo’eizus.

The time of the elites were more so legend than fact now. So, the thought of coming in contact with another being with spell-like gifts, but being from another dimension would be far from any of their minds. Even the technology Perkins used to get there wasn’t widely used outside of her team.

"Now the current champion is a different story," Abel continued. "How so?" Flex asked. "Manis has been on top for a long time. Longest run a champion has ever had. I think it's been a little over twenty," Abel counted in his head as he tried to run the calculations. He wanted to be as accurate as he could with his guess. "About twenty days." Flex fought the urge to laugh.

"That's it?" Flex asked. "Twenty days of fighting," Abel continued on. "Twenty days. Each day would have about three or four tournaments, each with a person trying to become the new champion of the cage. Manis defeated them all." Flex let this sink in and found himself smiling.

For all of his training and leadership skills, he always did enjoy a good fight. He would never admit it to Hunter, but even when they were more enemies than friends he had enjoyed when they had these physical interactions. When you were as strong as he was, a good fight was usually welcomed, and often won. Except for with Hunter.

No, when he and Hunter tangled those two times, they were stopped on both occasions. Even during training, neither of them went full power to really put it all on the line. "So, he must have one heck of a spell," Flex said. The roar of the crowd was getting louder, and as they continued to move Flex could smell what appeared to be sewage lofting on the air. "Strength," Abel said. "Just like you." Flex nodded.

"Although, you're certainly the better looking between you both. All that purple on him it's hard to tell what he truly looks like," Abel said. "All you have to do is win. You win and we all get paid." he continued. "Well we all get paid, but I will be getting paid better." Abel let out a long laugh at his own joke. "So, why don't you fight?" Flex asked Abel. Abel furrowed his brow and shook his head. "Your spell seems like it would be hard to beat," Flex continued. Abel released a slow and rusty laugh.

"You'd think so, but simply clog your ears, and I'm powerless. Then the rest of the fight, I'd just be trying to win on skill or luck. Too much risk. It's easier to be a betting man." Flex shook his head. "And that is working so well for you." Abel ignored his remark and continued talking. "I'll be your checker, naturally," Abel said to Flex. "My what?" Abel shook his head. "Just listen to what I say, when I say it." Abel took a deep breath and turned the corner in the hall.

As Flex did the same, he realized that they were out of the hall now. Instead, they were inside something much, much worse. They were inside a massive ribcage. Flex stood at the entrance and looked around him. It was hard to see from where he was, but from what he gathered, the entire area was constructed on the inside of the bones of a massive creature's skeleton, and they were currently in the ribcage. The area they had just walked through was some sort of tail with a hallway crafted on the inside of it.

Abel raised his hand in a grand gesture. "I give you, the cage." "I see. The name is unoriginal, but I see how it fits, nonetheless." Flex said calmly. Under the cage, a large hole was dug that had chairs all around it. Each chair had a person inside screaming and waving their arms around. The area was so crowded that people were even standing and cheering because there weren't enough chairs.

"The Wardens just let this happen?" Flex asked. "It seems too out in the open," he said as he looked around expecting to see food vendors of some sort.

"Omega takes a large portion of the profits," Abel grunted. *Omega,* Flex thought to himself. He kept hearing that name but only briefly. As if they didn't want to talk too much about the person, or organization, or whatever it was. "Alright, have at it," Abel said.

As he said the words, he casually placed a hand on Flex's back and pushed him forward. As he moved, he could see a worn path in the dirt that lead to the lower level of the large hole. Down below a single man who was shirtless like Flex, stood jogging in place and punching the air. "A new combatant emerges from the outside world."

The voice boomed around the fighting area and was so sudden that it caused Flex to pause in search of its source. On the opposite of the arena, in the middle of a crowd of chairs, standing on a platform was a man with a smile on his face that for some reason reminded Flex of a car salesman. His clothes were still as tattered as everyone else's but they were a pale gray color.

Flex assumed they were actually white once upon a time, and the ravages of time and dirt had slowly turned them. From what Flex could see, the man was broad shouldered with a bald head and a very wide nose. "Abel has returned, and is asking to use this new fighter to reclaim his lost glory," the man said. His voice once again boomed around the massive crowd. With each word from the man, the crowd seemed to get louder with hollers and cheers.

The man's voice exploded around the crowd again, and it did so on its own. Flex could see the man talking, but he didn't use anything to amplify his voice. Abel took in a deep breath behind Flex. "That's the conductor of the fights. His only job is to keep the crowd excited." "He seems to be good at it too," Flex said. "I'm guessing that his loud voice is his spell?" Abel nodded. "It's not destructive, though. Just loud. Took him a while to find a use for it."

Flex continued his descent down into the area. "And this person I'm fighting, any spell I should know about?" Flex asked. Abel made a clicking with his teeth. "Acid projectile saliva is what I believe it is," Abel replied. Flex laughed. "He spits acid," Flex said as a smirk spread across his face.

This time, Abel stopped walking as he watched Flex move. For some reason, the smile on his face made him look at his new hunk of a fighter in a new light. Flex walked into the area and heard Abel shout out to him. "This is as far as I can go." Flex gave a slight thumbs up and continued to walk over to the man. He had stopped bouncing around now. Instead, he glared at Flex and spat on the ground.

As the spit touched the ground it sizzled and created a hole underneath it. "Okay," the conductor said as he looked down on the fighters. "You know the rules. To the death unless one of you gives up." This caused Flex to jerk his head towards Abel, who in returned shrugged and sat in a chair. Flex wasn't going to kill this man for no reason. It wasn't his way, and it wasn't the hero way.

He was better than that and found himself suddenly thinking about his sister. He was pulled from his thoughts as two large globs of spit splattered against his massive exposed chest. Flex looked down at the spot where on a normal man would be two holes burning towards his organs. He heard a faint crackle, and then flicked the spit away.

The man on the other side followed Flex's flicking hand as he ignored his first attack. Now even some of the crowd had shut up and paid attention. The man charged forward and punched Flex in the face. As a result, his fist broke with a loud pop that made the crowd explode in cheers. "We have a bonified powerhouse from Abel's corner," the conductor said as the crowd began to clap.

Flex grabbed the man by his still intact hand and with ease slung him into the crowd about twenty feet away. Flex called for Abel to come into the area. After a few moments of hesitation, he ran to his fighter. "I want the other two at the same time," Flex said as Abel's eyes widened. "I, I," Abel stammered. "Trust me, they want to see the show, and I don't have all day. Make it happen," Flex told him.

"You're one good looking crazy fool of a man," Abel said as his eyes darted down to the exposed chest and ripped midsection on Flex. "I'll see what I can do," Abel said as he left the arena and made his way to the conductor. "Perkins, I hope you're doing your part. Whatever it is." Flex said to himself.

Perkins still had a look of worry on her face as she let her fingers dance on her shackles. The sound of cheers and screams were louder than they had been earlier, and even Martel remarked on it from outside of the cell.

"I hope Ryan is the reason for their excitement. They love it when a new guy is a real brawler." "You have no idea," Hunter said as he rolled his eyes.

He was tired of hanging around doing nothing. He wasn't as antsy as Danielle, but he was getting there. He wanted to snap those shackles, blast Martel, and get out of wherever they were. He was to the point that he felt like a fight with the Warden's Circle was better than just waiting for time to pass by. "So, what do you think?" Danielle asked Perkins. "This Manis really might be stronger than Flex?" "Maybe," Perkins replied.

"Manis is strong, of that I'm sure. His strength has become something of a legend in this world. We tried to recruit him for Bravado several times over," Perkins continued. "But he was addicted to chrome and became undependable for us to even consider anymore."

Hunter hung on to every word that Perkins said. After she told them that Flex might not be able to out- strength this man, Hunter could do nothing but stare blankly at her and shake his head. It just didn't seem possible. He believed in Flex but also wanted to see the fight happen, just in case his friend had met his match.

"Chrome?" Danielle said out loud. "Some sort of drugs?" "The worst kind. chrome destroys those that use it. Entire parts of some sections have fallen to chrome. Not like one of those drugs on your world that you told me about. Where you smoke it, feel great, get hungry, then go to sleep," Perkins replied. Hunter rolled his head to look at Danielle. "Really?" he asked.

"She was learning about the culture," Danielle replied. "You think I was going to leave that out?" Perkins looked through one of the holes in their cell and could see light outside. The sands still whipped around, but darkness wasn't there anymore. "Finally," Perkins said. "The patrols should be mostly gone now. It's time."

Instantly Danielle smiled and turned to her shadow form, and was freed from her shackles. She nodded to Hunter and then disappeared through the wall. Hunter, with a little more effort than Flex had to use, broke free from his restraints. As they clattered against the wall, Martel turned and looked in the cell. "How did you..." His words were cut off as a force field wrapped around him and lifted him off the ground.

The man began to squirm and scream like a child that had just lost its toy. Hunter wrapped his hands around Perkins' shackles and quickly set her free. She rubbed her wrist and smiled at him. "Thanks," she replied. "Spellborns look out for each other," he replied with a smirk. "Ready," Danielle shouted from outside the cell. She was in her normal form now, standing just below where Martel was being held by the force field.

With a flick of Hunter's hand, the force field faded away, and as Martel made his descent to the ground, Danielle balled a fist wrapped in dark energy and punched the man directly in the jaw. As he crashed into the ground he was still breathing, but not moving. "This certainly isn't his day," Danielle said as she stood over him.

"Yeah, he'll be just fine," Hunter replied as his eyes turned blue. "Now, step aside." Danielle looked at him with a brow raised. "Please. Can you step aside, please?" Hunter said as he rolled his eyes in an over the top fashion. Danielle stepped aside as she was asked and watch the blue energy collide with the cell door as it was propelled with so much force that it shattered when it hit the wall.

Hunter, followed by Perkins, stepped outside of the cell and looked around. "We just gonna leave him here?" Danielle asked as she pointed her thumb to Martel. "May as well," Hunter replied. "Unless one of you want to carry him." Neither of them responded. "Good," Hunter said after their moment of silence. "We find Flex, and then we get out. I'm done pretending to be a powerless damsel in distress." Hunter's words were cut off.

"My blasters," Perkins said, in a voice that was almost a shriek. "Well do you really need them?" Hunter asked. "We all can't punch a hole through a car with our eyes," Perkins replied. "You make a valid point,"

Hunter said. “Okay,” Danielle added in as she darted up the hall to look around to make sure nobody was coming. “Get your blasters, then we save Flex.”

Hunter stuck a hand out. “Whoa, whoa, whoa. Keep in mind he may not even need saving.” Danielle nodded, and locked eyes with Hunter. They both were hoping that Flex would be okay. He always was, but with the way Perkins spoke of this Manis fellow, it made them wonder. “Any idea where they would put your blasters?” Hunter asked.

Perkins, now standing over Martel, shook her head. “Not a clue, but I’m going to nerfing find out.” With those last words, she grabbed the unconscious Martel by the collar and slapped him so hard on the face that it left her hand sore. “Not his day at all,” Danielle said again to herself.

CHAPTER 12:
CHAMPION OF THE CAGE

For the first time that Abel could recall, the crowd was silent. The only sounds that could be heard in the arena now were the sounds of the occasional chair moving, and the faint vibration of the ground shaking. Abel swallowed to try and apply moisture to his dry throat, but it didn't work.

Had he not been there to witness it, he wouldn't have believed it possible, but he was there. He did witness it, and he realized that it was all too possible. The sensation of fear and excitement battled inside of Abel now. He was fearful at what he had just seen, and even more fearful when he decided that he would no doubt have to dispose of Perkins and the other two. There was no way he was going to part with this Ryan guy after what he just saw. That fear also included that Ryan would likely try to stop him.

Abel took in a deep breath. That wouldn't be good at all. Then the excitement came. What if this man, this random, talented, attractive man, was his ticket? What if Ryan was the one to propel Abel to the top of the world of arena fighting? His hands shook with the thought of the possibility.

Abel looked at his hand. No, there was an entirely different reason his hand was shaking. Covertly, Abel pulled a small vial from his pocket and untwisted the dropper cap after he filled it with a silver liquid. Abel turned in on himself, as he faced the most unoccupied portion of the area and allowed two drops of the liquid to fall under his tongue, and then dropped two extra droplets in his eye for good measure.

A few breaths later, he felt like a new man again. The shaking in his hands had stopped, and his focus was back. His ideas flowed smoothly through his head, and he was ready to take on the underworld again. Chrome truly was a marvelous gift, and Able loved every inexpensive drop.

Flex stood in the middle of the arena, breathing slightly faster than normal as he looked at the two men groaning on the ground. One of them was lean and muscular with dark skin, while the other was massive and built like a football player. Neither were dead, but both were too hurt to move without groaning and feeling pain.

The fight hadn't lasted long, and when the crowd found out his request to fight both contenders at once they assumed the night would end fast. They were wrong, and eventually, their disappointment transformed into disbelief, as the newcomer began to fight. Not only was he fighting the two men at once but he was winning, and shrugging off their attacks with ease. A feat that was unexpected considering both men had decent spell abilities.

"You both fought a good fight. Today just wasn't your day." Flex said as he extended a hand to the man with dark skin and tried to help him up. At first, Flex thought better of it. The man had displayed a spell during their fight that seemed to hinder his opponent's vision and induced headaches. This spell was a bother to Flex since it affected his vision and brain and not his physical body. Still, even once slowed the man was unable to hurt the invulnerable body Flex had.

In time one bad move allowed Flex to place his hands on the man, and then his time was over. The man stumbled to his feet as he slapped Flex's hand away. Despite prompts from the crowd Flex refused to kill the man. As he slowly limped away, Abel flashed him a passive smile.

When Flex turned to the other man on the ground he realized that he had already started getting up. He was a massive man and seemed to have a spell that gave him limitless endurance. During the fight, no matter what he did, he just kept coming. He never showed signs of fatigue. There was no sweating or heavy breathing. Endurance alone wasn't enough to topple an opponent like Flex, and in time the large man's back alley brawler style of fighting didn't last long against the trained fighting skills that Flex displayed.

He actually didn't even need to use much of his strength on the larger of the two men., but strong blows to the right location of the body got the job done. "Good fight," Flex said as he extended his hand to the man. He couldn't hear it but Abel groaned from the side of the arena. This time the man returned the gesture and shook Flex's hand.

He grunted out the words as he spoke. "Thanks for sparing me. I live to fight another day." "You may want to work on your style some first," Flex said as the large man lumbered away with a slight limp in his step. Flex didn't realize that as he put on a show and then stunned the crowd by allowing his opponents to live, that a pair of eyes were watching him from the crowd that didn't belong to the normal spectators.

Eyes that, unbeknownst to Flex, had slowly gotten closer and closer to the arena. "Well, that was...," the conductor's voice boomed around the arena. "Well, it was a little of a letdown huh, folks?" As Flex stood in the center of the Arena, shirtless and no signs of injury, the crowd began to scream and boo. The conductor motioned his hands for them to calm down as he continued to speak. Once the crowd was under control, the conductor licked his lips some and smiled as he began his intro. He usually put a lot of effort into practicing these the day before, so he always wanted full attention before he got into it. "We knew it would all come down to this."

As the conductor spoke, Flex glanced at Abel who, while still smiling, didn't look as confident as he did moments ago. His smile wasn't as large, and he was pacing now instead of standing casually. In the crowd behind Abel, Flex thought he saw a flicker of spiked blond hair moving, but as he adjusted his eyes, he couldn't find it again.

"It's time to find out who is truly tonight's champion of the cage," the conductor said, as he stretched out his final words. The crowd slowly began to chant one single word slowly. *Manis.* "Will it be the newcomer?" the conductor said as he did a little spin from where he stood and pointed to Flex. "A man given to use by Abel. A man who seems to be powerful and strong in his own right. A man with hand to hand skills that took down two worthy contenders!"

Flex looked around at the crowd that surrounded him as they continued to chant.

Manis. Manis. Manis.

"Or will it be our longest champion of the cage in arena history?" The chanting crowd exploded as one section of it slowly began to part and form a walkway. Flex turned to face the newly formed path and could see a large cloaked figure walking. "Will it be Mo'eizus' favorite son?" the conductor said as the crowd continued to chant.

Manis. Manis. Manis.

With each word, they seemed to chant louder. The cloaked figure stepped into the arena and stood on the opposite side of Flex. Even though they were feet apart, Flex still had to look up at the massive man. A hand slowly lifted from under the cloak that revealed purple skin, with a crystallized texture to it. "Our strongest son!" the conductor continued. Flex looked over his shoulder to Abel who was visibly sweating now.

Flex grimaced. He knew this was all an act and that he was only here to buy time so they wouldn't jump into another Warden's circle, but now he was curious about this Manis fellow. He hated that he was, and for a moment he felt like the jerk he used to be back in school. Back when he and Hunter had their first encounter.

The large purple hand finally unbuttoned the cloak, and as it fell to the ground the conductor screamed, "I give you, Manis!" The crowd went insane as the massive figure turned around and even did a little bow. Flex wasn't as shallow as Hunter often accused him, but he truly felt like less of a man as he shared the arena with this titan.

Flex wasn't small by any means, neither were his muscles, but compared to Manis, he looked like a malnourished child. "You know what to do," the conductor said. As soon as the words were out of his mouth the crowd was silent and watched Manis charge toward Flex. As he watched the giant approach, it took all of his control to not lift from the ground to fly out of the way.

Instead, he raised a hand to catch the punch that Manis sent his way. The crowd went silent again as they watched Flex do exactly that. As Manis' hand was held suspended in the air, he looked down on Flex. As their eyes locked, Flex could only hear the breathing of the man as he saw his purple disfigured skin up close. He tried to ignore the shaking in his arm as he held the attack back, but for a man like Flex, a man that had always been the strongest, it was hard to overlook.

He had only met one person stronger than himself, and that was Impervious. A man who even admitted that Flex was becoming stronger than him. Manis delivered another blow with his free hand to the face of Flex, that sent him lifting several feet in the air. Had this been any other fight, Flex would have used his flying ability to correct himself in the air.

Instead, he felt a massive hand wrap around his ankle and the world around him became a blur as Manis pulled him back down directly into another punch. This punch sent him to the ground with such force that the floor now had a tiny crater in it. Manis thrust his hands in the air as the crowd roared. Flex groaned as he pushed himself up from the ground as his tongue rolled around in his mouth. He could taste blood, and for a moment he was curious as to why. Then he realized he just had never been hit that hard before.

"Okay so he's strong," Flex said to himself as he stood up. "Nerfing right, he's strong," Abel said as he watched Flex get up. "It's that stuff on his skin," Abel continued. "It's braelium. The strongest mineral on the planet. It's fused through his body. He may not be a hit with the ladies, but a spell like that makes him stronger than anything." Flex chuckled some. "I noticed."

The crowd went quiet as Flex stood up and cracked his neck. His vision shifted some as he felt the room spin for a second. "Atlas, how hard did he hit me?" Flex said to himself. As he moved towards the purple goliath across from him, a single voice yelled from an unseen location in the crowd. "Hurry up, Ken Doll."

Flex smirked as he refused to lose with Hunter, and likely the others, watching the fight. "You take a punch well," an accented voice that sounded more like a bark came from across the arena. "But nothing is stronger than Manis." Manis tossed a punch at Flex that was dodged, as Flex delivered a solid blow to the purple mountain's stomach.

He had connected well too. Manis was hit so hard that his feet came off the ground. The crowd booed and hissed at this turn of events. "The newcomer isn't going down easy is he folks?" The conductor asked as he spun around and hyped up the crowd. "But can he stop Manis?" At the mere mention of his name, the crowd shifted and came alive again.

Hunter, Danielle, and Perkins moved slowly through the crowd, as they tried to avoid Abel's team that was spread out among them. Perkins had her newly found blasters secured in her trousers and hidden from view. No doubt there were various other weapons around her in the guests of the arena, but she didn't want to take any chances.

"We just have to make it to Flex," Perkins said. "I've heard how these fights get, and regardless if he wins or losses, once the battle is over it's going to get crazy here. Something that I hadn't considered until just now." "Why?" Hunter asked as they gently pushed people out of the way as they moved. "Flex has put on a good show tonight, even landed some good hits on Manis."

Perkins took a look towards the area to check to see how Flex was doing. At the moment he and Manis were exchanging blows in the middle of the arena, with neither giving a sign of slowing down. "A good show means more people are rooting for the favorite. So, if Manis keeps his title, then they keep their funds, and will likely explode in celebration. A celebration that usually turns violent from misunderstanding."

"And if our boy wins," Danielle asked as she followed behind them, bringing up the rear. "If Flex, an unknown suddenly wins then most of this crowd loses all of their funds, excluding Abel. If that happens, they will likely riot. Once the riot starts, bodies will drop. Of that I'm sure." "Sounds like a good time, and an even better diversion for us to get out unseen," Danielle said as she shoved a screaming man away that had bumped into her.

Perkins had finally stopped in the front of the crowd now. From where they stood, each of them had a good view of the fight and how Flex was doing. Each of them winced as they witnessed Flex for the first time looking tired, with a bloody mouth.

"It will be a good diversion," Perkins said. "The downside is that a riot this big will have to be squashed, and I'll give you one guess at who will be sent to do the squashing." "Those creepy ass Wardens," Hunter replied. Perkins nodded. "You win a prize," Perkins stuck her hand in her pockets and acted like she was looking for something and then pulled out her hand brandishing a thumbs-up salute.

Hunter was surprised at the state of Flex. The messy hair, heavy breathing, and blood were badges of honor worn by those in a fight, but Flex was just never one of those people. To think that this world could produce a person with strength on par with Flex was, well it was scary. While he and Flex may have started off as enemies, there was no doubt that they were friends now. Flex was his mentor, and Hunter made a mental note to kick this purple mountain's ass if he did defeat Flex.

He didn't know how or when, but he knew he would. Then he realized that maybe, just maybe, he wouldn't have to as Manis went to kick Flex. A single move that was the beginning of the end for the hometown hero.

Flex had seen his team watching the fight from the sides of the arena. Them being out meant that it was safe to leave and not be seen by the Wardens. All he had to do, was finish up with Manis. At that moment, a kick was rocketed to him. It was more so a purple blur than a kick. Flex was actually surprised a person with such size could move with such speed. Before the kick could land, Flex caught it with one arm and with as much power as he could create, he slammed his elbow down on the leg. At that moment several things happened at once.

First Manis screamed. A scream that echoed around the arena and caused the audience to go silent. They had never seen their champion in pain before. Why would they? Nothing was stronger or tougher than Manis.

The other thing that happened was the soft clinking sounds that could be heard as several purple shards fell from the leg of Manis and hit the ground. There were murmurs coming from all sides of the crowd now as they began to grasp what they were seeing.

Manis limped a little as he slammed one of his fists on his head to prep him for battle. "That hurt. You no stop Manis, though." Flex smiled back at him. "I think I will." The words were all it took for Manis who leaped from his good leg and sent a punch using his jump as momentum.

Flex didn't even dodge this time, instead, he caught the fist and applied pressure to the hand. So much pressure that the rock- like skin began to crack. "Do it," Abel shouted from the side as he leaped in the air. Hunter fought back the urge to wrap the man's head in a force field to see how long he could last.

"Looks like we can bet on that riot," Danielle said with a slight smirk as she watched the fight. With Manis still in his grasp, Flex did a leap of his own that sent him high in the air. So high that Hunter was pretty sure that Flex actually had flown some, and just used the jump to mask it. As Flex came down from the punch, he released the hand he was holding and buried his fist into the face of Manis.

As his punch connected, cracks rippled through the dense surface of Manis' face. The crowd was silent again. Only the jumping of Abel could be heard. Flex began to walk back to Abel, but then heard the crowd scream *Manis* as the conductor bellowed "this isn't over yet, folks."

Flex inhaled and spat blood on the arena floor as he turned to face Manis. “Stop. You will not win this fight.” The only reply Manis gave was to hold up his fist and take his stance. Flex did not. A gesture that Manis didn’t care for as he slowly approached his smaller opponent.

“You’re strong. Perhaps you’re even the Flex of your world,” Flex continued to speak as Manis inched closer. “But you have ventured into a fight you can’t win, against strength that you can’t match.” Manis continued his advance, and Flex slowly formed a fist.

“If you had a mental spell, you would probably win, but you don’t. You rely on hitting hard and being durable. I respect that, but in those two realms, I remain undefeated.” “Laying it on a little thick, pretty boy,” Hunter yelled from the side of the arena. It was at this moment that Abel and Hunter locked eyes.

Before he could even purse his lips to whistle, Hunter wrapped his head in a force field and slammed it to the ground several times. A smile of satisfaction stretched across his face. The crowd would have normally seen this and reacted badly, but Abel had few friends there. The friends he did have were too far away to help or care.

“Have it your way,” Flex said as he ran towards Manis, ducked below his punch and grabbed his injured leg. In comical fashion, he spun the purple mountain of a man around and then released him into the air as he was propelled from the arena, smashing bone from the ribcage of the beast as he went.

The crowd and conductor watched as Manis flew off into the distance and out of view. The only thing that could be heard was the sound of Danielle laughing, and Perkins saying one word. “Nerf.” then the conductor finally spoke. “We have a new champion of the cage.” After that, the arena exploded with anger, as the riot Perkins had feared, manifested.

CHAPTER 13:
THE GREAT BEAST

Hunter Monroe wasn't a person to run away from a fight. He normally charged right in. Being the son of a hero mother and infamous villain father usually left him as being a target for the greater super-powered community. The hate and cruelty came from both sides, so a fight, or two or five, was bound to happen, yet still, nothing could have prepared him for being in the center of a riot.

His time in Purgatory Academy had prepared him for a lot of things. That was the way of places that were educating heroes of the future, and riots were addressed. Riots on a different dimension, inside the skeletal remains of a giant monster sadly weren't on the syllabus.

As the events unfolded around him, Hunter was trying to figure out the best course of action. "What would Flex do, if he himself hadn't started the riot," he said under his breath. Instead of dwelling on the question for too long, he glanced to Flex who was tossing men aside with a single hand as he and Perkins were withdrawing from their embrace.

Flex kissed Perkins once more, and even as people screamed and raged around them, they found a second to smile about something. Seeing them made Hunter realize that Danielle wasn't with him anymore. His first reaction was to panic, then he thought better of it. As his eyes scanned the crowd around him, he saw her about ten feet away.

She had a fiendish smirk on her face and eyes that were as black as a windowless room. Tendrils of dark energy danced around her as she gladly took place in the riot. "We need to make a nerfing exit now," Perkins said as she and Flex ran over to Hunter. "We have to work on implementing our dimensions curse words into your vocabulary more. Nerf just isn't cutting it," Hunter replied. "Later," Flex said sternly. The tone he used was a solid indicator to Hunter that now wasn't the time for jokes.

"I really do hate to ruin her fun," Hunter said as he formed a force field around Danielle from where he stood, and pulled it towards himself. As the force field moved, Danielle allowed her darkness powers to fade away and she glared at Hunter who was now afraid to face his lover. "Atlas, she's gonna be pissed," Hunter said as the force field stopped in front of him. "No doubt, she'll be fine," Flex said as he lifted Perkins up in his arms.

"You couldn't give me a few more minutes for Atlas' sake?" Danielle said as the force field faded away. "Why should he have all the fun?" she asked as she eyed Flex whose mouth gaped open at her words. "He's out here arena fighting while I'm stuck in some rusty shackles, and as soon as I try to have some riot fun you cut me off."

"Don't look at me like that," Hunter replied. "You think I wouldn't like to mix it up in a riot?" Hunter tried to twist his face in a way to show that he was upset that they couldn't fight, but he felt that his ruse was easily seen through. Instead of discussing the issue more, Hunter instead created a large blue force field around himself and Danielle who rolled her eyes some as she watched the force field come into life around her.

Even over the crowd fighting around them, Hunter heard a faint booming sound as Flex, with Perkins in his arms, rocketed through the crowd and into the sky. Hunter glanced to Abel who was still scratching at the force field around his head. He had toyed with the idea of just leaving it on Abel's head but thought better of it.

Instead, Hunter removed it as he sent a salute over to Abel, and rose into the sky. Abel sat on the ground below, face flushed with anger and panting trying to catch his breath after being inside the small force field. "Later, Abe. Good luck not being an asshole," Hunter said with a smirk as he flipped the panting Abel off.

As they made their ascension into the sky, Hunter and Danielle could both see Flex hovering above them with a look of fear on his face. "What now?" Hunter groaned as he continued to rise into the air beside Flex.

As he came to a stop, he understood why Flex had such a look on his face. Once beside them, Hunter extended his force field to surround Flex and Perkins who now stood inside with them. Adding the size and effort needed to support a total of four people was less of a strain on Hunter than it was a year ago.

As they all floated in the sky, Hunter was finally able to see why he would feel a faint shake or tremor through the ground. Before them, or under them really, were five large creatures that to Hunter looked like they came directly out of a monster movie. Size- wise, each of them were larger than several football fields. Then Hunter realized that the skeletal remains that had become the arena, was much smaller than the beast now before him.

Two of them looked like they could have been dinosaurs that time had forgotten. Another had the shape of a turtle but the face of something much fiercer. Complete with yellow eyes that looked tired, and teeth that had no lips to cover how sharp and large they were. The last two were so unique that Hunter couldn't think of anything to compare them too, and he had a vast experience of seeing unique creatures on tv or even in video games.

What was more surprising to Hunter than even the monstrous size of these beasts, was what they carried. Each of the five monsters had large cities on their backs that stood several stories high. "Perkins," Hunter said as he broke the silence in his force field. "Want to give us a run down?" Perkins snapped out of her dream of watching the creatures and cleared her throat.

"Um, yeah. Sorry. I've just never seen the Great Beasts from so high up before," she stopped talking again and just stared at them. Only the obviously forced sound of Danielle clearing her throat snapped her out of it again. "Sorry. These are five of the six great beasts of Mo'eizus. Creatures of legend and longevity."

Flex narrowed his eyes. "Are they dangerous?" He slowly asked as he too continued to watch. Perkins shook her head. "Nope. Not at all. Well, we are pretty sure they were once before. They are older than anything else on the planet from what we are led to believe. Even in schools, we had to learn about them. Over time studies have been done on them and while they aren't dangerous now, it's safe to say they once were."

Perkins paused again to look at them. Such power and beauty all in one form. She had always been fascinated by them as a child but was never able to see them from afar. Only the resident of the sixth beast had that luxury. "The Sand Wastelands," Perkins said as she pointed down below them, "Is the only area where they live now. No other section has a Great Beast. Only the East section has that honor. Now, all sections have remains of their bodies scattered around, though."

The nonstop training had made him stronger. He would still be severely hungry when it was all over, but he was able to maintain for now. He also would rather struggle with a large force field than be comfortable with a small one. While a small force field was easy to maintain, he couldn't tolerate the small enclosed space well at all.

"I wasn't expecting that," Danielle said as she looked out in front of them. "Same," Flex replied. "Even after leaving where we just left. It's… they're…" "Beautiful aren't they?" Perkins said as she cut Flex off. "I was thinking terrifying," Hunter said to her.

Flex nodded as he took in her words. He didn't interrupt with questions or comments. He just listened. Hunter, on the other hand, had tons of stuff he had to fight to keep inside his head, and not his mouth. He, once again, found himself learning from the example Flex provided. Sometimes it still amazed Hunter at how much Flex had changed over that last year.

A stiff elbow to the side made Hunter grunt. "What?" he asked as he looked at Danielle. "You okay, boo? You're giving Flex the googly eyes. If anybody in this relationship is going to have a crush on Flex it's me," she said under her breath. "What? No. Pay attention," Hunter stammered as he tried to not laugh at the dumb look, she was giving him as Perkins continued to talk.

"Even these five have healed wounds on their bodies that couldn't have been made by any of the other living beasts. Because they have lasted so long, we always theorized that these five were the strongest once, even if they don't look it now. Only the strong survive."

Hunter snorted. "They look plenty strong to me." "They seem so, tamed," Flex said as he shifted in the force field to watch one that was walking directly under them. He had been watching each of the monsters as Perkins gave more details on them. Each monster walked single file behind another and continued to walk along a large worn path that was carved in the sand before them.

"That's because of the spires," Perkins added. "The harmonic spires generate a low humming sound that keeps them peaceful, and in order. Hunter remembered the sound from when they first fled into the spire from the Warden. Perkins looked around and then pointed to one of the creatures that Hunter had a hard time identifying. "We need to land on that one. That's where the base is. It's also my home city. A little slice of East Section heaven called Ventibell."

"Sounds like a plan," Hunter said. "I just can't fly us all there. I mean I could, but the chances of me crashing as we landed are pretty good. I'm hungry." Flex nodded and grabbed Perkins in his arms. "Okay," Flex said to Hunter as Perkins wrapped her arms around him tightly.

Hunter began to retract his force field. "Wait, wait," Perkins screamed before the force field was completely gone. "We can't just descend down in the middle of the city. We have to fly around the back of the beast, and," she paused for a moment. "You know what, just follow Flex." "It's what I live for," Hunter replied as Flex rolled his eyes.

"Okay, just lead the way." Before the words were out of Hunter's mouth Flex was already moving fast through the skies. Faster than he normally would, Hunter naturally felt like Flex was showing off. "You Ken Doll bastard," Hunter said with a smile as he kept his force field a little larger than needed and exploded through the open sky like a blue bullet. "Uh babe," Danielle said as she wrapped her hand in Hunter's.

"I got it. I got it." Hunter said as he followed Flex lower just below the Great Beast and flew around its legs. If Hunter was confused on if Flex was trying to show off or not, now he knew for sure he was. He could have gone around the legs of the monster, but instead, he bobbed and weaved between them with speed than an inexperienced flyer couldn't match.

Hunter, however, had been flying for over half of his life and matched the moves that Flex displayed easily. Flex did seem to be moving a little faster than Hunter though. Even though he was carrying Perkins in his arm, Flex's strength was so vast that she likely felt weightless. Hunter had Danielle, and even though he could manipulate the gravity inside his force field, she still was a drag on his top speed.

After looping around the back legs of the beast, Flex zoomed upward in the air around the rear and landed just behind a patch of trees in what appeared to be a field inside of the massive stone wall that encased the city. Flex gently placed Perkins on the ground and looked towards the direction where Hunter would appear. Sure enough, seconds later the blue bubble landed a few feet from them.

Perkins walked to the stone wall and placed her hand on it as she closed her eyes, and took a deep breath. She hadn't been in his part of the city in years. Mostly because of the smell. You couldn't be so close to the rear of a massive creature and not smell a hint of stench in the air. Yet she was still flooded with memories of herself running through this very field being chased by her brother. The thought of him made her open her eyes and snatched her happy memory away.

"Nice flying," Flex said as he smirked to Hunter. "I do what I can," Hunter said as he looked at Danielle who was bent over and breathing hard. "She almost hurled inside my force field, though." Hunter rubbed her on the back supportively, but she waved him away with a hand. "What in Atlas was with all the loops and shit," Danielle finally said, even though her face was still hidden. "He's still my intern. I have to test his skills whenever I can." "I knew you were doing it on purpose," Hunter said in a voice a little louder than he intended. "Had me flying damn near inside this thing's ass, which I'm guessing is why it stinks so bad around here."

"Would you shut up," Perkins said as she glared at him. "We just landed over a wall that people aren't allowed to be outside of unless they are officially allowed to travel. That smell is the only reason we were able to get in unseen. So, shut it." Hunter was so surprised at this outburst that he actually jerked his head somewhat before he apologized. "Sorry. I was just saying." Danielle smiled at Perkins so big that even her teeth were showing. "I like it when she's feisty." After she said this, she looked at Flex, who in return had a passive look on his face as he took in his surroundings.

Danielle exhaled. "Really Flex?" Flex turned to her with his brow raised. "What?" "I set you up for a perfect joke and you say nothing. Not even a *so do I* answer," Danielle said as she shook her head at Flex. "Shouldn't we get going?" Hunter asked as he tried to save Flex from embarrassment. "My thoughts exactly," Perkins said. "It's getting brighter and people will be out soon."

She took off at a quick pace and navigated through the small field of trees, and led them all to an abandoned, yet very clean street. Hunter looked down at the ground and was surprised to find millions of what seemed to be polished smooth stones. With the smell around this place, he was expecting a nastier looking aspect of the city but he was wrong. If this was the area that people avoided because of the smell as Perkins said, maybe that was why it was so clean.

As they ventured further into the city, and the smell faded away, he realized he was wrong. Every street, building, alley, and vendor cart was spotless. Not a single piece of trash was scattered on the ground. To be a city on top of a monster, it put their dimensions cities to shame. "It's not far now," Perkins said as she glanced over her shoulder to look at her team. Many of whom were looking around in amazement.

She stopped walking and asked "What's wrong? Our buildings, for the most part, look like yours, just from an older time." "It's just so damn clean," Danielle replied. "Like the city was just created clean." "I agree. I haven't seen anything quite like it. I always assumed the Diamond District was as close to perfection as possible. I was clearly mistaken." Flex said.

"I was thinking the same," Hunter replied. Perkins turned around and began to walk again and as she did, she quietly and quickly said "Omega demands it. Presentation is everything, and anything less than purity will not be tolerated." Hunter realized he had endured enough. He was tired of trying to figure out what or who Omega was.

"Can we finally get some clarification on what an Omega is?" "Yes," Perkins replied. "Finally," Hunter said as he raised his hands up. "Just not here," Perkins continued. "We need to get off the streets, and into some clothes that are fitting for people of the city. We look like commoners of the Sand Wasteland, and would stand out or be kicked out."

Hunter took in a deep breath. "Fine, the rescue mission, laced with suspense and half details continues." As they moved once more, Hunter noticed what looked like a flyer on one of the buildings. He was surprised to see it considering how clean the area was. He was even more surprised to see a similar flyer off in the distance about four buildings down.

He looked at the others walking and then quickly read the flyer before they were out of view. "In my shadow, or at my feet," Hunter said just below his breath as he looked at the flyer with its bird-like creature on it. "In my shadow, or at my feet," Hunter said once more to himself as he scratched the back of his head.

He wanted to think about the flyer some more, but decided it was better to catch up with the team. Perkins took them down a side road and came to a sudden stop as she stood in front of a building that to the rest of the team looked almost like any other. It was two stories high, square-shaped, and made out of what seemed to be clay or plaster. A small sign hung on the door and had very basic drawings of food on it.

“I thought we had to get off the streets,” Hunter hissed. “My questions can’t be answered but we can sight- see?” Flex glared at Hunter who in returned glared back and inadvertently flashed blue energy in his eyes for a second. “Everything okay?” Flex said as he leaned down to Perkins’ ear. “I thought we had to keep moving.”

Perkins nodded her head but didn’t say anything at first. “Is this it or something?” Danielle asked as she looked up and down the empty street. “Looks a little small for a base, but size doesn’t matter.” As she said these words, she earned a side-eye glance from Hunter to which she responded with an eye wink and blew him a kiss.

“No, it’s just a restaurant. One of my favorites actually. My brother and I used to come here all the time.” Hunter and Danielle both grimaced. “I didn’t know you had a brother,” Hunter said. “Neither did I.” Danielle chimed in. Hunter looked to Flex to see if he shared their surprise. He didn’t. If anything, he tightened his lips and looked to the ground as his shoulders dropped slightly.

“He died just before I came to your dimension,” Perkins said. She placed a hand to her eye quickly and then without a word began to move again. In the next few minutes, she stopped once more at a building only slightly larger than the one they recently visited. “Here we are,” Perkins said as she placed her hand on the knob of the front door. As she did so a slight buzzing noise was barely heard, followed by three clicks.

The door opened and Perkins stood aside. “Everybody in.” Danielle was the first to enter. Hunter and Flex then followed, and Perkins brought up the rear as she shut the door behind them. Once again, the faint buzzing sound followed by three clicks.

“I wasn’t expecting this at all,” Hunter finally said.

CHAPTER 14:
BRAVADO

Insects that seemed to be only alive in their current dimension crawled on the walls, and a smell of damp mildew lingered in the air. Various counters had faded and discarded chunks of unfolded fabric sprawled across them that were neglected over the years.

Danielle touched one counter and removed a layer of dust several inches thick. Flex eyed some machines in the back of the room that had spools of thread and clothing attached to it, and Hunter simply raised a brow as he tried to not touch anything. "Alright, I'll say it if nobody else will," Hunter started. "Your base needs some work. This entire place looks like a home for mold and rats."

"One, show some respect please," Perkins said. "This home for mold and rats, whatever those are, once was run by my family. It was passed down to my brother and myself from our mom." Perkins smiled as she looked around the room and them moved towards the machines in the back that Flex now stood beside.

While the others saw a place abandoned by time, Perkins saw her youth. A place where her family was once happy. Where she and her brother would play and get in trouble for said playing. It also still left a sour spot as she would remember her brother and the simple life he used to live. How everything had changed so fast, she didn't know.

"We had planned to renovate it into a house but clearly that didn't happen," Perkins said as she turned a dial on each of the machines. As she did her turning, she didn't speak but instead focused on her turns. On the final machine turn, a click could be heard and a section of the wall opened.

"And two," Perkins continued, "this isn't the base. This is merely the entrance. We just adopted the hide in plain sight model when we were trying to figure out where to set up shop, as you would say." Perkins motioned for them to follow her with a wave of her hand as she twisted some and moved through the new opening in the wall.

Flex looked at Danielle and Hunter and gave them a slight nod, as he followed Perkins. "How has she been in our world for a year, and not know what a rat is?" Danielle asked Hunter in a whisper. Hunter shrugged. "No clue. I am starting to realize we didn't know as much about our dear Perkins as we thought we did."

Hunter moved and held the door so Danielle could go inside. "Not that I don't trust her, but let's be careful while here." Danielle nodded her head a few times and leaned in to kiss Hunter. Even in their moldy surroundings, with unknown creatures crawling on the wall, Hunter still felt his heart skip as her lips touched his.

Once the kiss was over, he could hear himself release a long breath that he once again didn't realize he was holding. She didn't say anything, she just smiled at him and walked through the passageway. When they were finally inside, Hunter followed suit and closed the portion of the wall behind him. As soon as the secret door was closed, he could hear loud, unseen levers clicking into place.

Lights began to flicker on around them as the final levers of the closing door locked into place. "Now, this is an improvement," Hunter said as he moved past Flex and Danielle, both of whom stood in the corridor.

The smooth metal walls and floor clicked below their footsteps and was an overwhelming contrast to the dilapidated shop that they entered. This wasn't as nice as the base they had left behind in their dimension, but it was still a close contender. Perkins led the way down the corridor and quickly came to a spiraling staircase.

"I'll make sure you get the tour later. I just have to find Cord first." Hunter looked down different halls as they made their way down the stairwell. For it to be a large place, it seemed very empty. Danielle, as if she read his mind, voiced the same concern. "Where is everybody?" Danielle asked. "Most of them are dead," a deep voice came from the bottom of the stairs.

Perkins froze as she heard the voice, and then began to run down the steps towards it. Flex fought down the hint of jealousy he was feeling as he watched his lover run towards the voice of another man. "Cord," Perkins said in more of a sigh of relief than a scream.

Hunter, Flex, and Danielle found themselves at the end of the stairwell where Perkins still had her arms around a tall, brown skinned man, with short black hair. Flex watched the man's muscles bulge in his shirt as he released Perkins, and felt ashamed of himself when he smiled some at the fact that he himself was clearly more built than this man called Cord.

"I didn't expect you to bring help, but I'm glad you did. You must be the Imperial Lords that Impervious went on and on about," Cord said as he shifted towards the team. "I honestly expected more. You're nothing but children." Hunter glared at him as Perkins raised a hand to signal him to calm down.

"He has a direct way of expressing his thoughts. You'll get used to it," Perkins said out loud as she pointed to each of them and made introductions. "That's Danielle, Hunter, and Flex." Her words lingered in the air as she pointed to Flex. "My boyfriend."

Flex felt his stomach turn as he tried to not react to Perkins' words. Unbeknownst to him, Perkins was trying to control her reaction, too. It was the first time she had actually given what they had a title. Everybody just knew they were together. They didn't slap the names on it, because they felt they didn't need to. Now she had, and Flex felt all the concern he had about the good-looking, deep-voiced man, fade away in an instant.

Cord shook Flex's hand and gave him a smile. "The strong one, huh," Cord said in his deep voice as he looked Flex up and down. "And the nerfing boyfriend too," Cord said as he laughed under his breath slightly which caused Flex to frown at the man. "Impervious says you've got heart. I'm thankful that you came." Flex nodded.

"Wouldn't have missed it. We owe it to Perkins and Impervious." Cord said nothing in return. He had turned from Flex before he was even finished talking. The fabricated smile Cord had on his face shifted to almost a frown as he extended his hand slowly to Hunter.

He cleared his throat some. "Let's get something straight right now. I don't tolerate hotheads, and I don't tolerate egos. Cayden's enough to deal with. I won't have it from you, too. If you're here to help then I welcome it, but don't live up to the stories I've been told about you."

Hunter grimaced some as he glanced to Flex and Danielle. He already had to deal with a similar introduction from Commander Lopez, now this guy. "Take it down a notch, Cord," Perkins said from beside the man. Hunter was a little surprised at the picture Impervious had painted of him to the people of this world. A part of him even felt hurt that his uncle viewed him in such a way.

"I've changed a lot since Impervious has been..." Hunter was cut off by Cord's deep voice. "Good. Then maybe you can find a way to rub off on Cayden." Hunter's brow raised he as he gave a glance to Perkins this time. "I'm glad you came, more than you know," Cord added in. "Your blood could change our future."

Hunter quickly withdrew his hand. "Excuse me?" Hunter asked. Cord looked to Perkins after she slapped him on the head. "I was to understand that you were of elite blood too," Cord said as he rubbed the back of his head. Hunter exhaled. "I am." Perkins stepped in and placed a hand on Cord's shoulder. "He's only part Spellborn. He wouldn't be fit to lead. So, no ideas."

"Of course," Cord replied as he looked to Danielle. Hunter wanted to speak up but didn't. He had no intentions of being of any help in the royal leader department, but still, hearing Perkins say he wasn't fit for it, bothered him some. He wasn't a fan of being told he couldn't do something or wasn't good enough.

In his heart of hearts, it reminded him of when the world used to whisper that he was a half- breed or abomination behind his back. "I don't recall Impervious mentioning you," Cord said as he shook Danielle's hand and placed a light kiss on it. All the aggression and fire he displayed while talking to Flex and Hunter had evaporated.

Hunter casually placed one arm around Danielle, and with the other removed Cord's hand from hers. "I'm new to the team," Danielle said as she wiped the back of her hand on her pants. "Impervious likely only knew me as a villain that Hunter was banging. I haven't even taken the oath. Technically, I shouldn't even be here or using my powers." Cord furrowed his brow as he looked to Perkins. "Banging?" he asked.

Perkins shook her head. "Don't worry about learning the terms. It will give you a headache. Trust me." Cord nodded. "Well, let's get to it then," Cord said as he turned and marched up the hall. His large boots seemed to boom on the metal floor as he moved and ducked into another room. "That was a shitty welcome for a rescue team to receive," Hunter said. "While I would have worded it differently," Flex said as he eyed Hunter, "I do agree with him."

"I don't know," Danielle said as she forced a provocative switch in her steps. "He seemed to like me. I think he was pretty nice." Hunter's mouth dropped but Perkins spoke before he could. "Cord just has a no-nonsense way of doing things. He's a good man. Just direct is all."

As she finished speaking, she made her way to the same door that Cord had entered. Perkins was happy to be back home, even if she tried to hide it from her new team. Being back in the base she helped create years ago with Cord, made her remember what she had forgotten in her time away. Why she did what she did. Why she formed Bravado in the first place.

She had a mission, and as crazy as it was, it was hers. Perkins also began to worry. She instantly was feeling torn. She regretted leaving and what's more is that she didn't know if she would have the strength to leave again once this was over. She glanced over her shoulder and watched Flex enter the room behind her, followed by Hunter and Danielle.

She was fond of Hunter and Danielle. She really was, but she knew she could live without them. Flex, on the other hand, she didn't want to let go. Not just yet. She pushed her feelings down in her mind and told herself now wasn't the time to worry about something as trivial as relationships, but eventually, she would have to meet the issue head-on.

When Hunter finally entered the room, he found them all pulling out chairs at a long metal table. Cord sat at the head, with Perkins in the chair next to him, and Danielle and Flex were near the end closest to the entrance. Flex eyed Hunter and then darted his eyes toward an empty chair.

Once Hunter was seated, he noticed that there were a dozen more chairs at the table and that some had a layer of dust on them. They hadn't been used in some time. Cord shifted in his seat as he seemed uncomfortable in the room. "I haven't been in here since the mission," Cord said, without looking at anybody.

"I thought Cayden would be here but," "You know how he gets," Perkins said as she placed her blasters on the table. Cord lifted one the blasters and looked at it. "Not bad, you'll have to bring one for me next time." Perkins grimaced. "You hate guns. Weren't you always the one barking orders in defense class that guns jam, fists don't?"

Cord gently placed the weapon back on the table and kicked up some dust in the process. He let out a breath. "Things change." After his words, he paused for a moment and looked at the empty chair beside him and shook his head. "Things change," he repeated again.

Perkins placed a hand on Cord's arm, and against his will Flex felt his jaw clench. He glanced over to Hunter who in response patted the air and mouthed the words "chill out" silently to him. Behind Hunter, however, Danielle made a motion of sticking her index finger in and out of a circle she made with her opposite hand. "Not helping," Hunter whispered to her.

"Let's go over the mission you mentioned in the message," Perkins said. Cord quickly stood from the table and reached in his pocket, moving his hand around vigorously before withdrawing it with a small cube gripped in his fingers. He touched the side of the cube and then placed it on the table before them. In seconds, small cracks of light began to glow from it.

Hunter wasn't sure why, but for a second, he thought the cube was an explosive device. His thoughts were erased as Cord gripped a remote and aimed it at the cube. In a flash, a picture sprung to life showing a revolving building in blueprint format. "Well, isn't that cool," Hunter said in a tone that clearly implied that he thought it was anything but.

"No. It's not," Cord said in a bark. "Impervious spared no expense in telling us how the technology at his Imperial Lords' base put the Bravado base to shame. Sadly, one cannot have the luxury of grants and backers when leading a rebellion. So please save your comments." Hunter swallowed and shook his head. "Fair enough," he replied as he forced himself to remain on his best behavior.

In reality, he was getting tired of this Cord guy and his shitty attitude. Perkins may have liked him, but it was taking everything Hunter had not to Impact Blast this jerk between the ears. "Let's get this out the way now," Flex said as he slowly stood up and walked around the table to face Cord.

Each head in the room turned to watch as Flex and his lean bulk cast a shadow towards Cord. "Looks like the champion of the arena is going to make an appearance again," Danielle whispered in Hunter's ear. A smile played on her face as she hoped for a fight to break out.

"We came here to help you," Flex said calmly. "I understand you are a friend of Perkins, and Impervious was like a father to me, so I," Flex corrected himself. "We, want him back safe. But if you continue to talk to my team disrespectfully, then we are going to have a problem, and I assure you, you want to fight alongside me, and not against me."

"Damn," Hunter said under his breath, with his hand hidden behind his mouth as he stretched the word out and not for the first time, he wished Jen was here to give him a fist bump. Cord placed the remote on the table to his side. For a moment Hunter thought Cord was going to call Flex's bluff and try to fight him.

"I just lost almost every person I ever cared for. Dead, all of them in a matter of minutes. So sorry, if I don't take the time to form my words to caress your feelings." Cord said slowly. "I run the remainder of my team the best I can, and to do that I have to be myself. So, if you're going to help then help, but don't come at me, with your chest out, over how I nerfing speak.

Perkins stood and waved her hands, "Both of you shut up and focus on why we are here in the first place."

Cord looked over his shoulder to Perkins as he took a deep breath. "I'll choose my words more carefully. Now, if your moment of showboat is finished, take a seat." Perkins cleared her throat. "Please," Cord added in.

He didn't turn and walk away. Instead, Flex folded his arms and backed up to lean on the wall. "I'm fine just where I am." Hunter was surprised and impressed. He was usually the one causing a fuss, not good old Flex. He didn't know if it was just jealousy or if he really had enough of Cord's attitude, but Hunter supported it.

In return, Hunter also found a new slither of respect for this Cord guy. Clearly Impervious told him about each of them. So, Hunter knew that Cord was aware of just how strong and hard to hurt Flex was, yet he didn't care. Hunter smiled some. This Cord guy had brass balls, and Hunter supported this brash personality, too.

Cord picked up the remote again and looked at the still revolving blueprint of the building that floated in the air. "The mission was to be a simple one," Cord said as he looked at the building. "We had received a tip from our supporters in the city that a way to slow the Curse of Varo was being manufactured in this building but being kept from the people. After doing some research and recon, a few of my lieutenants confirmed the tip."

"Which lieutenants?" Perkins asked. "Sims and Levi," Cord replied without even looking at her. Perkins nodded her head and drummed her fingers on the table as Cord continued. "They also said that there were guards at the location so to expect push back. I took some of my best and a few of my worst, actually."

"Judging from the distress message you sent, things didn't go as planned," Hunter added in. "To say it didn't go as planned is an understatement," Cord replied. "Once my team was in place, three Warden's Circles emerged from the target location." Perkins' eyes grew wide as she stiffened.

"Not only that, but Levi killed three of the people in his unit." "So, this Levi was a traitor?" Danielle asked as she leaned in her chair. "No. He couldn't have been," Perkins said. "I recruited Levi myself. He devoted his life to Bravado. I can't believe he would turn on his own team." Hunter remained quiet. He could see the confusion on Perkins' face as her brain scrambled for a reason why her friend would do the things that Cord had said. Hunter felt bad for her, mainly because he was her, only a year ago.

He had felt the pain of finding out first hand that people you thought you knew for so long, weren't really who they said they were. "You're right," Cord added in. "Levi wouldn't do such a thing. Sadly, Levi had been dead long before that day."

The faces at the table looked at him with confusion. How could Levi be dead and there at the same time? "It wasn't until I confronted him that I saw Levi's face melt away and from the under the sludge emerged another," Cord said as Perkins let out a gasp. She then muttered a single statement. "It was Icaro."

CHAPTER 15:
CAYDEN'S GOODBYE

Seriously," Hunter said as he looked around the table. "A shapeshifter?" Flex let out a grumble from the wall. "That is an impressive ability to have. Even in our world, it's rare." Perkins shook her head and found herself rubbing her hands as she searched for words to say. "If it only were that simple," she said as she gripped her hands around her blasters.

She wasn't going to use them, but she found that holding a weapon open made her feel a little more at ease during tense situations. "His spell doesn't allow him to be the shape of another. Well it does but it's more than that," Perkins said as she looked towards Cord. He had just used his remote to change the floating display in front of them from a building, to a figure with a blurred- out face.

"Icaro is, for lack of a better word, a spy, assassin or killer," Cord said as he eyed the floating faceless man display. "His spell allows him to take the form, and memories, of any living thing he kills," Cord paused for a moment. "And consumes," he finally added in. Danielle sat up from her chair.

"He eats them?" she asked. "Not entirely, only a small portion. Usually, the brain or another internal organ," Cord replied. "To date, Icaro has over two hundred confirmed transformations. Those are the number for people he was paid to consume. We can only assume there are more. To be honest, we don't even know if Icaro is truly male. That is just the gender more commonly used."

Flex finally left his location from the wall and leaned in to look at the spinning figure of the man in front of them. He had never battled with a person like this Icaro before, but he had worked with and against spies. He knew the one thing they all had in common. "Who pulls his strings?" Flex finally asked.

"Pulls his strings?" Cord repeated with a frown on his face. "Who calls the shots, tells him what to do, pays him," Hunter added in. "Is, or was Bravado such a threat that a lone spy wanted to set up an ambush on you or was he likely part of a larger plan?" Cord took in a deep breath but before he could speak a young man barged into the room.

"Cord! Cord," Every eye in the room shifted to the man standing in the door. He was short and appeared to be no older than sixteen. His black hair was cut into a fade, and for the most part, he shared almost identical facial features with Cord.

As the young man stopped screaming Cord's name, he realized that there were several other people in the room. Breathing hard he said, "Perkins." The tone he used in his voice was more of an accusation than a question. Perkins stood up and raised a hand to the youth slightly. "Hey, Cayden."

Cayden glared at her for half a second and then promptly ignored her greeting. "Cord, it's Becca." Cord nodded his head silently and followed the boy out the room. He paused at the door as he saw the rest of the room stand. "You all wait here. This doesn't concern you." "It does concern me," Perkins said defiantly as she moved to walk pass Cord. "I assume she's in medical."

Cord didn't answer but his exhale was all that Perkins needed. As Perkins left the room, so did Hunter, Flex, and Danielle. "We go where she goes," Danielle said as she stepped by Cord. Hunter looked the man in the eye as he walked passed him. "Women, right?" he said in a joking manner. A manner that Cord didn't reply to.

Flex said nothing as he moved and placed a hand on Hunter's shoulder. "Not now." Hunter glanced at Flex but said nothing. Hunter was more so trying to deflect. He didn't let it be known but he had just a hard of time sticking to the heroic path as Danielle did. Well, maybe not as much as Danielle, but it was close. Some of the things the others cared deeply about, he could care less for. Had Perkins not forced her way to see this Becca, he would have been happy to just sit there and wait. Unfortunately, that wasn't the case and he was forced to care.

"How long has she been this way?" Perkins asked Cord as they all watched Cayden clean Becca up from inside an isolated room in the medical bay. "Not as long as you'd think," Cord finally replied. "The Curse of Varo is spreading faster and taking people down quicker than ever. Some people get lucky and can survive longer, but Becca noticed first signs of infection maybe just under two weeks ago. If that."

Perkins gasped as she looked from Cord to Cayden in the room that was inside of what looked to be a large plastic bubble. Her body relaxed some as Flex placed his arm around her shoulder. Hunter took a step closer to the bubble and leaned on it. As he took a deep breath, he realized that the room was completely quiet, apart from some of the medical equipment humming around them and the faint beeps that could be heard from the monitor at the bedside of the other single patient in the tiny medical area.

He looked inside the room and watched the young man called Cayden slowly maneuver around the pools of dark blood that were forming on the floor inside the room. With a cloth, he wiped the blood from the woman's mouth, nose, and ears.

She was sleeping now but was raging out when they had arrived at the room. Now her resting body was heavily restrained and strapped to the bed she was on. Hunter could only assume she, like the man they encountered in the desert wasteland, had grown violent. "Hurry it up," Cord barked from beside Hunter.

Hunter turned to him and noticed that the man's face was a blank slate. As if he had no feelings at all as he watched this person die in front of them slowly. Hunter almost envied the man's ability to keep his emotions away from the surface.

"Give me a few more minutes," Cayden replied as he checked the fluids running from a clear bag into Becca's arm. "Not like anybody else can do it. May as well do it right, so stop nerfing rushing me." Hunter felt his head jerk as he heard the way the youth spoke to Cord. It was rude, with a hint of arrogance in the tone. Hunter didn't want to admit it, but Cayden had reminded him of somebody at that moment. Himself.

"She looks a lot worse than the guy we saw," Danielle said to the room at large. "These are the final steps of the curse," Perkins replied. "As the insides of the body liquify, the person grows more violent. It usually takes months to get to this stage, not weeks." "We usually have them killed at this point," Cord added in. Flex looked at him and frowned.

Cord knew the question before it was even asked. "No cure, and at this stage, it's highly contagious. Better to put them at ease and save those around them," Cord replied. "Well, I sure as shit am not a medical professional, but if it's that contagious, should he be in there at all?" Hunter asked as he pointed to Cayden.

The boy was in the room dressed normally. He didn't even have on shoes or a mask, yet he was cleaning her up slowly without a care in the world. Taking his time to be gentle, even though she felt nothing. "Cayden will be fine," Perkins added in. "One of his spells is disease immunity. So, he is immune to the curse.

"Well that's a damn good ability," Hunter said as he looked at Cayden who stopped wiping Becca and turned to them and smiled. He shrugged his shoulders. "It gets me by. Don't be jealous or anything." Hunter frowned at Cayden, and said, "little shit," under his breath.

"That's enough, Cayden," Cord said slowly. "You've done all you can do, and I've made the decision. Spare her. She's too far gone, and we need to conserve the resources." Cayden turned to protest and was instantly cut off. "That's coming from me as your superior, not as your brother. Do what I say."

Cayden didn't reply. Instead, he threw the rag he was holding down on the ground and began to walk to each monitor in the isolated room, switching them off one by one. Each slower than the last. "I'm sorry Becca," he said faintly as he did so. "Have some of the others clean this up when you're done, and find us in the briefing room," Cord said to his brother. Cayden didn't reply. He just flicked the back of his hand towards them. The universal signal to leave so he could be left alone as he finished up.

Cord took one more final look at Becca's body and then turned to leave the medical bay. "Fifth person I've lost in four days," Cord said to them as they walked. Nerfing curse is destroying us faster than I can recruit. At this rate, Bravado will be a memory, not a legacy." "Becca was a good girl. I remember when she joined. Practically begged us every day until we let her in. She deserved better," Perkins said.

"Anybody deserves better than that." Flex replied. "Debatable," Hunter said as he followed them to the briefing room. Once they all sat down, Cord picked up his remote again. "So, he's your brother," Hunter said to the room at large. "So, he's elite blood too." "He is," Cord replied. "While I have no spells at all, my little brother has more than one." "What else can he do?" Danielle asked.

"It's not of importance right now," Cord replied as he turned to Flex. "Before we left you asked who pulled the strings." Flex locked eyes with Cord as he clicked the remote once more. This time the faceless man displayed vanished and was replaced by a youthful woman that had a smirk on her face, and a punk fashion style to her. Hunter looked at the spinning figure of the woman and noticed that Perkins had a balled fist resting on the table now.

"Empress Queen Omega," Cord said slowly. Flex looked at the spinning figure. He was thinking the same as the rest of his team. Finally, at long last, they knew who Omega was. "She's an empress and a queen?" Danielle asked with a grimace on her face. "What sense does that make?" "We know her birth name is Queen, supposedly," Perkins said. "Omega is just a name she gave herself, and Empress is the title she wields."

"The undisputed ruler of the East section of Mo'eizus. Creator of the Wardens and their circle, and highly considered the most dangerous being on this planet," Cord added in. "Well she doesn't look like much," Danielle said. "For Atlas' sake, she looks the same age as me."

"One of her spells allows her to age slowly," Perkins added. "She is actually closer to eighty or so years old, according to reports." "Live in my shadow, or die at my feet," Cord said to the room at large. Hunter remembered the flyer he had seen outside when they arrived on the Great Beast. *In my shadow, or at my feet.*

"What is that?" Hunter asked. "It's her oath to the people she rules. Live in my shadow, or die at my feet," Perkins replied. "There is no other option." "You said one of her spells," Flex said to Cord. "So, she's elite too?" Cord did a mixture of shaking his head with a slight shoulder shrug. "As far as we know, no. Her number of spells, or their power, can't be explained. Which added more intrigue to her Intrigue, she then uses as she wishes," Cord replied.

So, she's the one we have to stop," Hunter said. "Stop her, find a cure, save Impervious, and then get the hell out of this sand trap." Hunter looked around. "Am I missing anything?"

Cord exhaled and clicked his remote once more. The floating figure of Omega vanished. As he placed the remote on the table, footsteps could be heard in the hall, and slowly Cayden entered the room. He didn't speak and had his head tilted some as he removed a chair and sat at the table.

"You have the finer points," Cord said to Hunter. "But you are narrow-minded." Hunter fought back the urge to curse at Cord. He felt like he was going to have to set the man straight sooner than later. "We first need to replenish the ranks of Bravado. That includes recruiting and training. All under the eyes of Omega. She has people everywhere." Cord looked to Perkins.

She nodded her head slowly before she began to speak. "Omega is a threat, but Bravado is here for the people. We can't help them if we don't have the soldiers needed." "You're the authority on soldiers that are needed that aren't here and aren't you," Cayden said without looking up. Perkins stammered as she began to speak, but Cord raised a hand to cut her off. "Perkins is still your superior. Respect her as such," Cord said to his brother. "Yes sir, Cord," Cayden replied.

Cord's gaze lingered on his brother for a few seconds more before he spoke again. "Let's stop here. I'm starving and need to eat," Cord said as he made way to the room entrance. "We'll join you," Perkins said. "Alone," Cord barked. "I'd rather have some silence with my thoughts in my quarters," Cord replied.

He looked at the room and asked, "I'm sure everybody is caught up. If there are questions Cayden will fill you in." Flex stood up. "No, I'd rather you answer this one." Cord's jaw clenched as he crossed his arms in front of him. "What is it?"

Flex moved to stand in front of Cord, blocking his way through the door. "You told us everything except for the one question that any sane person would ask," Flex said. He looked passed Cord and then glanced at Danielle who in return shrugged her shoulders. "How about you Paragon?" Flex said to Hunter. "Has a certain question been burning at you this entire time? One that our host with horrible manners has left out?"

Hunter cleared his throat as he stood up to stand behind Cord. To the room at large, it was clear that the two men were positioned around Cord in a way that he was overpowered if he tried to do anything. Cayden quickly stood up. "What are you doing?" he asked loudly. Perkins placed a hand on his shoulder, that Cayden quickly knocked off and away.

"It's okay," Hunter said without looking at Cayden. As he did so, a large force field separated the three of them from the rest of the room. "The question he didn't answer," Hunter continued. "With all the killing at the ambush. With several Warden's circles and even a spy in their midst, he still survived. A man with no spells what so ever, and who prefers fists over guns. The question we should be asking is, how did he get away."

Flex smiled "give my intern a prize," he said. "Well Cord, answer the man."

CHAPTER 16:
FROSTY BITCH

Power Prince walked down the hallways of the New Lords' base and thoroughly wished that Flex, Hunter, or even Danielle were back. Considering the task before him, he would rather have Flex back a little more than the others. He hadn't realized it before but the base was rather creepy when it was only being used by one or two people. He felt that perhaps his boredom was the main reason that he felt it was creepy. When you have nothing to do you tend to notice long dark hallways, or random noises from unknown sources.

What was even worse was that he found himself talking to Prism more and more since he returned from seeing the powers that be with the I.C.E. officials. Jen was so fast to run off with Sasha, that the only thing around to listen was Prism, and the hologram seemed genuinely interested in how the meeting went.

All in all, the trip he and Jen made went well. As the only true member of the New Lords, who was also around when the Imperial Lords ran the show, Power Prince had done much of the talking, with Jen adding in some points of view here and there.

Despite her lack of experience, she proved to be a help as they tried to win them over for approval. Power Prince stopped at a door and placed his hand on the scanner. A yellow, slow moving light encased his hand, beeped and then the door opened. He jumped when he saw there were people inside the room waiting for him.

"Atlas dude, you gotta give a guy some warning." Power Prince said as he walked into the room and stood in front of a monitor. "I didn't even know you were here yet." Power Prince looked the two men before him up and down. He hadn't seen him in a while, but Life-Line still looked the same. Same stern jaw that a boxer would envy and the same old-fashioned buzz cut. Life-Line placed a hand on Power Prince's shoulder. "Sorry. I used my credentials to get in and then Terry here," Life-Line said as he nodded his head towards the man standing beside him. "Teleported us directly in here from up top."

Life-Line had on his traditional costume. A gray suit that covered him from neck to toe, boots of the same color gray, and a green cape that fell down to his feet. Power Prince hadn't seen Life-Life for the better part of a year, and it was his understanding that Hunter hadn't either.

Since the events with Infinity, and secrets of the Imperial Lords past coming to light, Life-Life, and his healing ability, moved into civilian life. His healing clinic was generating more money than some tech companies, and for a company with only three members of the staff, that was impressive. What Power-Prince did notice was that there was a rounder midsection in the gray costume than he remembered.

"I know. I know." Life-Line said as he caught Power Prince's eyes look at his stomach. "I'm not as active as I used to be," Life-Line said as he topped off his words by placing both hands on his stomach a few times. Power Prince shrugged as he extended a hand to Terry.

The man was short but muscular and the purple costume he had on was a contrast to his dark skin. "Shall I call you Terry or would you prefer Gleam?" Terry looked to Life-Line, smirked some and then turned back to Power-Prince. "Gleam is fine. Marcus didn't think you would know who I was," Gleam said through a nasal voice that didn't reflect his muscular appearance.

"Come on, dude," Power Prince said as he ignored the glare Life-Line sent his way. Life-Line knew Power Prince was one of the more relaxed Icons he ever worked with, but still, he expected him to show a little more respect to Icon legends. Calling them *dude* didn't cut it.

"One of the most popular teleporters around and I wouldn't know him?" Power Prince asked as he shook the hand with enthusiasm. "Well, the retired life makes it easy to fall out of popularity." Gleam replied as he turned to Life-Line. "We all don't have jobs that make the masses seek us out."

Life-Line cleared his throat some as he clapped his hands and stood before a panel of glowing buttons. "Don't start that shit, Terry," Life-Line said. "I am but a humble healer. Some people want the benefit of meeting an Icon, being healed instantly, having no scars, or recovery time. It's not a bad deal." "And they pay through the nose for it," Gleam said. "You could do the same with travel services," Life-Line replied as he pressed some buttons. He had to stifle a laugh as he did so. "I know some people would pay top dollar to travel the world in seconds instead of hours."

Life-Line was facing a monitor and as such couldn't see the look on Gleam's face at this joke. "Insult me like that again and I'm going to drop you in the middle of the ocean." "Point taken," Life-Line said with a laugh he didn't try to hide.

Power Prince moved to stand in front of the panel to the opposite side of Life-Line and brought several additional screens to life. Each screen either had news feeds running on it or multiple smaller security camera feeds on them.

"If I'm being honest dude, it's because of Charmed that I'm such a fan of yours," Power Prince said to Gleam as he continued to hit the glowing keys. There was silence in the room, which prompted him to look at the two men. "Charmed. The cult classic show about witches?" Still, silence occupied the room.

Power Prince took in a deep breath. "They have these beings called Whitelighters that teleport from place to place, and the special effects they use on the show is exactly what your power looks like. You know what, never mind."

Before he could say anything else, Prism flickered into view which caused Gleam to jump. "Nice to have you back in the base, Life-Line," the holographic butler said with a slight flickering bow to the man with the green cape. "It's good to be back, Prism. Even if only until we resolve the issue at hand."

"Gleam, welcome to the New Lords' base. If you need anything simply call upon me and I will be there." Gleam gave a silent thumbs up toward the hologram as he continued to watch the monitors. "Clearly manners aren't only skipped by the younger heroes," Prism said loudly. Gleam ignored him.

"Power Prince, the information you requested has been uploaded to the personal computers in your room," Prism said. "Perfect," Power Prince replied. "Do the same thing for the one in Flex's room, and send a copy of the file to Life-Line." The hologram did a slight bow. "As you wish sir," Prism said before he flickered out.

"You know you don't have to include me on this," Life-Life said as he typed on the panel in front of him. "Yeah, I do," Power-Prince replied. "Trust me. Those I.C.E. guys at the meeting said a lot of shit, and one of the things they kept coming back to was for us to recruit at least one new member. Two if possible. Said we were too small, and you're the highest-ranking member of the former team so you have a vote in who we accept."

"Well, they aren't wrong." Gleam replied. "Two full-time members, two interns, and then two random consultants that haven't even taken the oath won't cut it. I'm surprised they didn't ding you on the oath part alone. They must be getting soft." Power Prince fought the urge to look at Life-Line who had clearly shared their current team roster with Gleam. He even told him that officially, Perkins and Danielle were still labeled as *consultants*.

Flex had decided to make them official members once Hunter and Jen completed their internship. "Found her!" Life-Line said as he tapped a few of the glowing buttons with more pressure that was needed. As he typed, all of the screens fused into one. "Yeah, that's her alright." Power Prince said as he looked at the paused face of Zeva Greene become enhanced to the point that it consumed the entire screen.

"Where is she?" Power Prince asked. "Looks like she is on the unsavory side of town in Millwater," Gleam replied. Life-Line pressed a few more buttons and then looked to Gleam. "Damn, Terry. You're right," Life-Line said. "How in Atlas' name did you know that just by looking at one still video?"

Gleam smirked. "I'm a teleporter. I get around. And unlike this amateur she's running around with, I don't have a limit on where I can go," Gleam said as he snorted, "five-mile radius," under his breath. As he spoke Power Prince realized why Gleam was here. He wasn't just support and transport. His second power would be vital to their success.

"Where is Jen?" Life-Line asked. "She's out with Sasha celebrating that we made it out alive from that room full of government suit-wearing types," Power Prince replied. "Good. I don't want her anywhere near this frosty bitch." He typed a few more keys and then closed the screen. "I just sent word to some of the local Icons in Millwater. If they can, they will help. Detach had friends there, so I'm sure we won't be alone."

Power Prince nodded as he looked at the screen and let out a shallow sigh. "You okay, son?" Life-Line asked. "Yeah," Power Prince replied. "I just wish it hadn't come to this. Or that Flex was here." Life-Line rubbed his chin for half a second as he placed a hand on the young Icon's shoulder and clamped down gently.

"Flex knew it would come to this, the moment she did what she did in Vincula. He made his choice to leave and left this here for you to handle because he trusts you. He may be the leader, but I remember both you boys when you joined the Lords. You've got just as much ability as him. You know how the public is. Give them a good- looking Icon with super strength and they eat it up."

As Life-Line spoke, Power Prince was running over their options in his head, and he found no other outcome that would work. What he had decided to do had to be done. If this were anybody else, he wouldn't even be having these second thoughts. Flex's sister should be no different and he knew it. Not to mention that he had always loved Detach. He even had a crush on her when he first started, and a reoccurring fantasy about a night of bliss with her and her clones.

If anything, she deserved justice and her killer shouldn't be free. "If you need to sit this one out," Life-Line began but Power Prince shook his head quickly. "No, I'm good," Power Prince replied. With his lips tightly pressed together, Life-Line took in a breath before he spoke.

"We've got permission to use extreme force. After the breakout taking her alive is an option but not a must. She likely knows this so don't hesitate." He made it as if he was talking to the room but internally, Life-Line hoped that Power Prince was paying him undivided attention. He was their only defense until other Icons arrived.

"Let's hit it," Gleam said as he placed his hand on their shoulders. Power Prince felt a surge of energy wash over him and then instantly he was standing on a dirty street between two buildings. "Welcome to Millwater," Gleam said as he popped his back. He closed his eyes for a moment and then opened them again. "It's done. They aren't going anywhere."

Power Prince was expecting more from this part of the plan. Gleam was a famous teleporter, perhaps even the most famous teleport. He had earned a reputation for being the guy you called when you wanted to catch a hero that was hard to lock down because they could fly or teleport. While his teleporting power was often caught on camera, his second power wasn't.

"That's it?" Power Prince asked. Gleam nodded. "Dang dude, I was expecting something flashier." "Flashy or not, Slingshot can no longer teleport as long as I'm here," Gleam replied.

As they stepped onto the street, they saw various vendors spread around them. Most of them looked as filthy as the street they worked on. Ragged carts, and flimsy stands full of junk. "Why would she come here?" Power Prince asked as he scanned the crowd. "Variety of reasons," Life-Line answered.

"It's very crowded, which gives her the ability to blend in. These vendors clearly don't seem like the type to ask questions, and would likely give her what she wanted without a fuss if threatened. She can't have much money on her fresh off of an escape from an Icon prison."

Power Prince nodded and had thought some of the same things, but for some reason was cautious to voice them. He didn't like playing the role of leader. That's why Flex ran things but after hearing those supportive words from Life-Line in the base, he was slowly seeing that he had what it took to play the lead role too. Even still, having Life-Line here allowed for a more experienced Icon to step into the role that he was slowly warming up to.

"We need to get some of the people out of here," Power Prince finally said. He didn't want to be a leader, but he refused to have a street full of bodies on his heart because he was shy about being in control or speaking up.

"We don't have the resources just yet to get them out so we have to be as cautious as possible until help arrives," Gleam said. As he spoke, the locals on the street began to notice the three Icons standing among them. How could they miss a man dressed in purple, or another with a green cape on? Not to mention the young man dressed in black with orange highlights.

"I have eyes on her," Power Prince said as he focused his attention on a cart halfway up the street. "As do I," Life-Line said. "Gleam, give us support from up top." Gleam didn't say anything. Not even a slight nod. A dazzling rainfall of bright light appeared for half a second, and then the man dressed in purple was gone.

"He'll cover us from there if needed," Life-Line said before he asked Power Prince a question. "How do you want to proceed?" Power Prince bit his lower lip for a moment before he considered a few things in his head. From where he was, he could see Zeva even though she didn't look like her normal self. Instead of her normal black hair, she now had short blond hair.

He couldn't tell if it was a wig or a dye job. She also was dressed in more casual clothes. Large jeans, sneakers and a tank top that exposed her toned upper body. All this aside, he knew it was her. He had seemed that face around their base a lot a year ago and if you squinted, she even looked like Flex some.

Power Prince and Life-Line flinched some as a sudden burst of wind touched them. As they turned around, they could see a woman towering over them both. She was dressed in a costume of teal and white with yellow trim. Most of her face was covered, and her brown short hair stuck out on top.

"Vicky Velocity," Life-Line said with a slight smile. "I take it you heard the call for additional help." "I did," she said with a smooth voice that had a slight accent. "What's up?" Power Prince said to her with an upward head movement. He hadn't worked with the speedster before. When the Imperial Lords were around, they had no need for her. Impervious was their resident speedster and was considerably faster that Vicky Velocity.

"Power Prince," she said with a slight nod as she looked at him and then in the direction of Zeva. "That her? Blond hair over there?" "Yeah," Life-Line replied. He knew Vicky from when she was a newer hero on the scene, and the way he knew her, made this situation a little more difficult.

"I know Detach and your mom were close, but," Life-Line tried to finish his words but Vicky wasn't having it. "Close, she was my godmother," Vicky said with a hiss. Power Prince closed his eye for a few seconds and then opened them again. He remembered seeing Vicky at the service for Detach and she hadn't taken the death well. Now he knew why.

"I know," Life-Line replied, "but our priority will always be the safety of the innocent first. So, do what you can to declutter the street." After a loud sigh, and a burst of wind, a sea of teal streaks washed over the crowded street as one by one, the area became less crowded. From across the street, Zeva looked around her, and Power-Prince felt the temperature in the area drop some.

"Bingo," Power Prince said as the head of Zeva finally turned in his direction. The glowing green hands of Life-Line were placed on Power Prince's shoulders as the glow consumed him for an instant. "It's all on you now," Life-Line said.

Power Prince could feel the difference in his body. It was as if every fiber of his being was tingling. What Life-Line had done to him, was a new discovery he had figured out while in his healing practice. Some of his clients didn't have the need for immediate healing and requested a subscription healing plan.

Life-Line wasn't familiar with the request, but the rich are prone to come up with out of the box ideas. The rich man in question was an extreme sports junkie that wanted to have a healing aura running inside his body at all times. That way if he got hurt, he would in theory heal from it, as if Life-Line himself was there. It had taken a few attempts, but Life-Line got it done.

Just like that, a new avenue of healing on the go was created for his clients and colleagues. It was short-lived, usually around twenty- four hours, but in a situation like this, it got the job done. Unfortunately for Life-Line, Zeva didn't know about the recent discovery, and he became her first target.

CHAPTER 17:
ENERGY VS ICE

Zeva had tried to push the voices away from her mind. She had been trying since she was a child, and for equally as long she had been failing. Her pills used to help, but not in the way she wanted. While the voices, or her demons as she called them, weren't heard quite as often she still knew they were there.

To her, it always reminded her of being in one room, and people were in the next room beside her, and those same people were screaming. She couldn't hear them clearly, but she could hear enough to know they were there. She could hear them enough to want them gone. Her pills were her wall, keeping her and those loud angry voices separated in their personal rooms. Take them away and the wall comes down. Take them away and she was free to listen, a thing that she enjoyed more than she wanted to admit.

In Vincula they forced the pills on her, but near the end, she didn't take them as much. Having a guard on your side had many perks. Now that she was free, she could take them as she wanted. If she wanted the wall up, then she would take some pills. If she wanted freedom, and to be washed over by her true potential then she would ignore the pills altogether. Working out proved to be a buffer for her.

She found herself working out daily for a number of hours, sometimes twice a day. That combined with her pills made her mental wall thicker. For right now though, the wall was paper thin, and she needed her pills. She knew if she was overtaken by the voices before she got herself and Slingshot to safety, she wouldn't be any good to either of them, especially when the heroes came.

That's why she came to Millwater. The vendors there sold everything, and if you asked the right questions, sometimes you could find what wasn't even advertised. Slave labor, sex, and even drugs were in the grasp of some of the vendors for a price.

"How soon can you get them to me?" Zeva asked the vendor as she scratched her neck and looked around. The vendor, a man with tanned skin, a hump in his back, and thinning brown hair, continued to move his hands and show Zeva some of the assorted clothing his cart had. One must keep up the ruse at all times.

What he had in his hand now, was a red silk shirt, and from a distance, he looked like he was talking about the shirt at great lengths. "Meet me back here tonight. Bring cash," He looked Zeva up and down as he kept talking and moving the shirt around. "Unless you would like to pay by other means."

His smile faded as he shivered some. He suddenly found himself unbearably cold. The voices were clawing at the wall now as several began to get through. The demons inside of Zeva were angry the man had dared to insult them. Dared to insult the body they called home. Ice covered in blood was the only form of payment that the voices would accept.

Zeva took in a breath and closed her eyes." No, cash is fine." she said as she opened her eyes and looked around for Slingshot. She was supposed to be getting them some food and coming right back. What Zeva saw instead, were three men dressed in colorful clothing. She recognized Life-Line and Power Prince at once.

The man dressed in purple she didn't. As she tried to figure out what to do, Power Prince locked eyes with her. She didn't know the Asian youth well, but she knew he had made it to be a full member of those liars of a supergroup, The Imperial Lords. That alone spoke volumes to his skill and add to it that her brother spoke highly of him so he wasn't to be ignored. "If you were good enough for Flex to accept you, then you won't be easy," Zeva said to herself.

"Huh," the vendor asked as he finally put the redshirt down. Several people around Zeva had suddenly begun to shiver, and some were begging to realize that they were seeing their breath as they talked now. She thought it over for a second, and she knew how the Imperial Lords worked.

Suddenly, the man dressed in purple was gone after a minor light show. "They brought their own teleporter," Zeva said to herself as her throat felt a little dry. It's hard to run with a teleporter on you, especially if it was a good one and it likely was. The Imperial Lords had reach, money, and connections. They could get the best help, even after they fell. Disgraced or not, they could still call in favors. "And all I have is a junkie, among other things, that I met in prison," she said to herself in a tone that sounded like she was scolding her actions.

They were here to take her in. Not kill her. It wasn't the heroic way. Then she heard the voices again. The demons in her had a point. She had killed one of their own and escaped prison. An escape that involved killing a few people in the process. A peaceful surrender wasn't going to help. The voices were right.

She could feel the sliver of the wall falling down inside her mind as she listened to them more. They noticed that her brother, the mighty Flex, wasn't even with them. He didn't want to see her die. So, he left her to the wolves. Killing them all was the solution. The voices knew it and she did too.

As she slowly turned to face them a woman appeared. She was tall and in full costume. Moments later she became a blur and people around her, vendors and customers alike were being plucked off and whisked away.

Zeva could feel her breathing increase as the last remnants of the wall came crashing down and her voices were set free. There was no walking away now. Not for her, and the first person to fall would be the healer. "It's always the healer," she said to herself as she created several daggers of ice in her hand and sent them towards Life-Life.

Before the shards could impale him, a streak of teal moved across the street, and in a second, he was gone. Power Prince went from cautious to full blown pissed off. She had just tried to kill Life-Line. She had the nerve to try to kill another Lord. As he controlled his anger, he could see the pink glow from his fist. He took a stance, and in boxer fashion put his guard up. So much energy was in his fist now that he could hear it crackle as sparks of miniature lightning bolts began to dance up his forearms.

"Where is my brother?" Zeva shouted as she encased herself in a suit of ice. "I'd focus on me if I were you," Power Prince replied as he aimed his fist down and released some of his energy and propelled himself into the air.

Being the living battery that he was, he had enough energy inside him at any giving moment to power two cities. The more energy he used, the more his body produced. He had a limitless well of power on a supreme scale, and all he had to do was be smart and patient and he would avenge Detach.

He came crashing down like a pink meteor and flooded his fist with energy as he connected with Zeva's armor of solid ice. It was thick, several inches thick, but his fist melted through her ice with ease. He couldn't see her face inside the arctic armor, but he could imagine that she was cursing.

The downside, as Power Prince removed his fist to throw another punch, was that the ice had begun to reform. It seemed that she could generate ice as easy as he could energy. "Frosty bitch," he said under his breath. He kept on the pressure even still.

Sending combo after combo to her frame as he chipped away huge shards of ice. He wanted to scream at her, but he kept his emotions in check. That was one of the first rules he learned early in his hero career. A level head and no witty banter unless needed. Focus on the goal and your opponent.

Focus he did, and he quickly realized this was getting nowhere and needed a change of attack. Power Prince quickly aimed his fist down and blasted in the air again. This time only slightly as he flipped over Zeva and landed behind her. She was too fast for him, though.

As he landed, several shards the size of water bottles exploded from her back. They all found their mark as Power Prince screamed in pain and fell to the ground. Zeva turned around and looked down at him. One shard was in his leg, and two in his stomach. While he couldn't see her face, he could only imagine that she was laughing inside the armor.

What Power Prince could see though, was a large fist raise into the air. As the fist rose, several large shards of ice formed around it creating an arm of impaling danger. He flooded his fist with energy once more and pushed himself back on the ground. The spiked fist exploded as it hit the solid ground where he just was. "Okay, that was embarrassing." Power Prince said to himself as he began to pull the shards out.

He fought the urge to yell out in pain as he did so, but as soon as the shards were gone, his body healed. "Oh, thank Atlas," he said as he looked at the newly- healed skin. A part of him was cautious about this new ability Life-Line said he had found, but apparently, it worked. As he stood, he was greeted by several ice figures that Zeva had created.

Not only that, but it had begun to snow. His teeth chattered as more and more snow came down. He hadn't seen her use snow before, but it made sense that she could. Snow and ice weren't that far from each other on the spectrum. What he also saw through the falling snow was that the area was clear. There were no longer vendors or customers on the street.

Somewhere between fighting and getting his ass kicked, Vicky had removed everybody from the scene. He wondered where she was now, and why she wasn't joining in the fight. He ignored it and put his fist up as he smiled.

"Seriously?" he heard a voice say as the armor around Zeva's head formed an opening. "I'm pretty sure we can beat you," she said as her ice imps all began to form daggers of their own. "I always thought you were more so a battery, not a bruiser anyway. Guess I was right." Power Prince didn't speak. Instead, he ran forward and clapped his hands together.

It took only a second, but she reformed her armor just in time before the wave of pink energy from Power Prince's hands was sent forward slicing through each imp and leaving large puddles where they once stood. The heat from the wave melted right through the snow, too.

"The kid's holding his own pretty good." Gleam said from atop of a nearby building. As he said this, he extended his hand over towards Vicky. "You owe me ten bucks." "Has it been enough time?" She asked as she reached in a pocket. Life-Line nodded his head as he refused to take eyes off the fight. "I told you to not join the fight because Power Prince needed to do this on his own. He's more capable than he thinks," Life-Line said.

"You responded saying that you didn't think he could last ten minutes. Even called him Battery Boy," Life-Line added. "That's when I bet you ten bucks he could, and that was ten minutes ago," Gleam said. "So, pay up." Vicky no longer protested as she gave two bills to Gleam who looked at the front to back in a mock fashion to check that they were authentic. "Now both of you focus," Life-Line continued.

"I have faith in him, but I still want to be ready." They all remained quiet as the fight unfolded below them, and then they all gasped as the wave of pink energy exploded from below them and carved a path through the ice. "Holy shit," Gleam said as he winced at the bright flash of pink.

As Power Prince ran, he sloshed through puddles around him. Zeva was taking steps back as she peppered the area in front of her with tiny slithers of ice. They should have been cutting him but many of them were melting before they could get close enough.

She could feel her heart pounding in her chest now as the pink glow from her opponent's fist increased in intensity, and the snow on the ground literally turned to water as he ran towards her. She focused, and more snow began to fall, but now large bowling ball size hail was mixed in with it.

This didn't stop him but it did make him slow down. It slowed him enough that Zeva reached out and controlled the snow around him and made several large shards rip through his leg. Blood spattered on the snow around him as he fell, and his glowing hands faded. He screamed, but it was hard to hear over Zeva's laughter.

"Not yet," Life-Line said as they continued to watch the battle. All of them were standing a little closer now as the cold had reached them too. "Marcus, I think," Life-Line silenced his friend with a simple look. "Okay. Have it your way, but it's on you," Gleam replied.

"I watched this boy train. I've seen the amount of damage he can do and energy he has both physically and mentally. He has this well within his grasp. If he's doing what I think he is, then he is playing a dangerous game."

Vicky didn't speak. Instead, she looked at the two older Icons beside her and began to bite her nails. She didn't like this type of tension outside of a movie theatre. As Life-Line watched, he felt bad for wishing Zeva hadn't gone bad. She had come from purestock and like Flex was rather powerful. She would have put fear in many under the right guidance. Yet, here she was on the wrong side of justice just the same.

"I don't know how you healed earlier, but that trick seems to be a one-time thing," Zeva said as she walked towards the sprawled body of Power Prince. As she took her steps, she kept her armor on but exposed her face again. She was stupid enough to think the battle was over simply because the target was down.

Her mouth moved but nothing came out as she heard the voices again. She grimaced some then created a large knife out of ice. Power Prince groaned as he looked to her. She walked around him, and only the crunching sound of her weight on the snow was all Power Prince could hear.

"We have decided to take your head," Zeva said as Power Prince tried to figure out who *we* were that she kept talking about. "Next time my brother should just come himself. I'll never stop. I can't stop. They won't let me. In the end," Zeva said as she raised her sword up in the air. "It will only be me and them. Me and my demons. I'm fine with that."

Her words were cut off as a blinding flash of pink exploded around her. It had happened so fast that she wasn't sure how she missed it. When the light cleared, Power Prince still had his fists touching each other. The second wave of energy he created wasn't as wide as the first one. He had to focus to keep it tight. As her mouth gaped open, the sword she created fell to the ground and caused snow to fly up as it landed.

The remaining armor she had on her slowly cracked from the middle where a massive thin crater was. The focal point of Power Prince's attack. Power Prince gritted his teeth so hard that saliva rolled down his chin as he removed his leg from the ice shard that was locking him to the ground. As he lifted it up, it began to heal but not as fast as his previous wounds. It hadn't been twenty- four hours but it seemed that the healing boost from Life-Line was close to its natural limit.

He stood over Zeva and looked down on her. Once the ice armor was gone, the gash he had created on her was larger than he thought. Had he not controlled it so well, the attack would have sliced her in half. Instead, she lay there in front of him. Unmoving with lifeless open eyes looking up to him and pooling blood on the snow she had created moments earlier.

A burst of wind and a flash of light happened behind him. "It's done," Power Prince said as he turned around. His words came out slow as he avoided their eyes. "I see that," Life-Line said as he looked towards the young woman's body on the ground. "Flex," Power Prince began to speak but Life-Line spoke over him.

"Flex will be fine. This was," Life-Line wanted to select his words carefully. "Your first kill in the field. That comes with some feelings that no amount of training can prepare you for. And I wish I could say it would be the last time you feel this way, but it isn't." Life-Line placed a hand on his shoulder.

"You did good, Kevin," Vicky said from the side. Power Prince nodded towards her as he turned to look at Zeva's body one last time on the red snow. Zeva Greene had taken her last breath that day, but because of him she couldn't take any more lives, and he found peace with that. "Let me be the one to tell Flex," he finally said.

CHAPTER 18:
EARLY STAGES

Cord looked from Flex to Hunter who still stood behind him. Then he looked at the force field around him. He had seen force fields like it before, but usually, they came from devices, not from people. He fought the urge to touch the pale blue bubble that swirled around. "Any day now," Flex said to Cord.

After cracking his back and taking a deep breath, Cord looked to Flex and for the first time showed a faint smirk. It only lasted for a second, and Flex saw it, but it was there. "Sorry, I left that out because I assumed you were smart enough to put that part of the puzzle together," Cord replied.

He slowly turned and looked to Hunter who was oddly relaxed at the turn of the conversation. Beyond Hunter, Cord could see Danielle with a smile on her face, and Perkins with her eyes wide. Then there was Cayden. He had moved from where he was sitting at the table to standing just beyond the barrier of the force field.

"I made it out because Impervious saved me," Cord said. "As you may have gathered, I'm normally not a fan of guns. During the mission I only have these," He balled up his fists and shook them slightly. "And a sword. That's it. Had I known three Warden's Circles were to be there I would have rethought that decision. I fought with Icaro, but he is," Cord shook his head as he looked for the words he wanted. "He's very adept at hand to hand. He doesn't need the weapons apparently."

Perkins' mouth gapped some from across the room. "He beat you in a fight hand to hand?" she asked. Hunter looked at Cord a little differently after hearing the surprise in Perkins' voice. Cord must have been one hell of a fighter to generate such surprise from announcing that he had lost.

"He did," Cord replied. "Once that was over, he made me watch as my team was wiped out. Saving me for last, I can only assume. But then Impervious arrived," Cord said as he grinned and rubbed his chin. "The Swordsmith and Gunner of the Warden's Circle couldn't hurt him. Even the Pain Conduit didn't hurt him. Nerfing guy is immune to everything."

Cord laughed slightly under his breath as he met Flex's eyes. "His speed ripped through their forces in almost an instant. When he found me, I was on the floor, beaten badly, and a Warden and Icaro had escaped somehow."

"Well, you have your answer," Cayden said from outside the force field. "So, taking this nerfing barrier down." Hunter looked to Flex who gave him a slight nod. Instantly, the pale blue dome that surrounded them faded away. Cord looked at Flex, and then to Hunter. "You may be a good leader after all. Question everything. That's the only way you'll make it in this world."

Cord pointed to Cayden. "Show Hunter and Danielle to where they can set up and get some rest after they eat. Perkins and Flex will be fine on their own. I assume Perkins remembers her way around." Perkins gave a slow thumbs up as she tucked her blasters away. "I do," she replied without even looking to him.

Cayden sucked his teeth some but then nodded his head after Cord glared at him. "Sure. I'll get them wherever they need to be." Cayden said as he looked to Hunter and Danielle. He loved his brother, he really did. For as long as he could remember it was always them. Together against the world. Their parents had been killed so long ago that Cayden couldn't even remember them, but he knew it was because of their elite blood that they were taken away from them.

He even often wished Cord was the one with powers and not himself. Maybe then the right brother would be destined to lead. He thought that maybe Cord would have been able to save their parents if he only he could have done then what Cayden could do now.

Instead, it was him. Cayden. The second born. Born with powers that indicated his elite blood like a beacon glowing in the night, and he was still treated like a glorified lackey. That was also why he respected his brother so much. Many of the other members, well former members of Bravado often treated him in an unnatural way because of his lineage. Not Cord, though. His brother gave him a harder time if anything.

That's same love and respect that Cayden had for Cord, were driving forces of why he suddenly felt sweat on his brow, and a tremble run over his body. He took a single step and could feel a rolling stomach that he didn't have only seconds ago. "Cord," Cayden said as his words came out in a stammer.

His eyes were expressing the fear that his words couldn't. Cayden was the first to see it, but the rest of the room soon followed his eyes and found their attention directed at Cord. Cord let out a sigh as he wiped a single drop of dark blood from his ear. Flex and Hunter took a step back from him.

"Don't worry," Cord said as he wiped his hand on his pants. It only affects the people of our world. Our studies show that those from your dimension shouldn't be harmed at all by the Curse of Varo." "Just the same, I'll keep my distance," Hunter replied. "I'm still part Spellborn." Cord nodded his head in agreement. "That's true."

"How long have you known?" Cayden asked with a steady tone to his voice. His words weren't adept at hiding the anger that consumed him. "How long have you known and not told me?" "Relax," Cord said as he moved his hands to calm the room. "Only a week or so, and it's slow acting so we have time to figure something out, or get stuff in order." His last words hit Cayden and Perkins like a kick to the stomach.

"Get stuff in order?" Perkins replied. "Look it's still early and we have you here now. We will figure everything out. These are very early stages, so spare me the sad looks," Cord said as he turned around and motioned beyond Flex. "I'll see you all later. Get some food and rest if you need it. It's going to be a long day."

The room remained quiet as his boots clicked off down the hall, growing silent as they continued. "Plot twist," Danielle said to nobody in particular. "I didn't see that coming." She moved to the door and looked down the hallway in the direction Cord had walked. "Should he be walking around freely like that? I mean knowing that he is sick and all?" she asked as she turned to face Cayden and Perkins. "I was curious about the same thing," Flex said.

Cayden rubbed his hands over his now reddish eyes. "Early stages of the curse aren't as easily spread. All the same, you and Hunter should keep a decent distance from him," Cayden said as he looked at Perkins. She silently nodded. "I know it will be hard to stay away from his award-winning personality, but I'll do it," Hunter said. Perkins slowly walked over to Flex who put his arm around her. "Come on," she said as she looked up to him. Flex looked down into those green eyes that he had fallen for and for the first time saw a sadness he didn't think could live in a place where he normally saw so much joy. "It's going to be okay," he said slowly. "We will figure it out." Perkins withdrew from his embrace and slowly walked out of the room, with Flex behind her.

Hunter turned to Danielle and then to Cayden who was oddly standing still. "I'll show you where you will be sleeping. You'll both also have a change of clothes there." Hunter nodded. "Cayden?" Hunter asked as they followed the young man down the hall. "What?" his snappy tone was almost as bad as his brother's. Hunter looked at Danielle who made a face at the aggression in the remark but said nothing.

"This Omega lady," "Empress Queen Omega," Cayden snapped back quickly. "Right," Hunter said. "How much of a badass is she? I know your brother said she formed the Warden's Circle, and ages slowly, but outside of that he didn't go much into detail. I guess I'm just trying to figure out what we are up against, and how Impervious, a man that can shrug off anything, was captured?"

Cayden lead them down an additional hall and stopped to look up. Danielle and Hunter followed his gaze but didn't see anything outside of the ceiling. "Empress Queen Omega is more so a mystery than anything. We don't know her lineage at all, but despite her gifts, she had been vocal that she isn't elite like you or I. A normal Spellborn with such power shouldn't exist, but yet she reigns."

Cayden opened a door to a small room that was fully stocked with a small bed, and some clothes. It had a funny smell, but Danielle fought the urge to comment on it. "She is above us in every way," Cayden continued. Even her home, the fifth Great Beast flies above us all. Forever placing us in their shadow."

"Their shadow?" Danielle asked as she dropped down on the bed to test it out. It felt more like a detention cot to her, and less like a bed. In her youth, she had spent several years sleeping on such a cot, and would likely still sleep fine on this one, but still, the difference was noticeable.

Cayden took a deep breath as if he was irritated with their questions. "Acropolis, is the city of wealth and only those in favor of Empress Queen Omega, are permitted to live there. In her presence. In her glory." Hunter grimaced at Cayden. For all of their efforts to liberate the people, Cayden still spoke of Empress Queen Omega as if she was a higher being. Almost as if she was a god of some sort and not just a Spellborn that had risen to power.

"All of that is well and good, but that still doesn't explain how she stopped or prevented a person like Impervious from returning. Sure, she had formed the Wardens' Circle, and ages slowly but big fucking deal. Even if you add in the wealth and power. It still was," Hunter's words were interrupted by Cayden. "Created. Not formed."

"Huh," Hunter asked as his brow raised. "Created, not formed. *We formed* Bravado. Impervious and his team *formed* the Imperial Lords. Empress Queen Omega created the Wardens' Circle." Danielle finally stood up from the bed and looked at Cayden. "Are we missing something?"

Cayden moved from the room and placed his hand on the door. "Empress Queen Omega wields power like none other. Elite or otherwise. Slowed aging is great, and so is wealth, but Empress Queen Omega has the power of creation, and to some that is more than life itself." Cayden cleared his throat some.

"I'm going to talk to Cord. He claims he wants to be alone, but I know my brother and that's not like him. Change and rest. Some food should be in the dresser over there. The day will be long." With those final words, Cayden backed out the room and shut the door with more force than was needed.

Hunter swallowed and could hear it loudly around the silent room. Danielle had already made her way to find food in the dresser. What she held up looked like some sort of candy bar. Hunter remained still as he compared his powers in his head. Surely what he could do was more impressive than creation. For that matter, all of their abilities seemed more impressive than that.

What bothered him was how Cayden still spoke about her. Even though he was a member of a rebellion with the sole purpose of liberating the people, he still spoke of her with respect. If that was how an enemy spoke of her, Hunter was afraid to think of how a supporter would speak of her. Not only that but with a power like creation, these same supporters would likely damn near worship her. His time on his own world had shown him all too well the lengths people would go for those they worshipped.

As he heard Danielle open the candy and begin chewing, he felt that this situation was a lot more complicated than they expected.

CHAPTER 19:
EMPRESS QUEEN OMEGA

Empress Queen Omega could feel her body stiffen while she tried to hold the pose perfectly as she spoke. She sat at a long wooden table trimmed with golden edges, and large chairs that were rumored to be the most comfortable in all of her kingdom.

"How much more do we need to discuss Maridian?" She asked loudly to the man standing behind her while never looking away from the young painter standing in front of her. She wanted to turn and look at her subject but refused to break posture for anything.

She had been sitting in the same chair several hours all to make sure everything was perfect. "We still have recent developments inside that awful cage arena, chrome distribution, the public request with the people, and new tributes to discuss, Empress."

The man called Maridian was a naturally tall man with a silky beard. A man that always made it a point to walk with his head held high and eyes forward, that was unless he was in the presence of his Empress. Then his posture and form were even more sharp than normal. She demanded it to be so. Excellence or nothing else. That was what their ruler expected and for Maridian he felt she deserved it and so much more.

Empress Queen Omega took in a deep breath and repeated the words back to herself. "I didn't expect chrome to be on the agenda for another day or so." She relaxed her posture, and the painter standing before her flinched some as the brush visibly began to shake in his hand. Omega stood from her chair at the table and walked over to the life-size painting.

As she did so, she tore away the cream-colored dress she was wearing only to reveal a white shirt, clean yet tattered pants, and large boots. As she stood in front of the painting, she cracked her back and took the knot out of her hair and allowed the pink layers to fall down to her shoulders. "That's better," she said out loud as she snapped her fingers several times. "Oh, sorry Empress," the painter said as he quickly put down his paints and passed her a green jacket.

The painter wanted to act quickly for his Empress but made every effort to not let a single paint- covered finger come in contact with the jacket. He feared he would not be making it back home if he did. "Thank you," she said as she put the jacket on and adjusted it.

It was larger than her thin frame needed, but it was the jacket she had always worn. The jacket protected her once, and now it meant the world to her. Not to wear it now after all this time would leave her feeling naked, no matter how clothed she was.

Omega stood and took in the painting. "Maridian," she said over her shoulder as she adjusted her pink hair. The man quietly moved closer to her. Despite taking several steps, he made no sound and his robe barely moved.

"Yes, Empress?" the man asked as he looked her directly in the eye. His empress loathed when her subjects didn't respect her enough to look her in the eyes. The man who held the position before Maridian was rumored to have died for forgetting to do so. His family was taken care of, sure they would never want for anything again, but still, their husband, father, or brother was gone. Such was the risk while working for Empress Queen Omega.

"Do you think this looks like me?" she asked as she looked at the painter. Even though she was talking to her aid, the painter felt things would turn bad for him if Maridian didn't give promising feedback on the work. "I do, Empress," Maridian said as the painter slowly began to breathe again. "This young man managed to capture your essence entirely. Even the strong cheekbones and tan complexion of your skin are mirror images of the person before me."

Omega took in a breath and tapped her finger on her side as she looked the painting up and down. "So be it," she said as she dropped to one knee to tighten one of her boots. Once done, she looked over across the room and snapped her fingers. One of the two Wardens waiting near the entrance turned and walked over with its hands clasped behind its back, and stood near the painter.

While most people feared the Wardens the painter actually felt calm as the faceless metal creature stood beside him. There was no need to fear the pet when the master was around, and the same went for a Warden when Empress Queen Omega was around. They listened to her without question and without hesitation. She was their creator. Their ruler and mother. Her word was their law throughout the land, and to her subjects her presence was divine.

"See that he is paid for his service and that the painting goes to one of the medical facilities close by. The one with the children. I want them to know that I am thinking of them and watching over them in their times of sickness and pain," Omega said as she began to turn away. "How generous of you, my Empress," Maridian said as he looked at the Warden take a slight bow.

Try as he might, Maridian couldn't hide the snarl on his face. "Play nice, Maridian," Omega said as she opened the balcony doors in the room. Maridian watched as the Warden walked away with the painting beside him. "My apologies, Empress. You know how I feel about your pets." "Children," Omega snapped in response. "Children. Extensions of my being and you will respect them as such, or I will have you replaced with someone that will." Her voice only rose a little but it was enough to make the room stand still. Even the painter walking away flinched as his faceless escort remained passive.

Maridian could suddenly hear himself breathing loudly in the newly quiet room. Even the swallow he took before he spoke seemed to echo in the silence. "Apologies, Empress," Maridian said as he pulled a large book and metal pen from under his long crimson robes. She didn't reply to his apology. Instead, she stood on her balcony and watched over her city. Her palace was the largest building in Acropolis and from here she could see everything.

Below her, people walked the streets dressed in the finest clothes in all of the East Section. Clothes that Omega herself didn't even wear often. Laughter and celebration could be heard in the distance but couldn't be seen because of the large homes that covered the lands. Had the residents suddenly been forced to live on any other of the Great Beast, or the Sand Wastelands, they would surely perish as their life of luxury was taken away.

Omega smiled and nodded as several of her subjects below stopped to waive or bow to her as she watched over them from above. Many of her subjects thought she had her palace stand so tall to signify her rule over them, they were wrong.

Omega simply wanted to be closer to the stars. Her kingdom as ruler on of the East Section of Mo'eizus was vast and yet she still wanted more. Until the time came, she would wait here in her palace and watch the stars as she ruled. Her glance above her allowed her to watch the sky roll by as the winged beast her city rested on moved effortlessly through the sky, never landing, and never stopping.

The creature was a marvel. One she didn't know if she would ever be able to create herself, but should the beast ever need it, she would try without question. Omega loved all those that chose to live in her shadow and the great Beast was no different.

"The children in that medical facility," she said as she turned to Maridian "make sure their funds are covered and that their families want for nothing until their children are released. They are dealing with so much that the burden of enough funds, or food, or shelter shouldn't be a worry. Make sure their taxes are covered as well." Maridian smiled and made notes in his large book.

As he added the remarks, he smiled to himself. His Empress was unlike anybody he had met before. The ability to rule while making those beneath you love you for it was no small task, yet for the most part, his Empress did so with ease.

Omega placed her elbows on the balcony rail and rested her face in her hands. "Let's start with chrome," she said. Maridian flipped some pages in his book as he began to speak. "The original creation of chrome was so that we could systematically spread the drug throughout the other sections of Mo'eizus. Doing so would weaken their people and their rulers. Leaving us virtually unopposed when we began to move against them with your pets," Maridian cleared his throat. "With your children." He looked up from his book to see if he would be disciplined for his slip.

"And according to previous reports, the plan was working. Slower than we anticipated, but working," Omega said as she continued to look at the stars above her. "Yes, but unfortunately Empress, the reports of chrome being in the East section have increased by thirty percent." Maridian glanced up from his book once more to see Omega slowly stand from the casual position, she had held seconds ago. He also noticed the slow clench of her fist that she held a few seconds, and the repeated rise and fall of her shoulders before relaxing and turning to face him.

"We have made it abundantly clear that chrome is illegal in the East Section no matter the location. Yet they refuse to listen and live peacefully in my shadow." Omega took in a deep breath. She hated this part of being a ruler, but she knew it must be done. "Then at my feet, it is. Assemble several Wardens' Circles to descend on these locations where the chrome has become a problem. Any resident of the East Section with chrome found on them is to be terminated on the spot. Their families are to be terminated as well."

"And if the targets of your wrath have children?" Maridian asked slowly. He knew this part above all others gave his Empress the most sorrow. To leave a child alone with no family, love or protection. She wouldn't have it at any cost if she could help it. "Find Lex or Abraham," Omega said finally.

Maridian used the hand that held his pen to stroke his beard once before making notes. He knew of the men. Free contractors that altered memories for a price. The loss of a family member or separation of a loved one weighed heavily on the heart. Lex or Abraham could make a person forget about it altogether.

"I'd prefer Lex as opposed to Abraham. Lex has a more experienced touch with his spell. He doesn't leave marks as his student does," Omega said as she tried not to think about the children whose lives were about to change because their parents refused to follow simple demands. "The children are to have their memories altered, and placed with a new family. The family's memories are to be left alone, but they will receive an increase in funds from work to aid their new addition."

"Yes Empress," Maridian said as he smiled and made several notes in his book. "Don't smile at their guardian's deaths Maridian. I regret taking the life of those I rule. No Empress should want a kingdom with dwindling subjects, but they have made their choice." Omega walked back to the table and poured herself a single glass of water. "Would you like some?"

"No thank you, Empress," Maridian said as he finished writing in his book. "Then there is the issue with the cage," Maridian said as he finally looked up to her. "Percentages from recent fights are lower than projected. Omega took a drink and rolled her eyes. "I allow those sand vermin to have their little fights, and all I ask is for a small chunk of the funds for taxes. Dismantle the cage, and terminate all those involved. Take the fighters to see if they can pass for tributes." Maridian slowly raised his hand. "What is it?" she asked as Meridian began to move a little closer to her while turning a page in his book.

"The Wardens' Circle in that area have reported that funds are low because Manis lost," Maridian said his last words with a brow raised. Omega frowned and then took another drink. "Lost?" she repeated.

"Indeed," Maridian replied. Omega thought about this for a few moments. She knew Manis by reputation. He was the only Spellborn to ever receive a direct invitation from Omega herself to become a tribute.

He refused several times, and with reason. He was plenty strong and powerful all on his own. He didn't truly have a reason to want to become a tribute. Several ideas began to form for Omega. Any strong enough to defeat Manis would have to be monitored closely, they could cause a problem if not watched.

"Do we know who defeated that purple brute?" she asked. "Not currently. They managed to escape the cage before the circle could arrive. We do have an idea though. Another Warden reported beings with impressive power nearby in that part of the Sand Wasteland. We haven't confirmed any accounts as of yet."

Omega nodded her hand as she sat down and placed her boots loudly on the top of the table. "If only they were all linked as we claimed they were. I wonder if," she began then stopped herself. She decided to keep this thought internal for now. No need to let her aid in on the plan just yet. "Have we still not heard from Icaro?" she asked. "No. Not for some time now. I fear he…" Maridian's words were cut off by a loud laugh from his Empress.

"Don't worry about Icaro. He will be fine and is likely exactly where he needs to be." she clapped her hands together and smiled. "First," Omega said, "Find Manis. Tell him I want to see him. Second take care of his family and anything else he needs. He may be an idiot that has refused my advances, but he has always been loyal and supportive. More so than some that even live in Acropolis. I want him to know that we appreciate that and his service he has provided in my shadow."

Mardian did a slight bow and made some marks in his book. "Next we see the people," Omega said as she stood and gently took off her jacket and placed it on the table. She made extra effort to make sure that it was perfectly flat. Not a single wrinkle. As she moved from the jacket, a single drop of dark blood dripped from her nose and on the table.

She stiffened some as she quickly wiped the blood away and focused her power. She was using her internal abilities to continue to fight the curse. She had used the same gifts for so long not to age, and now she was literally fighting for her life with the same power. No matter. She had been doing this for months now, a few more days wouldn't hurt anything. If everything went according to plan, it would be over soon and she would have a cure. Another gift to give to those that served her and worshipped her as she slowly stretched her power across the planet.

"Are you okay, Empress?" Mardian asked as he saw her wipe her nose. He was the only one that knew of her internal battle and was proud that she trusted him above all others with her greatest secret. "I am," she replied with a smile. "Now, shall we begin?" She asked as Maridian followed behind her.

The remaining Warden standing at the room's entrance opened the door for her, only to reveal two more Wardens standing outside in the hall. Maridian took in a deep breath as they walked towards the main room of the palace with the Wardens on their heels. He tried to remain calm as he mentally told himself that the brief journey would be over soon and then he wouldn't have to be in such close proximity to the creatures.

He didn't know why he despised the Wardens as he did. He just knew that he did. It wasn't their faceless appearance or their metal skin. It wasn't the raw powered they wielded or even the countless acts of violence they had carried out in the name of their creator. Maridian just didn't understand the creatures. He knew how they came to be, but never could understand why they had chosen the life they did.

He himself had devoted his life to Omega. That was a noble profession, and he wouldn't judge any that did the same but to become a Warden was to lose the one thing that made a human, human. Their humanity. "Here we go," Omega said as her words forced Maridian to focus once more on the world around him.

They hadn't made it quite to the large opening ahead of them, but even from where they were, they could hear the sounds of voices speaking. Maridian tried to mentally calculate the number of people waiting for them based off of the noise they created, but this task he was horrible at. Still, he always tried, and always was wrong.

As Omega stepped into the room, silence fell on the crowd instantly. She didn't have to command it or signal it. It was out of respect. It was out of fear. And in some cases, it was out of worship that the sight of her resulted in attention and obedience.

She didn't really like meeting the people of her section for their request, and because of this she only did it once every few days. Maridian organized the meetings and spread the word throughout the East Section when it would happen. Omega simply had to show up, and listen. Still, this was the part of the day she dreaded, yet resulted in her praise the most.

As she moved beyond the crowd, she slowly sat down in a large chair she had created for this sole purpose. While other rulers on Mo'eizus ruled from a throne, Omega wanted to be comfortable. Instead, she had a larger than life, purple, cushioned chair made. She could stretch out in the chair with ease, and the color radiated harmony through the large room. Purple was her favorite color, and she found it to be comforting to her as she listened to her people.

Maridian stood at her side, while her Wardens slowly spread out through the large room. Each went to a corner where the rest of their circle waited for them. Omega gave a single nod, and the entire room took a knee and bowed their heads. *"Forever in your shadow, Empress,"* said by the entire room in unison. Only the faceless Wardens remained quiet, but they did take a bow.

Maridian stepped forward and flipped to a new page in his book. While the room was full, many of these people were simply visitors. Those who wanted to be in Omega's presence and praise her. To witness her greatness and divinity. On the page before him, Maridian only had around ten names. Each with a request that only Omega could help them with.

"Shaw, Lorenzo," Maridian said loudly. "Please step forth and address our Lord and ruler. Speak freely from the safety of her shadow." As Maridian spoke a large bald man from the back of the room quietly stood and made his way to the front. Once in front of the large purple chair, he dropped to his knee again. "You may stand," Omega said. Lorenzo stood and wiped his brow.

"Empress, I request that you do something about the gangs on the Great Beast Izax." Lorenzo had a rather nasally voice that spread through the silent room. "How long have these gangs called Izax home?" Omega asked. "Quite some time, Empress. Several cycles."

Omega glared to Maridian and then back to Lorenzo with a smile. "Thank you for bringing this to me. I was not informed of such activity. An oversite I will handle personally." As her last words sounded more menacing, Maridian felt a single bead of sweat roll down his face.

Omega moved her hand slightly. As she did so, a full Wardens' circle stepped forward and stood with Lorenzo. "Escort Mr. Shaw back to the Great Beast Izax, and swiftly handle the gang activity there." "Thank you! Thank you, Empress." Lorenzo said as he looked around with a large smile on his face.

The Pain Conduit of the Warden's Circle placed a gentle hand on his shoulder, and escorted him out, with the rest of the circle in tow. As they left the room, the Warden closed the door behind them. Omega let out a slight sigh. If only they all could be so easy.

Without hesitation, Maridian looked to his book and called, "Spencer, Regina. Please step forth and address our Lord and ruler. Speak freely from the safety of her shadow." A woman with a thick scarf on, from the middle of the crowd, stood and with her rose a small boy. Empress Queen Omega leaned forward and furrowed her brow as they walked to the front.

The boy continued to limp as he held Regina's hand. Once in front of Omega, they moved to bow. "Don't," Omega said quickly as she looked at the boy before her. "Empress, I request that you help my son." Omega focused on the boy's numb of a leg, and the burn marks on his arm. Even his eye sported a fresh dark circle around it.

What bothered Omega almost as much as the sight of the boy, was how he and his mother were dressed. Their clothes weren't the tattered garments of the Sand Wasteland or even the worn clothes of those that lived on the other Great Beast. No, they were clean and elegant. Form-fitting and soft. They were clothes of the people of her city, Acropolis.

Omega stood from her chair and walked to the boy and took a knee beside him as she looked at what should have been a full leg. Then she moved to the burns, and lastly the eye. "What happened to him?" Omega asked as she began to unwrap the leg.

Regina began to sob and stuttered. "Speak freely," Maridian said. "You are in the safety of her shadow." "My husband does things. Hears things. Sees things. He can't help it." Omega turned to Regina. This time she had a glare on her face. "You allow these things to happen?"

Regina shook her head and began to sob more as she removed her scarf to display a large bruise that looked like hand prints. Maridian closed his eyes for a moment and turned away. "I cannot heal your wounds, but I will see that you get medical care," Omega said. "I can, however, fix this." She said as she placed a hand on the disfigured leg.

She looked the boy in the eye and then to his mother. "When you are old enough, you will come to serve me. Be it in my court, or as a tribute. That is all I ask." The boy nodded as his mother vigorously did the same. "Yes, Empress. Thank you." The mother was eager to accept these terms.

Her son would be whole again and was guaranteed a job when he was of age. Their Empress truly was a giving god.

"What's your name?" Omega asked as she placed her hand on top of the boy's shoulder. "Miles," he said slowly. "This will not hurt Miles. Just breathe normally and relax." She applied pressure to her hand and closed her eyes. It happened in an instant, and several members of the crowd looked up. Seeing their Empress create was merely a hope. Not just for those in the room, but to all that worshipped her. They all knew she could. They all believed in her and her power without question, even though they had never seen it.

In seconds Miles' stump from his leg began to transform into a leg that looked healthy and whole. It was metallic, just as the skins of the Warden. Miles' eyes grew wide as the sensation of his new limb registered with the rest of his body and he began to move his foot. A sight that caused his mother to cry harder all while thanking Omega.

With a slight move of Omega's hand, Regina and her son stood and moved towards the exit in the room. Regina opened the door for Miles as he waved back to Omega and left, followed by his mother. As she put her hand down from the wave, she sent Miles, she moved to a member of a Wardens' Circle close by. The Swordsmith with the colossal sword stood at the ready. "Follow them, and find the husband." The man nodded slowly. "Do not kill him quickly. Cut off his limbs first, and then burn him slowly over time. Make him experience what his son has. I want him to beg for death, and when he is within an inch of his life, have him healed. Then repeat the process indefinitely. Any man that does that do a child doesn't deserve to live in my shadow, and will not be granted the mercy to die at my feet."

The man, sword in tow, gave a slight bow to Omega, and then to his Warden, and left the room. She stood alone off to the side for a moment. Her heart was heavy at the thought that one of the people of her city, they ones she cared for the most, would be capable of such a thing.

Omega turned to face the crowd, all of whom were still kneeling, and then found her seat in her chair. "Maridian," she said but found her aide was already writing in his large book. "I have already made a note to assure the family is able to survive with the father gone. Funds will be given to aid in the process."

Omega smiled briefly. "This doesn't make up for the gang oversight, but it is a start." She took in a deep breath and then crossed her legs and allowed her booted foot to swing freely. "Now, let's finish your list so we can be done here, and I can face my tributes." "Yes, Empress," Maridian said as Omega began to truly smile with the thought of her new tributes and the children, she would gift the world with, from them.

CHAPTER 20:
NEW RECRUITS

A loud noise caused Danielle to wake up. She hated being abruptly forced to wake up, and yet she found herself always waking up this way lately. If it wasn't for her training, it was from Prism. That damn hologram had it in for her and she knew it. Deep down, she felt Prism had never truly accepted the new leaf she had turned over to be a hero. Honestly, she didn't know if she had either.

Danielle loved Hunter. More than she had ever loved anything else, but deciding to be a hero a year ago with him was more so his idea and not hers. She had always considered it, but also always found a reason to not go through with it. Even if she hadn't done anything villainous at the time, she always knew that deep down, she eventually would.

Now, she walked the straight and narrow. A life of boredom and mediocrity. A life where she at best could hope for her own line of merchandise, maybe even a cartoon. She would never be infamous. People wouldn't shake at the mention of her name, and the only people that would fear her would be villains. People she related to all too well.

As she sat up in bed, she felt herself getting frustrated. Funny how a single loud noise caused her to spiral down the path of thinking about her recent life decisions. Clearly, they were weighing on her more than she thought. "Did you hear that, boo?" She said as she looked to where Hunter slept.

Or, where he was supposed to be sleeping. His spot on the bed was empty, though. She frowned as she rubbed her neck and then looked around the tiny room they shared. The door was still closed, but they hadn't been there long. She ran the recent events through her mind.

Cayden showed them the room. Hunter asked him some questions. Cayden left. Then she ate a candy bar while Hunter started talking about how things didn't add up. She told him to relax, and he sat down on the bed. One thing led to another and twenty minutes later they were both breathing heavily, and tired. Naturally, they fell asleep. "So where in Atlas did you go?" she said to herself as she jumped from the bed.

She tossed her clothes on and then opened the door. They couldn't have been sleeping that long. There were no windows around so it was hard to tell, but it still had to be early. Didn't it? Once in the hallway, she found her first decision to make. "Which way, which way?" Danielle said as turned and looked down both sides of the hall, and then to the third hall directly across from her.

She realized this place was damn near a maze when they didn't have a person leading them. "Who the hell makes a base this complicated to navigate around?" she said to herself. Then suddenly, she thought about it. What if Hunter didn't leave? What if they took him and she somehow didn't hear it?

"That doesn't make any sense at all," she said to herself as she started walking down the hall to her left. She felt that was the direction the noise came from. "He's too powerful for something like that to happen," she muttered.

Danielle had been walking down the hall for less than a few minutes when she heard a voice behind her. "Where ya headed?" The sudden voice caused her to jump, as she turned around with dark tendrils springing to life around her hands.

Cayden stood before her with a spoon in his hand and vigorously chewing. "So, you just what? Blast people with energy when you are startled? They sure raise heroes differently on your world, huh?" he said as he looked at her. Danielle dropped her hands and caused her powers to fade away.

"Where in Atlas did you come from?" Cayden pointed his spoon to a door she had just walked past. "My room," he said as he put the spoon back in his mouth, took a bite, and began chewing again. Danielle frowned and took a step back. "Are you, eating that?" she asked as she leaned in some to make sure she was seeing things clearly.

"Obviously," Cayden replied. Danielle liked being a rebel as much as a person could, but even she was getting tired of the way Cayden and his brother spoke to people. "But why? I mean how?" she said as she stumbled to find the words. Cayden finished chewing and took another bite of the spoon, and then tossed the last portion in his mouth as if it was a chip.

"One of my spells," he said behind a burp as he reached in his pocket to reveal another spoon. This one was old and rusted. "I can eat anything for energy. Literally anything. My other spell consumes a ton of energy when I use it, so I'm pretty much eating all the time. Lucky for me, it doesn't have to be food."

Danielle looked at him as he explained to her this weird ability with a straight face. He was pretty much a billy goat, but she kept that thought to herself. "So where are you going?" He asked as he moved closer to her. She looked down the hall and pointed. "I uh," she stammered. Hunter had gotten to her and she didn't know how much she trusted these people either.

She knew she trusted Perkins, but then again, she had only known her for a year. Then she heard it again. A loud sound followed by a screaming male voice that caused her to look in that same direction. "That," she replied as she turned and walked towards the sound. "I heard it from my room, and Hunter is missing. So I, decided to sneak down a hallway in an unfamiliar base to find out what the noise was?" Cayden added.

"Not a great plan, but I get it," he said as he walked by her to take the lead. "Cord is training the new recruits." Danielle followed him down the hall toward the sound. "New recruits? That fast?" she asked.

Cayden took a bite of his rusty spoon and nodded his head. "Yeah, we have a running list of people we rejected over the years. Usually, Cord is dead against them joining. Says they are incompetent, untrainable, or just plain old failures. But this time he was eager to let them join."

"Why?" Danielle asked. "It doesn't sound like a smart plan." "It isn't," Cayden said as he shook his spoon in the air. "Same thing I told him, but he has his mind set and we need troops. Not like him to move without thinking, so I'm sure he knows what he is doing. Or I at least hope so. I don't want to have to be the powerful one, and the smart one too."

Danielle looked around as she continued to follow Cayden through the maze of a base. They went down another hallway and passed a few people in what looked like a kitchen. They weren't much in the looks department, and she hoped for their sake they weren't soldiers in Bravados movement. From the tired looks on their faces, they had seen enough of whatever they recently faced, and wanted out.

Even when she waved at them, they just avoided eye contact and shuffled away. "Can I ask you something?" Cayden said from up ahead. "You just did, technically," Danielle replied. She heard a faint laugh from up ahead but couldn't see Cayden's face.

"Your boyfriend's name is Hunter. But he goes by Paragon. According to Perkins, your leader's name is Ryan, but he goes by Flex. They're your hero names." "We call them true names," Danielle replied. "Essentially the same thing, though." Cayden took another bite of his rusty spoon and finished it.

"So, what's your true name?" This question caught Danielle off guard. She had been here before, though. Hunter and she had discussed it at length if she would ever find a true name. Some cool names were tossed around in private, but she never chose one. For a while, she didn't know why but now she did.

Once she chose a true name, she would feel like a hero. A true hero. Sure, heroes could go bad, but she just didn't feel she was ready for that yet. She wasn't like Zeva. Oh no. As far as Danielle was concerned Zeva was a monster. A monster that she hoped Power Prince was having success with tracking down.

Danielle wasn't like that, but she just didn't go all in with the hero stuff. She liked the gray zone. That was one of the main reasons she feels so hard for Hunter. He practically lived in the gray zone. The middle ground between good and bad. He would still visit that area here and there as he struggled to fit in with her life, but more and more she found herself there alone.

"I don't have one. Not yet anyway," she finally replied. "So, you're not a hero then?" Cayden asked. "What's with the questions you little shit? You writing a book or something?" Danielle snapped. "Wow," Cayden replied as he pulled out a spoon and took a bite.

"I guess that's a sensitive topic. But take it from a guy who is being forced to be a potential ruler, that wants nothing to do with command. I get it. Sometimes it's hard to figure out which path to take."

Danielle began to feel bad for snapping. She didn't intend to, but damn sure wasn't going to apologize for it. "Here we are," Cayden said as they entered a large room that smelled like sweat and eggs. "This is where we train."

He said it as he opened his arms. As if he was revealing a masterpiece. To Danielle, a person that was accustomed to training with cutting-edge technology back in the New Lords' base, this room was a shit show. More or less, it was a large room with some mats on the floor, a high ceiling, some lights, and a pile of weapons besides a row of chairs. That was it.

In those chairs, she saw Hunter sitting beside Cord, talking animatedly with his hands imitating a person throwing punches. As they spoke several people, likely the new recruits, stood before them breathing hard and sweating. Most looked tired and some even had shaky legs, but still they stood tall. "These are the recruits?" she asked as she looked at them all.

Cayden sighed and nodded. "Slim pickings, but we need the manpower for the plan Perkins has cooked up." "Cooked up?" Danielle repeated. She had begun to wonder just how long she was sleep if they had time to create a plan and draft new recruits. "Well let's go see how this unfolds," she said as she took the lead and made a direct line to Hunter.

"Oh shit," Hunter said as he looked up. "Is shit a bad thing?" Cord asked as he looked to Hunter and then saw a glaring Danielle walking towards them. Hunter swallowed loudly.

"Hey, babe," Hunter said as he stood up. His reply was a darkness-encased fist to the stomach. The recruits standing in front of them jumped back in shock. Some of them eyes wide at the powers Danielle gave them a sneak peek at. "Sleep well?" Hunter said as he caught his breath.

From where he was bent over, he could see Cayden walk by him and sit down beside Cord with a smile on his face. "You could have at least told me you were leaving," Danielle said as her voice got loud. "It's not like we are on a strange world, with people we barely know or anything." Hunter looked at the recruits and then to the smirking Cord and Cayden.

He slowly positioned himself in front of them. "I figured you were tired, so I left you to sleep." "You're damn right I was tired, I did all the work," Danielle replied. Behind him, Hunter heard Cayden conceal his laugh in a cough. He turned to tell him to shut up but was confused when he locked eyes with Cayden.

"Is he eating a spoon?" Hunter asked slowly. Danielle glanced at Cayden who had yet another spoon in his mouth. This one was golden with a curved design. "Don't worry about him," Danielle said as she gripped Hunter's face and turned it to herself. "What are you even doing here?" Hunter stepped closer to her and moved her to a spot where they weren't as close to Cord and Cayden.

"I told you, none of this felt right," he whispered. "Impervious is, well Impervious. A guy that can literally stand up to anything." "So," Danielle replied. "So, why isn't he here? There's no way this Omega lady defeated him. Even with those Warden goons. Something is up. So, I went to look around. I figured it was no need for us both to get caught so I didn't wake you. That's the truth."

Danielle avoided his eyes as her anger began to slip away. She took in a deep breath as she nodded slowly. Making sure to not let the others see her face. "You find anything?" Hunter shook his head. "I do know Perkins and Cord have a plan. That and he trains these damn recruits harder than Flex trains us."

"That a bad thing? I hear they aren't that good anyway," Danielle replied. "They aren't. Not even close, but it's like he's trying to force skill on them instead of teaching them. It's like he just wants," Hunter's words were cut off. "Hunter!" Cord said from behind them.

He and Danielle turned to look where Cord was sitting, but only found Cayden with a spoon in his mouth. He gave Hunter a hand gesture, one Hunter only assumed was an insult, and then pointed to the recruits. Standing with them was Cord.

"Yeah?" Hunter responded as he took a few steps toward the center of the room. Danielle watched. She didn't know what was going on, but for the rest of the time she was here, she was going to keep her guard up. "The easy way to say it is that our new batch of recruits isn't much to look at. Especially compared to our previous batch," Cord said out loud.

Hunter eyed some of the faces standing near them. A mix of men and women ranging from youthful to early twenties. They all were sweating, dirty, and breathing hard. Still, they stood at attention. Backs straight, chins up, and eyes forward. "I don't know," Hunter replied. "They need some work, sure. But they still have tons of potential. I'd go to battle with them any day."

Hunter said these last words with a forced smile. He didn't truly believe what he was saying, but he didn't want to join Cord in his verbal assault. Encouragement was what they needed. Even if it wasn't entirely true. "I'm sure you would," Cord said as he walked up and down the line in front of the recruits.

"But you're a special case, aren't you?" Hunter felt his brow raise. "I don't follow," he replied. "Of course, you don't." Cord said. Hunter took in a breath. He was just starting to like Cord too. When they were both sitting down discussing hand to hand skills, they seemed to get along fine. Now he was back to being a dick.

"Recruits," Cord said loudly. "Hunter here, just like my brother and I, come from a rare heritage. An elite one at that." The recruits all looked at Hunter. For the first time, they broke their perfect posture. Many of them had brows raised and gapped mouths. "Now don't think the old days are coming back. His bloodline is all but extinct. Only two members remain in it. One is missing, and one has no intentions of taking the role of leader. Still, he has tremendous powers. Powers that would allow him to be just fine in battle. Regardless if you're there or not."

"Really?" Cayden said from the side chair. "Tremendous power? Laying it on kind of thick, aren't you? I mean we only know what Impervious has told us. For all, we know it's a nerfing lie." "You trying to trick me into fighting you, kid?" Hunter asked. Cayden stood up from the chair.

"No tricks. We can go at it if you want." Danielle took a step closer, but Hunter stretched an arm out. Cayden was in front of him now. He was shorter than Hunter was, but he had a devilish smirk on his face. He wasn't scared. Even with what Impervious told them, he was ready to fight.

Hunter found himself seeing something in Cayden again, and this time it didn't surprise him. Something that made him like the boy a little more. Hunter saw himself. Young, more powerful than those around him, fearless and eager to show off. Yep, that was him, or who he used to be. Hunter looked to Cord.

"So, you cool with this? It's not my fault what happens to him next." Cord, standing behind his recruits smiled. "Sure. A demonstration from the men they will be fighting beside in the field could be good for this sorry batch of losers." Danielle winced at the insult directed to the recruits.

"He may be cool with it, but I'm not." Hunter closed his eyes and took a breath as he heard the voice. Danielle watched Flex and Perkins walk into the room. Flex had a smile on his face, and Perkins' hair was clearly the result of trying to fix it up quickly. She could tell that they had the same evening activities that she and Hunter had.

Perkins' stood beside Danielle as Flex put himself in front of Hunter and placed a hand on Cayden's back. "Take a seat kid." Cayden laughed. "Who do you think?" "Shut up and sit down," Cord said. Cayden glared at him and then returned to his seat as he took a huge bite out of his spoon. "Did he just?" Flex started but shook his head as he left the question for another time.

"Cayden may have power, but he is inexperienced and young," Flex said. "If we are going to give the recruits a demo, then it's going to be a good one. One where the combatants are equals. Even if one is slightly better than the other."

Through his smirk, Hunter could see a bit of the old Flex shining through. The Flex that he used to be before he was forced to become a leader. "You sure you want this Ken Doll?" Hunter asked. Flex stepped back and opened his arms with a smile.

Danielle leaned over to Perkins. "Are they really about to do this here? With everything else we having going on?" Perkins shook her head. "Men and their nerfing egos." "So, what do you say, Paragon?" Flex said as he slowly rose in the air. Seeing him fly made some of the recruits gasp out loud and whisper.

Then in reply, Hunter called his force field to life. More whispers came from around the room. Even Cayden was paying attention now. Danielle looked and could see more people piling in from outside and joining halls. Clearly, Bravado had more soldiers left that she had originally thought. "One last go, to settle the score. A tiebreaker." Flex said as he raised his fist.

"Oh, you think you won the second time?" Hunter said. "Fine. let's do it." Hunter allowed the room to turn blue as energy danced in his eyes. In an instant, he released his Impact Blast and was surprised to see that Flex didn't even flinch when it hit him in the chest.

CHAPTER 21:
DARKNESS BECOMES HER

Hunter knew it would happen eventually. He had always known. Icons like Flex, born with invulnerability always eventually did what Flex had just done. The thing with invulnerability was that it was a growing power. As the Icon got stronger and older, so did the invulnerability.

When Flex first got his powers, a small caliber bullet wouldn't hurt him too much. It would leave a damn good bruise, or even puncture the skin a little, but as he got older those same bullets bounced off of his skin in comic fashion. Not just small caliber bullets either.

Heavy- duty stuff like bombs, armor piercing ammo, energy blasts, and much more left barely a scratch on Flex. The only comfort Hunter had was that his energy, his special kind of energy could still hurt the titan of a hero that Flex had become at such a young age. "Well those days are over I guess," Hunter said as he and Flex both looked at Flex's chest.

"When in Atlas did that happen?" Danielle said from the side. "What are we talking about here?" Cord asked. "Normally Flex's invulnerability doesn't do so well against Hunter's energy. It seems that his growing invulnerability has reached a point that Hunter's Impact Blast no longer leaves damage," Perkins said.

"Well, well, well," Flex said as he stood a little taller and stuck out his massive chest. "It's not too late to back-," another beam of blue energy roared towards Flex's face. Instinct took over. He had been hurt several times before by Hunter's energy and found himself guarding his face out of habit.

The energy slammed into his raised arms, sparing his face and eyes from the blue burst. Hunter wasted no time now. If his energy attacks didn't work, this would for sure be a one-sided fight. His pride was hurting as he moved towards Flex. Every fiber in his being was screaming for him to quit, to admit that Flex truly was the superior Icon, and deal with it.

Hunter couldn't. He knew he didn't have the raw power of Flex but his powers were more versatile. As he ran towards Flex, Flex himself formed a fist and charged towards Hunter. Then, in an instant, they both slowed down. When they were only feet apart from each other their steps became slower as they lost momentum. Hunter fell to his knee, as Flex began to wobble on his own.

"What's going-" Hunter groaned as he clenched at his stomach, unable to finish his question. His bones began to hurt and his body started to ache. Flex coughed as his vision became blurry, and spasms spread throughout his back. "That's enough, Cayden," Cord said as he glared at his now standing brother.

Danielle looked at Cayden. The casual, smart-mouthed, spoon eating youth she met in the hallways was gone now. Replaced by a young man, standing with his hand stretched out and a smirk on his face. "Cayden, he said that's enough," Perkins repeated from behind Danielle.

Danielle glanced at Perkins. She had forgotten her friend was behind her for a second. She then looked to Hunter on the ground. He was looking at Cayden and had energy in his eyes now, but Danielle could see a difference. The energy wasn't is normal raging beast clawing at the cages to be set free. No, it was more a flicker. As if the energy wouldn't come to its call.

Her eyes fell back to Cayden whose hand was still stretched. Only a few seconds had passed since Cord told him to stop, but that was far too long in Danielle's mind. She summoned her powers quicker than even she knew was possible. As darkness consumed both of her arms, her eyes became pools of eternal blackness.

She didn't think, she simply reacted and as the room seemed to go dark, black energy exploded from her arms and poured over Cayden. His screams filled the rooms he was lifted off the ground and slammed into a wall several feet back. Cord watched his brother fly and barely reacted. He had no care in the world for what just happened.

Danielle took a step forward to advance on Cayden. She wasn't done yet. She wanted him to feel her anger. The recruits in the room had huddled together as if they were afraid to stand alone in this room of powerful people.

As she inched closer to Cayden, she felt a small hand grasp her arm. As she turned her head, her eyes became normal again and she found the green eyes of Perkins looking back at her. "Easy," Perkins said. "He's down."

Danielle looked to where Cayden was slowly being helped up by the recruits. Hunter and Flex were finally getting to their feet too. "What?" Danielle's voice trembled some as she tried to ask the question. She could see Cayden standing to his feet now, but was being assisted with walking by a recruit.

Danielle watched them walk away as she fought back tears. She was afraid of how far she could have gone had Perkins not stopped her. She wanted him to feel fear. Feel pain for what he had done to her team. The people she loved. No, it wasn't even for them. She just wanted to keep going. That feeling inside her as she slowly moved from the gray zone of bending the rules to the darkness that came with breaking them scared her.

"I'm a hero," Danielle said to herself strongly. Perkins tilted her head. "I'm a hero," Danielle said again, but this time not with as much certainty as before. "You're nerfing right you are," Perkins said softly as she moved to stand in front of Danielle who quickly wiped at her eyes. "And don't you ever forget it. Okay?" Perkins said.

"What did he do to them?" Danielle asked as she took in a few breaths and avoided Perkins' gaze. Perkins went to move her mouth but the two loud thuds beside her caused her to stop. As they both looked towards the sound, they could see Flex and Hunter slowly breathing on the floor, unconscious.

CHAPTER 22:
TEAM A AND TEAM B

Beeping and a smooth humming noise was all Hunter could hear as he slowly opened his eyes. He could feel a stiffness to his body as he propped himself up in his bed. "What the…" he slowly said as he realized that he was dressed in white and on a medical gurney. "Welcome back, boo," he heard a voice say from the side of the room.

As he turned around, he could see the rest of the room around him a little better than before. His eyes finally focused to the point where his brain could connect the dots again. He was in the same medical bay from earlier. Danielle placed her hand on his forearm and kissed him on the cheek.

Hunter closed his eyes for a moment and felt the energy from the kiss spark a fire in his body. It felt, good. "Hey," Hunter finally said. He realized his voice was lower than he wanted it to be, and his throat was dry. "Why am I in the medical bay?" he asked. "And why am I facing a wall?" "Same thing I asked when I woke up." Hunter heard the voice but couldn't see where Flex was. Slowly, his gurney began to slowly pull away from the wall, and spin around.

"You," Hunter all but hissed as he saw Cayden sitting at a square white table in front of him. "Easy. Easy," Perkins said as she stood up. They were all in the room together. Danielle walked back into view, for it was she who spun Hunter around. She stood beside him and gently rubbed his arm as he looked at Cayden, Perkins, and Cord sitting at the table. Just to the side of the table was Flex.

He was also dressed in white, and on a gurney similar to the one Hunter was on, but he was sitting with his feet hanging from the side. Hunter ignored them all and just glared at Cayden. The boy tried to avoid his eyes, but Hunter didn't care as the room turned blue.

The energy rushed to his eyes so fast that he got a slight headache but Hunter ignored it. For him, it was worth it to blast this little bastard into oblivion. "Whoa," Danielle said as she stood in front of Hunter and put her hands up. Behind her, chairs could be heard screeching as the residents of said chairs leaped up and out of the way. "What did he do to us?" Hunter hissed as he tried to lean around Danielle.

"Babe, you need to relax," Danielle said. "Relax?" Hunter yelled. The slow footsteps were heard before he saw Flex pop into view and stand beside Danielle as he rubbed his neck. "Just calm down," he said.

Flex looked over his shoulder towards the rest of the room. "I'm sure they will explain everything," Perkins nodded as she moved to grab Flex's hand and led him back to his gurney. "Cayden," Cord said in a flat voice. The boy let out a sigh. "Sorry for attacking you a few days ago. I-" "A few days?" Hunter let out as he looked to Danielle. "How long have we been here?" he asked her.

"Just over sixty hours," she replied. Hunter cracked his neck and felt his hand form a fist as he moved his legs to stand. Danielle shot a hand out. "Let him finish," she replied. Hunter didn't speak. He felt he didn't need to. His anger was filling the room like a thick fog and it was hard to miss.

"Cayden," Danielle said as she raised her brow to the boy who was now eating what appeared to be a small plastic pipe. "I wanted to show Cord that I could, under the right conditions, hang with you two power-wise," Cayden said between chews.

Hunter was becoming more and more pissed at this kid with every word he said. It wasn't exactly what he said, it was how he said it. It was his tone. That casual, matter of fact, I don't give a rat's ass how you feel, tone. Yet again, Hunter was seeing bits of his old self in this brat, and he wondered how his friends tolerated him for so long before.

"By the right conditions you mean, to ambush us with," Flex paused as he spoke. "Whatever that power was that you used." "Time," Cord said finally as his brother took another bite out of the plastic pipe. Cord looked toward the entrance of the room and moved his finger, causing the young girl standing at the door to disappear in the hallway.

"Time what?" Flex asked. "Time is what I used on you," Cayden said as he burped. Hunter could feel his eyes narrow. "Say what?" he asked. "That was my reaction too," Danielle added in. "Time manipulation is one of Cayden's spells," Perkins said as she sat on the gurney beside Flex now.

Hunter didn't speak. Instead, he looked from Perkins to Danielle, to Cayden. 'Bullshit," he finally said. To which Cayden leaned over and pulled a small fruit from his pocket. At first glance, it looked very much like a tiny apple, except it had a purple tint to it. He took a bite of it and then placed what remained on the white table in the room.

With his hand stretched out, the fruit suddenly went from bright and lush to withered and decayed in seconds. It was as if some unseen force had pressed the fast-forward button in real life and only the fruit was affected.

"Some smaller, less complex items, are affected faster," Cayden said as he looked at the fruit then turned to Hunter. "That's is pretty much what I did to you two. Not at full power, or anything. Just a little bit. I sped up the time in the space you both occupied. I may have started off too strong, though. That's why it hit you so fast."

Flex whistled slowly. "You're still not on my good side, but that's a pretty good ability to have." Hunter quickly turned to Flex with betrayal etched on his face and brows raised high as they could go. "Oh, come on. You know it is." "It may be, but it consumes a ton of my energy. That's why I eat all the time. Hence the random stuff I keep in my pockets as snacks." As he said this, he pulled out a small metal cube and tossed it in his mouth.

"Disease immunity, advanced consumption, and time manipulation," Hunter said as he leaned back to rub the side of his head with his hands.

"Anything else we're missing?" "Stealth," Cayden replied. Hunter rolled his eyes. "What do you mean- stealth?"

"I can create an aura in a small radius that blocks those in it from being seen by anything," Cayden casually replied. He didn't even look to Hunter when he answered him. The only other thing he could have done to show how much he didn't care was shrug his shoulders. A gesture that would have pushed Hunter over the edge.

"Sounds like a long and fancy way to just describe invisibility," Hunter replied. "Actually it's-" Danielle began to say, but a glare from Hunter caused her to reconsider. "Never mind," she said quickly.

Those weren't flashy powers. Well, they were, but not like his. Still, they were good powers to have and Hunter knew it. He just refused to admit it to Cayden. "Dodged the fight again, Ken Doll," Hunter said to Flex. "You did see the energy from your blast did nothing to me right? Just how did you think that match would end?"

"Actually," Cayden interrupted. "The blast was caught in my area of effect for my time manipulation," Cayden said slowly. "I was pretty much-making everything in that area advance in age. Your energy was no exception. So, from the moment it left your eyes, it was being aged so it was weaker. Your bodies just hadn't reacted yet." "Ha," Hunter said with a genuine smile. "That explains it." He felt relief wash over him. Flex wasn't able to stand up to his blast after all. Not yet anyway.

His thoughts and Flex's retort were interrupted by the clanging of wheels being rolled towards them. A large chalkboard was being wheeled into the room by the same girl that left moments ago. "A chalkboard?" Danielle said as she leaned in and touched it. "Where in Atlas did you find one of these old things?" "We have several," Cord said as he began to write on it.

"Normally we do this sort of thing in a briefing room, but since we are all here anyway, this will have to work." Cord jerked his head towards Flex and Hunter. "Your clothes are beside your beds. Feel free to get dressed when you're ready." Cord continued to write on the chalkboard, as Perkins and Danielle found their seats.

Flex all but leaped from his gurney and began getting dressed. Hunter wanted to do the same, but he didn't have that invulnerable body and endurance that Flex had. He couldn't shake off time being increased on his body with such ease. "Need a hand, Hunter?" Cayden said through a smirk. "Fuck you," Hunter replied as he slowly placed his feet on the ground and grabbed his pants.

Cayden glanced to Perkins. "It's an insult," she said to him. "I see," he said as he sat back in his chair. The loud clicks of Cord drawing on the chalkboard filled the room as Hunter and Flex finally joined the rest of them at the table.

"A quick layout of the land," Cord said as he pointed to the small picture he had drawn to the side. The picture has three sections on it. "At the bottom, we have the Sand Wasteland," he wrote the words on the bottom portion of the picture. "The wastelands are where the real scum dwell. The lowest of the low, that the East section of Mo'eizus resides."

Cord then moved his chalk to the middle. "Here is where we are. Above the sands on the back of The Great Beast Arzi." "They have names?" Hunter said out loud. "Why would they not?" Cord shot back at him without turning from the chalkboard. Hunter sucked at his teeth but said nothing.

"The cities on the back of the Great Beast are considered the commonplace. It's where regular citizens work, play, and do everything in between to live a normal life in the shadow of Empress Queen Omega. Naturally, that's where we are." His chunk of chalk finally touched the top of his little picture.

"Where we need to go is here." He punctuated his last word with a quick tap of the chalk. "We need to make way to the Great Beast Sonah.

This is where Empress Queen Omega lives in Acropolis with her chosen." "Chosen?" Flex repeated.

Cord took in a deep breath and glared at him. "Does it really matter what they are called? All we need to know for the purpose of the meeting is that this is where we need to get to, in order to save Impervious. We can discuss meanings of names at a later date." Flex nodded his head at Cord.

"Very well," he said. Hunter was impressed. That old Flex that came out to issue a challenge to him had been replaced by the facade of a leader again. "This is where Perkins and I disagree on how the plan should unfold." Cord wrote out the words *Soldier A* and *Team B.* "I think it is better to send in one single soldier to infiltrate Acropolis. This soldier would make their way to the city, and be able to investigate without being seen. This also makes for an easier exit."

Cord paused and looked at the room. Perkins was the only one looking at him dead in the eyes. "I believe Hunter would be the ideal person for this-" Cord found his words sliced as they left his mouth. "Why me?" Hunter asked. Cord cleared his throat. "Well, considering that you're from another dimension, you don't have to worry about the Curse of Varo." "You think I won't have to worry about it. Think. Nobody is sure," Hunter said.

Cord ignored his comments as he continued to talk. "You can also, and most importantly fly and defend yourself if need be."

"Why not Flex, or Cayden?" Hunter asked. He wasn't trying to get out of going. Why would he? Hunter was confident enough in his abilities to get things done, but none the less he felt that there were better options for the job that for sure could become cursed or infected.

"You do realize Flex can fly and is damn near unable to be harmed right? You do know your brother is immune and can turn stealthy right?" Hunter said as he laughed as he said the word *stealthy*. "So why in Atlas did you pick me to go?" Cord rubbed the corner of his eyes with his forefinger and thumb. "I'm not in the habit of leading the show, but I'll do it just this once,"

It took all the energy Hunter had recovered to not flip the table over right then and there, and try to beat Cord to a pulp. His hand skills be damned. "Well Flex would stay back to defend our understaffed base, and Cayden," Cord stopped and looked at his brother who sat at the table but was eating another fruit. "Well Cayden is my brother and I want to watch him." Cord said finally.

"What's gotten into you?" Cayden said. "Normally you can barely stand me, but now you're leaving me off missions?" Cord cleared his throat into his hand. "I wanted to, yes. But Perkins had more plans for you all. A plan that I agreed to go along with."

With that, Cord used his hand to erase the word *Soldier A* off the board and replaced it with *Team A.* "Since I'm tired of being interrupted, I'll let Perkins explain her plan for you," Cord said as sat in the chair that Perkins had just gotten up from.

"So, Team A will be the combination of Hunter, Danielle, and Cayden," Perkins said as she wrote the names on the board. "Team B will be me, Flex, Cord, and basically anybody else we have left in the base." Once again, she wrote their names down as she spoke. "It's unlikely that anybody will try to attack the base, but unlikely doesn't mean impossible."

Flex watched as she continued to explain the plan to them, and glanced to Hunter who was actually paying attention completely. He was happy to see his intern stepping up, thinking, and above all else controlling his anger. He really had changed a lot in a year. Flex smiled some. This made him happy because if he had to do what he was thinking he was going to do, it would make things much easier.

"So, once we fly there, then what?" Danielle asked. "Do we try to take out Empress Omega Queen or whatever her name is?" "Empress Queen Omega," Cayden said from across the table. "Yeah, her," Danielle replied casually. "What's the end goal once we get there because I'm sure there will be Wardens and a bunch of other flunkies around."

Perkins nodded her head. "Indeed, there will be, in theory. That's why we want you to be as low- key as possible. Between your shadow form, and Cayden's ability to conceal Hunter, you all should be able to get around rather easily. So for now, this mission is strictly to search and rescue. Try to find Impervious, and if able, free him."

"Free him from what?" Hunter said out loud. Perkins paused for a moment and then glanced from Hunter to Flex. "We don't know," Flex said. "We have to assume that he is either captured or unable to return to us." "But he's Impervious," Danielle said. "What in Atlas could stop him?"

"We don't know. We just have to consider all options," Flex replied. Danielle thought to herself, all of this seemed damn near impossible. She knew Impervious, mostly by legend and from Hunter's stories, but one thing they all had in common was that he was one major badass. An unstoppable force that you couldn't contain. She shuddered slightly at the thought of something or someone with the power to do just that.

"Sounds almost like a suicide mission," Hunter said finally. "No. Remember don't engage." Flex said as he looked Hunter in the eyes. "Do. Not. Engage. As your leader, your safety is most important to me, but still, this is the job. You all have the skills to get this done, and the ability to protect yourselves if needed, but make that the last resort."

Flex turned his gaze from Hunter to Danielle who had a smirk on her face. He rolled his eyes some. He had known Hunter for so long and seen him go from rebel bad boy to hero that he forgot that his better part was still getting used to the hero side. Between the two of them, Hunter had the temper, but Danielle had a swing first ask questions never attitude. "Do. Not. Engage," Flex said to Danielle this time.

"Cross my heart," Danielle said with a smirk. Flex took in a breath. "Good enough." "Now can we begin?" Cord said as he stood up. Cayden stood with him and for a second, they looked at each other, gave a slight quick hug, and then faced the rest of the room. Hunter looked at Flex as he stood up. "You know, I bet the rest of Purgatory Academy is having normal internships. Even Jen is having fun. But for me? Nope. I'm off-world on a rescue mission. I should have stayed home with Power Prince."

Flex extended a hand to Hunter. A hand which Hunter shook with a look of suspicion in his eyes. "Look at it this way," Flex replied. "You'll be the better hero in the end. Stubborn, and hotheaded as you are, your potential will take you far."

Hunter was surprised at the words. Flex was a great guy and a better hero. Few could compare to the name he had created for himself in such a short time. Sometimes Hunter even forgot that Flex was only a few years his elder. Still, he rarely spoke to him this way. "Now get your ass in gear, Paragon. We have a mission to do," Flex replied as he punched Hunter in the shoulder a little too hard.

Hunter rubbed the shoulder as Danielle stood up. "It's me and you again, boo," she said as she glanced over to Cayden. "Yeah us, and the jackass," Hunter replied.

CHAPTER 23:
ROOFTOP RENDEZVOUS

Hunter stood on the roof of the base, close to the ledge with Flex and Danielle, as they waited for their new gadgets provided to them by Cord and Bravado. Cayden, still not on Hunter's good side, decided to wait alone and leaned on the roof door that led back inside of the base's upper level.

As he yawned, he caught Hunter looking at him for a second before he turned back to Flex and Danielle. Cayden just didn't understand it. Flex and Danielle seemed to be fine with him and how he had shown his powers during the fight for the recruits. Hunter on the other hand, still seemed like he would attack him given the chance.

Was it because he had attacked without their notice? If it was, Cayden really didn't care. Many battles were to be won by any means. It was what he was used to growing up in Mo'eizus. Born of elite blood almost made you a target, and he and Cord had to fight a lot before Bravado came along. Many of those fights weren't fair and the way to victory wasn't either.

He had no issues with that. Deep down Cayden felt that Hunter was simply jealous. Why wouldn't he be? The way Cayden saw it, Hunter was used to being the powerful one. Used to being the one getting the attention, and now he wasn't. Now he was against a power he couldn't stop. Time came for all things that were living, and Cayden controlled time better than any other.

"You're better than him. Maybe better than them all." Cayden said to himself as he dropped down from leaning on the wall to sitting down. With just that slight movement, Hunter's head turned quickly towards him. "Damn, he really doesn't trust me," Cayden said under his breath.

He personally had no real issues with Hunter and as far as he was concerned, they were fine with each other but he would never be the one to bend to another's ego. So instead of looking away from Hunter's glare, Cayden pulled some long steel nails from his coat pocket and began to chomp on them. All while smiling and waving back to Hunter. "Hi, Paragon! My dear sweet friend," Cayden said as he continued to eat on his nails.

"That prick," Hunter said as he turned from Cayden to Flex and Danielle. "Really?" Flex said as he leaned and looked back at Cayden. "I don't understand what your issue is with him but let it go. We are all on the same side now." "You don't understand?" Hunter repeated as he glanced over his shoulder towards Cayden.

"That metal- eating freak jumped us. He could have killed us with that damn attack," "But he didn't," Flex replied. "He has just as much control over his abilities as any of us." Flex paused for a moment and looked at Hunter. "What?" Hunter replied as he jerked his head back. Flex shook his head in return as he laughed slightly. "It's just that of all people, it's funny to hear you call somebody out of their name. Metal- eating freak is no better than being called spawn or abomination. He can't help what he is."

Even though Flex was merely speaking, the words hit Hunter with the strength of a punch. Hunter had been the target of people's verbal abuse for years just because of his birth. The names Flex had mentioned, Hunter had been called for as long as he could remember. When he became Paragon, the names stopped mostly but still, some people saw him that way.

At that moment, he looked to Cayden. Sitting alone. Eating his nails, and seemingly carefree. Now Hunter felt differently for being so aggressive towards him. He could remember the pain that came along with being called a name that he wasn't or being made fun of based off of things he had no control over. Most of all he knew the pain that came with being different.

He took in a deep breath. "Fine," Hunter said as he returned back to their huddle. "I'll cut the kid some slack." Flex nodded. "I thought you'd see it my way." "You really are getting this leader thing down," Danielle said as Flex smirked some.

"Don't let it go to your head, Ken Doll," Hunter said. "We still got plenty of time for you to screw stuff up when we get back." Flex nodded, but didn't reply as his smile faded slightly. A reaction that Hunter didn't notice, but Danielle did.

"I'll go easy on him, but I still don't trust a lot of this," Hunter continued. "First Impervious, now we have to sneak in a base that they just happen to have blueprints to? How in Atlas do you even get blueprints to a city built on top of a flying monster?" "I get it. It all sounds ...," Flex searched for the words as his eyes darted a little.

"Hard to believe. We all know Impervious. We know how he earned his status as an Icon that nothing could stop, but still, he hasn't come back so we have to go. We owe him that much." "You sure are tossing that *we* word around a lot for a guy that is staying behind in safety," Danielle said.

Flex narrowed his brow at her. "Lady has a point," Hunter chimed in. "I'm literally the only major defense the base will have when you guys are gone." Hunter shrugged as he replied. "I saw the video of you catching a plane out of the sky. You'll be fine." "That aside," Flex continued. "I trust Perkins."

"Sex will make a guy do that," Danielle said as she licked her lips slowly. Hunter tried to ignore this attractive gesture. "Lastly, they have been planning to take Omega's base for years. Obtaining the blueprints was just part of the process.

The door to the roof swung open and nearly hit Cayden in the process. Flex, Hunter, and Danielle turned quickly to the sound. "Calm down," Cord said as he stepped through the door and saw Hunter's blue eyes facing him.

He was holding a stack of black clothes in his hands, as Perkins follow him out of the door with a small metal box in her hand. As she moved, she put something in her ear and twisted it. Behind them, Cayden pushed himself from the ground and joined them all in the center of the roof.

“I know we wanted to get this done as soon as possible, but I needed some time to get some things,” Cord said out loud. “I had to go to one of my nests in the city. So sorry it took so long, but it was worth it. Put these on,” Cord said as he tossed each of them some bulky padded clothes.

Hunter looked at the clothing in his hand. Both the shirt and the pants were black and felt odd in size with the pads made into them. “What is this?” Danielle said slowly. Flex and Hunter wore her confusion on their faces as they looked around from the clothing back to Perkins and Cord.

Cayden, on the other hand, had already started removing his shirt and getting dressed as his brother instructed. They’re the uniform of Empress Queen Omega’s palace staff and guard,” Cayden said as he slipped his pants off. “It will help you blend in up there,” Perkins said. “Danielle, yours may be a little big, but that was the size that fit me the best, so I figured it would work for you.”

Danielle nodded as she moved to stand behind Hunter and get dressed. Hunter noticed Cord moved his head slightly to the side as if he was trying to get a peek of her undressing. He cleared his throat loudly and Cord smoothly returned to his normal position.

Perkins dropped down on one knee and opened the case. “Put these in your ear,” she said as she gave them a small black circle. “Hunter, Cayden, and Danielle each did what they were told. You will be able to hear us back here at base automatically. On the outer side of the com is a button. Press it once to speak to us back here at the base.” “So easy even you can do it,” Flex said as looked at Hunter.

“Ha, fucking, ha,” Hunter said as he placed the com in his ear. “These go on your eye,” Perkins said as she passed out small circular cases that she pulled from the box. Danielle took her case and opened it to reveal what looked like a contact lens inside. "Make sure it's the left eye," Perkins said.

"Your map will be displayed on these, and for some reason, they pick up better on the left eye instead of the right." Danielle once again did what she was told. So did Cayden, but she could see Hunter moving slower than she was.

Unlike her better half, she trusted Perkins. Maybe not Cord so much, but she had grown to know Perkins over the last year. She never had a reason not to trust her. "It looks like a video game," Danielle said as she blinked a few times and looked around them.

As her head moved a small, circular, rotating map appeared in front of her. On the map were various halls and large squares. "Perkins thought you might say that." Cord said as he watched Hunter and his brother both move their hands in front of them trying to touch the map that they were seeing.

"Once you arrive at the palace, you will see three dots appear. As I'm hoping you are smart enough to guess, those dots will be you. At that point, we will be here if you need us at the base. You shouldn't get lost, but we really don't know where to send you once inside. So, if you have to split up, at least you will be able to see each other. Understood?"

They all gave a gesture or few brief words to signify that they understood what Cord had just said. "We can see you. We can hear you. But once you get inside, you're on your own," Cord said as he paused to see if they had questions. Nobody spoke. Instead they all just glanced at each other. "Good," Cord said. "Off with you then. Time is wasting."

He said the words, gave his brother a quick nod, and then turned and walked towards the entrance door. In a fluid motion, he opened and closed the door behind him without looking back. "Not big on goodbyes, is he?" Flex said as he looked at the recently slammed door.

"That nod that I got," Cayden said as too looked at the door. "Was more than I was expecting." Perkins motioned her head towards Flex and he gave her a slight nod before he turned to them. "Good luck up there. All of you. I would say play it smart, and don't be a hero but, well that's what we are."

Danielle avoided his eyes as they fell on her. "Yeah, yeah we got it," Hunter said as he stepped forward between Danielle and Cayden. He turned and looked towards Cayden. "We good?" he asked as he stretched out his fist to him. Cayden looked down at the fist in confusion.

Normally when a fist is aimed at him it would be coming from a punch. Not just hanging in the air connected to a person with a smirk on their face. "Yeah," Cayden replied slowly as he looked from the fist to Hunter. "You gotta just," Hunter grabbed Cayden's fist as everybody around them laughed gently.

Hunter balled Cayden's fist up and then touched his own. "We'll work on that," Hunter said as he called a large force field to life, making sure to give him enough room as always. As they began to lift off the ground Cayden squealed a little as he felt weightless, as Hunter's control over the gravity inside the bubble took over. His hand touched the force field from the inside and felt a slight tingle as the mix of warmth and cold touched his skin.

"This is amazing," Cayden said slowly as he let his other hand touch the force field. "I am aren't I," Hunter said proudly as Danielle slapped him in the head. "We have force fields, but they don't," Cayden said as he paused to put his face on the force field. "They don't feel like this."

"Okay, you just made it weird," Hunter said as he grimaced. "Remember," Perkins said from below them. "Once you get up there, look for the big flying thing. You literally can't miss it. The palace is in the center, so you will have to navigate through the city to get there. Just like we did here, come up around the back end. Should be fewer people there."

Hunter gave them a thumbs up, and then with all the power he had, shot the force field through the sky like a pale blue cannonball. From that moment, he was no longer Hunter. He was Paragon now, and he had a mission. He was going to find his uncle. Impervious. The only true relative he had left. He was going to find him, and figure all of this out.

He didn't know why, but he felt everything would be better once Impervious returned. The only thing that stood in his way was a flying monster and a ruler that had people that worshipped her like a god. How hard could it be? Hunter cursed himself for thinking such a thing. He knew right then and there, that he had just jinxed himself, and that hard times were coming.

CHAPTER 24:
STEALTHY

That's Sonah," Cayden said from inside the force field as he pointed to the large winged creature in the distance. "Well, I'd hope so," Danielle said in return. "Otherwise there would be just another dragon-monster thing hanging around up here." Hunter wanted to laugh but he was too busy focusing his energy and power on navigating the skies.

The speed in which he was flying combined with the weight of Danielle and Cayden was no easy feat. In fact, the feat wouldn't have been done with such speed and ease a year ago. Virtual nonstop training for a year had its perks after all. "We are approaching it now," Hunter finally said in his ear com.

"Good. Just remember to fly around the rear just above the tail," Flex said through the coms. "If you're confused about which end that is, it's opposite from the head," Cord's gruff voice came back. "Asshole," Hunter said under his breath. "We can still hear you," Perkins said back. "He knows," Danielle said as she watched Hunter give her a grin.

As he looked ahead of him, the grin on his face faded away. As the Great Beast called Sonah came into view only one word came to Hunter's as he tried to voice his shock. "Whoa," he said slowly. The monster was larger than he could have ever imagined. Its bright orange skin could be seen perfectly, even though it should have been barely visible in the darkness.

Large black scales covered over half of the muscular body. Two large leathery wings were on each side of its torso, that flapped slowly and with grace. Hunter found it hard to believe that a creature of this size could contain momentum with such slow wing movement, but it did. Then there was its face.

With bright red eyes that burned through the night around them, the head of the beast seemed the most out of place. It was smaller than expected, with tentacles extended from the bottom, and what appeared to be gills on each side. On top of all that this monster was, rested various buildings that stretched to the skies. Hunter slowed the force field down as he gathered himself.

"Imagine all that this creature has seen," Danielle said as she moved closer to the force field to look at the beast. "People debate about the age of the great beast, but many believe that Sonah is the eldest of the five," Cayden said casually as he looked in awe. He had never seen the great beast before. Only the special were able to live in the city, and only those selected were allowed to visit. He was neither.

"Perkins," Danielle said through her com. "Go ahead," Perkins came back through their ears. "Just how in Atlas did you guys ever get cities built on these things?" "Damn good question," Hunter said as he shot the force field towards the monster. As with before, he dipped low enough that nobody should have been able to see them and gained altitude once more when near the back.

"Not sure, to be honest with you," Perkins said. "It's believed that when the planet was young, many of its inhabitants had spells that were equal to those with elite blood. With such abilities in abundance, they came together to build the cities. Eventually, disagreements began," Cord said through their coms. He had paused on the word disagreements.

"Disagreements led to fights. Fights led to wars. Wars that forced those without great spells to flee. When everything was over, those that survived declared themselves to be elite. To be royal. Once those that fled returned, they were allowed to live on the beast and serve under the royals' lines." "None of that is actually proven, though," Perkins added in once Cord had stopped speaking.

"Thanks for the history lesson," Danielle said. "Shit!" Hunter screamed out as he tried to move the force field in time before the large, plated tail of the great beast came flying towards them. "What happened?" Flex shouted over the coms.

"We're fine. We're fine," Hunter replied. "Damn thing tried to swat us away with its tail." "It was nearly successful, too," Cayden added in. Hunter glanced at Cayden through the corner of his eye. "Landing now," he said as he lifted them through the air and finally placed the force field on the ground in front of a massive metal wall.

"Hey guys," Hunter said as he tapped his fist on the wall. "The wall surrounding the city is reinforced." "Fly over it," Flex said. "Too high," Danielle said through her com. "If we go over the top we risk being seen. I can use my shadow form and walk right through, but that still leaves the boys outside."

Silence filled the air as both teams allowed their gears to turn. "I think I can use an impact blast, but-" before Hunter could finish Cayden stretched his right hand out, while at the same time eating a large purple stone.

Cayden caught Hunter and Danielle looking at him. "I got it," he said over a mouth full of whatever he was eating. "You have enough energy?" Cord came back over the com. "Plenty. I've been eating brailium most of the day." The word made Flex laugh as for a second, he thought about Manis and his brailium- covered skin.

Cayden narrowed his eyes and as he did so, Hunter could feel his widen. Across from where Cayden had his hand extended, a large portion of the wall quickly went from a strong, resilient, thick steel to old, weathered, and rusted full of holes. Hunter felt his mouth drop and he hated himself for it.

He didn't like to be envious of another man's ability, but every now and again he found himself in just that situation. Now was one of those times, as he saw Cayden with as much effort as it was to blink, accelerate time on this chunk of wall. For a second Hunter felt himself get angry again that this same ability was used on himself and Flex, but he let it go.

"I aged it few hundred years," Cayden said. "Tough stuff. It has to be laced with brailium." Hunter stepped forward and began to clear open the hole with his hands. His enhanced strength was enough to make a way for them. Had Flex been there with them, he could have easily done the same with the wall prior to it being aged.

"We're in," Hunter said as he smirked to Danielle. "I've always wanted to say that." "Stop talking and move." Cord's voice said over the coms. "You're dressed like them, but you're not one of them. Under investigation they will realize just that, so make your way to the palace and try not to draw attention to yourselves."

"We all can hear that right?" Danielle said. "It's not just me?" "No, I hear it too," Hunter replied as he tilted his head to hear the music better. It was faint, yet still soothing. He couldn't tell where it was coming from but harmonious music lived in the air around him. It almost made him feel like they were in a spa.

"Oh, so the rumors of the music are true," Perkins said over the coms. "People always said that Acropolis was so loved by Empress Queen Omega that at night music plays to put children that are afraid of the dark at ease." Hunter tutted as he brought up his map. Cayden and Danielle followed his lead.

"It looks like you've stopped moving," Cord said. "This isn't the time to stand around." Each of them looked at their floating map in front of their eyes with a beacon for the palace being a yellow blip in the distance. "Calm down," Cayden said. "We know what we are doing." "You'd better," Cord replied.

Hunter took lead and started walking towards the yellow blip on their map. The part of the wall they came through was in the shadows, nestled between two large buildings. Once they made it out of the alley and stepped foot in the city Hunter stopped walking so fast that Cayden slammed into Danielle as she bumped into Hunter.

Hunter looked over his shoulder to Cayden. "None of Bravado has been here before?" Cayden shook his head. "No. I don't think so." "None," Perkins said. "Hm," Hunter said to himself. "What is it?" Flex asked over the coms at the same time that Danielle said it from behind Hunter. "See for yourself," Hunter said as he stepped aside.

Danielle moved passed him as she looked around the city in front of them. "Shit," she said slowly. "What?" Flex asked. This time his voice was louder. Danielle was expecting a lot of things when they arrived at the flying beast city but not this. While the buildings back on the beast they had left were nice and intact, they weren't built like the ones before them.

This entire city looked, modern. They weren't just buildings, they were composed of steel and glass. There were street lights and hanging signs. People that were out and about at night, walking around holding cups and eating. Laughing and having conversations. "This entire city," Hunter said as a wide-eyed Cayden looked around. "It looks almost like our cities back home. Minus the traffic and pollution. I could pass this place off for a burrow in Atlas City with ease."

"Empress Queen Omega has rebuilt the city with a vision in mind," Cord said . "We still believe that once, the city looked like all others on the beast." "Noted," Hunter said as he began to move through the semi-crowded area. He didn't speak about it, mainly because he didn't know what to say, but something about the city bothered him. It looked too much like his home dimension. Maybe a little dated, but still the resemblance was uncanny.

He knew the Spellborn people had the technology to come to their world. That was established long ago with the Battle of Ages. Still, why design it to look that way? It wasn't a big deal but it nagged at him, and he didn't know why.

There weren't many people out tonight, but it was enough to make him cautious. As they moved, however, the citizens of Acropolis seemed to give them room with ease. One look at the uniforms they had one and people would smile and then step aside. Some even raised their cups to them as a form of salute.

"Forever in her shadow." one bald man with dark skin said as she smiled and walked passed them. Two younger blond women followed behind him, and both smiled while giving the three of them plenty of space as they passed. "We're taking a turn up here," Hunter said as he pointed and followed his map.

As they turned around the corner, Hunter felt his body stiffen against its will and had he been a weaker man, his knees would have trembled. He saw the sword first. It was attached to the slender man standing beside the larger figure with a gun that normally would require several men to lift.

"Shit on a stick," Danielle said as she rounded the corner with Cayden in tow. "Report in," Perkins said. Hunter ignored them all as his eyes fell to the shorter female in the middle. One thought from her and pain would consume them all like a raging fire scorching the land. Yet still, she wasn't the one to be feared.

No, that honor belonged to the one in front of them all. The one dressed in black with the metallic skin. "Warden's Circle," Cayden said in just over a whisper in his coms. "How far away," Flex asked. "About five feet," Cayden said as he slowly raised his hand. Quickly Danielle wrapped her hand around his wrist and shook her head.

There were too many people around for Hunter to react the way he wanted to. He could have easily released an Impacted Blast that would have obliterated the Pain Conduit, and then systematically handle the rest of the Warden's Circle. In theory anyway. The risk of hurting those around him was too high, and as a hero that was a concern. He raised his hand slowly and with his index finger, swirled it in a semi-circle to signal his team to turn around.

As he took a single step back, the Warden paused, and with unnatural speed turned around on the spot. Had it had a face with eyes they would have been looking directly at Hunter and his team. Slowly, the rest of the Warden's Circle turned and looked in their direction. "Nobody move," Cayden said in a voice that was surprisingly normal. He didn't whisper this time. Danielle and Hunter barely heard him a few moments ago, and yet this time he spoke without care.

A few seconds passed, then the Warden turned again and began to walk away in the direction it was heading. When they were out of hearing distance, Hunter turned to Danielle and Cayden. "What in Atlas just happened?" Cayden was wiping sweat from his brow with the back of his hand and searching one of his pockets. "I made us stealth," Cayden said slowly.

"Good Job," Perkins said. "Thank Danielle," Cayden replied as he looked to her. "I was about to try to age them but she stopped me." "Good thinking on your feet," Flex added in. "Follow them," Cord said finally as he decided to not compliment the team on a job that wasn't completed yet.

Silence filled the coms once more. "Come again?" Hunter replied. In his mind, he could mentally picture Flex glaring at Cord back at the base. "They are likely headed to the palace. Follow them inside. If they are your escort, even if the circle doesn't know it, it will be easier for you to get in beyond their defenses."

Hunter let his eyes follow the circle as they steadily moved away from his team, but closer to the yellow blip of their maps. They were indeed headed towards the palace. Cord was a prick, but he was right. "How long can you keep this stealth thing going?" Hunter asked as he turned to Cayden. "Long enough," Cayden replied as he moved in front of Hunter.

"As long as you're in the radius of my energy, you won't be seen or heard from those beyond the field." Hunter nodded as he realized this power may have been better than he thought. Especially if it covered the sound they made, too. In seconds they were all running in unison, under the protection of Cayden's stealth field, until they closed in on the Warden's Circle.

Despite not being able to be seen or heard, Danielle still could feel her heart pounding in her chest, and it had nothing to do with the running. Once they were close enough to be a few feet from the circle, they started to walk again. Hunter looked to his map and realized they were almost at the palace now.

"I'm not a detective, but I'm guessing that's it," Hunter said as he looked at the tower- like building that loomed over the city. The design was unique. Slim at the bottom and extended at the top. For those close to the building, they were in its shadow on all sides. Hunter began to think this design was done intentionally to drive the mantra of Empress Queen Omega.

Several normal guards, all dressed in the same garb as Hunter and his team stood near the front entrance. One look at the metal- faced creature approaching and the guards quickly stood aside and allowed the Warden's Circle to pass. The motions were so smooth that none of them had to even slow their steps.

Danielle wondered what it must have felt like to be so feared by those below you. None of the guards even looked in the direction of the Warden's Circle. They spread away and looked away. Danielle hated that she felt the way she did, but she knew a part of her wouldn't mind having people be so afraid of her in such away.

Then a voice in the back of her head told her that it could happen. Even as a hero, one could still be feared. She knew plenty of people feared Flex. And he was as good as they came. "Took you long enough," Cord's voice came across the coms as they entered the palace grounds.

"He means 'good job' team," Flex came back. The Warden's Circle stopped walking almost at the exact same time as Cayden took in a deep breath and almost lost control of his power. "You okay?" Hunter asked him. Cayden didn't speak. He wanted to. He really did. He wanted to tell them to run. Tell them they needed to retreat because their end was approaching.

Instead, he did all he could do. He pointed at the young woman with pink hair and large boots approaching them.

CHAPTER 25:
ALL SEARCH NO RESCUE

"Wait, that's her?" Danielle said as she looked to Cayden and pointed her thumb towards the woman approaching the Warden's Circle. Cayden said nothing. The slow nod and increased rise and fall of his chest said it all. This was their divine ruler through and through. Danielle looked at the woman with narrowed eyes.

She could remember being told that despite how young she looked, the Empress Queen Omega was rather old, and now that she could see her in person, she realized that the lady held up well over the years. Her skin was flawless and seemed to radiate even in the darker surroundings.

Her pink hair bounced when she walked and her passive posture displayed a woman that had nothing to fear from anything around her. She was in charge and there was no need to fear those who owed their lives to you.

"Who is that with her?" Hunter asked as he leaned his neck to the side and could see a tall, thin man with a well-maintained beard walking slowly behind Empress Queen Omega. His long robes touched the ground and he had a large book in his hand. The people around them seem to shy away from his presence as much as they did Omega herself. "Her aide, Maridian," Cayden said from beside him. "He's the most trusted person in her empire."
"He gives me the creeps," Danielle said as she watched the man clasps both hands around his book and sneer at the Warden.

The Warden's Circle motioned to take a knee as Empress Queen Omega approached, but she quickly signaled for them to stop. "Enough with the theatrics," she said with a slight laugh in her tone. "I know, I know, forever in my shadow. Now that that's out the way did you find what we were hoping for?"

The metal face warden shook his head slowly. With this simple answer, Omega took in a deep breath. "Step forward," Omega said as she looked at the Pain Conduit. This conduit moved slowly and with hesitation as she gave a quick glance to the Warden. "Don't insult me," Omega said quickly.

"The Wardens are the authority to you but are servants to me eternally. You fear them, and they fear all that I am." Hunter watched as the man called Maridian took a slight step away from Omega as she continued to speak to the Pain Conduit. "The next time I give you an order, and you look to another for direction I will have the very Warden you look to, eviscerate you on the spot."

As she finished her words, the same Warden she mentioned turned and stood by her side to face the Pain Conduit and removed its hands from behind its back. The other two members of the Warden's Circle took strides to not be beside their colleague. "Do you understand?" Omega asked slowly as she looked into the other woman's eyes. "Yes, Empress."

Hunter had never heard any of the Warden's Circle talk before. In fairness they were too busy trying to kill him to speak. The Pain Conduit had a low hiss of a voice, that had almost a click like echo to it. "Now, step forward," Omega repeated. Before the order was from her mouth the Pain Conduit had already moved. "Report." This time the words came not from Omega, but from Maridian.

"All of the tests proved unsuccessful. The new serum still only serves as a way to temporarily halt the Curse of Varo, not cure it." Omega's fist clenched as she bent over slightly and screamed out. Maridian looked to her and for a second considered reaching out to his Empress to touch and comfort her, but caught himself.

Instead, he continued to grip his book. "Our efforts outside of the East Section were successful," the clicky voice of the Pain Conduit quickly said. "The addiction of chrome has increased in all sections of the world, and not just ours. Combined with the curse's spreading, and our numbers, we should be ready to mount an assault on the South Section first, followed by the North and then the West." The man Maridian opened his book and began to write some things down.

"And those that were guilty of using chrome inside our section?" Maridian asked. "Disposed of," the Pain Conduit said as she added the words "painfully and slow." to her verbal report. Danielle whistled from inside the safety of Cayden's spell.

"She may look like she works in a comic book store, but this Omega is one cold bitch, and she runs a tight ship." "You don't know the half of it," Perkins said in their coms. "Well, that is good to hear," Omega said as she clapped her hands together before placing them in the pockets of the green jacket she wore.

"Had your report been different, I would have taken away your ascension from all of you. It can be rather messy and," Omega paused to look at the Warden beside her who, while not having a face, seemed to become a little stiffer from her mention of taking away their ascension. "You know how I like to keep things clean."

"One of the guards out here has a minor spell that allows them a brief burst of speed and endurance. Makes him an efficient guard, and an even better person to clean up the mess," Maridian said with a smile from the thought of disposing of this Warden Circle filling him with joy.

"You're free to go," Omega said as she flicked her hand away without even looking at the Warden's Circle. As a unit, with footsteps in almost perfect timing with each other, the Warden's Circle did as they were told. Only their leader, The Warden himself didn't move. As the members of his unit put more and more distance between them, Omega spoke softly.

Hunter looked at Empress Queen Omega as she leaned in and spoke to her Warden. "Return whatever we have left of the new serum to the lab. Check on our guest, and then return to the rest of your team. Do you understand?" Empress Queen Omega asked as she stepped away and returned to stand near Maridian. There was a slow nod from the Warden, and then the creature turned to walk towards the palace.

"Would you really destroy them my Empress?" Maridian asked. "Children must be loved as much as they must be disciplined," Empress Queen Omega said as she turned away. Maridian, however, did not move. "Come Maridian, we have much to do tonight, but first I have something I want to show you."

Maridian bowed and did what he was told as he fell into step behind Omega leaving only the entrance guards. All of whom looked considerably more at ease now that Omega and her creations were gone.

"You guys are getting all of this right?" Cayden asked through his com. "Every word," Flex replied. "I think our best bet is to follow the Warden," Hunter said. "Agreed," Danielle said at the same time that Cayden said, "as do I."

"Follow him for what?" Cord finally asked. "He is going to their lab, but then is checking on their guest," Hunter answered. "That must be Impervious." "We hope it's Impervious," Flex responded. "We have no proof that it is him. What we do know for sure is that they have a supply of a treatment serum for the Curse of Varo. Follow the Warden to the lab."

Hunter looked at the Warden walking off in the distance. From inside the safety of Cayden's field. He hadn't gone so far that he couldn't still be followed. Hunter wanted to protest that Impervious needed them. That they could free him, and then find out about this serum. He knew that wasn't the right frame of mind to be in, though.

There was no way to be sure that this guest was truly Impervious. He had just wanted to free his uncle so badly that it seemed logical, even while it wasn't. "Okay," Hunter finally said. "We'll follow the Warden to the lab." Cayden nodded and then began to move in the direction of the Warden, as Hunter and Danielle kept in step with him.

"Retrieve as much information as you can once inside," the voice of Perkins said to them. She sounded, different to Hunter but he didn't know why. She wasn't her normal calm self. Perhaps being on a mission that involved following one of the most feared creatures in her world didn't leave room for a person to be calm.

"These Wardens don't really do much, do they?" Danielle said from inside the stealth field as they walked behind the Warden. "What do you mean?" Cayden replied. "It's just that they seem to be so feared around here, and I'm not sure why." Hunter had noticed it too. As the metallic creature roamed around the grounds and halls of the palace, people stayed away. In some instances, people would even turn around and almost run away to avoid being alone with the creature close by.

"We fought a Warden's Circle when we arrived, and the Warden himself did the least amount of fighting. It just makes me wonder if people fought back how they would -" "We have been fighting back." the cold voice of Cord came through the coms.

"Many of us have lost family and loved ones to stand up to Omega. Some eventually giving up, and even joining her. We may not have much, but don't you dare assume we haven't been giving it our all." "Sorry," Danielle said after a few seconds of silence. "Lastly, pray that you never see a Warden display the power for what he is feared. My entire team is mostly gone because of it." Cord said, but this time in a voice that was softer than any of them had heard him speak since their arrival.

"He seems to be slowing down," Hunter said as he raised a hand. They all stopped moving and watched as the Warden removed a slender tube from inside his jacket and stood as a light appeared and covered its faceless head. A light above the door turned from red to green. The Warden performed several more feats and with each, a single red light turned until all four of the lights were green.

With a slight hiss, the door opened and the Warden stepped into a room that apparently had smoke inside of it because some seeped into the hallway as the door was open. “Wait for him to leave and then find a way inside that lab,” Flex said over the coms. “Quietly,” Perkins added in. “I have an idea,” Hunter said as he glanced over to Cayden. The boy was standing tall, but had a visible sheen of sweat on his forehead.

“Perhaps I couldn’t keep this up as long as I thought,” Cayden said as he wiped his sweat away. Just at those same moments, the door to the believed lab opened and the Warden emerged from within its darkness. As the doors shut, the Warden smoothly continued down the hall and out of sight. “Okay, we should be good,” Hunter said as the Warden left their view. “Danielle head inside and see if you can find a way to let us in.”

“On it,” Danielle said quickly as she shifted into her shadow form and sprang from the safety of the stealth field. If there had been another person near them, they would have seen a ghostly dark figure appear out of the nothingness, and then run through the door of a lab.

“Whoa,” Danielle said as she shifted back to her normal form. “There should be a lever just beside the door to open it from the inside,” Cord said. Danielle looked at the horror around her in the lab, and fought the urge to not scream or throw up.” Danielle,” Hunter said as he spoke into his coms.

“Are you there? Do you see the lever?” Hunter was beginning to worry. On their map, he could see the dot that was Danielle. It was still very close to their location, but the dot hadn’t moved at all. He could feel himself beginning to panic, and had to fight the urge to not blast through the door to make sure she was okay.

Then the door to the lab opened with Danielle silently, and frantically, motioning for them to head inside. “We just hit the creepy scientist jackpot,” Danielle said as she released the lever and locked them inside the lab.

Hunter took several steps inside the lab and looked around as what appeared to be cool air filled his lungs. It wasn’t smoke as he originally thought, and the lab was virtually freezing. None of them were dressed to be in such an environment and Cayden was literally shivering. This realization made Hunter wonder were Wardens immune to things like cold and heat, but the thought faded away as he looked around the large lab.

It was dim inside, and from what Hunter could see, the lab was more so a very large, two-level, square room. "Thank Atlas," he said to himself. The last thing he wanted was to be in some tiny lab and have his phobia set in.

Each step Hunter took sounded like he was walking on steel and echoed around the room. To his surprise, when he looked down to the floor, he could see his reflection looking back up at him.

One side of the lab had several monitors, all flashing things that he couldn't understand. One monitor had a DNA chain revolving on it. He had seen enough science fiction films to be able to point that out. Near these monitors were several small tables with beakers, tubes, and syringes.

Many of which had what appeared to be blood inside them. To the other side of the room, where most of the cool fog was originating, were five human size tubes. Even though there were five tubes, only one had an actual body in it. For a second, Hunter was afraid that the body belonged to Impervious but quickly realized that it was too small a frame.

As he turned around, he glanced up to the second level of the room. It was a small area that had a single set of stairs leading up to it. Danielle was already up there and looking over the shelves of books. She grabbed one and then quietly placed it back on the shelf. "I think I found it," Cayden's voice came from across the room as Hunter could hear a click and then lights came to life inside the lab. "Sweet mama," Danielle said as she stood near the railing on the second level and looked around with eyes wide. "What in Atlas are they doing in here?"

"Really wish these coms came with cameras," Hunter said as he looked around and took a step to the center of the lab. No reply came back from the base. "Flex," Hunter said again as he looked to the others. "Cord.

Perkins." Danielle touched her com a few times in her ear. "I can't hear them either." "I'm guessing it's the lab," Cayden said.

He wasn't as surprised that their signal was blocked from in here as Hunter and Danielle were. "We should do what we need to do and hurry out. If I know Cord and Perkins, they are already planning a rescue attempt."

"This is where they are trying to figure out the curse's cure," Danielle said from upstairs. "How do you know," Cayden called from beside one of the human-sized tubes. Her feet clicked as she trotted down the steps. "They have it written up there on a glass board. There are a few more monitors up there too. All with monitoring videos of people that look like they are already infected. Each with a number on the screen. I'm willing to bet boobs and biscuits that those are some of the subjects our Warden friend had to visit."

Hunter was walking towards the middle tube now to look at the man inside. "This should be enough to make more people join our cause. Now we have proof that they at least have a treatment that they aren't sharing with us." Cayden said. "It's not a cure but," his words faded away as he fought back images of cleaning up the mess that had become Becca. All that time he stood by her, watching her insides bleed out and the madness consume her. There was a way he could have helped her. Could have made her last moments peaceful, but Omega kept it for herself.

Hunter leaned into the tube and squinted his eyes, and then they popped open. "Atlas no," he said as he stepped back some and then looked at the tube. "You okay. boo?" Danielle said as she walked over to the tube. Cayden now pulled from his inner thoughts of how much the treatment could change things, turned and looked at the tube also.

Hunter had expected a lot of things, but this wasn't one of them. He hadn't seen much of the man in the tube, but he knew him. Now that he was close, he could see that he recognized the man's face. Not all of it though. Just the bottom half, but it was enough. He had dealt with dreams for months about that face.

The face of a man with power that couldn't be matched. The face of a man that wanted to see their world come crashing down. The face of a man that was partially covered by a white mask as they fought a year ago. The face of his cousin, and Impervious' true son.

"It's Infinity?" Hunter said slowly. Danielle gasp as she took a step back and flickers of black tendrils danced up her arms in reaction to the moment of fear. "Are you sure? How? Why?" she fired off her questions too fast for Hunter to answer.

All he could do was shake his head for a moment. "I don't know." "Infinity," Cayden repeated. "Wasn't that the name Impervious' son used? He told us that part of the story shortly after he arrived. He offered to show us the body, but most of us refused. All but Perkins."

Cayden stood closer to Hunter and looked inside the tube. Hunter walked around the tube and could see various cuts and holes on the back of the floating body. In the center of the back was one single slender tube that was red and leading out of the chamber he was held in.

"I think they are doing something with his blood. Testing it maybe?" Neither Danielle or Cayden replied. Instead, Hunter heard two loud thuds hit the ground. "Guys?" Hunter said out loud as he walked slowly from behind the tube. Hunter was a lot of things, but stupid wasn't one of them. He may have still been on his internship, but he had extensive tv and cinema knowledge. A knowledge that while not on the level of Power Prince, it was still vast enough that he knew things were about to enter cluster fuck mode.

Anytime a person heard a loud thud, and then calls for their friends, only to hear nothing in reply, that person should prepare for a fight. As he stepped from behind the tube, his force field came to his call. Sure enough, Cayden and Danielle were both on the ground unconscious. Well, they were safe for now at least. As Hunter was stepping out, two Wardens were picking them up off the ground and tossing them over their shoulders.

"I promise you, your friends will be delivered off-world to a safe location close to their base." Hunter's throat suddenly became dry. "Yes, I know the general location of the base. They will be safe, only if you stay behind so we can have a chat." Hunter swallowed and felt the sound was amplified by the lab itself. He glanced from side to side at the metallic henchmen. There was no chance he could take them both, but still, it took a lot to fight the urge away from trying.

Doing so would just get his team killed. He nodded to the person talking. She smiled at him and turned to walk away as she motioned her index finger for him to follow. Hunter took in a deep breath and followed Empress Queen Omega out of the lab.

CHAPTER 26:
FOREVER IN HER SHADOW

Hunter looked over his shoulder as he followed her through the palace. There was a single Pain Conduit with them. She looked exactly like every other Pain Conduit he had seen in this world. Shorter than the rest of the Warden's Circle, solid, covered in some sort of body armor and moved with a determined grace. Not just her, but the entire Warden's Circle, in general, all seemed to move with focus and grace. It was almost cat-like.

As Empress Queen Omega began to hum as she walked down the hall, Hunter realized he had bigger issues to worry about. At first, he thought that if done right, he could end this all right here in the hall. He could quickly handle the Pain Conduit and then confront Omega. His plan was flawed, though.

For one he still needed answers. Answer to where Impervious was. To what they were doing with the body of Infinity, and those were just the first two questions that came to mind out of about ten. "So, uh what now?" Hunter finally asked. Omega placed her hands in her jacket and continued to walk. "You keep following me," she said with a slight pep in her voice.

Hunter took in the woman in front of him. He was upset and disgusted with himself for finding her attractive. He had even glanced down at her butt in front of him at least twice since they had been walking. He loved Danielle. He really did, but to believe the body bouncing around in front of him belonged to a woman in her eighties was both impressive, and slightly off-putting to him.

As they approached a door with two men dressed in the same outfit that Hunter had on, Empress Queen Omega gave a slight nod, and the men opened the door. Inside the room was a large table with a lavish assortment of food spread out. Soft music played, and a man and woman walked around the room to pour drinks to those at the table when needed.

Sitting around the table were no less than ten men and women, all barely dressed in nothing more than undergarments. In the corner of the room, sitting down and reading a book while sipping on a glass filled with blue liquid, was the man Cayden called Maridian earlier. He looked to Empress Queen Omega and raised his glass slightly, tilted his head and then returned to his book.

As she moved closer to the table, the men and women motioned to stand up but she raised a hand and stopped them. "No. Eat. You've all earned this." she said as her finger danced on the table as she walked by and picked up a grape to pop in her mouth.

The Pain Conduit moved to the opposite side of the room and stood with a Warden that Hunter hadn't noticed when they first entered. "You having an orgy or something?" Hunter asked slowly as he watched the men and women at the table laugh and talk to one another. Empress Queen Omega, looked at him with a smirk. "No. Something much more sacred and fun," she said as she placed her hands on twin knobs that opened a door to a balcony.

"I'm glad we got this chance to talk," she said as she looked out onto the city. Hunter could still hear the music lofting in the air, but it seemed fainter than when they first arrived. "Why did you come here tonight?" She asked as she gently took her jacket off and placed it on a nearby table.

She applied extra effort to make sure the jacket wasn't ruffled. The extra attention she paid to the garment made Hunter frown slightly. That combined with her blunt question caught him off guard. "I'm here for Impervious," Hunter said finally. He knew she knew of Bravado, but he wasn't sure yet of how much she knew.

He would rather seem like the three of them mounted a failed rescue mission than to let her know they were equally interested in a cure. Or did she know that too? If she knew enough to know the general area of the base, then she likely knew more. "For Atlas' sake, that man is a thorn in my side," Omega said slowly as she pulled her pink hair back. The words made Hunter's eyes widen as he slowly looked at her in a new light. No. It couldn't be what he was thinking. Could it?

"I assure you. Impervious is fine. He, like us all, plays a part in my plan. Once they are fulfilled, he will be released." "Interesting choice of words," Hunter said as he felt his body was stiff for the first time. He didn't even realize his jaw was clenched until he felt the soreness when he went to speak. "Caught that did you?" Omega said as she lifted a hand towards the man walking close by. The man walked over so quickly that his silky white clothing flapped.

He, and the other server, were dressed completely. A stark contrast to the guest at the table. Omega took a glass from him and sipped the green liquid. "It's just that many people here don't speak that way," Hunter said as he locked eyes with her. "True. They don't say the word void here either." She took another sip.

"I know you don't have a reason to believe me, but you also don't have a choice. Impervious is fine. He's being taken care off and held in a secure part of the palace." Hunter's gears began to turn. Now at least he knew that Impervious was alive and somewhere on the palace grounds.

"Hunter," a whisper of a voice came into his ear so suddenly that he almost jumped. It was Flex. "If you can hear me, clear your throat." Hunter listened to Omega speak for a second and then cleared his throat.

"Perfect. We can hear everything now. We lost signal to you a while ago and have been trying ever since. Cayden and Danielle's coms seem to be down, too. When knew they were captured, but coms should still be on. Keep Omega talking. Try to find where Impervious is. If you can get to him, then do so. If not, then get your ass out of there as soon as possible. Clear your throat again if you understand."

Yet again, Hunter cleared his throat. "Would you like a drink for that itchy throat?" Omega asked casually. I know it looks odd, but it's fantastic I assure you." Hunter shook his head. "Nope. All good."

A feeling of relief took him over as he felt comfort in knowing that Flex and the rest of the team were back with him. Seconds later that relief vanished as he tried to not worry about why the coms of Cayden and Danielle were no longer active.

"Enough about good old Impervious," Omega said finally. "As I'm sure you guessed. I'm not from around here." Hunter laughed. "This palace and the people that damn near pray to you says otherwise." Omega shrugged. "Do I rule the East Section? Yes. Was I born here? No. A long time ago, maybe about seventy years or so, I came here with my brother. Like you and I, he too was an Icon."

And there it was. If he hadn't been so shocked Hunter felt he would have let out a gasp. Empress Queen Omega was an Icon. A chunk of information that Perkins, Cord, and even Cayden had failed to mention. Hunter still had his reservations about Cord, but Cayden was growing on him, and he had spent a year living with Perkins. It wasn't a detail she would have left out before heading here. Was it? He was sure Flex was questioning them back at the base right now about such a discovery.

The only conclusion Hunter could draw was that they didn't know. Perhaps none of the people of this world did. He did the math in his head. If what Omega said was true then she arrived here when she was no more than nine or ten. "We traveled everywhere together. My brother and I were like this," Omega said as she held up her fingers twisted around each other.

"He was able to open portals to anywhere. He was much slower than a standard teleporter so he never went into the line of hero work. When our parents died, he became my guardian. No time to be a hero while you're suddenly a parent." Omega paused as she swirled her glass some, creating a mini vortex with the green liquid inside.

She stopped and then took another sip. "Anyway, we went all over the world, and then one day my powers came. At first, we just thought I could create stronger powers that the Icon already had. We had a friend back then that, when I used my power on her, her power tripled. In the end, it was too much for her body to deal with. She wasn't a powerful person to start with, and that type of change needs to be introduced slowly to weaker Icons. A lesson I learned over time, but needless to say she died from it. I overloaded her because I barely knew what I was doing."

"Murder at a young age huh," Hunter said slowly. "Don't be rude," Omega snapped back. "I didn't know how to control it then, but my brother taught me. He risked his own life to let me practice on him. Eventually, I got it right," she said as she shrugged. "Time and time again I created a newer, stronger version of his power for him. It was just done slowly over time. That's when he realized that he could create portals to other worlds, not just to locations in our own."

She stretched her drink free hand out into the air and waved it out to the city. "The wastelands have always been a rough place. Lawless with no order. It was worse then. When we stepped into this world, our luck placed us in the sights of men who believed only a person with elite blood could do what my brother had done. These same men, oppressed by the current rule, felt the only course of action was to attack,"

Omega took a deep breath. "My brother wasn't a fighter and the attack was over before I barely knew what happened. Then they turned their sights on me. For the next few days, they took turns." Hunter felt himself fighting the urge to want to comfort her as she began to speak slower than before.

"They did things that," she stopped talking and took a gulp this time, not a sip. "Well, there's no need to mention. When it was over, I was left alone in the dark cold of the wasteland with only my brother's corpse to comfort me. I took this jacket from his body," she turned her head to the jacket on the table and smiled slightly.

"And went out into the world. My new home. With only his scent from his jacket to comfort me in my darkest hours. In time I was found by a young boy wise beyond his years. He was only sixteen, but he was raising a group of children. Children that were victims of the way the world was run back then. He told me that if I wanted to survive, I could join them. As long as I followed their rules for survival. Keep to the shadows. Keep your head down, and above all else, if you have gifts, don't use them in public."

Empress Queen Omega let out a sound that could have been a faint laugh, but it was so brief Hunter couldn't tell. "I remember asking him who would want to live like that. His response was; either we live in the elite's shadow, or we die at their feet. There is no other way."

Omega paused as she bit her bottom lip some and shook her head as if agreeing to something only she could see. Lost in her own memories. "Those words have been with me since. I built my empire on them," Omega said as she forced a smile towards Hunter. "My rise to greatness is a sad story that I won't bore you with any longer."

"Then why spare me? Why bring me up here to talk." "Because you have elite blood. Your family is one of the oldest. Was one of the oldest. The elite among the elite families that time has forgotten. Imagine what we could do together." Hunter's mouth moved a few times but nothing came out. "Do, do together?" he stammered.

"Yes," Omega said gently. "I have several plans in motion that will have me as the ruler of this world totally, not just a section. War will come, and people will die. A price I'm willing to pay on both fronts. When it is all over, I will need a partner to help me rule. A partner to give me an heir."

Hunter's heart skipped a beat as he saw a flickering image of Danielle in his head. Full of anger and bathed in darkness as she screamed at him. He found it funny that how even in this situation, his first reaction was to think of an angry girlfriend. "I," Hunter said slowly, but Omega spoke again.

"I know it isn't ideal. Impervious was against it, but eventually told me some of what I needed to know, and how you wouldn't agree to this. That man can be impossible sometimes. I had to show him what was for his own good several times."

Hunter began to wonder just how a person that was impervious to any and everything could be forced to go along with a person like Omega. "Sorry to bother you Empress, but it's time." Hunter turned and saw the bearded man standing at the balcony entrance. His hands were at his sides, and a fake smile was on his face.

"Finally," she said out loud. "Come with me," Omega said as she glanced to Hunter as she stepped off the balcony. He did as he was told and followed her into the room. All of the servers were gone now, and so was most of the food. Each man and woman sat silently in their chairs and seemed genuinely happy to see Omega enter the room again.

She walked around the table slowly, as she left Hunter standing beside Maridian. "You know I was against her bringing you here," Maridian said as he leaned over to whisper in Hunter's ear. The man's breath had a surprisingly sweet smell to it. Perhaps it was from the colorful drink Hunter had seen him with earlier.

"You can't be trusted. Not with your history of rebellion." Hunter found himself again wondering just how much Impervious had been forced to tell them.

"Exterminate them all was what I suggested," Maridian said as he took a sigh. "Alas she didn't listen to me," Maridian watched Omega walk around the table and shake each hand and exchange a few words personally to the people at the table. "I've seen her order the slaughter of entire villages without thought, and in the same breath order every child in the city to be given fresh clothes and for their parents to be given funds." Maridian smiled and shook his head. "She is a mystery, my Empress. A graceful gift from divinity for some, and an unstoppable wave of death for others."

He turned slowly and looked Hunter in the face now. "Why she would want to join you in a union is another mystery." As he finished Maridian turned back to face the table. Hunter couldn't wrap his mind around any of this and felt that his only action should be to save Impervious. To find Impervious. That or make it home to the base. He just needed to wait for his moment.

"I am thankful for you, and the service you will bring to my order," Omega said as she finished her walk around the table. Now she stood just in front of Hunter and faced those at the table. Hunter fought the urge to glance down at her perky backside. *She's old enough to be your grandmother*, he thought to himself. "You're my tributes, and today is the day of your ascension." She pointed to a dark-skinned man, covered with muscles, and a wide chin.

The man rose from the table and walked forward. Beside him, Hunter could hear Maridian take in a deep breath and whisper the words, "*and here we go,"* under his breath. "You see Hunter," Omega said as she moved to stand behind the kneeling man and placed her hands on his shoulders.

"As I grew older, I realized two things about my ability to create. Some of which I can't even explain. One was that I could create new life within myself. I couldn't heal from wounds like a person with regenerative abilities, but I could slow down my aging and heal my body internally." Hunter watched as she clamped down on the man's shoulders so tightly that her fingers turned red.

Slowly, the intense orange glow began to pulse from her hands and spread over the man's body. The orange power made Hunter think of Power Prince. Of his vibrant pink energy and how they left him behind. How he missed the man that was his superior but also got along with so well. "I also realized, much by accident, that if I tried to create new powers in people that had none, I could create whatever I wanted, and what I wanted was an army. A powerful one to help me and my friends escape the harsh world of the wasteland."

The glow had consumed the man entirely now and was flowing up Omega's arms. The people at the table looked on in amazement and Maridian had returned to his seat and began to read a book. Utterly unimpressed by the events unfolding in front of him. In a flash, the orange light was gone. For that matter, so was the man that was kneeling before Omega.

Hunter's brow furrowed as he watched the metallic man stand up. As with all his kind the creature was faceless. The lights around the room danced off of its metal skin, and Hunter realized that between the creature's legs was nothing. He was clearly male before, but now the figure of the Warden resembled a doll and not a man.

"Welcome, Warden," Omega said with a smile. "Your new life starts now. Your powers will mirror one or more of the true elements of Mo'eizus. Your power was gifted by me, and as such cannot harm me." Hunter let this information sink in and hoped they were getting it all down back at the base.

"You are to serve me for your life and are to protect me with that life. Should I perish, your gift of ascension will perish with me, and so would your life." Hunter looked around the room at these words. Omega couldn't be hurt by those she created. This explained why none of them got smart and tried to take over. Their powers wouldn't work on her. It also explained why they followed her words to the letter. If she were to die, so would they. Hunter had to admit, it was a damn good business model. One that guaranteed obedience.

What was more concerning is the smile that still remained on the rest of the people's faces. The other tributes as she called them. None of them seemed to care about the rules of their ascension. Hunter could only assume that they knew the rules already, and didn't care one way or the other. "You are my child now," Omega said as she placed a soft kiss on the Warden's metallic cheek. "I will protect my children for as long as you are in my shadow."

As soon as she said these words, the rest of the table in one group chant said out loud. *Forever in your shadow.* Hunter took in a deep breath. No doubt about it, these people were crazy. As Omega shoot a glare to Maridian, he stood from his chair to stand beside Hunter once again.

As the next few minutes passed, Hunter witnessed much of the same process take place. No more Wardens were created, though. Instead more members of the Warden's circle were created. Two Pain Conduits, a few Swordsmiths, and a Gunner or two. The process was faster than he expected, and the act didn't take much out of Omega. Normally the extended use of any Icon's abilities would cause some sign of fatigue, but not for Omega. Hunter wondered if that internal creation power was the source of this seemingly unlimited endurance.

With her newly created soldiers quietly waiting as they were fitted with clothes, and men with papers began to speak to them, Omega turned back around to face Hunter. "So, you've heard my story, seen my power, and even got a taste of my vision to unify the world." Hunter leaned on the balls of his feet as he raised a brow.

"Unify the world by creating war? You may have been raised here, but you'd still fit in back home." Omega shook her head. "The people in my section are happier, smarter, and receive better treatment than any other section combined. Nobody starves, the people have jobs, and many live good lives," Omega replied.

Hunter shook his head. "The people here may, but from what I've seen in the wasteland, not so much." Maridian raised a slender finger and cleared his throat. "Even by those comparisons, the people here still live several levels more comfortably than those in the wasteland of other sections."

The man chuckled slightly. "A visit to those other areas would confirm this in mere seconds." Hunter paused for a moment. He had no idea if Maridian was telling the truth or not. He hadn't seen other parts of the world yet.

Omega spoke and ripped Hunter away from his internal conversation. "Those who reside in Acropolis are different. They are the chosen and their descendants." "Come again?" Hunter said.

"It's hard for an outsider to gain hold in a new world. When I showed people my power back then, most of them feared me. Some even tried to kill me. But some believed. They believed so much that they thought I was a second coming. A person of divinity to save them. And I did. My children and I protect them. Those who believed in me, their descendants, and their families, were allowed to live by my side in Acropolis."

Hunter nodded his head. He knew Omega was the bad person in all of this. One couldn't kill, withhold cures, and create addictive drugs to topple nations and not be a bad person. Still, she always seemed to have a logical backing for what she did. Rewarding those who supported her with a city of beauty and advancement was a nice touch. No wonder they worshipped her. "I just want the rest of the world, to experience what the East Section has. Will you join me in that?"

Hunter stood silent for a moment. Many people continued with their normal tasks around them, but a few were watching him. None stronger than Maridian and Omega. "I can't." Hunter said finally. "I have a life and responsibilities of my own. My duty is to my own world." Omega sighed as she shook her head and walked away from him.

She reached the table on the deck and placed her jacket on once more. She was silent as she adjusted the clearly too large jacket around her, and placed her hands in her pockets. "I offer you something none other has been given. Not to live in my shadow, or to die at my feet, but to rule by my side." "I can be a rebel sometimes," Hunter replied. Omega nodded as she pursed her lips. "Impervious said you were stubborn."

"If you're not by my side, then they are to be at my feet. Maridian proceed to your plan. Have our forces descend on their base. No survivors. Once he is alone, maybe he will reconsider my offer." Hunter couldn't breathe as he quickly turned to Maridian. The man had a smile on his face that could cut through steel. "No," but before he could get the word out Maridian turned to a body of smoke and disappeared. Empress Queen Omega was being escorted out of the room by her newly created Warden and several Swordsmiths.

"You little," Hunter's eyes turned blue as he prepared to attack, but at that moment pain exploded through his body like a rocket. Sending him to his knees, and causing him to scream so loud that his throat started to burn. He didn't have time for pain. He didn't have time to even try to fight them. He needed to get to Bravado. He knew Flex was there, but he could only do so much.

As he rolled on the ground in pain, he could only hope that the members at the base were doing whatever they could to escape the death that approached them. He didn't even know where Cayden and Danielle were. With vision blurry from tears in his eyes, Hunter reached out with as much power as he could and wrapped a force field around the Pain Conduit. He tried to close it on her, but he couldn't focus.

The force field faded away for a second, as a new idea formed in the home of pain that was now his mind. He needed to hurry. He could feel this Pain Conduit playing with him. Increasing the pain tenfold and then reducing it just before he passed out. Eventually, she would end things. For the first time in his life, he made the decision to kill. Not to stop or to hurt, but to outright kill.

Instead of wrapping her entire body in a force field, he instead encased only her head. In an instant, he caused the gravity inside the bubble to rip apart. In a flash, blood splattered on the inside of the force field as the pain in his body stopped, and the Pain Conduit fell to the ground. The sound of grunts and guns buzzing to life were the only warning Hunter got as he scrambled to his feet.

A force field the size of a small car manifested around him only seconds before bolts of energy bullets began to bounce off of it. He didn't know where the gunners came from, but they came in force. So much force that his force field was hurting, and he could feel it. Dozens of tiny cracks appeared on the surface and Hunter forced the field to expand and pushed it back on his attackers.

At the same time, he pushed himself fully to his feet, ran to the balcony and leapt over the edge, as he began to fall to the city below.

CHAPTER 27:
CAYDEN'S PLAN

Hunter loved flying. It was long considered to be his favorite power. It wasn't the power that first manifested for him, but it was the power that gave him freedom. Freedom from a world that judged and teased him because of his parents, and their unaccepted union. Flying gave him the means to escape it all.

It was the first power he learned to truly master. That's why, as he was falling down towards the city, he found it surprising that he couldn't fly now. He could barely focus with his head still spinning from the number that Pain Conduit had done on him.

Slowly, as the ground below rushed to meet him, he could feel his world return to normal. He could feel the power flowing around him as he began to slow down as the power of flight returned to - "Ah," Hunter grunted out as something solid and strong wrapped itself around him.

Hunter struggled in the air and turned to find a Warden latched onto him. This Warden wasn't wearing the normal black suit that the creatures dawned. "Eager to prove yourself, huh," Hunter said as his vision shifted to blue. He could tell this was the newly- created Warden from inside of Omega's party.

He must have been sent after him after the others failed. Before Hunter could release the energy from his eyes, several things happened at once. First, the Warden wrapped its hands around Hunter's head. The metallic touch felt cold to Hunter's skin and the pressure made him feel like his head was going to explode.

The Warden's must have possessed some sort of super strength because try as he might, Hunter couldn't move away from the grip around his head. The next thing that happened was an utter shock to Hunter. The wind around him came alive with air and heat. Where he was once falling, he was now being lifted by this heated air current. Hunter had been in the Icon world long enough to know air manipulation when he saw it, and apparently, that was the elemental force that this Warden controlled.

Hunter wrapped himself and his attacker inside a force field as he braced himself and prepared for the worst. It was all he could do considering he still couldn't see. He had seen an Icon back home called Lobo with the same power, snatch the air from a person's lungs. He waited for something along those lines to happen but it never did.

This Warden didn't seem to have the style or precision to pull off such an attack. Instead, he resorted to good old fashion body blows. Hunter's vision returned and for a second one of the vice-like hands removed itself from his head, formed a fist and punched him in the stomach. Pain almost as intense as the feeling created by the Pain Conduit flooded his body.

Despite the Warden's size and bulk, it moved fluidly inside the force field. In the blink of an eye, the Warden detached itself from Hunter and shifted the hand wrapped around his face to his neck, and applied pressure. Hunter was having a hard time breathing now as the grip increased in strength. His force field around them flickered in and out of life, as the continued to rise in the air.

Hunter didn't even know whose power was pushing them up anymore. His or the Warden's but he could feel his grip on his own ability slacken. In a horrible effort, he released an Impact Blast full to the face of his attacker. The attack connected, and he could feel the grip on his neck release slightly.

The air around them came alive again as the Warden sent two punches to Hunter's body. He could taste blood in his mouth now. He wasn't even sure where it came from, but he knew he had to stop this beast, but it was just too strong. It was becoming harder and harder to keep his eyes open now. There was no doubt in his mind that only the rushing hot air created by the Warden was keeping him in the air.

His force field had long gone, and he was too weak and in too much pain to fly. Once the Warden decided to let go, he would die. They were up higher than before. Hunter could make that out as his eyes fluttered and struggled to stay open. Even the Acropolis wasn't directly under them now.

With all the effort in the world, Hunter lifted his head up. It felt like it weighed a ton now, and looked the Warden in what would have been its face. The skin wasn't as polished and damage free as once before. It appeared to be chipped and cracked slightly. So, his Impact Blast, his own unique brand of energy had left a mark. Between pain and lack of vision, Hunter smiled to the best of his ability and spat on the Warden's face.

Apparently, that did it. The grip around Hunter's neck released completely and he began to fall through the open sky. As he did so, he heard a faint pop but he didn't know where it came from. He could barely keep his eyes open. There was just so much pain, and he was so tired. He tried and tried to form a force field. He was determined that he wasn't going to die on some sand- covered planet.

The force field would absorb most of the impact. It flickered around him and lasted seconds then faded away. "Fuck," Hunter muttered out. He was too tired to scream. Too tired to show one last form of defiance to this godforsaken planet. He had begun to accept his fate and then, he wasn't falling anymore.

Instead, he was snatched out of the air by strong hands and slumped over a person's shoulder. "No slacking on the job, intern." a voice called from under Hunter. He had never been so happy to hear Flex's voice in his life.

"Ken Doll," Hunter asked slowly as his eyes drifted open and then closed again. Flex laughed. "At least you haven't lost your ability to joke." "How are you here? Where-" Hunter asked slowly as he was lifted off of Flex's shoulder and placed on something solid. "Before your com went out, we heard the attack ordered on the base. We made it out just in time to an alternate base. We found Cayden and Danielle headed our way as we made our escape."

Flex looked Hunter over and couldn't see any major damage, outside of the trickle of blood in his friend's mouth. He removed his shirt and balled it up into a makeshift pillow. "Anything to take your shirt off," Hunter said through a cough. "Perfect. Just keep talking, I don't want you to fall asleep. Just in case." Flex said as he placed the pillow under Hunter's head

"Once we were all out, I got here as quick as I could to back you up. I saw your force field going in and out and figured you were in trouble. I caught you just in time." Flex turned his head and searched the skies. He could see him, still up there. Looking and floating like a guardian of the skies around him.

He took in a deep breath and balled his fist. "Wait here, and try to stay awake. I'll make it quick." Flex said as he stood up. "Sure thing," Hunter said through a cough and a shaky thumbs up. The ground shook some as Flex exploded into the sky. Hunter was in too much pain to turn around and try to see what was going on, but his ears did all of the work.

The silence of the sky was soon full of what sounded like loud explosions going off one by one. Hunter knew the Warden was strong. The punches he received were evident of that. He was sure that he could have put up a better fight had he not just been mind-raped by a Pain Conduit, and a part of him was embarrassed that Flex had to save him like he was a damsel in distress. But as he heard the sounds coming from the sky, he realized that Flex was the better person to be fighting the Warden.

The Warden was strong, but compared to Flex the metal monster was a mere infant learning how to throw a punch, and Flex was Mike Tyson in his prime. "All set," he heard a voice say from behind him. Before he could comment, Flex had Hunter over his shoulder again. "Let's get you home."

"Thanks, pretty boy," Hunter said slowly. "Don't thank me just yet. Wait until I tell Power Prince about all this." Hunter groaned as he felt his head drop and against Flex's wishes, and his own attempts to hold it off, Hunter closed his eyes.

It seemed like only seconds had passed by when he opened his eyes again. He jumped as he found Danielle leaning over him with hair pulled back and a smile on her face. "Let's not make this a habit," she said as she helped him up. "Me having to wait for you to wake up in a medical facility isn't exactly fun."

She removed her hand from Hunter's back as he looked around. Cayden was sitting beside his bed as well. Actually, Hunter realised it wasn't a bed he was on. It was more so a table. "How ya feeling?" Cayden asked as Hunter rubbed his stomach. "Not too bad." Danielle applied pressure to his stomach and caused him to wince in pain.

"Could be better though, I suppose. Where are we?" he asked as he looked around the room. It was large and seemed to have everything needed for a base. There were monitors, although many weren't powered on. Across the large rooms were several small cots, and to the side of them were blankets on the floor.

Some tables nearby had several seats and boxes of food on them. As he glanced up, he could see dozens of lights, but only half were powered on, and while the floor seemed to be tile or some sort of polished stone, there was a layer of dust so thick that it had footprints in it.

"This is the retreat base," Cayden said. "It was supposed to be completed a long time ago, but it's hard to do construction while trying to free the people from a ruler that has them brainwashed to not see the harm she is doing." Hunter nodded. He wanted to comment on how Cayden had begun to see Omega differently than when he first told them about her. Instead, All Hunter could do was wince and groan some more from the pain in his midsection.

"I take it, Bravado doesn't have good medical stuff in this base." Danielle shook her head. "They don't have *any* medical stuff in this base.

Except for Cayden." Hunter raised a brow and looked from Danielle to Cayden, and then to Danielle again.

"It's not totally accurate, but if I focus and take my time, I can speed up the time around you just slightly, which will cause the natural healing of your body to take place." "Atlas," Hunter said as his eyes got big. "That's -" "very complicated," Cayden said.

"I only did it about a little over half way. Enough to get you back up and moving and in the fight. You should be at about eighty percent." "So, you're a healer too," Hunter said as he slid off the table and looked around the room once more.

"Sometimes it seems that way," Cayden said slowly as he glanced to Danielle. "Even when I try not to be," he added. Far across the room, Hunter could see Perkins leaning on the wall as Flex and Cord exchange words.

Flex could have been shouting, but it was hard to hear from this distance. Hunter could clearly see he wasn't happy, though. "What's that about?" Hunter asked. "Parents are fighting again," Danielle said as she sat at the table and opened one of the boxes. She pulled out something that looked like a thick graham cracker and took a bite that sounded too hard on her teeth.

She quickly spat the food out of her mouth and looked at the box. "The food has been here for a long time," Cayden said. "Even I don't like eating it, and that's saying a lot." to emphasize his point he picked up a stray chunk of metal from the ground, blew the dust off, and took a large bite. It had considerably less crunch than Danielle's graham cracker.

"Fighting about what?" Hunter asked. "Perkins and Flex want to wait and form a plan while giving us all time to regroup. Cord wants to take the few troops that we have and attack Omega head on. He feels that if Flex is strong enough to take on a newly- born Warden then he should be able to take on several others if the Pain Conduit is out of the way." Cayden stopped talking and took another bite of his metal snack.

"Perkins just got on Flex's side though. When she heard he had killed a Warden she was all quiet and stuff," Danielle said. "Why?" Hunter asked as he moved around some to get an idea of how much pain he was left in. "Get this, that brother she had," Danielle said as she leaned in. "The one that died?" Hunter asked.

"Turns out he didn't die," Danielle replied. "He left her and went on to be a Warden. Gave up his life to serve Omega after his chrome addiction became too strong to tolerate." "Atlas," Hunter said slowly as he looked at Perkins across the room. "She was afraid that Flex may have killed her brother."

"How many people made it out?" Hunter asked. "Mostly everybody," Cayden replied. "All of us, and all but one new recruit. They're in one of the other rooms. We're in the main room now. There is a secondary room, and then like a closet for storage. Some base, huh?" Hunter shrugged his shoulders, and then felt a hint of pain from it, but not much.

"So, what are we going to do?" Hunter asked. "I'm down for a fight, but that Warden kicked my ass up there." Cayden shook his head as he finished chewing. "Newly created creatures are different. The creation process results in increased power for a short amount of time. We don't know why. Either way, a normal Warden wouldn't be as hard to control as the one you fought."

"Flex still wiped the floor with his newly metal ass, though," Danielle said. "True," Cayden replied. "Flex may possibly be the strongest being in this world after seeing a display like that." Hunter rolled his eyes. "Please don't tell him that to his face. The last thing I need is him reminding me that he is the strongest person on two worlds combined. That aside, we still have to figure out something. I'd bet Power Prince's movie collection, that Omega will find this base. She is determined to make me join her, and I'm not sure why."

Danielle's eyes went dark as stray tendrils moved around her hands. "Oh, I heard how she wants to make you her royal baby daddy. Give her an heir and all that. Cord played back what we missed while you were asleep."

"Yeah, it seems odd," Hunter said as he glossed over Danielle's comments. "And just what were they doing with Infinity back there." Danielle shrugged. "We told Perkins and Cord about it but had zero ideas. We know that the lab is where the cure is made and tested, but outside of that, we haven't the slightest clue. Then there is the million- dollar question." "How are they holding Impervious?" Cayden said to complete Danielle's statement.

"Flex is having the hardest time with figuring that out," Danielle said. "The leading theory is that somehow Icaro was able to assume Impervious' form and is playing as a way to control him," Danielle said.

"Well, however they are doing it, he is being very chatty. Apparently, he told her boatloads about me. But if Icaro is in the mix, then he would have access to Impervious' memories," Hunter said as he looked at their leaders all arguing. "They need to come up with a plan, and fast."

"Oh, I have a plan already," Cayden said. "I'm just waiting for them to finish. If they don't like it, I'll do it anyway." Danielle and Hunter looked at each other slightly as their gaze fell to Cayden. Cayden in return started eating another chunk of debris found on the floor. "Well," Hunter said as he waved his hands. "You want to fill us in?"

Cayden swallowed loudly. "Simple. We kill the Great Beast, and bring Acropolis to us."

CHAPTER 28:
HORN OF BOOMING

"Are you nerfing crazy?" Cord said as he held his hands on his brother's face and looked at him. He was squeezing his face so hard that it looked like his cheeks were going to explode. Finally, Cayden slapped Cord's hands away and moved his jaw a few times to get the feeling back. "It's not crazy. We need to rescue Impervious, get to Empress Queen Omega, weaken her numbers, and have access to her data for the cure they are working on."

Cord grunted as he turned away from his brother. "It's not even a full-blown cure, Cayden. It's treatment according to the conversation you three recorded." "Treatment that could have kept Becca here long enough to find the cure," Cayden shouted back. "I don't want to keep mopping up the blood of my friends, only because I'm the one immune. If there is a way to help them, then I'm going to do it."

Up until this moment, Hunter, Flex, and Danielle had stood quietly to the side as Cord and Cayden argued about his plan. Flex turned his head and could see Perkins frantically typing away at one of the few working monitors in their new base. What was she up to? His eyes narrowed as he quickly crossed the room and stood by her side.

"What's going on?" he asked her. Flex made sure to adjust his tone so that he sounded more like a boyfriend that was concerned, and less like a leader that was annoyed. Once he had a hard time separating the two. For him, it was all one and the same, but he had gotten better. "Cayden's plan," Perkins said quickly.

"You agree with him? You think that this is the best way to handle this?" Flex asked and made sure to focus on Perkins' face as she responded. He loved her, more than he could have ever expected, and one thing he had learned about her was that her face always gave away her inner thoughts. "I do," she said slowly as she shook her head.

"I must be losing it if I'm agreeing with Cayden. Kid barely likes me and I'm taking his side. Funny thing is, he wasn't the first to come up with the idea. If I could just find," her voice trailed off as she continued to type quickly. Flex took in a deep breath. "What about the people on Great Beast Sonah, though." "What about them?" Perkins asked as she stopped typing and almost glared at Flex.

"Won't they die if the beast falls?" Perkins shrugged. "Perhaps." "And you're fine with that?" Flex asked. "Not really. But I also have to tell myself that those people have lived above us all for as long as I can remember. Both literally and figuratively. They turn a blind eye to the harsh treatments of any others in the East Section." Her fingers came back to life again as she started to slam them against the keys once more.

"As far as I'm concerned, if they stood by and did nothing, then they are just as guilty as Omega and her inner circle." "Don't you think that is a little-" "A little what, Flex?" Perkins asked as her voice rose some. "A little harsh? A little cold? You know there hasn't been a single Curse of Varo death there in a year? A year. Meanwhile our studies show that everywhere else is averaging several a week. Even Cord is starting to have the signs more."

Flex turned his head slightly to see Cord, still going at it with Cayden and then realized Hunter and Danielle had disappeared. He looked around the base and couldn't see them anywhere. "What about?" he said as he thought the next few words out in his head before he allowed them to leave his mouth.

He leaned in closer to Perkins. "What about your brother? What if he's up there. Aren't you worried about him being hurt?" Perkins slammed her hands on the keyboard so fast that, while Flex didn't jump, he did glance down to the sound of the noise quickly. She closed her eyes and remained silent for a moment. Only the sound of her breathing and rise of her chest showing the anger she felt now.

"I don't have a brother. Not anymore. He chose those things over his only family left. He can burn with them all as far as I'm concerned. Now can we please drop it?" She turned and pulled Flex in by his shirt and kissed him. "I love that you're concerned, but trust me. This is the right call." Flex nodded his head as she returned back to her keys.

"Maybe," he said slowly as he heard a door open to the room. As his head jerked up, he saw the smiling faces of Danielle and Hunter walking back in the room. Danielle's hair was visibly messy and Hunter's shirt was inside out now as his hand nursed his pained ribs. There was a visible bounce in both their steps as they made their way over to Flex and Perkins.

"So, what's up?" Danielle said as she ran her hands through her hair. Flex looked from her to Hunter, and then back to Danielle. "Really?" He asked. "Like now? Of all times. Even with your body in pain?" Hunter looked down at his shirt and realized it was on incorrectly. "I almost got killed up there," Hunter said slowly.

"That kind of thing makes you stop and take a breath for the good things in life." Danielle nodded her head slowly as she leaned on the table beside them. "Villain in the sheets," she said under her breath as Hunter shot a smirk at her. "I found it!" Perkins finally said as she punched the air so hard that her goggles almost fell lose from her head.

"Cord, Cayden, get your asses over here and stop arguing," Perkins said without even looking away from the screen. The brothers stopped arguing on command and slowly walked over to the monitor where Perkins was standing. "What's all this?" Cord asked sternly. "More nonsense?" "No," Perkins replied. "It's Cayden's plan." Cord took in a slow deep breath that was so intense that Hunter felt like the recruits in the other room could hear it. "Oh, so it is more nonsense? Well, don't keep me waiting. Get on with it. What have we got?" Cord said finally.

While Cord asked the question, the furrowed brow of confusion rested on Cayden. In front of them, in classic blueprint fashion was a design of something that looked like a mixture between a gun and a horn, or perhaps an instrument. "Fine, I'll step to the ledge," Hunter said finally.

"What are we looking at Perkins?" "This was one of Arwen's designs," Perkins said as she manipulated the keys to zoom in on the image. "Arwen's!" Cord shouted. "Now I know we've gone crazy." "Who is Arwen?" Flex asked. "You took the words right out of my mouth," Danielle chimed in.

"Arwen was one of our top technical members. Very gifted," Perkins said. "He was also," Cayden looked to the sky as he searched for the words. "To call him strange is putting it mildly. He was almost an expert marksman, though." "You're nerfing right that's putting it mildly." Cord said as he looked at the screen. "No matter what he was before he was killed, he was one of our most gifted," Perkins said.

"He had the idea of killing a Great Beast when we first formed Bravado. I told him it was a drastic idea, and would only serve in the worst of cases. Still, I gave my approval to have him design the machine. So that in a few day's time, he could construct it if needed." Perkins thrust her finger to the screen.

"And here is what he came up with. A gun that hits them with a sound that hurts them, or kills them, or something." Perkins said. "Or something?" Hunter asked. "It was a long time ago, so his explanation isn't exactly fresh in memory. Point is, Cayden's plan isn't as far-fetched as he thought it was, and this is how we do it."

Danielle raised her hand slowly as if she was in a classroom. Perkins gave a slight jerk of her head toward her. "Okay, so we have the plans from this guy," "Arwen," Flex said. "Right. Arwen," Danielle continued. "He was pretty much a tech genius. I get that, but that doesn't do dick for us now. We have some heavy hitters that are strong in the abilities department, some very new recruits, the always nice Perkins, and the ever- rude Cord."

Danielle looked around the room. "so, blueprints are nice, but who is going to build this-" she leaned into to the screen and looked at the name on the file. "This horn of booming." Danielle rolled her eyes. "Genius and that was the best name he could come up with?"

The room sat silent. While she had a blunt way of pointing it out, Danielle was right. They had a pretty talented team, but none of them were tech people, and from the looks of those plans on the screen, a tech person was exactly what they needed. Then Hunter slowly began to form an idea in his head. An idea that even he truly didn't know where it came from, but there it was. Swimming to front of his mind. Maybe it was the near-death experience, or the storage room closet sex with Danielle, but he had a plan that would turn this all around. He knew how to get the horn created, and likely with some extra features too.

"Perkins, do you have another multibox around here?" Hunter asked. Perkins rubbed her chin and thought about it as Flex narrowed his eyes at Hunter. "A multibox for what?" he asked. "I think we may have one or two in storage," Perkins added in. "They wouldn't be new models if they have been here all this time, though. A few years old, but should still work."

Perkins quickly walked away toward the storage closet, and Hunter followed behind her. Cayden shot a glance to Danielle who shrugged her shoulders. Flex looked around at them all and his confusion turned to anger, as Hunter and Perkins got further away. "Am I a damn ghost? What in Atlas' name do you need a multibox for?" he shouted to Hunter.

The smile Hunter displayed as he turned to face Flex made him afraid for a second. Flex could stand up to a lot of things, and while he never openly said it, he often believed reports and news articles that said he was likely one of, if not the strongest Icons alive. Still, this single smirk from his teammate, his intern, gave him a chill.

Hunter finally spoke as he turned to follow Perkins again. "We're going to see our dear old, fast talking friend, The Mechanic."

CHAPTER 29:
OLD FRIENDS

Let's say he does, help us," Flex said slowly as Hunter waited for Perkins and Cayden to prep the multibox. Danielle sat on top of a table swinging her legs back and forth as she watched the supremely strong hero walk in so many circles that there was a newly formed path on the dust- covered floor. Hunter exhaled loudly as he rubbed his hands through his hair.

"Why wouldn't he help us?" "Well for starters when you first met him, you punched him in the jaw," Flex said without cracking a smile. "Stuff like that people aren't quick to forget." Then suddenly he stopped walking in his circle, and all the worry he had about The Mechanic helping them faded away.

The world around he seemed to turn to a blur as Flex had focus for nothing else but Perkins. Hunter was speaking to him, no doubt defending his reasoning for striking The Mechanic, but Flex heard none of it. From where he stood, Flex likely would have missed it. Had he not been looking in that direction at just the right time, he would have.

As he looked beyond Hunter sitting in a chair, and pass Danielle on top of the table he could see Perkins and Cayden standing around a large book shaped, metal box. As Cayden turned away to reach for one of many tools sprawled on a table, Perkins quickly pulled a stained towel from her pocket and dabbed at her nose and ears.

As she wiped the dark blood away, Flex felt his stomach lurch. As strong as he was, and as invincible as he seemed, he didn't have the strength to shrug off what he had seen. "Atlas, no," he said through a shaky voice that cracked on the last word.

Hunter's brow raised as he looked at Flex, and then followed his eyes to Perkins and Cayden. She had put her stained towel away now. To Hunter, it simply looked like Perkins was working on the multibox with Cayden. "I miss something?" Hunter asked. "He trying to move in on your turf? I was just starting to like him too."

Flex shook his head as he swallowed and found his mouth was suddenly dry. "No," he hesitated as he began to lie to Hunter. "Everything. Is fine." As the broken words left his lips, he couldn't help but wonder why. Why hadn't Perkins told him she had caught the Curse of Varo. How long had she had it? Judging from that towel color, it had been long enough.

"I think we are all set to go," Perkins said as she walked over followed by Cayden. Cayden himself was holding the multibox in his hands as Perkins wrapped her right arm around Flex's waist. She looked up to him with those vivid green eyes, and Flex felt himself fight back tears. He actually had to look up, in a fake stretching motion to keep the tears at bay.

"You okay?" Perkins asked. She sounded normal, but then again So did Cord and he had been sick longer. She looked okay and everything. Flex couldn't wrap his mind around why she would keep such a secret from him. He didn't want to bring it up. Not now. For now, he would play the role of the unsuspecting boyfriend. "I'm fine," Flex replied as he flashed a perfect smile that masked the pain he was feeling.

"Okay, so we figured out the major issues and fixed them. I think," Cayden said as he placed the multibox down on the table beside Danielle. She looked at the box and then back to Perkins. "You think?" she said slowly. The slight tilt of her head and single brow raised alerted the room that she wasn't too confident in their proclaimed fixed device.

Perkins smirked. "It will work. But only twice, and for only two people. We pick two people, send them back to your world, use The Fixer," "The Mechanic," Flex said as he corrected her with a laugh. "Right," Perkins replied. "Talk to him, and then open a portal again head back. We set it so that the first portal will open up at the location you gave us, and the second will open and bring you back here." Perkins looked around the room as Cord slowly entered.

"Where you been?" Cayden asked. "Scouting," Cord said gruffly. "Don't make a habit of questioning me. Somebody has to make sure we aren't found here." Cord didn't stop moving as he spoke. Instead, he crossed the room quickly without looking at them. "I'm checking on the recruits." In a fluid motion, he slightly opened the door that lead to the room where the new recruits were held up and then took a step back.

From where they sat, the team could see Cord count to three on his fingers and then delivered a strong kick to the door so fast and loud that Cayden jumped some. "Off your nerfing butts recruits," Cord shouted as he walked in the room. "Be alert at all times! I could have been a Warden coming to-." His words were cut off as he slammed the door behind himself. "Well, okay then," Hunter said as he stood up from the chair.

"So, who is coming with me?" he asked the room at large. "You're going?" Danielle asked. Hunter nodded his head eagerly. "The Mechanic and I go way back," he said as he smirked at Flex. To Hunter's surprise, Flex didn't respond. Not even an eye roll. His leader seemed to be in another place, even though he was only inches from him.

"Then I'm going too," Danielle said. "Wait, what about me?" Cayden said. "You live there, let me see this new world." Danielle fought back the urge to curse at the young Spellborn. "Perkins' is going." Flex finally said. Perkins looked up to him. "I am?"

It took a minute for him to respond, but he wanted her as far away from this disease- riddled world, even if for a short time. For some reason he felt that would help things. He knew he wasn't being rational. That if she was sick, then she was sick. Location wouldn't change it. Still he had made his decision.

"She's going." "Our leader has spoken," Hunter said as he stretched a hand out to Perkins and did a slight bow. She leaned in and kissed Flex on the cheek, and as her lips touched his skin, he closed his eyes for a second and tried not to think about a life where he wouldn't be able to feel her touch. In the last few minutes, he realized that he cared for her far beyond what he thought he did.

As she pulled away from him, Flex fought the urge to reach for her to hold her back. "Okay everybody, stand back." Perkins said as she tossed Hunter a blue backpack. "Put this on." Hunter did as he was told and watched her lift the multibox off the table and press a button on its side. The older model device began to hum and click as if something inside was moving.

Then in an instant, a large swirling portal sprang into life in front of them. Hunter had forgot about the portal on the inside. While he was quick to volunteer to be on the mission back home, he had forgot about the trip to Mo'eizus in the first place. His biggest issue being how cramped it was on the inside. He could feel the sweat forming on his brow now as his phobia reared its ugly head.

He took a few deep breaths and gave a slight nod to Danielle. "Here we...," before he could finish his words Perkins leaped inside the portal. He rolled his eyes, and without thinking about it too long, grabbed the multibox off the table, and leaped inside after her.

The Mechanic let the water flow over his head for a few more seconds before he turned the shower off. He had spent the last year of his life living in the Ebony District, laying low, and taking odd jobs here and there. After the bombshell scandal with The Imperial Lords, he felt that it was best to distance himself from the brand and their base for a while.

That was then, and he felt he had slummed it enough in the Ebony District. Those were dark times for him. Not now, though. He was back in The Diamond District now. His penthouse was downtown, had a view, top of the line appliances, countertops made out of stone created by an Icon several cities over, and even had a doorman in the lobby. For most people this would be considered *the life.* Sadly, The Mechanic wasn't most people.

As he dried off and rummaged through his large walk-in closet to find clothes to put on, he glanced to the opposite end. That end of the closet was spotless, and only housed one thing. Several long, full body, microfiber outfits all colored in a dark navy blue. His hero uniform was crafted to look like that of a standard mechanic, and even had *The Mechanic* stitched over the chest.

He smiled as he stood and looked at the outfit. He remembered once that Life-Line told him, maybe one day he should have one of the outfits made, with his real name on it. It was a running joke they had because very few people, especially those he worked with, even knew his real name. They all simply called him The Mechanic. Those were good times. Time full of complicated test, and building gadgets that would cause villainous Icons to shake in their spandex.

He took a deep breath as he pulled the red shirt over his head and exited the closet. Now he only built stuff covertly for tech companies. They would pitch him an idea, he would build it in less time that some people took to prepare a standard dinner, and he would be paid handsomely for it. He had a builders' fee, and a small percentage of sales. In the year he had been in the public sector of work he had amassed a net worth somewhere in the hundred million range.

The money was great, but it didn't bring him joy. Not really. As he moved through the large luxury home, he still had to side step the many tools and gadgets that lay around. He had considered purchasing the unit above and below him for the extra space. He could fashion a means to enter and exit all three units in no time, and with the right amount of money paid, nobody would care.

The sound of brewing coffee filled the room as the smell tickled his nose. Coffee was just another part of his dull, mundane morning. While he was an Icon, he wasn't one of the flashy types. He couldn't fly or lift cars with ease, and bullets would tear through his skin as easy as it would a piece of paper. Unless a team came to him with a special need, he really didn't get that much excitement in his life.

Pouring himself a cup of coffee, he strolled over to his living room and lifted a remote. With a single click, the entire wall transformed from a solid object to a living picture. The images on didn't remain flat against the surface of the wall. Instead, they sprang to life and moved around as if he were in the studio watching as the show was being made. This form of viewing pleasure was limited to himself. It was his own personal invention and made video games amazing.

For now, he just watched the news. Yet again they were talking about how Power Prince, had killed the sister of Flex, and that Flex himself still hadn't made a statement. The Mechanic watched for a little bit and then flicked the channel. He didn't want to hear the story for a tenth time in the days since the events happen. Maybe it was because he knew all of the parties involved.

Maybe it was because watching made him miss the life he used to live. He had considered several times reaching out to Power Prince, Flex, or even Life-Line to talk about joining the newly- formed group that he had heard about. The New Lords, but once he found out they were still in the same old base, he couldn't bring himself to do it.

He sipped his coffee and clicked the remote a few more times, and then something unexpected happened. There, right in his living room, a swirling green portal came to life. "What the,-" The Mechanic said so fast that it was hard to determine where one word stopped and the other started.

He placed the coffee down on the table, leapt from the couch and pressed a button on the wall, that had he not installed it himself, it would be easy to miss. As he moved his finger from the button a section popped from wall with a hiss. Inside was a silver gauntlet with red lights blinking on the bottom. He slid the gauntlet on his hand and made a fist. As he did so the gauntlet swirled and formed a metallic sleeve that went to his elbow, and several mini blasters extended beyond his fist and formed a circular disk of red spinning energy.

The Mechanic stretched his hand out and aimed it at the portal as he took cover behind the couch. He had seen these portals before and knew what to expect. For all he knew, it was Impervious coming back. He had heard he left after the showdown with Infinity, but he couldn't be sure. An enemy could have been stepping out instead of a friend.

A young woman with spiky blond hair finally fell to his floor, and groaned as she rolled over. "Who are you, and what do you want?" The Mechanic quickly said from behind the couch as he stood up and aimed his weapon at the woman on the floor. He heard a thud hit the ground beside him, and as he turned around to face the new arrival, he found himself lifted off the ground and suspended in a pale blue force field.

"Hey buddy," Hunter said as he stretched his hand out and pinned the force field holding The Mechanic to the wall. Hunter was happy to be out of the cramped portal but found the home he stood in was almost just as crowded with gadgets, and debris that he was wishing he had more room to move.

"Hunter Monroe," The Mechanic said in more of a question instead of a statement. "What's going on? Put me down. Did Impervious send you?" "Slow down," Hunter said as he raised a hand.

He hadn't seen The Mechanic in a year, but he still looked the same. Same pointed chin, greasy black hair, and strong cheekbones. He seemed to speak faster when he was confused, though. "I'm going to let you go, but put the hand canon away," Hunter said as Perkins pushed herself to her feet. "Yes, of course," The Mechanic said quickly.

Hunter lowered his hand, and as he did so, the force field faded away and The Mechanic dropped to the ground. "This is a nice place," Hunter said as he looked around and waited for the Mechanic to get off the floor. "Messy as a college dorm room after a party, but it has potential."

"I must say, Mr. Monroe, we never have pleasant introductions." "Nerf, he does talk fast," Perkins said as she sat down on the couch. "Sorry, who are you?" The Mechanic quickly asked her. "I'm Perkins," she replied as she slapped her feet on the table, after placing the multibox down first to check it. The Mechanic looked from Perkins to Hunter.

"Why has the mighty Paragon came to see me?" The Mechanic asked. "Hunter's fine. No need for the Paragon stuff," Hunter said as he pulled a piece of paper from the bookbag he recently placed on the ground. "I know you left the hero stuff behind, but we could use your help. The short version we need you looks over some designs to create a weapon, and help us kill a giant monster that has a city on its back so we can rescue Mr. Impervious. You in?"

The Mechanic's eyes grew wide as he quickly looked from Hunter to Perkins. "Is he. Are you? Serious." "As serious as you are weird," Hunter replied. The mechanic bit his lower lip and quickly said: "I take offense to that but I get your point." He removed the gauntlet from his hand and dashed out of the room.

"Is he running away?" Perkins asked as she stood from the couch. "No," she quickly heard a voice from the other room say. In a time that Hunter didn't think was possible, The Mechanic returned back to the room in his Icon uniform. "Still fits!" The Mechanic said quickly. "Now, let's see those plans for the weapon." Hunter gave the paper to The Mechanic who in return spread it over the counter in his kitchen.

He placed some glasses on his eyes that, after he tapped the side of them suddenly had three additional lenses on them that were all different colors. "Hm. Basic plan," The Mechanic said to himself. "Several changes will need to be made to improve the design. Implement an energy core, and add a cooling chamber perhaps." as he quickly spoke, Hunter turned and gave a slight shrug to Perkins who looked confused as to what was happening.

"The frequency for the sound should be adjustable. Perhaps to incapacitate and not kill," The Mechanic said. "Is this standard steel for the frame? No, no, no, that will never do. I have some developmental alloys that will help keep the weapon from overloading with power." The Mechanic finally slammed his hand on the table as a smile covered his face.

"So, you in?" Hunter asked. The Mechanic thought to himself for a moment. If he agreed, that meant he was back. Back in the hero life. Back creating things that made a difference. Saving people, and not just people, Impervious himself.

The thought of such a powerful being needing saving was both scary and exciting. He had been in the public sector for too long, and Hunter Monroe, of all Icons, was the one to pull him back into the world he had been far too long away from. The Mechanic took a deep breath and looked to Hunter. "I'm in, but only if I can come back with you."

CHAPTER 30:
HER TRUE NAME

Flex entered the main room of the incompleted base to find Cayden asleep on a table with a chunk of plastic, with a large bite mark, hanging lazily from his hand as he snored. In the distance, he could still hear Cord training the new recruits, and Danielle sat alone at a table looking at one of the boxes of stale food.

Seeing her sitting there gave Flex a plan. "You busy?" He asked her as he approached with a grin. Danielle leaned up in her chair, looked around and spread her arms wide. "I think I can spare a minute." Flex nodded his head. "Good. Come with me." He said as he flashed his perfect teeth and turned to head to the entrance door.

Danielle stood and followed. Normally she would ask where they were going, or why he had even offered, but she really didn't care. Anything was better than sitting around and waiting for Hunter to get back. Flex slowly opened the door, and stepped inside of the small entrance, with Danielle behind him.

On their side of the door, it appeared to be just that. A metal door with a single knob. On the entrance, however, it didn't look like that at all. While the base wasn't completed, some of its defenses were. The interior of the base seemed more like a large warehouse, but on the outside, some sort of device disguised it.

To a person outside, it looked like the two young heroes had just appeared from a solid chunk of wall that surrounded an even larger building. The wall had some art on it, that was both beautiful, and allowed them to remember where the door was. There weren't many people on the streets and most that were seemed to be in a hurry.

They all wore worn clothes, and looked down as they walked. Barely making eye contact or speaking to each other. For Danielle, this was the first time she had actually seem this many people out. By chance alone, most of the times she had ventured outside while on this beast, there were no people around. What was more disturbing for her was that now she truly was able to see how the less fortunate lived.

Compared to Great Beast Sonah, this city looked horrible. There were no signs of technology advancement, no music playing in the air, and most of all, none of the eternally happy people. She felt her stomach churn as a little boy, no older than ten, walked by with dried blood on his upper lip, and ear.

As he walked by, he caught her eye for only a second and gave her a slight wave. A wave that caused her eyes to water. He was so young, and the curse had already claimed him. Empress Queen Omega had treatment, but she didn't share it. She wondered how people could still support her. Still, worship her. "What going on?" Danielle finally asked to take her mind off of the child she had seen. "

"Figured it be good to go on a quick patrol around the area," Flex said. "It is, but why with me?" Danielle asked. Flex shrugged as he looked around and squinted as the dry heat and light touched his eyes. "We, don't actually get a chance to talk much," he said slowly as he walked with a steady purpose through the people. While he was dressed in the ragged attire as the rest of them, he still stood out. His tall muscular frame, and untarnished good looks, made him look like a slither of light escaping through the darkness. He was very hard to miss and more than once people turned and watched him as he walked by.

Danielle didn't get the same amount of attention. Something she was thankful for. She kept close to him, though. The last thing she wanted to do was get separated. "You're usually with Hunter. That or we are training or something like that." Flex said. "I guess you're right." Danielle replied.

She had never thought about it because Flex was always around in one way or the other, but they really didn't talk. Not on a personal level anyway. The few words they had normally exchanged dwindled once he began dating Perkins. "Let's say we make it back home and everything goes fine," Flex continued as he held up a hand to stop a man from approaching him with a bag of fruit that he appeared to be try to sell.

"What then?" he asked. "You've been with us for a year, but you're only Hunter's girlfriend. He told me you finished school early, so you clearly are smart, but you decided right away that you wanted to be a villain." "Sounds about right," Danielle said. She had been worried that one day this conversation would come. That one day Flex would change his mind and not let a person like her, with her history, hang around the base anymore.

Telling her alone, when Hunter wasn't around to react was a smart move. She had to respect the way he planned this out. "Yeah, but you weren't a villain really," Flex said. Danielle's brow perked up a bit. Flex looked down to her as they walked side by side. "I mean saying you're a villain doesn't make it so. Same goes for a hero. For Atlas' sake, I can say I'm a musical genius, but it doesn't make me the next Young Pyro."

They made a turn down a street and began to walk again. Flex held his comments for a moment as he looked around the area to make sure nothing seemed out of place. No metallic faces, or guys with large guns or swords. Most of all, no Pain Conduits. Strong as Flex was, he was worried about the next encounter for those. He had a plan in his mind on how to deal with them, should he need to, but he was hoping this his team would have his back when the time arrived.

After determining that this area was mostly clear he glanced back to Danielle. "So, I say we do this right." Danielle looked up to him, fearful that the swift, verbal boot out of the base was headed her way. "First, your internship officially starts now. You will take the oath when we return," Flex said as her heart seemed to skip several beats per minute in her chest.

He wasn't kicking her out. He wasn't making this a covert attempt at getting her guard down. He was doing the opposite. He wanted to keep her around. " You'll have to do the same paperwork that Hunter, Jen, and-" his words cut off. He was about to say her name. He hadn't mentioned his sister in a while. He didn't even try to think about her or the havoc she was creating back home. He couldn't.

He needed to be at his sharpest and best while here on Mo'eizus. Zeva Greene would be an issue for later. Danielle didn't miss the stumble as Flex almost walked into the issue he was trying to forget. "I remember the forms," Danielle said. "I'll have to pick them up from my school and then have my guardian sign them. I um. Well-" Flex shook his head. "Normally you do, but remember we are starting late. You're of age now, so that wouldn't be a problem." Flex was quick to get beyond this point.

As far as he knew, Danielle didn't have parents. None that she had mentioned anyway. As if she was inside his head, she voiced the same. "Not like I have parents or anything anyway. The people who raised me were more so long- time babysitters." she let out a fake laugh. "I used to tell myself, I'd become a big- time villain, find my parents and see if they even cared. If they were villains, they'd be proud, and if they were heroes they'd fear me. Loving Hunter messed that up, though."

"Hunter has a way of messing things up from time to time." They both laughed some and turned down another street. Danielle could see the area on the wall from where they made their exit up ahead. "Still nothing," Flex said as he looked around. He wanted to fly up just to make sure, but that would have more eyes on him than even now.

"Once the paperwork is done, you'll be mentoring under Power Prince." "Why not you ?," Danielle asked. "You only take on the interns that come in already famous?" She gave him a punch to the side that actually hurt her hand a little bit. As she opened and closed her fist, she began to feel like Flex likely didn't even notice she had struck him. "No. Power Prince needs the experience. I want him to experience stuff early in his career like the Imperial Lords did for me. We aren't much older than you and Hunter, but we have a world of difference experience- wise. This isn't to brag, but we are also more capable heroes because of that experience. I want the same for you all."

They stopped in front of the art- covered wall and waited for people to pass them by. "The very last thing you really need to do is find a True Name. Even Jen has one. I'm not a fan of it, but then again plenty of people don't like mine." The nearly invulnerable hero shrugged. "In their defense, Flex was certainly a name I wouldn't pick for myself now if I had to do it all over again." Danielle rubbed the back of her neck and tried to avoid his eyes. As she turned her head, the hot air caught he black hair and caused it to spread over her face. Flex narrowed his eyes. "What's wrong?" She cleared her throat and looked down to her feet.

"I kind of already picked out a True Name. I'm mean I think so. Like I've been playing around with it in my head here and there." Flex stood tall and crossed his arms. "I'm listening."

Danielle didn't want to tell him. She was nervous enough about her name as it was. Hunter hadn't even heard about it. Truthfully, he didn't even know she was picking a name.

"When I first got here," Danielle slowly began. "I was still feeling like I didn't fit in. Like there was a darkness inside of me that didn't have anything to do with my powers." "Flex nodded his head half-heartedly. "I noticed it when I first killed that Pain Conduit bitch back in the wasteland. I thought because I killed her with no remorse, that I was still destined to be a villain. I felt that way for a while until I realized that I killed her for you. For my team. To protect. I may have been more open to it than most, but I did it for a reason."

"I'm glad you realized that, but what does it have to do with the name you picked?" Flex asked. "Well, I wanted a name for a while but didn't spend time thinking about it until then. I wanted a name to reflect the darkness of my powers, and the darkness inside of me. That same sharp darkness, that I can master, control, and shape for the benefit of those around me. Then it hit me." She took an extra moment to go silent. Danielle wasn't about to let this perfectly timed dramatic pause moment pass her by.

"Obsidian," she said as she looked up to Flex slightly. For the first time, Flex realized that she was slightly blushing. He didn't even know Danielle was capable of such a thing. He nodded his head a little and mouthed the word back and forth. "Obsidian. Hm. I like it." Danielle perked up some.

"I'm sure in time, the villains of the world will tremble when they realize, Obsidian has been summoned to deal with them." A slight smile played on her face and then her eyes got wide. "Don't tell Hunter I told you first." Flex laughed. "Oh, no chance in hell. I'm snitching that as soon as I can. I won't tell him the name, but he'll know I knew first." He chuckled slightly and jerked his head to the wall. "Come on. It's finally clear."

With those words, Danielle glanced around and then leapt into the wall and seemingly was absorbed into as she passed through the generated illusion. "Obsidian," Flex said with a smile to himself, and then he too leapt into the wall and vanished from the street.

CHAPTER 31:
LARGE GUNS INDEED

Perkins stood up as Hunter gave her a long glance. He didn't know exactly how to tell The Mechanic that he couldn't come and felt that his normal brash approach wasn't the right way to go, especially since the fast-talking Icon had just agreed to help them out.

"Well, Mr. Mechanic," Perkins said as she stood up. "Oh, please. No Mr.," The Mechanic replied quickly. "Just Mechanic is fine. Or you can call me The Mechanic too, but it will no doubt sound weird. That is what most call me, though." Perkins nodded her head and exhaled as the Icon blurted all the words out in what seemed like less than a second.

"Either way," she continued, the multibox is only able to bring two people here, and bring two people back. So, if you came, then one of us would have to stay and that can't happen." As she finished her words, Hunter extended his hands and shrugged in a *there you have it* fashion, and then whistled slightly as he leaned back and forth on the balls of his feet. "Sorry, man. Really I am."

The Mechanic shook his head with a slight laugh and turned from the plans he was studying to point to the large box on the table. "Is that the multibox in reference?" he asked quickly. "Well, yeah," Hunter replied slowly as he looked to Perkins with a brow raised. "I will improve it. It, it looks clunky anyway."

He took several long strides across his crowded living area and picked up the multibox. As he did so, he could hear several parts inside seem to roll around and could feel dust below his fingertips. He looked to Hunter and then sucked his teeth. "Typical," he said quickly.

"We also have another problem." The Mechanic said as he placed the multibox down just beside the plans for the Horn of Booming. "Of course, we do," Hunter said through an exhale. "What's wrong now?" "If this monster is as large as you say it is," The Mechanic began and then paused for Hunter to confirm.

Hunter slowly nodded. "Did you miss the part where I said it has a damn city on its back?" "Precisely," The Mechanic replied. "Any creature with such size and strength will need to be hit from several sides at once for the device to work. Not just at the head either. All sides. So, I will have to craft several guns. They will be perfect, small and powerful. One, perhaps two, likely three, will, of course, be rather large and imposing but that comes later in design. Either way, much more impressive than these childish plans you have provided."

"Those plans aren't childish," Perkins insisted. She had only met the man, but for some reason, he reminded her of Cord. The person who created those plans was a friend to her. A good man and she refused to let his designs and his genius be referred to as childish. "I'm sorry, perhaps childish wasn't the correct word. The designer was clearly intelligent, just not on par with myself." The Mechanic raised his hands quickly and shook his head. "Merely an observation." he quickly added.

While Perkins and was still taken aback by his words, something else The Mechanic said had stroked her attention. "You mentioned one of the guns would be rather large?" "Or two, likely three but yes. Very large indeed," The Mechanic quickly said. Perkins didn't respond. Not verbally anyway. The large grin that found a home on her face was enough to let Hunter and even The Mechanic know, that she would have dibs on the larger weapon.

"So how many people we talking?" Hunter finally asked as he dropped down in a chair and rested his elbows on his knees. He was ready to get this show on the road and over with. He didn't realize just how much he had missed his world until he landed back in this luxury apartment with a fabulous view, that he was trying to avoid. He was also reminded of a special task he had set into motion before all of this save Impervious business started, and was eager to get back to it.

As crowded, and phobia-inducing as The Mechanics place was, the undertones of wealth well spent was playing a number on Hunter, and he was not looking forward to going back to live in a semi-completed lair. Still, he had a mission to complete, and he would see it through. "Two for the head on each side, one on each side of the body, and lastly three at the end of the body. This will be the location for the larger guns." The Mechanic said quickly.

Hunter took in a breath and leaned back in the chair. Seven people, seven people were going to be needed for this to work. He then rubbed his temples and sighed. Nothing ever seemed to happen easy. Then again, if he wanted easy, he could have just been a painter. Instead, he wanted to be a hero. He wanted greatness, fame, to help people, and do the right thing. Complications came with the job.

He adjusted himself in the chair and ran through a tick of names in his head. Seven people. There was himself, Flex, Cayden, Danielle, and Perkins. No way she was going to miss out on that big gun. Cord was sick, even though he tried to hide it more and more, so he was out, and Hunter didn't really trust the recruits. He knew what he had to do, but didn't really want to involve them in it. "Hey," Hunter said as he sat up.

The Mechanic, sprawled on the counter, and talked to himself as he made notes on the side of the designs before him. He didn't look to Hunter, but he did raise his brow to signify that he heard him, and for the most part was paying attention. "To make the gun, horn, thingies and to replace the multibox. How long we think that will take?" Hunter asked as he eyed The Mechanic.

A slight laugh came from The Mechanic's mouth as he continued to write down some numbers. "Once I'm in the back in my lab, very little time at all." "What's very little time?" Perkins asked as she reached for the remote and adjusted the TV. "About Five hours or so," The Mechanic replied.

"Damn," Hunter said to himself. That was pretty fast. Much faster than he expected at any rate. "What if we needed a device that would grant limited flight to some people. Five people to be exact. How long would that to make?" Still, The Mechanic didn't miss a beat and continued to make corrections on the paper before him.

"Do they need to fly as you do? Do they need to exit the sound barrier? Or do they need the basics? By basic I mean up, down, hovering in the air. Nothing too fancy." Hunter thought about it for a moment. He and Flex would be there. So, the fancy stuff would be covered by them. Everybody else just needed to get in position and stay there.

"The latter works but allow them a little speed just in case," Hunter finally replied. "Oh, I have several devices like that in storage," The Mechanic said. "So, we are all set if that is what you need." Hunter didn't respond. He wasn't a fan of The Mechanic. Their original introduction was too rocky for that, and one didn't get a second chance at first impressions. Still, he continued to prove to be an asset, and even if Hunter didn't want to admit it, he was glad they came to the fast-talking Icon for help. He was even more glad that The Mechanic was so board that he would jump at the opportunity to do almost anything.

"Okay, I need to borrow your phone," Hunter said. "Phone, living room." The Mechanic said out loud. From across the room the sound of items being knocked over startled Perkins and Hunter. The Mechanic didn't even seem to notice. From the direction of the sound, slowly rose a floating item, that for a moment Hunter thought was a remote.

As the item drifted to the living room and began to hover in the air, however, he realized it was, in fact, a phone. "I have the same design for the remote controls and my keys." The Mechanic stated. "These bad boys hit the market in a month and are gonna be targeted to buyers with multiple children or people living in large homes. Affordable, and guaranteed to save your time looking for your crap." The Mechanic blurted out in record time.

Hunter stretched his hand out and grabbed the phone. For some reason, it had a rubberized feel to it that was slightly warm. He didn't know if that was normal or if it was part of the design that allowed it to listen to voice commands and fly. Flipping it over he muttered to himself, "he better pick up the damn phone, too."

He dialed the numbers and waited for the phone to ring. "Nerf!" Perkins screamed as she stood up. "Nerfing, nerf." Hunter quickly hung up the phone before it could even ring once, and took a few steps to Perkins. The Mechanic, completely oblivious to Perkins or her squeals, grabbed his plans and dashed off to another room.

Hunter realized what had caused the reaction from Perkins, she had landed on a news channel as she was looking for something to watch. Zeva's face was now on the screen. "Hunter could feel his brow furrow as he read the bulletin.

Zeva Green, sister to popular hero Flex, dead at hands of former Imperial Lords member Power Prince. He swallowed to try to kill the sudden dryness of his throat, but it didn't work. Flex had no idea that his sister was now gone, and that the man he tasked with taking her down, did just that. Hunter didn't actually feel bad for Zeva. He had fought her a year ago and had he not won, she would have gladly killed him.

She was a villain through and through. No way around it, and after seeing her in the prison, he knew that she would go on to do horrible things if not stopped. Power Prince did what he had to do. What he took an oath to do. Flex may be hurt about it on the inside, but he would harbor no ill feelings towards his second in command. At least that was what Hunter was hoping for.

"Should they just be blurting out that she was Flex's sister like that?" Perkins asked. "What about his privacy? His safety." Hunter all but laughed at her. "You're referring to his secret identity. Like in the comics." He shook his head some as he looked at the phone to dial again. "Some heroes do keep who they are secret. Mostly for the safety of themselves and loved ones.

Flex on the other hand, is no pushover and his family is loaded to the limit with Icons. So there really was no need. Same goes for me, and my parents. Some things just can't be private, sadly."

"Oh," Perkins replied as she looked back to the images from the television that moved around her as if they were on set. Hunter looked at the phone once more and hit the redial button. It rang a few times, and then he heard a voice answer the phone with a loud tv blaring in the background. "Hey, glowy hands it's me. Paragon. Hunter, whatever." Hunter turned away from the tv and closed his eye. From where Perkins was standing, she could hear the other person on the phone unloading words almost as fast as The Mechanic.

"Wait. Wait. Slow down." Hunter said as he moved his hands to punctuate his words. "Yeah, I just saw the news. Busy indeed." Loud sounds came from the phone again. "Look we'll talk later. Grab Jen and get over to The Mechanic's place." More loud sounds came from the phone, as Hunter nodded his head slightly and agreed a few times. "Okay, see you in a bit, and tell Jen to bring her sword. Oh, if Jen drives over here then Atlas be with you." Hunter smiled and then hit a button to end the call.

In what seemed faster than should have been possible, a knock came to the door. When it did, Hunter glanced at the clock on the stove in The Mechanics kitchen. "Ten minutes?" he said to himself. Perkin leaped up and ran to the door, opening it with a smile as she saw Power Prince first and gave him a hug. A hug that he gladly returned. "Glad to see you two are still kicking," he said as he let her go and entered in the living room. His eyes got wide as he looked around. "Dude, this place is messier than the Sanford and Son house."

Hunter laughed as he understood his tv show reference. "I suppose it is," he said as he crossed the room and extended his hand out to him, while at the same time trying not to panic at the thought of the cramped area being more occupied. "Good to see you," Hunter said.

Power Prince shook his head but avoided Hunter's gaze, and it had nothing to do with Hunter being taller than he was. "We need to talk," Power Prince finally said. "Nah, we don't," Hunter replied.

"You did what you had to do. Nothing more." Power Prince exhaled. "I have no idea how I'm going to tell Flex." "With your head held high, and confidence in your voice," Hunter replied. Power Prince shook his head. "I'm supposed to be the experienced hero that gives the advice around here." Hunter shrugged. "I trust the meeting with the stiffs at I.C.E went well?" Hunter asked.

"Yes and no. We can get into that later though," Power Prince said as he moved to look through the home, and disappeared into another room. "Hey Paragon," Jen said as she left Perkins and moved his way. "I didn't want to break up the bromance reunion or anything," she said with a smile.

She extended her fist out to Hunter who in return bumped it with his. He then plucked the brim of her baseball cap. "Couldn't leave it at home, huh Mystic?" He asked as he said her True Name a little louder than needed and gave her a hug. "Heck no. When he told me, you requested I bring this personally," she held up Big Whopper concealed in its sheath and gave it a slight shake. "I figured my luckiest cap would be needed."

Hunter rolled his eyes. "I know the green one with white trim. Same cap you had on when you told your folks you liked men and women, wrecked the car, and turned Jr. invisible and now you couldn't find him." Hunter suppressed a laugh. Now that he thought about it, that cap was always around when Jen delivered news that could have earned her months of grounding or scorn, yet she came out unscathed each time.

True, she could have just looked at it as having very understanding, supportive, and forgiving parents, but no Jen figured it must have been the luck of her green cap. Either way, here she was, sporting it proudly. "So, first things first," Jen said as she shoved her sword into Hunter's hands. "Let's check out this fridge."

She grinned and clapped her hands in mock fashion as she moved to the kitchen, opened the large stainless- steel refrigerator, and leaned inside. "Jackpot on so many levels," she said from the inside. Perkins followed her into the kitchen. "I could use some food, too." Hunter was about to proclaim the same thing, but heard footsteps behind him and found Power Prince entering the room again.

"Now that the introductions are out of the way, and Jen has found the fridge, tell me from the beginning what's going on, and why we needed to help." Power Prince said. Hunter glanced over his shoulder and saw Perkins gawking at the size of the sandwich Jen was making. "I'm going to make you one too. Just wait a minute," Jen said to her.

Hunter turned back to Power Prince and then motioned for him to take a seat. "I'll just start from the cluster fuck of events that have happened since we left, and landed there." "Sounds good," Power Prince said as he fell to the couch.

CHAPTER 32:
THE GANG'S ALL HERE

I honestly expected this to be going better," Cayden said as he looked at yet another recruit getting tossed to the ground with a loud thud. He had finally decided to head to the room where the new recruits had turned into their quarters to check on them. His brother had left some time ago to make his rounds in the city and check some contacts.

Or so he told Cayden and the rest of the team. Secretly, Cayden had feared that his brother's condition, as strong as he was, was getting worse. Because of his immunity to disease, Cayden had seen first- hand just how quickly the Curse of Varo could ravish a body. The fact that his brother was dealing with it for so long was a testament to his strength.

While Cayden was just now checking on the recruits, Flex had given the same task to Danielle almost as soon as they returned from their own scouting mission. In the time that followed Danielle gave a brief introduction on who she was, what her powers were, and how she liked to fight while in battle.

The demo was great for the recruits. Having to face an enemy with superior power would make them strong, but first, they would suffer. Danielle held nothing back as time after time she was rushed by the new recruits. Bolts of dark energy, mixed with her shadow form, made her hard to lock down. Throw in that she was decent in hand to hand combat made her a force to be feared.

Cayden also could tell she was going easy on their recruits. He had noticed several times that she pulled punches when she had direct openings and could have caused serious pain for the recruits, but instead would have simply blocked or countered their attacks.

"No, they're doing fine," Danielle said as she ducked down spun around and swept the legs from under one of the recruits. The brown- haired boy she was facing fell over in a comic fashion and groaned as he went to stand up. "I've been on the receiving end of getting my ass handed to me several times. Once you guys get in a better base and have more time to train, you'll be on your way."

"Will there even be a need for us once we are finished with Empress Queen Omega?" A dark-haired and tan skinned recruit asked from the corner where she rested. "I mean if you think about it, Bravado was formed to defeat Omega and give back freedom to the people that didn't even realize they were being oppressed. The real people, not the high and mighty people in Acropolis."

Danielle removed some sweat from her brow and eyed the girl, then she turned to Cayden. "You know what, she has a point." Cayden pulled a small, protruding nail from the wall and proceeded to bite into it as he shook his head. "You'd think that, but once Omega is dispatched with, that is when the real fight starts."

Every recruit in the room adjusted and turned towards him as his words shocked them. "Think about it," Cayden said. "Once she is gone, there will be a void left in the East Section. Not only that, but once she is gone, so are her Wardens and their Circle. With them goes their power and protection. Other leaders will likely war for her kingdom, and normal people will be caught in the middle. Normal people that we will protect, and fight for if we have to. In time our numbers will grow, and even you all will be Generals in Bravado."

At these words, a few of them perked up. The thought of leadership and respect rushing through their sore bodies. "Unless somebody of elite blood decides to take action," Danielle said slowly. "Wouldn't that prevent the war?" All the recruits turned their heads from Danielle to Cayden. Danielle smirked as she could see Cayden visibly struggle with what to say. His posture changed, and his lip quivered slightly as he tried to select his words carefully.

Danielle had grown fond of Cayden in the time they had been here. He was a smug guy, but having such power among people that couldn't compare could often do that. Her time with Hunter was living proof of that. Still, Cayden had turned out to be an okay person. "I," Cayden stammered.

"Hey look alive," a sudden voice said as the door to their quarters was swung open with force. Flex stood tall in the opening. "They're back." He turned and quickly exited, leaving an open door that led to the adjoining room where most of the interactions went down. "Keep training and running your drills my future Generals," Danielle said as she motioned for Cayden to follow her. Several of the recruits nodded together as they stood up and paired off with each other to continue practicing.

Flex stood alone in the center of the main room of the base and watched the portal swirl, as the familiar odor it produced radiated from it. Before the portal came to life, he had been alone with his thoughts for a while since Cord left, and Cayden went to join Danielle in her recruit's training. He needed the time, though. So much was going on, and he barely had time to think about how he was going to approach everything and handle his team.

As he watched the portal swirl, he let out a sigh. For the first time in a long time, he wished he had a senior member of the Imperial Lords around to talk to. He had missed Detach, and her calm demeanor most of all. She always seemed to have a plan for what to do next. Impervious would just have to do, and for what Flex was planning, he felt that Impervious would support him completely.

He heard footsteps behind him and glanced over his shoulder to see Danielle and Cayden trotting over. "They're not here yet?" Danielle asked. Flex shook his head silently. He had begun to wonder what was taking so long too. Before he could say anything, a single baseball cap fell from the portal and landed on the floor.

It was a darker shade of green than the portal itself, and its sudden appearance made Cayden jump some with surprise. Danielle and Flex had a different reaction to seeing the sudden appearance of a baseball cap. Flex shook his head and smiled some. "Oh, now it's a party," Danielle said as she smiled so hard her teeth were showing. Seconds later, a girl with long black hair with red highlights, blue jeans, and a white shirt fell to the ground.

"I made it!" she said with more surprise than joy, as she looked around. "Flex! You pretty bastard." Jen said as she stood up, grabbed her ball cap off the floor and ran to hug her leader. "What are you doing here?" Flex asked slowly as he gave her a hug. The question didn't get answered as one by one more bodies continued to fall out of the portal.

Perkins stood as tall as she could with a massive gun in her hand that looked almost like the creation for a science fiction movie. It was black with blue markings on the side, several inches long with a circular shape, and had a faint wisp of cool air falling from it. It seemed like it would have been too heavy for her, but she carried it with ease as she walked over to Flex and gave him a kiss on the cheek. "What in the name of Atlas is that you're carrying?" Flex asked as he looked down at her and laugh slightly.

She looked comical moving a weapon that was almost as large as her. Perkins smiled as she moved the gun around to show how light it was. "Little bit of an upgrade from my blasters. I call her," She paused for a moment. "Well, I don't have a name for her yet." "Her?" Flex asked. Perkins rubbed her hand along the large gun as if she was stroking a cat, and smiled slightly as she nodded her head. "Nerfing right it's her."

"No judgment from me," Flex said. "Well, that's a first," Hunter said as he walked by carrying two weapons identical to the one Perkins had and a bulky bookbag on his back. "I send you off to get a weapon fixed, and you return with multiple weapons and several additional people?" Flex questioned. In return, Hunter smirked. "World's best intern, right?" Flex opened his mouth to speak but stopped when he felt a hand on his shoulder.

"My fearless leader," Power Prince said from behind him. Flex turned around and, all formalities gone hugged his friend. While the hug may have had too much strength in it, Power Prince didn't flinch. He wanted to cherish this moment. He had decided to talk to Flex about Zeva after the mission. The last thing he wanted was for one of their big guns to be underperforming because of personal issues.

"Glad to see you came," Flex said as he released him. "Although, I'm not sure why you all came," he added. "Because I am a genius," The Mechanic said quickly as he moved around the room and looked at several monitors. "This place is, well. Less than welcoming, but I'm sure anything is compared to the luxury of the Imperial Lords' base." "New Lords' base," Jen said from across the room.

She was being introduced to Cayden by Danielle. "Oh yes. Yes. The name change." The Mechanic said. "I'll make a note to help upgrade this," He stopped talking as he looked at the layer of dust on the floor with several dozen footprints in it. "Base if time permits," he finally finished.

"Hey, when this is all over, let's take a moment to catch up," Power Prince said. Flex looked at his friend and could see that something was bothering him. While Power Prince wore a smile, he didn't seem to truly mean it. He wasn't his normal bouncy self. Flex nodded his head slowly. While he didn't know what was on Power Prince's mind, he respected him enough not to question it. Power Prince had been a hero for a few years now, and he knew how to handle things. Flex new that whatever he wanted to talk about, would be better addressed once they were safe, and the task at hand was completed. "Sure thing. I was actually thinking the same thing," Flex finally said. "I have some ideas that I wanted to run by you."

Power Prince nodded his head and smiled again. In the next few moments, everybody got situated as those that fell from the portal gathered up their things and placed them on the center table. Jen only had her sword, but Hunter had a backpack loaded with assorted gadgets that were now sprawled on the table in front of them all. "Should we wait for Cord?"

Cayden asked the room at large as they were standing and sitting around the table.

As the question left his mouth his gaze darted towards the door where his brother would normally enter. "I'm sure he will be here soon. Let's just go over the main parts of the plan and give him his time. I'm sure he is dealing with somethings he'd rather none of us see," Perkins said. As she spoke, Flex looked at her.

He couldn't help but wonder was she talking about Cord, or was she relating the issue to herself. She still hadn't told him that she was sick. She had no idea that he knew, and as with Power Prince, he refused to address it right now. It was hard enough to keep his mind in the game, and he didn't need the possible impending doom of the woman he loved adding to it.

"Alright, I think that's all of it," Hunter said as he placed Perkins' twin blasters on the table in front of her and looked inside the bookbag once more. It was empty and he tossed it to the ground. "Mechanic, take it away," Hunter said as he stretched his hand out towards his fellow Icon. "Explain everything."

CHAPTER 33:
ASSAULT

Several hours had passed. In that time, Hunter and Flex took the extra steps to explain everything to Power Prince and Jen. They gave detail on the trials that they experienced once they arrived in this world. How Flex encountered a Spellborn named Manis, that was almost as strong as he was. How the disease was ravishing the land, and how Cord was its latest victim.

They told of Hunter's narrow escape from Empress Queen Omega after hearing about her offer to rule by her side because of his elite heritage, and how Flex had to save him soon after. When Jen moved to make jokes about this part, Hunter quickly cut her off or flat out ignored her comments. Then there was The Mechanic.

After he and the rest of the newcomers were caught up, he went on to give details about the devices he created, and how they were to be used to bring down the Great Beast Sonah. Several times he was requested to repeat himself because even if he tried, he simply couldn't slow down his speaking. Shortly after, everybody was given their roles in the assault to come. Even the recruits were to play a part.

Now, they all stood on the roof of their current base. While not as tall as their previous location, this base was more private. Sure, on the streets below people moved around at almost all times of the day, but at night there was virtually no life around them, and neighboring buildings were as dark as the night sky above them.

Danielle was perhaps the only one that felt eager to get the show on the road. Her extra strength she received for using her powers at night coursed through her. Every fiber of her being felt like it was hyper-charged, and she needed an outlet. For the first time, she was hoping for a Warden to show.

This time they would be fighting her head on at her best, on the equal ground while she had as much support as the Warden's Circle did.

Through some quick thinking by the recruits, additional outfits of black were secured. They weren't guard uniforms like Hunter, Cayden, and Danielle wore, but they still helped them all look like more of a team. Even Cord, who turned up last minute before the original briefing ended was dressed in black.

While he told them he was fine, his body told another story. His hands were stained from the blood he had been wiping away. His movements were slow, and his face seemed a bit gaunter. His current health issues were likely why he took so long on the last patrol he made. His body was slowing down as the Curse of Varo increased.

Flex glanced from Cord to Perkins. He refused to let this be her fate. If there was a cure or even an improved treatment somewhere in the palace, he was going to get it for her, and Atlas help any that tried to stand in his way.

As they all lined up beside each other, The Mechanic stood in front of them joined by a recruit. The recruit in question was dark- skinned with blond hair and held a bag in front of him. The Mechanic spoke, the recruit walked behind him and did as he was told, and that was to only pass out the items in the said bag when given a nod from The Mechanic.

"We have already gone over the items and your roles in depth," The Mechanic said quickly. "I don't foresee any, but if you have questions then-" his words were cut off as Jen's hand punctured the air. The clicking sound of his boots on the roof stopped as The Mechanic exhaled and turned to Jen with his recruit behind him.

"Yes?" The Mechanic said without evening trying to hide his impatience. Jen wrapped her hand around her wrist and touched the glowing gold band around it. Each person, aside from Hunter and Flex, had one on. "How fast can these make us fly?" she asked. "Your top speed will be around sixty miles per hour. Perhaps a little more," The Mechanic said quickly.

Hunter let a slight grunt escape from his mouth, and Flex slapped him on the back of the head for it, yet Flex too had a smirk on. "Naturally it isn't as fast as those who wield supreme flight," The Mechanic said as he glanced to Hunter and Flex, "But it is enough to get you to where you are going. Remember the bands allow flight by manipulating the gravity around you. Since you all will be spread out and leaving the roof one by one, there shouldn't be any interference from bands in close proximity." The Mechanic cleared his throat some. "At any rate, the main purpose is for you to hover alongside the Great Beast and move accordingly. Much flight shouldn't be needed."

Without even giving Jen time to ask another question, The Mechanic continued to move up the line of spread out heroes. He gave a slight nod to his recruit and the young man started handing out small weapons from the bag. Power Prince, with a massive cannon he would be using by his feet, watched as the first weapon was passed out. The weapon was circular, and about twelve inches long. Composed of brass, and some allow he couldn't identify, it glowed a faint green when powered on, and had several buttons on the side.

"Is it just me or does that look like a sonic screwdriver?" Power Prince asked out loud to nobody in particular. Once again, the other people on the roof simply looked at him in confusion. "Okay, I get that some of the stuff I watch you may not have seen, but Doctor Who? Seriously?," Power Prince said in more of a plea as he looked around. "The Time Lords? The Tardis? The show has been on for decades, and no-" he let out a sigh as he stopped speaking mid-sentence. "You know what, never mind."

While she didn't know what a Tardis was or who this Doctor Who person Power Prince was talking about was, Perkins did notice that the weapon her colleagues held wasn't a gun. She spoke but didn't raise her hand as Jen did. "What happened to them looking like guns? Those things look nothing like the plans we gave you."

Quickly and bluntly The Mechanic spoke. "After all of my improvements, the original design had to change. Once you're in position and fire the weapon, the results will be the same I assure you." Perkins shrugged her shoulders and looked down to the massive cannon at her feet, identical to the ones that would be wielded by Power Prince and Cayden.

The three of them would be at the rear of the Great Beast. They had the largest weapons that would create a larger cone of sounds. She was happy. She wasn't an enemy of their new fast- talking colleague but had he tried to give her one of those small devices, while others had a cannon, he'd be in a world of hurt.

The Mechanic stood to the side with Cord and his recruit and each member of the teamed walked closer to the edge of the building and spread out some. "That's all from me," The Mechanic said. "My recruit has given out everything. Seriously I wish we called them by their names. Calling them all *recruit* is off-putting." The Mechanic said quickly. "What's off-putting is how you talk like a robot and seem to be a master of tech," Cord replied. "If I were the jumpy type, I'd assume you were a droid and end you."

The Mechanic's eyes widen as he cleared his throat again, but said nothing. "We call them recruits so as not get too attached," Cord continued. "If they die during training, an early mission, or decided to leave and have to be terminated, the connection is minor." "I see," The Mechanic finally said, as he avoided Cord's eyes.

"You sure it's up there?" Power Prince said as he looked in the dark sky above them. From where he stood the sky looked peaceful and empty. Nothing but stars. He found it hard to believe that an entire city was up there on a monster's back.

"Oh, it's up there," Perkins said as her green eyes glowed slightly. "I can see it." "Everybody spread out, and remember your positions," Flex said sternly. They did as they were told and as they moved away from each other, those wearing flight bands could see their new wrist- wear glow brightly.

"Make sure your coms are on now, so we can keep contact while we are up there." As he said this several hands flew up to their ears and pressed the tiny device inside.

The Mechanic flinched as he watched them activate the ancient device. He had pleaded for more time to improve those as well but was denied the request.

"Hunter doesn't need his force field to fly," Flex continued. "But he will have it on so you can know where you are going. He'll be our beacon and focal point up there so we can at least know where to head to." As Flex spoke, Hunter summoned a force field around him that glowed in a faint blue. A faint blue that radiated several times more than the bands they wore. "Let's bring Impervious and that cure home," Flex said. "We need it. The people of this world need it. The iron grip Omega has over this land ends tonight. Not by people in her shadow, or at her feet, but by those at her neck."

Around him, several people gave silent nods, and Danielle smirked. Jen gave Hunter a fist bump as she adjusted her strap around her chest that held her sword in place. She secretly hoped they would be back on the ground before she would have to use it. Flex gave a slight nod to Hunter. "Take it away, Paragon."

With those few words, Hunter touched his power and took off into the sky like a rocket. His exit was so strong that several people took steps back and tiny cracks formed on the roof. "That people, is what supreme flight looks like," he said through the coms. Several people swore and cursed at him in response. While he couldn't see it from his position in the sky, the rest of his team one by one were making their way up into the vast nothingness of the sky following his lead.

For a moment he didn't see anything, but as he passed the clouds, there it was. Flying slowly through the sky. A king, in a kingdom that few had entry to, The Great Beast Sonah. Ancient and resistant to time, the monster had lived unopposed for so long. Hunter wondered how it would react to what was about to happen to it. He wielded himself to fly alongside the monstrous head and spoke into his coms. "In position,"

"Same," Perkins responded. Slowly each member of the team confirmed that they were ready. "This is incredible." Power Prince said as he flew alongside the beast. "As I made my way up here, I was able to see the other Great Beast, but this is. It's." He couldn't find the words to express how in awe he was over the creature. He knew they were there for a purpose, but he was making a mental note to try to learn the history of the monsters before they left.

"Don't go all fanboy on us," Jen said through the coms. "Quiet, intern." Power Prince muttered. "Ready your weapons," The Mechanic said through the coms from below. "According to your current location you should be in position soon. My calculations, based on data given by Perkins and Cayden, use the estimated size, weight, and strength of the Great Beast and compare it to the speed you're moving. Everything lines up, and the monster should safely land in the sand instead of crash."

"Just say the word," Flex replied. "We are all good up here," "I know this is off topic, but I'm pretty jealous," Danielle said through the coms. "Flying is amazing. Like orgasmic amazing, and you two dorks get to experience it all the time." From his position in front of the Great Beast, Hunter frowned.

"You've flown with me plenty of times." "Yeah but that was more like a pity fly. Like being driven around in a car is great, but getting behind the wheel and driving for yourself is always better," Danielle replied. "How about we all just focus on our task at hand," Flex said through the coms.

"Agreed." The Mechanic added. "Approaching the target location now. Activate and aim weapons." None responded, but all around the monster weapons were being raised and activated, and at the tail end, Perkins had a smile on her face as she hefted her ultra-lightweight canon. "Three, two, one. Go!" The Mechanic said so fast that it took the team several delayed seconds to actually fire their weapons.

For a second, as his finger squeezed the trigger to his cannon, Cayden thought his weapon had failed him. Nothing happened. He repeated the motion and pulled the trigger several more times, and even gave the weapon a slight shake for good measure. Still nothing. "Nerfing tech genius my ass," Cayden said over the coms. "Nothing happened," Hunter said, only seconds before Cayden could.

"Same here," Perkins replied as she glanced at Power Prince to see him looking as his weapon in confusion. "No. No. everything is going to plan. The weapons are working." The Mechanic said from below. "It's like a dog whistle, you just can't-" the sound that roared through the sky was so loud and intense, that none heard what The Mechanic was saying. They all looked at the Great Beast as it twitched and screamed in the air, dropping several hundred feet as it tried to right itself.

As the beast, Sonah, dropped chaos manifested in the city of Acropolis, as expected and planned. Even from their positions outside of the beast Cayden, Power Prince, and Perkins could hear the scream from the residents as their world began to fall. On her side of the beast, Danielle rose higher into the air to see the city. Buildings were starting to crumble as their foundations gave way, cracks were spreading in the streets, and from where she was the residents of the floating city looked like ants fleeing a flood of carnage.

Jen finally regained her senses after being taken aback by the scream of Sonah. As she floated back a few feet her eyes widened as she slightly felt bad for the monster. The double wings on both sides flapped but weren't in perfect harmony as they were moments ago. The tentacle-like appendages on the head flared in all directions, and that banshee-like howl bombed again.

"Sorry," Jen said slightly under her breath as she gazed at the creature that was helpless against their assault. Then the Great Beast Sonah stopped flying completely and began to plummet to the ground. All members of the assault team had to spread out fast to get out of the way of the massive falling beast.

"What in Atlas," Hunter said as he looked at the beast plummet through the sky. As it fell chunky of debris from the crumbling city began to plummet below and spray through the sky around them.

"There was a miscalculation." The Mechanic franticly voiced through the coms. "You think?" Danielle screamed to him. Flex's eyes darted around as the beast fell. "I don't think the smooth landing we planned is going to happen," Flex said over the coms as he began to fly towards the falling monster. "Paragon, with me. The rest of you stay here and handle the falling debris if you can. That's an order."

As Flex's words came through the coms, each member reacted. Danielle's eyes turned black as dark energy exploded around her, and she darted off as fast as her flight band could take her. She finally had an outlet for her growing power. Perkins dropped her massive cannon, and drew out her twin blasters, and tossed one to Jen. They began to fire in different directions, hitting anything falling that they could.

Power Prince had long dropped his weapon, and currently had glowing pink orbs of crackling power where his hands should have been. So much power flowed through the Icon known for being a living battery that could have powered several cities. His hands had a spark in them and as large portions of a building fell, Power Prince clapped them together.

A pink circular wave of power tore through the dark sky that was so bright that it made some of the heroes around him flinch. "Damn, double P," Jen said from across the sky.

Cayden popped two purple cubes in his mouth and began to chew rapidly. Then he stretched his hands out in front of him. A landslide of debris falling through the sky turned from massive boulders into brittle dust as the time around them was rocketed forward. "We got you guys covered from here," Jen said through the coms.

Hunter wasted no time as he took off behind his mentor and began to look like a blue bullet ripping through the sky as he dodged falling chunks of the city. "Mechanic, how off were the calculations?" Flex asked. "Very. The Great Beast Sonah is on a path directly for the great beast we currently occupy. Not the open land we originally planned." "What!" Hunter yelled.

"If impact is made, casualties will be over eighty percent. The death from both cities will be, catastrophic." The Mechanic said quickly. "I'm sorry." "You're sorry?" Perkins screamed through the coms. "These are my people. And you're sorry." Silence filled the coms, as Flex gritted his teeth and pushed himself harder.

Around him, all he could hear was wind rushing by and his team giving their all to reducing the falling chunks of the city that were going to destroy everything below. He didn't know if he could do what he needed to, or if he was strong enough, but it was time to put his title to the test. It really was time to see if he was the strongest Icon.

He realized that for the first time in his days as a hero, he was scared. Scared he wasn't strong enough be the winner. This was much more than catching a plan out the sky. This was an ancient beast as large as a city, and with the added weight of a city on its back.

He could feel his stomach roll as his throat seemed dry. Flex glanced over his shoulder and saw the pale blue force field of Paragon come into his view. His intern gave him a slight nod, and surprisingly, that nod put him at ease. "I'm here Ken Doll, let's show 'em what the New Lords can do," Flex smirked and nodded, as they tore through the sky and rushed towards the falling city.

CHAPTER 34:
THE POWER OF PARAGON & FLEX

From where she hovered in the sky, Jen began to feel tired. This flying around and blasting stuff put a strain on the body, even if there was a device that allowed her to fly. As she caught her breath, she looked down and felt her heart skip. Flex and Hunter were both flying through the sky alongside the falling city.

"What in Atlas are they doing?" she said to herself, not knowing it was loud enough to be heard through the coms. "What they were born to do," Danielle grunted through the coms. She sounded strained but oddly happy as she unleashed wave after wave of her dark energy and destroyed all in her wake. "Flex gave us an order. Get back to it,"

"How large can you make a force field?" Flex asked as he flew alongside Paragon. Hunter didn't miss the worry in Flex's eyes. "Pretty big," he replied as they both had to split to avoid a chunk of rubble in the sky. They were approaching the falling beast. "I need you cover the city. All of it, and the Great Beast Arzi too," Flex said. "The fucking city?" Paragon replied as he glanced down to the slowly moving beast on the ground. As he flew through the air, it only looked like a tiny dot that was slowly getting bigger. There were thousands of innocent people down there. People that didn't know death was falling down on them from the sky, because of something *they* did.

"Cord, have the recruits reach as many people as they can and tell everyone to get somewhere safe, and to brace for impact," Flex said. "Cord already left," The Mechanic said back into the coms. "Where did he go?" Cayden and Flex said in unison. "I'm not sure, but I have already sent the recruits out to alert the city." "Good," Flex said as he reared off from Paragon in the sky.

"What in Atlas are you going to do?" Paragon screamed as Flex flew towards the falling beast. The question was pointless. He knew what Flex had been planning from the moment he began to fly to the city. The crazy bastard was going to try to lift it. The entire city and the best itself. Tens of tons, maybe even hundreds. Paragon took a breath. Was Flex *that* strong?

"You have your orders," Flex screamed as he vanished under the size of the falling Great Beast. As Paragon moved through the sky, he glanced below to the city on top of the falling beast. Buildings were still breaking apart as the residents scattered. Fires roared throughout the city as the destruction continued to spread.

Then, his head jerked so fast that it caused Hunter to stop flying all together. As he hovered above the city falling, he saw it again. A streak of something. Moving fast throughout the city. It wasn't only moving, but it had purpose. As people fled the carnage of the collapsing city they were whisked away by the blur. Even fires were put out as the streak formed mini air funnels. "Impervious," Hunter said with a smile. He didn't know how, but the legendary hero had broken free, and was saving those on the city.

"I don't see that force field," Flex said. His voice wasn't normal, though. It was strained and forced. His words were enough to make Hunter focus. "Anytime, Paragon," Flex added. "On it," Paragon said as he flew through the air, beyond the great beast, and came up on the city below. He had seen the Great Beast from this point of view before, but now it looked larger. As he took in the sheer size of the monster, he took a deep breath and raised his hands.

The motion wasn't needed to create the force field, but he often felt it helped him focus his efforts, and for the most part, it looked good on camera. Slowly, a pale blue bubble came to life at the highest point of the city and began to spread. It was easy at first. Almost like spreading a blanket over a large area

Then the area seemed to continue to go, and the blanket was too small. Still, even though it seemed like a pointless act, Hunter continued to push.

Continued to slowly spread that force field larger than he ever had too. Larger than he thought he would ever need to, and he realized that if he made it out of this mess alive, he would add force field size to his training. He naturally just made it large enough to cover a few people or to fill a room, but never an entire city.

Under better circumstances, an Icon would join forces with other heroes with a force field power and just cover various parts of the city in a precise and planned out manner. He didn't have that luxury, though. "Holy shit," Jen came through the coms. "I see it too," Danielle said. "Same," Cayden replied through the coms. They all floated in the sky in different positions. The debris had been handled, and from where they were the Great Beast was too far away to catch.

They hovered as slowly, they watched two things happen. On one side, the falling Great Beast Sonah, began to slow and turn slightly. Its wings weren't moving, and the large tentacled head of the beast hung limp. They didn't know if the monster was dead, or had just passed out from pain. Either way, its shift in momentum wasn't from its own power.

On the other side, they could see a force field larger than anything they had ever seen began to form. "If we can see it from here," Cayden said slowly. "It's massive." Jen said with a tremor in her voice. "He's never had to-" "You can do it Paragon! I love you, you blue bubble- forming bastard," Danielle screamed through the coms so loud that it caused all listening to jump. Somewhere down below, Paragon smiled as sweat rolled down into his eye.

"I second her statement. The city is almost completely covered if my calculations are right," The Mechanic said. "Don't get me started on your calculations," Cayden said in a hollow tone that sounded almost identical to his brother's.

"They really are freaks of nature," Perkins said over the com. She sounded weak. Far weaker than the others, and from where she was in the sky, she wiped the blood from her ear. Happy that none could see her. As she gathered herself, she took a page from Danielle's book.

"You guys see my man? Moving an entire city and the mountain of a monster below it? Manis never had a chance." His muscles were pushed harder than they had ever been. So much force was being exerted that Flex's fingertips had pushed through the armor like skin of the monster.

He felt like a slap from a feather would take him down, but he kept pushing, and through all of the force and energy he was spending, he found a little more power to smile at the words from Perkins.

The sweat rolling down his face wasn't his problem. No, Hunter could deal with that. It was a pounding headache and moments of blackness that took over his vision that was becoming a problem for him. He dipped a few times in the air against his own will. His team in the air above him could hear the heavy breathing that he and Flex released through the coms.

It had taken so much from him, but he had done it. He even urinated on himself in the process, but Hunter swore to tell nobody that secret. Not even Danielle. As he slowly lowered his hands, he could see the blue force field cover the entire city and the beast below it, forcing the monster to stop walking entirely. His timing couldn't have been better as massive chunks of debris and rubble that his team was unable to dispatch hit the force field like meteors falling from the sky. With each collision Hunter could feel the damage on the force field.

His fear was beginning to come true. He thought it would. His force fields were strong. Massively so, but those were normal force fields. He had a theory that the larger the force field, the less damage it could take before it was destroyed. In theory, this worked like a muscle, and the more he created such large fields, they in time would become stronger. Unfortunately for Hunter, he went from semi-personal force fields, to covering a city with no training in between.

"This isn't going to hold long," Hunter said. Even as he spoke, he could feel the cracks spreading in his force field below. He turned in the air to see the Great Beast falling towards him still but at a slower pace and in a slightly different direction. "Atlas," Hunter said slowly as his mouth gaped.

Flex really was doing it. For the first time, Hunter realized just how strong Flex truly was, and even in the world of the powerful, Flex truly was a force to be respected. Hunter often overlooked it because of their past, and because of Flex's youth. Seeing him literally moving a city and the beast it rested upon put things into perspective and made Hunter realize something that he never had.

In their previous fights, Flex had held back. Every time. If he released his true strength, things wouldn't have been as close as they were between the two friends. "Ken Doll, you son of a bitch," Hunter said over the coms with a slight smile. "Huh," Flex said faintly through the coms.

"Nevermind," Hunter said as he began to fly through the sky towards the bottom of the Great Beast. "Guys, I need you to help the force field I put over the city below us," Hunter said as he moved around the slumped wings of the Sonah. "Why? What's up?" Power Prince came back as he signed for the others to move towards the pale blue dome over the city below.

He didn't know why Hunter had given the order, or why Hunter was even giving orders, but he trusted him. An act that Hunter didn't miss as he saw his team fly by them in a slightly different direction towards the city below them.

"The force field I created is large, but not as strong as my smaller ones. Every time it gets hit, I can feel it weaken. Take out any additional debris that you can and then join us when we are finished. Then we enter the city."

"You heard the man," Danielle said as she found a good position above the dome over the immobile Great Beast. She clapped her hands together and began to create a swirling ball of spiked dark energy. Bullets covered the sky from Jen and Perkins, as she continued to form the ball. There was an entire building falling towards her.

She had seen it break away from Sonah as they moved into position. The shift in direction had caused the tall building to break clean off. Not a piece of debris, or a large chunk of rubble, but an entire building. She didn't know if the ball she created would be large enough to take it out, but as the thought ran through her head, Power Prince and Cayden rose in the sky to her side.

"Atlas, I hope the building is empty," Danielle said. "Doesn't matter." Power Prince said slowly as his hands began to glow brighter. "If it hits the force field, they are dead anyway. If it destroys the force field and makes an impact, plenty more will die. It's a tough choice, but one we have to make."

He was right, but Power Prince hated being in these situations, but it was what he signed up for. It was why he took the oath and trained. So that he could make the tough decisions. It hurt him inside, but it was all he could do. "Atlas forgive me," he said slightly under his breath so low that even the coms didn't pick it up.

"Now," he screamed as he clapped his fist together and released a wave of energy that sliced through the building. It destroyed some but left two large halves that kept falling. The smaller pieces were sprayed with the blast from Perkins and Jen.

Danielle released her channeled energy and watched it obliterate one half of the building with such force that she and Power Prince had to cover their eyes. Cayden on the other side had his hands out, and as if time was being fast forwarded, the building rapidly turned to dust. "How does that power work again?" Power Prince said as he looked at the dust field sky.

"Tell you later," Cayden said through gasp of air.

Below the Great Beast Sonah, Flex could feel his fingers going numb. His arms burned as if they were on fire from the inside, yet he found the strength to keep pushing. He could feel the monster shifting and was certain he had done enough to prevent it from crashing into the other Great Beast. Still, he pushed for good measure.

Then he saw another pair of hands near his. "What in Atlas are you doing," Flex said slowly as Hunter, barely able to keep his eyes open, smiled at him. "Helping. Out." His words came out so slow that they barely made sense.

Flex noticed Hunter's eyes close and saw his head dip. "Guys, the force field over the city just vanished," The Mechanic said quickly. Those on shield guard duty all looked below them to see the defenseless city. Most of the debris was handled and any additional chunks seemed to be mere target practice for the trigger-happy Jen and Danielle who seemed to have ample power to burn.

"The city will be fine," Power Prince responded. "Hunter," Flex shouted as he watched his intern fall through the sky unconscious. He wanted to reach for him, but he had to continue to guide the city. "I'll get him," Cayden said as he moved to fly through the sky, even though he feared he wouldn't be able to catch him. Oddly enough, his assistance wasn't needed.

As Hunter fell through the sky something happened. Something that was unexpected, and caused fear in Cayden heart. A wisp of sand seemed to come alive in the air around Hunter and began to swirl in a violent circle around him. As the circle grew large, Hunter's momentum slowed to the point that he was just floating in his newly formed prison of sand.

"Hunter," Danielle said in a gasp as she watched in horror alongside Cayden. The sand swirling around him began to move him closer to a large floating chunk of debris, or perhaps simply a large rock. From their distance, they couldn't tell. What was clear to Cayden and Danielle was who was on top of the rock.

Standing in the front center, her pink hair could be seen even through the night, yet they didn't know how. Surrounding her were four metallic men, each flanked by their Warden's Circle. A loud crashing sound exploded in the silence around them as Flex came over the coms. "It's. Done."

He shook his arms to relieve the pain in them and turned around to see what they were all looking at across the night's sky. While his team was in shock of Omega's sudden appearance, he could feel fury forming in his sore body. They had him. Paragon. Hunter. His friend was being held by a Warden now.

His body looked as if he was a child in the metal creature's hands. Then he dropped him. Not off of the rock to plummet to his death. No. He dropped Hunter at Omega's feet. The same position where countless others ended their lives.

CHAPTER 35:
REUNION

They were all too shocked and tired, to speak. The use of their powers to such a degree had left most of them drained save for Danielle and Power Prince. Danielle was fuelled by the darkness around them, giving her power reserves beyond her normal limits. Power Prince, well he was a living battery. As far as he knew he couldn't run out of energy. While his energy may have been limitless, his body wasn't. It still had limits, and even though he wasn't tired, he knew eventually he would have to slow down to recover. Even Perkins and Jen were feeling like they could use a breather.

In the distance, the sounds of buildings could still be heard crashing as the cries and screams from across the Sand Wasteland filled the air slightly. The residents of Acropolis were doing all they could to survive as their world literally came crashing down.

One by one, each member of Flex's team slowly landed on the ground as they saw Omega do the same on the large floating platform she occupied. Flex was the last to arrive at a scene that looked like a classic showdown between two forces. As he began to descend, he allowed his anger to hold as he looked at his team.

He couldn't say it, not right now, but he was proud of them and what they had accomplished. Even Jen and Danielle, by far the biggest rebels of the bunch, now that Hunter was coming into his own, had performed without question and to the best of their abilities. As they waited on the ground below him, all he could see were their stone faces. Neither woman was joking or cracking smiles like normal. Danielle, with eyes as a dark as bottomless pits, stood prepared with her hands up as if she was going to enter a boxing ring.

Jen, large sword drawn and in hand, had more of a crouching stand. Her time training with Sasha really had paid off. The blaster she used while in the air was back with Perkins now, as she aimed both of the weapons across the sand towards Omega. Even from where he was above them, Flex could see her green eyes glowing as she analyzed the darkness around them.

A faint glow of pink light pulsed below. Causing shadows to dance on the sand. Power Prince, his second in command, his team member able to generate raw unmatched energy on a supreme scale was standing there. Hands at his side and his body tilted so that his shoulder faced the enemy.

A slight smile tugged at the corners of Flex's mouth. Power Prince, his obsession for tv and movies aside, always was smart in a fight. Now he was just trying to make himself a smaller target. No doubt he had seen several of the large Gunners in each Warden's Circle, and the imposing cannons they held like toys in their hand. Flex let out a sigh. Even a smaller target wouldn't help in this fight.

Cayden was the only one that seemed out of place. Flex didn't know why but the young Icon had a confused look on his face. Like he had seen a ghost, but he had seen Omega and a Warden's Circle before. What could he- "Why don't you come on down?" A voice hissed through the silence.

Flex quickly turned his head and looked down to the source of the suggestion. She had a passive face as her hands were resting in the pockets of the green jacket she wore. Flex could feel his anger reignite as he could see that she had placed her large boot on Hunter's neck. Everything inside of him wanted to rip their entire force apart, but he couldn't. As he began to descend, he could see the four Pain Conduits in their midst.

They were oddly close to each other. Standing, as if they were covering someone up, but Flex couldn't see anything. He had descended too close to the ground before he had noticed it. Had he still been in the air, maybe he could have figured out what they were up too.

“Four of them,” Flex said to himself. A whisper came back over his coms. “The women are the Pain Conduits, right?” It was Jen. “Yep,” Cayden responded under his breath. “I’ll handle them,” she replied calmly. Flex admired her confidence, but she hadn’t seen or felt the power of even one Pain Conduit, not to mention the combined might of four. “Hold your ground. Nobody moves until I say so.”

Omega clapped slightly at hearing his words. “Smart.” As she spoke four of the Wardens around her seemed to spread out as they leaped off the platform that now rested on the ground. They all took steps and moved as if they shared a single mind. Perkins swallowed as she saw the metal creatures seemingly come to life. She told herself she didn’t care, but deep down she wondered. Was one of them him? Her brother that had abandoned her. Was he among them now?

She raised her blaster that had dipped slightly and shook her head. None of that mattered and she had a new family now. One that needed her protection for as long as she could. “I take it, you’re the one who defeated Manis,” Omega said as she leaned in closer without actually moving her feet. The distance between them wasn’t great but she wasn’t directly in Flex’s face either.

“I always thought Manis was strong. One of the main reasons I offered to help his power was that I knew he could be great. Stronger than anything or anyone. Even my Wardens.” She glanced to the Warden closest to her and shook her head.

“I love my children, but facts are facts. They’re strong, but Manis with my help...” She shook her head and sucked her teeth. “Special.” She stopped talking and looked to the side as the glow from the fires in her city lit the skyline. “Now I see I was wrong.” “Give me-” Flex’s words were cut short as Omega applied pressure to the boot on Hunter’s neck. As she did so, her Warden seems to come to life.

One suddenly had swirls of sand spinning around him, as he floated off the ground. Another had fire dancing in one hand, while cool tendrils of ice encased the other, all while a body of water moved around him like a serpent. The remaining two Wardens still did nothing. They simply stood there. Faceless creatures that were positioned to look directly at Flex.

"You know how many people you've killed tonight? How many of *my* people perished because of what you did to Sonah?" Omega asked. This time she wasn't as smooth with her tone. "Far fewer than the amount you have killed throughout the Sections of Mo'eizus," Perkins replied from behind Flex. "Let's not forget, they're not even your people. Not truly."

Omega pursed her lips and nodded her head. "They chose to be at my feet, and not in my shadow." "Don't nerfing try it," Perkins screamed. Her reaction caught several of them by surprise. The Gunners all aimed at the blond spikey- haired body of Perkins across from them. Still Perkins continued her verbal carnage.

"None of them chose The Curse of Varo. You chose to not help them like you did your precious residents of Acropolis. Then any who tried to oppose you, tried to give a slither of power back to the people were wiped out. Don't talk to me about choices." Perkins was breathing hard now, and Cayden glanced at her through the corner of his eye.

He thought that his brother would have loved to seen what just happened. "This is going nowhere," Danielle said as she stepped in front of Flex. "Either give us Hunter or we take him." Omega's brow raised as Flex repositioned himself to stand in front of Danielle. She may have been brave and fueled by anger, but Flex was nearly invulnerable.

"Sorry, but I can't do that." Omega said slowly as she looked down at Hunter. "I need him." Danielle's eyes narrowed. "You're still stuck on this King and Queen shit?" As she spoke Flex could have sworn, he saw the darkness around them ripple. Not some energy generated by Danielle, but the literal darkness around them seemed to pulse. He looked at Danielle again, but this time he had confusion on his face. The question found its way in his head. Just how strong was Danielle really? For most of the time she had spent with the lords, she never really showed how much she was able to do, but since they had arrived on this new world, time and time again she was letting her true power shine.

"You know when I realized you were attacking my city, I put plans in motion to send a message," Omega said as her audience looked at her in confusion. "To be so bold as to attack Sonah, to try to destroy Acropolis, couldn't go unanswered. Right now, my forces are in place on the Great Beast Arzi. Mostly normal guards, but they have a little surprise with them." Flex and Cayden both moved to advance, but as they did so Omega smirked and shook her head while leaning in and pushing her boot down harder on Hunter's throat.

"Your home will be destroyed. Blood will paint the street red, fire will rain down on those below, and every Spellborn will know that Bravado brought my fury down on them," Omega said with a slight eye roll. It was as if the destruction of an entire city was normal practice for her.

"Oh no. Oh no." The rapid voice of The Mechanic came over the coms. Several members of the team looked toward Flex for direction on how to handle the new development. Power Prince thought it would be better to divide forces, but at what cost. He felt they were screwed on all fronts, and he didn't like that *surprise* that Omega spoke of.

Omega release a long sigh, removed her boot from the unconscious Hunter's neck, and placed a hand on his head. The pure orange glow from her hands covered his entire body in seconds, and was gone just as fast. Flex and his team didn't even have time to react before gasps filled the air, and Hunter shot straight up from his slumber.

He was breathing hard now. As if he had just run tens of miles in the last few minutes. The sound of air rushing from his nose seemed to boom around them. He looked up at Omega standing above himself and could see her smiling down on him. He scampered backwards to move but then, something happened that he didn't expect.

As he placed his hand down to move, it crushed the stone surface below him into dust. He looked at his hand, still breathing so hard that he could barely hear anything else. "What the?" he began to speak. "It's going to take some getting used to, but I needed you strong for what comes next," Omega said as she extended a hand down to him.

Hunter looked at the hand in front of him and then across the sand to his friends, all standing there as confused as he was. Against his better judgement, he extended his own hand and allowed Omega to help him up. The mere contact of their skin was enough to make Danielle advance, but Flex had an iron grip on her shoulder in seconds. "Not yet," he said slowly. "Something is going on here."

Omega rubbed the access debris off of Hunter's chest and looked him up and down. "You're going to save us all." Hunter's eyes narrowed. "I took your powers and created newer versions of them for you." Omega continued. "Whatever you could do before, you can still do, but at a far greater scale."

Hunter looked down to where he was moments ago and at the destruction, he caused by simply placing his hand down too hard. "My strength," he said as he looked at his hand. "Far beyond your normal limits," Omega said as she looked at him. "I dare say you might even be able to give him a run for his money." Hunter let that sink in for a second. He was almost as strong as Flex?

"Naturally your new abilities won't work on me," Omega said as she took a step back from Hunter and extended her hand towards his friends. "That's part of the package. Although, because of the part you play in our future, I gave you a bonus. Unlike any of my other children I create, your power will not leave when my time finally comes to pass. I could be long gone, but you never know just what Mo'eizus could need from its savior." Hunter looked at Omega.

He was confused at what she was saying. None of it made sense to him. In her eyes looking back at him was something he didn't expect. It was hope. The same look of wonder a child gave Santa at the mall. The same look of a mother watching her child graduate. Whatever Omega needed from him, she truly believed in, and it was more than just the hope of giving her a child.

Then it was gone. In an instant. The look of hope, that made Hunter think for a moment that Omega wasn't as bad as he thought, was wiped away as she gave a snap of her fingers. Instantly the Pain Conduits leaped forward. Flex's eyes went wide as he prepared for the onslaught of pain to wash over them all, but nothing came.

Instead, the Pain Conduits, all four of them changed one by one. They became intangible. Sinking through the sand below them as their arms moved frantically. Flex quickly looked back to Jen, and instead found an empty space. She had ignored his orders, and turned invisible during all of the commotion of Hunter's return. Flex couldn't see her, but he was willing to bet that she was across the field and was the cause of the Pain Conduits sudden intangibility. "Guess she really could take care of them," Cayden said.

"What a woman," he continued. "Easy, lover," Danielle said while never taking her eyes off of the growing tension in front of them. "She's spoken for back home." Omega looked around in surprise as her Pain Conduits seemingly turned to ghosts and descended through the sand- covered ground. While surprised, she didn't lose her composure. Hunter had scampered away and run towards Flex and Danielle. He wanted to fly towards them, but with his new power, he feared how that would turn out.

The last thing he wanted was to end up in the atmosphere. "Nice to have you back, boo," Danielle said as she winked at Hunter, but never dropped her guard. Hunter looked at her and gave a slight nod as he took up position behind Flex. "What are you doing?" Flex asked.

"Helping," Hunter responded. "New powers or not, I have to try. Plus, didn't you hear? I'm stronger than you now. I'll be fine." Flex rolled his eyes. "Not how I heard it, but-" his words were cut off as the wind rushed past them.

In a sudden pop of sound, he was there. "I knew it!" Hunter said as the sand storms created from the new arrival died down. He looked almost the same as he did when they last saw him. Tall and muscular with an inhumanly large chest. His salt and pepper hair was longer now. The shaggy layer covered his ears and was accompanied by the thick beard he now sported.

He wasn't in the expensive suits or hero gear he was known for. No, he wore white tattered clothes. Similar to those of Acropolis. Hunter suspected that the clothes were perfect before the fires and destruction caused by the city falling. "Impervious," Flex said as he looked at his mentor and friend.

"You're..." his words were cut off. "I'm fine," Impervious said. Danielle and Perkins seemed to be the only people who were concerned by the power in his voice. "Flex," Perkins said as Danielle took a step forward and stood beside Hunter. Before they could voice their concerns, Jen reappeared beside them.

Her sudden shift to visible from invisible caused Cayden to jump. "Call me crazy but he doesn't look like he needs saving," Jen said. "My thoughts exactly," Power Prince replied. The young hero had been quiet up until now. Even Hunter's return didn't earn a response. Power Prince had been a hero longer than most of them. He knew there was time for celebration and reunions, but that came after they were all home and safe.

Something that for now, they weren't. As he stood there, he noticed how Impervious looked very healthy. Normally a person held captive showed signs of malnourishment, muscle atrophy, or even pale skin. Impervious had none. True, it could have simply been that, like everything else, he was Impervious to those effects too. Still, Power Prince was weary.

He knew how fast Impervious was. For Impervious the world moved in slow motion when his speed was used. So, he could have joined either side, but he chose to stand with Omega. Power Prince wasn't sure how his friends missed it. In the back of his head, he realized that he was still thinking like a leader.

"The city's in ruins," Impervious said to Omega as he glared at Flex. "The lab?" she asked. "Secured," Impervious replied. "The data, research, everything." Omega didn't speak and instead nodded her head. "Atlas no," Hunter said slowly as he looked over at his uncle. "You're working with her?" He said slowly. "We thought," "you thought exactly as you were supposed to," another familiar voice said from behind the remaining members of the Warden's Circle.

Cayden gasped as he stepped forward. Earlier he thought he was simply seeing things. That all the adrenalin was getting to him. He now knew he was wrong. He had seen exactly what he thought through the Warden's Circle. They all knew that voice, but couldn't understand why it was coming from across the sand where their enemies were. Perkins frowned as the owner of the voice stepped forward.

There he was, dark-skinned and menacing. The same eyes Perkins and Cayden had known for so long. The eyes of a friend. A brother. "Cord," Perkins said slowly in a cracked voice. Cayden, couldn't find the words to express what he was feeling. His knees suddenly felt weak, and against his own will, he could feel his lip quiver. As Cord walked closer to where Impervious and Omega stood, his face began to melt.

Power Prince and Jen both grimaced their faces as they watched a man seemingly turn to wax and melt away. From within the wax face came a new voice of laughter. "Not quite." The voice had an odd accent to it. As if it had spoken in a dozen different languages, and created a new one in the process.

"The man you knew as Cord, died in that building ambush so long ago." "Icaro," Cayden said as he finally found the power to speak. He didn't say the man's name in the calm fashion of a statement. It more so sounded like he was accusing the man, the way he spat the name out. Hunter's mind raced for a moment.

Where had he heard that name before. Then it hit him. When they first arrived, and had the debriefing with Cord. He mentioned that they were betrayed by a man posing as one of their own. A man called Icaro. A Spellborn assassin that could shape shift into the figure of people he consumed. "Atlas, it's been you all the time." Hunter said out loud.

"Well, I'm lost," Jen said. Power Prince felt the same way but remained quiet. "All the random disappearances to scout, the time you needed alone to think. Everything," Hunter continued. "You were passing information to them." Cayden's eyes widen as Hunter's conclusion finally set in. He had seen it all along and didn't even notice it.

How many times had he said his brother was behaving differently. Was treating him in a way that wasn't normal. He had assumed that the ambush, and losing their team had changed him. In reality, it never was him. His brother was gone. Dead, and discarded. There wasn't even a body to pay respects to.

He wiped a tear from his check that he didn't realize was there. "So, the pieces fall into place at last," Icaro said. His face was hard to see through the wax-like sludge from when he was Cord. Flex felt this was done intentionally to conceal his true face.

"No, they haven't," Impervious said as he used his speed to move from beside Omega to in front of her in an instant. The Warden's Circle around her didn't even have time to react. Before they could move, Impervious' hand was impaled in her chest. Her gasp cut through the air as blood flowed from her mouth and she dropped to her knee.

She tried to speak, but her words came out gurgled as Impervious removed his hand and left a hole in the place where only moments ago it was solid. The Wardens dashed towards him, but their movements were pointless. As Omega's life faded, so did their power. Each member around them slowly began to change.

With each step, they took, the glass- like formation that took them over spread through their bodies. In mere moments they were surrounded by glass statues of what was once several Warden's Circles.

Hunter's eyes darted from side to side as the events unfolded. "I can't keep up with all of this," Power Prince said. His glowing fists were up and alive with energy, but he had no target. Icaro looked down to the lifeless body of Omega and at the glass statues around him. He didn't know what was going on, and for the most part, he didn't care.

He had only one goal in mind, and that was his survival. "Doesn't this change our agreement?" the wax-faced man asked. Impervious wiped the blood from his hand on his white pants as he shook his head. "No. When the cure is perfected, I will summon you."

"Well as much as this reunion was fun, I think I'll be leaving now." He moved to take a step and found a bolt of energy hit the ground where his foot would have been. "Stick around," Perkins said slowly as she kept her gun raised. "This, reunion as you call it, is far from over."

CHAPTER 36:
FROM IDOLS TO RIVALS

Icaro turned slowly and faced Perkins who stood beside Cayden. The two people who knew his recent persona the most. Likely the two who were hurt the most. Icaro had dealt with this sort of thing before. In the past, he would have just killed them, but this damn Curse of Varo had made him weak. Literally.

He could feel it as the bleeding increased. He wasn't as formidable as he once was. His only hope rested with Impervious, and this plan he had. This plan that he had assured him would work. Although a crashing city wasn't part of said plan. He had begun to think that they had underestimated these brats from the start.

Icaro had warned them what the team was going to do, and they still just barely made it out in time. Seeing as how Impervious just killed Omega, his efforts to pass on the information was pointless.

"Impervious. Davis," Flex said slowly as he stepped towards the man that he once looked up to. "What in Atlas is going on here?" Impervious put his hands on his hips and then rubbed them through his beard. He looked at Flex and it genuinely hurt him how the young Icon looked. He was confused, scared, and angry all in one yet he still played the role of leader for the team. A role that he had left for him to fill.

His eyes looked at them all one by one. His old team and interns, along with two of the young rebels he had met when he arrived here. "I suppose I do owe you answers," "I'd say so, yes," Hunter added in.

Impervious took a deep breath. "When I arrived here, I found a planet, not like the one I left. The elite families were all but forgotten, and this damn curse was spreading. So, I wanted to help. I had turned my back on the Spellborn before, and as a result, the Battle of Ages took place."

Hunter felt a slight prickle of goosebumps as the event that killed his parents was referenced. "I couldn't let that happen again. I wouldn't betray my people twice. So, I joined Bravado. I figured with my help they could regain control from Omega and slowly, with me at the head, I could restore order. Save the people. Cord and Cayden were elite but they didn't want to lead. Who else but me could? Perkins was holding the rebels together, but she was burnt out, and still hurting from her brother's actions. So, I sent her to your world. Figured maybe she could get a breather, and learn somethings in the process."

He paused for a moment and a glance went toward Perkins. "I didn't expect her to end up with Flex, though." For a moment Flex wondered how Impervious even knew about him and Perkins. Then he realized that Icaro must have been very detailed in his reports back. Impervious continued talking, despite the looks on some of his former team's faces. "Then the ambush came, and Icaro entered the picture."

Impervious glanced to the wax-faced man, who in turn did a slight bow. His movement, slight as it was, was met by a single shot from Perkins. "Stay still," she said. "I was about to kill him when he told me that Omega had a treatment for the Curse of Varo. That he was just doing his job to secure treatment, and that the rumors were true, and that if I spared him, he would share all that he knew. So, I agreed, and decided to look into it. Then I found out the truth and with it, an alliance was created."

"And what exactly was this truth?" Power Prince asked. Impervious fought a smile. Power Prince had come so far from the boy that joined the Imperial Lords just after an internship. Impervious always knew that Kevin had potential, and the name Power Prince would eventually go down in history books beside the big guns of their time. As Impervious saw the young man now, bursting with power at his fingertips, clearly upset, but unwavering in battle, he knew he had made the right decision to ask him to join the Imperial Lords. He truly hoped that Kevin's future wouldn't end here. On some other dimensional planet in the sand with forgotten beast.

"The truth was that Omega was dying. She too had caught The Curse of Varo. She had it for ages, but her powers kept her healthy. It was becoming harder and harder for her to heal, so she got desperate. When people get desperate, they do unthinkable things. I confronted her, and she confessed to having a cure, but at my expense."

Hunter could hear the shift in his voice as Impervious paused and looked down slightly. "She had Will didn't she." Hunter finally asked. Impervious nodded as several people looked at Hunter at once. All but Cayden and Danielle seemed confused. They had seen the body in the lab. Had seen the tubes, and test. "What does Infinity have to do with anything?" Danielle asked.

"His name was Will," Impervious said slowly but in a strong tone. He shut his eyes for a second and turned away from them slightly. "He was my son, and I abandoned him all those years ago." He took another deep breath. "When I returned here with his body, I buried him in the Sand Wasteland. In the same spot where my family's garden once was. Somehow, she found out, and in her desperation, she ran a test on him. She knew what he was. While Will didn't live in the East Section, many knew of the power he had wielded. Omega thought that one as powerful as Will could have hidden abilities, or stolen powers, to defeat the Curse of Varo."

"Atlas," Jen said slowly. Impervious shook his head and raised a hand. "In the end, she was right. Through Will, a treatment was created. Turns out the blood from a Spellborn and human hybrid does the trick. If done correctly it produces a potent treatment to keep the disease away. That's why the people of Acropolis never seemed to have it. The cure was available to them without hesitation."

"None of this explains why you vanished. Why you created the story that you had been captured. Why you sent Icaro back to them as Cord." Hunter said, as he looked his uncle in the eyes. Flex was the first to answer this time. "It was for you." Hunter and Danielle looked at Flex in confusion. "Me?" Hunter asked. "I'm not sure why," Flex said. "But you and Will have one thing in common. You're both Spellborn, human hybrids."

The weight of his words slammed into Hunter like a slap to the face from an angry lover. He could remember what Cord or Icaro said to him when he arrived. How he could save them all. He thought he meant because he was elite, but now he wasn't so sure. "Flex is right," Impervious said as he looked at Hunter slowly. "Will is dead. Has been for a long time. All of our studies show that, if the blood comes from a hybrid that is alive, it will be strong enough to cure the virus."

"And that's why she wanted you," Cayden said as he made effort not to look at Icaro. "She needed you by her side and strong to provide her with the cure. You're blood. You're the only other hybrid of your kind." Hunter glared at his uncle now. "So that's it? You want me to be a lab rat? Your only living relative?" Impervious shook his head.

"I don't want that, no. But my people need it. I told you, I turned my back on them once, and nobody will make me do it again. Nobody is going to die this time because of my actions. Not anymore."

"Well, sorry to break it to you, but Hunter isn't going to be plugged up and drained just for your magic cure. You can suck a bag of zebra dicks before I let that happen," Danielle said. "Let?" Impervious asked.

"Looks like some decisions still need to be made huh?" Impervious said as he looked at Flex. "Omega wasn't joking. Plans are in motion to destroy to the city on Great Beast Arzi. The guards are manageable. They likely could be stopped by a normal citizen if they banded together. But that Manis," Impervious said as he shook his head and whistled. "Omega gave him a similar boost to Hunter's. It wasn't permanent, but it wasn't set to die if she did. Manis was more of a trial case. He got the new powers created for a few hours to try them out, and was given immunity on any carnage he could create in that time."

As Impervious spoke, he glanced at Flex whose eyes were wide now. He remembered Manis from the fight they had. While Manis wasn't as strong as Flex, he damn sure wasn't as far off as his team was led to believe. The purple, stony skinned man was plenty strong then, and with am augmentation from Omega he would be leagues stronger now.

Flex turned to Hunter. "I need you to fight." "What?" Hunter began to ask, but Flex cut him off. "I know your powers are new now, but with Manis in the city, we need to have somebody there to match him, and that's going to be me." Hunter didn't speak but he shook his head.

"I didn't train you to run away, Flex," Impervious said. Flex fought all the urges in his body to lash out at his former mentor. "Power Prince, Danielle, and Jen. You're with me to protect the city. Paragon, Cayden, and Perkins can keep things under control here." "Seriously," Danielle began to protest, but Flex shook his head. "Not now."

Danielle gave a pleading glance to Hunter, who in return gave a slight nod to her. She took a deep breath and her flight band on her wrist began to glow as she rose in the air. Power Prince and Jen followed her. Flex looked across the sand at Impervious once more.

"I expected better from you," Flex said to him. "And you're right. You didn't train me to run away. You trained me to value life, and to know how to use my resources. You trained me to be a hero." Impervious looked away slightly as Flex rose into the air, and took off towards Arzi.

After he was gone, Impervious seemed to regain his composure and inhaled once more as he looked at the team before him. He knew them all. Loved them all, and to a certain extent would fight to the death for them all. But he had a loyalty to his people. "I'm sure none of you missed the fact that Flex left all the Spellborn together to work out their differences. Either way, if Hunter comes with me, none of you will have to die. None will suffer. Under my rule, the cure will be given out for free. The murders, and plotting on the other sections stop. I will reclaim this world in a way that only an elite Spellborn can. Can't you see that?" His words came out as a plea as he stepped towards them.

Sadly, they didn't move, and Hunter didn't step forward to sacrifice himself. They all stood their ground. Weapons were drawn, eyes wide, and powers at the ready. Perkins kept her blaster pointed at Icaro, and Cayden popped several tiny cubes in his mouth and began to chew. "As you wish," Impervious said in little more than a whisper. Then it happened. He was gone in a blur of speed as he began his assault on the very people he once trained and called his friends.

CHAPTER 37:
DUST AMONG THE SAND

Perkins, during the entire conversation, never truly let her gaze or her guns fall from Icaro. She couldn't. A person with his abilities could be there one second and gone the next once he consumed another person. It had long been suspected that the spy would keep portions of prior victims preserved and on his person, if he needed a quick escape. Her never-failing watch over the spy came to an abrupt stop when the blood-stained white shirt suddenly appeared in front of her.

Impervious was a mountain of a man. Something made evident as he stood and towered over Perkins. From pure reaction, Perkins looked up at Impervious and unloaded both blasters in his chest as she leaped back. She may as well had been shooting a wall of steel with rubber bands. The bolts of energy destroyed his shirt, but left skin that was pure and damage free. There weren't even faint red spots from the heat.

In an instant, Impervious snatched both blasters from Perkin's hand and crushed them with as much effort that was required to crumble paper. For a split second, she looked at her now empty hands and felt rage that her favorite blasters were gone. Had this been normal circumstance, she would have been making a plan in her head on how to replace them. Sadly, she didn't have the time to do much of anything, because everything that was happening to her, did so all in the span of a few seconds.

One minute she was pointing her guns at Icaro, the next she was defenseless, and being lifted into the air by an inhumanly strong hand. Perkins swung at Impervious, but the powerhouse caught her arm and broke it quickly. Pain that could have only been matched by the Pain Conduits rushed through her body.

Her head was suddenly throbbing, and she was finding it hard to focus. Behind her, she could hear air rushing around her, and she realized she had been thrown with such force that the sand below her dispersed. How could he be that fast? To do so much to her in less than a minute's time. She expected to crash into the sand, and with the speed at which she was moving, it was going to hurt.

Instead, she found herself being snatched out of the air by a force field. She was still in pain, tons of it, but she was thankful that the force field was there for her. As she tried to regain focus, Perkins realized that the force field she was in, wasn't the pale blue energy from Hunter that she had come to love. Instead, it was a vibrant, pulsing white orb of energy with blue swirls here and there.

It wasn't painful for her, despite the random streaks of white electricity that pulsed from the field. "You're fine," A voice said as the force field faded away after she was placed on the ground. Cayden was speaking while Hunter was standing over her.

"No, I'm not," Perkins said through gritted teeth. Hunter was surprised to find that his force fields now appeared to be white, and not the pale blue color he had known most of his life. These new powers created by Omega must have been so much more potent than his own that they looked different. Now that he thought about it, he could remember the energy feeling different when he created it.

Across the sands, Icaro realized that he had gone from being in the crosshairs to being free. Impervious for some reason or another chose to attack Perkins first, even though she posed almost no real threat. Icaro played back what he knew about Impervious compared to what he knew about his fellow Spellborn that were fighting him.

None of them truly posed a threat to Impervious. His name said it all. He watched as a beam of white light ripped apart the night around him. Hunter was unleashing blast after blast of the white energy from his eyes, as Impervious approached and swatted them away with little effort.

Cayden, the man who he had acted like was his brother, was crouched over the injured Perkins. Icaro felt bad for them slightly. They really weren't of any use to Hunter. Perkins was injured, and Cayden didn't have power suited for the type of enemy that Impervious proved to be. Icaro took several small steps backward from the fight.

He kept quiet, as he reached into his pocket, looking for the slither of jerky he had stashed there. It was the skin of a man he had killed before he became Cord. A normal man. A nobody. Somebody that could move through the world and people wouldn't notice him. The perfect form to use as he got some things in place to leave the East Section, and wait for word from Impervious once he finished with these children. Icaro only hoped that he could last long enough.

As he continued to move back and chew the jerky something began to happen. The darkness from which he moved began to change. It was almost as if a pink light was being aimed directly towards him. The ground around him suddenly went from dark to being a beacon of vibrant pink. Icaro looked up above him, his waxy face slowly beginning to take shape of the new form.

From where he was, it looked like a meteor was falling through the sky with pink trails behind it. He narrowed his eyes and realized that it wasn't a meteor at all. It was a person. A person with glowing fist of energy and a smirk on his face. Before he could react, the falling force was upon him and the ground exploded as impact was made. Sand peppered the area as Impervious and Hunter continued to fight.

Power Prince stood in the round crater he had created with Icaro's lifeless form below him. His face was half wax, and half middle-aged man with long white hair. "Well, that's one problem solved." Power Prince said as he turned and witnessed Paragon going toe to toe with his own uncle. A few feet from them, Cayden was leaning over Perkins as if he were some sort of human shield.

With his hands glowing, Power Prince released some of his energy and was propelled into the air as he was sent flying to the two Spellborn. "I thought you were with Flex," Perkins said as she squirmed in pain. "I made an executive decision in my leadership role. How you two holding up?" Power Prince asked as he looked Cayden over.

He couldn't see anything wrong with him. The kid didn't even really look shaken up. He was clearly strong for his age. Growing up in a rebel group likely did that to a kid. Losing his brother wasn't going to make life easier on him either. "All things considered, we're fine," Cayden said as he looked beyond Power Prince to Hunter.

"We need to help him." Power Prince nodded. "I'm on it. Keep her safe," he said as he ran towards the fight. From where Cayden watched he couldn't help but be in awe. Watching Hunter and Power Prince fight Impervious was a sight to behold. Not because of how strong they were, but because of how resistant Impervious was. Nothing seemed to be able to stop him.

"We can't win this. Not against him," Perkins said as she propped herself up from the ground. Cayden tried to keep her flat, but she pushed his arm away. "I've got a broken arm, not a gunshot wound," she said. She hoped that the rest of her friends were having better luck in the city because as of now, the fight wasn't going their way.

Hunter slowly got to his feet and could see Power Prince stretched out on the ground. His fist had turned back to normal now. Impervious was walking slowly over to him at first and then ran, jumped, and drew his fist back to deliver a blow as he fell. Hunter stretched his hand out and created one of his new force fields over Power Prince. Impervious' blow struck the force field and sent him back several feet.

He turned and looked at his nephew. "You do know this is pointless? Right?" Hunter could see the glow return to his fallen friend's fist, and he removed the force field. Impervious glanced over his shoulder and nodded his head. "Kevin, fancy entrance considered, I still think you were better off with Flex. Leave this matter to the Spellborn people while you still can."

Power Prince wiped some blood from his mouth and blinked his eyes a few times. One was beginning to swell, and from where Hunter stood, he could see the eye change color slightly. "So you're just going to kill me? Kill us?" Power Prince asked. "I don't want to, but I will to save my people and this world," Impervious said. "I wish-" His words were cut off as a force field wrapped around his head and slammed him to the ground. Impervious wasted no time in attacking the force field. Hunter could feel the blows but was happy to see that the energy barrier remained strong. "Thank you, Empress Queen Omega," he said under his breath.

With eyes full of crackling white energy, he ran towards his uncle. The landscape looked different for Hunter now. Back when his powers were blue, everything around him just looked like he was wearing blue tinted glasses when he summoned his Impact Blast. With this new power though it looked as if he were looking at the world through a black and white filter. A filter with flashes of blue here and there.

As he ran towards Impervious, He slung the force field around his uncle's head towards Power Prince and then removed the force field. As the force field faded away, right on time Power Prince with a fist glowing with so much energy that it seemed like they were in pink daylight, delivered a direct punch to Impervious' chin.

The punch connected with such force that while not loaded with super strength, it still sent Impervious a foot or two in the air. At the same time, Hunter released his Impact Blast aimed directly at Impervious' face. The blow should have least landed and given them some breathing room to think. Sadly, things don't always work how they should.

In seconds, with speed beyond what the eye could see, Impervious corrected himself in the air, reached out and grabbed Power Prince, and hurled the hero into the beam of oncoming energy. Hunter's eyes went wide as Power Prince screamed as the energy pummeled him. He was sent several dozen feet into the distance. A pink dot could be seen where he landed, and then faded out.

Impervious looked at the spot where the light was and then turned back to Hunter. "Are you done? Or should I stop taking it easy on you all?" Hunter balled his fist. This was taking it easy? "Come with me, and nobody has to die," Impervious said as he moved closer to Hunter.

Instinct taking over, Hunter moved and stood in front of Cayden and Perkins. "Hey guys," he said as he stood over them, trying his best to sound positive and unbothered. "I respect them sticking by you like this. My team did the same for me when I decided to do what I did. Those that didn't eventually come around. So, I get it. But at the same time nephew, you have to think about them."

Hunter titled his head slightly. "You're going to let them die for you? The way I see it, you don't come with me willingly, they fight, they die, and eventually, you tire. Then I take you to the lab and the testing starts. You'll be taken care of, feed, clothed, housed, -" "You'd turn me into a pet?" Hunter shot back.

Impervious laughed. "I'd say well taken care of savior to his own people. If you come with me willingly, then they all live for now. I say for now because eventually, they will try to stop me. Force my hand, and then they would die. Either way, time is on my side. Nothing you throw at me can hurt me."

Hunter took a deep breath and prepared himself for the fight to continue. The best he could do would be to try to hold him off, and not get captured long enough for the others to arrive. Even still, what could they do to Impervious? He was, and always would be a force of nature. Nothing could hurt him. Time truly was on his side.

Or was it. Hunter's brow raised. Something that Impervious didn't miss. In the distance, Hunter could see a figure walking slowly toward them. Power Prince had survived. Hunter took a slight step back. "You can still hear me, right?" he said under his breath.

Cayden and Perkins both responded at the same time. "I think I have a way out of this. It will either work or be utterly pointless. Cayden be ready." Confusion took control of Cayden's face as he looked from Perkins to Hunter. "Okay," he said slowly, not sure of where this was going.

With those words, Hunter created a force field the size of a small arena, stopping it just before Power Prince, and locking him outside. Power Prince stumbled as the sudden force field pushed him back some. "Let me in," he screamed as he pointlessly banged the bottom of his fist against it. "Who am I kidding?" he said as she slowly slid down the force field and stretched out in the sand. A few seconds passed, and then he got an idea. Quickly he jumped to his feet and began to run around the dome, ignoring the pain that his body was in.

Impervious looked around him as the crackling white orb pulsed around them all. "What's this? An attempt at a final effort?" "Not at all," Hunter said. "Just keeping you in place. I honestly thought we were fucked until you said something. You said time was on your side. Then I realized it wasn't. It is on our side though. Literally."

Impervious' eyes shifted from Hunter to Cayden who was now standing beside Hunter. A smirk came on his face, that was replaced by a snarl. He took a slight step forward and Hunter created yet another force field. This time in front of himself, Cayden and Perkins. Impervious moved across the distance separating them in the blink of an eye, only to find the force field in his way.

Hunter took a few slow breaths to keep himself focused. He tried not to look around at the newly tiny space he had locked himself in. "I know what you're thinking," Impervious said from behind the force field. "It won't work." Hunter smiled for the first time and fought back the urge to wince from the pain his entire body felt from the fight.

"You say that, but those gray hairs you flaunt say differently. I remember the picture you showed me last year of yourself and my dad. A younger, and less gray you. It made me realize that you do age. Finally, something the mighty Impervious can't stand up to. Something as simple as time. Fitting that one force of nature can eliminate another."

As Hunter said his last words, another force field came into life behind Impervious. He was locked down like a rat in a box. "I'm sorry it came to this," Hunter said as he gave Cayden a slight nod. Cayden raised both hands, as a small opening was created in the force field wall in front of them.

"Have at it," Hunter said slowly. Cayden didn't speak, he simply took a breath. Through it all Impervious didn't show fear. He stood tall, with a smile on his face and flashing perfect teeth. Then the smile faded as Impervious grunted, and his knees buckled. His eyes were wide as something he felt for the first time in a long time touched him. Pain. He could feel it, slowly at first, then it spread through him like a fire.

Hunter fought the urge to turn away as he watched his uncle age in front of them all. Even Perkins on the ground was watching with her mouth gaped. She knew Cayden's power but never had seen it like this.

What it was doing to Impervious was almost hard for her to watch. The locks of salt and pepper hair turned completely gray and then began to thin. The inhuman muscles that covered his body began to shrink, leaving loose skin in their place. His eyes became yellow and then milky and slowly those perfect teeth turned discolored and fell out.

Cayden was visibly under strain now. His arms began to shake and his face was contorted with concentration as he willed the time inside the force field box to rapidly push forward. Hunter looked at the young Spellborn as he began to breathe hard, and had a forehead covered in fresh sweat.

The mountain that was Impervious was little more than a withered hill now. Power Prince stood only a few feet from them as he watched in horror as the unstoppable man he knew, withered away in front of him.

Impervious, or the thing that was once Impervious, was on all hands and knees now. Skin so thin that it seemed transparent. "Ah," Cayden said as he leaned in closer and stretched his fingers wide.

With his screams, the bones began to visibly break down in front of them all, and then they continued to break. Bone after bone, crumbled, as the body was stretched in the sand. Each broken bone continued to change, and in seconds only dust covered the area where the once mighty, and unstoppable Mr. Impervious stood.

"Cayden," Perkins said loudly. He still had his hands stretched out. "Cayden, it's over," Perkins slowly slid towards him from the ground. "We. Won," she said in a whisper as she watched the force fields around them fade away.

Power Prince moved towards them, making sure not to step in the dust that was once Impervious. "He's gone." Power Prince said as he looked from the sand to Hunter. "He is," Hunter replied as he watched the win around them whisk up what was left of his last true relative.

He had saved hundreds back home. He was a hero known the world over and had touched the lives of many. Yet here, he was just a man trying to do right by the people he had abandoned a lifetime ago. Hunter took a deep breath. "Goodbye, Mr. Impervious."

CHAPTER 38:
CONFESSIONS

Power Prince moved slowly around Hunter, making sure to not look at the pile of ash that was in front of them. For some reason, he could feel his stomach turning, and for a moment he thought he would be sick. He had seen some crazy things in his time, but never anything like a person being rapidly aged in seconds.

He extended a hand to Cayden who had dropped down to his knees and rested his hands on the ground. Sweat was still gleaming on his head, and he could barely speak from exhaustion. "Need a hand?" Power Prince asked. Cayden moved his hand slowly, and then reached into his pocket and pulled out a chunk of purple rock, and tossed it into his mouth.

"I'm good. Help Perkins." Power Prince nodded as he stretched his mouth and jerked his head while saying, "Alrighty then!" He fought a laugh as he stretched the words and wished Jen was there. She would have understood the Ace Ventura reference.

She didn't share his love for all things movie and cinema, but she did love a good Jim Carrey movie. True to his word, Power Prince dropped down slowly and hefted Perkins up from the ground, careful not to cause more pain to her injury.

As they turned, he tapped his com. "Flex come in." There was silence over the coms for a moment. Even though it was short-lived, it was enough for the people around him to pause and listen for a response. They feared that they would have to go join another fight and push their already tired bodies to new limits.

"Hey, you guys okay?" Flex finally came back. "We just got done with Manis and are en route back to you." "Don't," Hunter said through the coms. "Impervious is dead. Get The Mechanic to Acropolis. We need to see if he can come up with a solution in that lab."

"He's dead?" Flex asked slowly. "But-" His words were cut off by Power Prince this time. "Cayden used his ability to speed up time around him, once Hunter locked him down. Only dust is left of him now." "Holy shit," Danielle said back over the coms. "What about Icaro?" Flex asked. "Taken care of." Power Prince responded as he slowly walked with Perkins to where Hunter stood looking at the ashes.

"Looks like you guys had a blast," Jen said. "This Manis guy was a pushover." "That's easy to say when I was doing the pushing." Flex came back over the coms. "We all have our strengths," Jen replied. "Your strength just happens to literally be strength."

"Mechanic!" Flex suddenly blurted out. "I know you're listening." "Yes. Yes. I'm here. I have my things ready for transport to the Acropolis lab. The recruits are still spread throughout the city working with civilians." "Good," Flex said. "I'll come to get you and fly you over. Jen and Danielle will stay here and help the recruits with clean up and civilian control." "Also known as the dull part of being a hero. I noticed you aren't jumping up and down asking to stay," Jen said in a groan that was easily heard over the com.

"We all have our strengths," Hunter said to her slowly. "Very fucking funny, Paragon," she replied. "I'm not staying here," Danielle said suddenly over the coms. "I'm going to be where Hunter is. You get to see Perkins, and I want to see the person I love after a fight too." He knew she was talking to Flex, but he couldn't help but smile some at her words.

As he looked over to Power Prince, Hunter saw him mouth the words *she loves you* with a goofy face. Perkins rolled her eyes at him as she stretched her arm out to Hunter. He dipped a little and lifted her up off the ground.

She felt almost weightless. He had always had enhanced strength and had lifted people before, but he normally could still feel them pulling on his muscles some. That wasn't the case now. Now he felt like he was holding nothing. He couldn't even feel his arms strain from being held in place.

He made a mental note that when he returned and had time, that he truly needed to test these new powers Omega created within him to see how strong he was. He lifted up slowly off of the ground and as he did so, he looked at the spot where Impervious' remains were. A part of him felt like he should have gathered up the remains and did something with them, but in the end, he decided to leave them there.

In time the heated winds from the wastelands would spread the remains. Impervious would truly be a part of his world now, and Hunter felt like he would like that. Then again, what did he know? At the end, he saw that he knew so little about what made his uncle tick. Still, deep down, he knew he would miss him and the slim connection that Impervious provided to his father.

The Mechanic moved slowly around what was left of the lab. It was easy enough to find but had a steel defensive wall around it. That must have been the measures taken by Impervious to secure the lab. Under normal conditions, it would have worked but with Flex, and a newly stronger Hunter, the security measure stood little chance.

The tube housing the body of Infinity was now empty. Each person looked around the lab, but there was no sign of his body on either level. Jen stood guard outside of the lab with Cayden, just to make sure there were no other surprises left waiting for them. When they arrived, they found the body of Omega's aide, the one called Maridian.

His body, much like Omega's had been destroyed by one likely faster and stronger than he. His book was clutched in his hands but now rested in the one good arm of Perkins. She drummed her fingers over the book slowly as she bit her lip.

"What is it?" Flex asked her slowly. He stood beside her with his hand on her shoulder, wishing they had a healer around to mend the broken limb she had. Power Prince and Hunter could deal with their bruises from the fight. So could Jen and Danielle, but he hated seeing Perkins in pain.

Pain that she had an unusual tolerance for. Had he not known the arm was broken, he wouldn't have been able to tell by her actions. Only the never moving, limp limb gave her away. "This book," she finally said to answer his question. "It's got everything in it we need. Locations, ledgers, goals, personal notes on people in Omega's employ, and methods to destroy the leaders of the other sections of Mo'eizus. It even talks about secret stashes of funds this guy had hidden over the city under Omega's nose."

"That is quite the resource." Flex said slowly. "It's your golden ticket." Power Prince said from across the table. Danielle, who was sitting in Hunter's lap laughed. Power Prince glanced at her with a brow raised. Danielle shrugged. "I loved Willy Wonka as a child." "As a child?" Hunter replied. "We watch that movie every other week. I know every damn line."

She turned and glared at him with a fist balled. "Want a punch to the nuts?" "And I look forward to it every other week," Hunter said quickly as she dropped her fist and leaned on his chest while saying. "Good boy," as she pinched his cheek.

"I just don't think I could trust it with anybody if," Perkins' words faded slowly. "If what?" Hunter said. A single tear fell down her cheek as she held onto Flex's hand that was on her shoulder. "Cayden. Jen. Can you come in here," Perkins said over her shoulder in a voice just under a scream.

On cue, Cayden and Jen darted in. Jen had her sword raised. "What's wrong?" Flex motioned for her to put the sword away. "Since we are all here," Perkins said slowly. "I. I wanted to tell you about me. There is more going on than my arm."

Flex took a deep breath. He knew it was coming. The secret she had been keeping from them. Well, the secret she thought she had kept from them. "I'm sick." As she said the words Hunter leaned up in his chair and even The Mechanic who was reading a file across the room looked in her direction.

"I've known for a while now but didn't want to mention it until we finished with Omega. I have The Curse of Varo." Not a sound could be heard as she delivered the news and turned to look at Flex with pink eyes. "I'm sorry I didn't-" He leaned down and kissed her and caused her already shaky words to be cut off.

"I already knew," he replied as he pulled away from her lips. "You? But how? For how long?" Perkins asked. "Doesn't matter. I figured if you wanted me to know then, you would have told me. So, I waited until you were ready. Until now. It actually helped me with a decision I was trying to make. Well, it was one of the things that helped me anyway."

"Decision?" Hunter said slowly. "What decision?" Flex locked eyes with his intern and then scanned the room before talking. "From the moment we arrived here Perkins fell right back into her role of leader or co-leader of Bravado. I could tell from the start that she wasn't going to be able to leave them again."

Perkins took a breath as she wiped her eyes. She hated feeling so vulnerable, and wondered if the curse flowing through her made her that way. "I had wondered about the same thing," Danielle said slowly. "Maybe it was woman's intuition. Maybe I'm just super smart. But I felt something inside of me telling me that when this was over Perkins wouldn't be making the trip back with us."

"And neither will I," Flex said slowly. Questions and comments exploded around the room from all sides. All except for Power Prince. The young Icon watched as Flex looked to all the people in the room except him. Above all others, Flex looked at The Mechanic more than the rest of the team.

"What was the other thing that helped you decide to stay?" Power Prince asked. Flex took a deep breath and released his hand from Perkins' shoulder. Walking around the table slowly, he finally looked Power Prince in the eye. "The other thing that helped was learning that I didn't have a sister to return home for and try to capture, because you killed her."

"Oh shit," Hunter said as he gently shoved Danielle out of his lap and stood up. He was likely the only person in the room that could slow Flex down if he decided to attack Power Prince.

Mouth gaped open, Power Prince stood from where he was sitting. "Flex. I was going-" His words were cut off as he felt the muscular arms of Flex wrap around him. Not with aggression, but with a hug. As Power Prince looked over Flex's shoulder at the other people in the room, Jen shook her head. "I was expecting a punch."

She looked around the room. "Oh, don't act like I'm the only one." "I don't understand," Cayden said slowly. "He is happy that his friend killed his sister?" "It's complicated," Hunter said from across the table while still keeping eyes on them. "Wait," Danielle said slowly. "How did you know?" "The Mechanic told me." Flex said as he released Power Prince from the hug and gently placed his hands on the man's shoulders.

While he was looking at Power Prince, he was clearly talking to the room at large. Only The Mechanic, who was now reviewing some files on a computer and then writing on a board, wasn't listening to his every word.

"My sister was disturbed and had been that way since we were younger. She's killed more than once and would likely have done it again. She needed to be stopped and you made the hard decision. A decision I forced on you when I decided to come here." Power Prince stammered as he tried to get words out.

"You protected the people. You met with the I.C.E jerks, and you kept things in line while I was away. You even reviewed files for new members. I'm thankful for you, and I love you like a brother. That's why I'm sorry to place two more burdens on you."

Power Prince raised his brow. "What burdens?" Flex released him from his grip and returned to Perkins. "I'm staying here with Perkins. I love her, more than life itself, and regardless of what happens, I'm going to be here with her. Helping her and Cayden rebuild Bravado. This world will still need protecting as the balances of power shift. While I'm here, the New Lords will need a leader. A permanent one."

Power Prince's head jerked slightly. He had fought an internal battle within himself for so long about being a leader, and second in command. How it was easy because the buck didn't stop with him. Now here was Flex offering him the title permanently. How could he say no? He didn't actually say anything. Instead, he nodded his head first and then spoke.

"I'll do it. I'll have to find a second in command, but I'll do it. What was the second burden?" Power Prince asked. Smiling, Flex turned his head to Hunter and then to Jen. "You agree to take the role, right? No turning back." Flex asked with a grin. "You now have two new interns under your belt. For whatever time is left of their last year. Teach them well, you're welcome, and I'm sorry." Flex said with a laugh." "Funny," Hunter said under his breath as he rolled his eyes and sat back down.

"This is all well and good, but there is a bigger issue at hand here," Cayden said as he looked to Perkins. He found it odd that when she returned, he couldn't stand her, and now he was here fighting back tears at the thought of losing her. He had already lost a brother, and he didn't want to lose her too. Despite their differences, she was like family.

"How long have you been sick. How quickly is it advancing? We need to set up a place for you to rest and be monitored." Perkins went to answer but was interrupted. "Won't be a need." The Mechanic said quickly.

"What do you mean?" Perkins said slowly. "Well. The data is all here. Percentages, procedures, theories, test results, everything." The Mechanic said quickly. I have enough here to make a machine that can generate the cure. I'll need a few samples of Hunter's blood, though. Then I'll synthesize the blood and use it to create a cure. Based off of these notes it seems rather doable."

The Mechanic moved his finger down the paper in front of him and then tapped twice on the bottom. "There are two additional names on here of researchers. We will have to find them, or at least one of them to help, but that shouldn't be a problem. If they were important, they were likely guarded and protected."

He finally looked up from his work in front of him and saw a room full of smiles looking at him. "How long are we talking here? Cure wise," Cayden asked. "I'll be taking my time of course," The Mechanic said. "I want to avoid any calculation errors, but about a week." Perkins walked over to the slender man and gave him a hug.

She stepped back and looked at him as he smiled slightly. "Thank you. Not only are you saving me, but you're saving my people," She glanced at Hunter and Cayden. "Our people." The Mechanic nodded. "Indeed. However, that means that I too will not be returning." The room had already come to this conclusion once he said at least a week.

For those in the room that new him personally, they knew before then that he would be staying. The Mechanic loved what he did. He loved his work and inventions. It was his power after all. It made him the Icon that he was. Tech was his life, and from what he had let slip from time to time, he wasn't very happy with that life back home. Now he had a purpose, and to him, that meant more than any amount of money he'd be missing back in his own dimension.

"Well, I'm pretty sure there aren't any other surprises to drop on us are there?" Hunter said as he looked around the room. For the most part, everybody either shrugged or shook their head. "I'm pregnant," Danielle said out loud. The room went silent as Hunter's mouth gaped open. "Kidding. Kidding," she said quickly with a laugh. Hunter glared at her and then he noticed Flex smirking from ear to ear, and glancing to Danielle.

Danielle caught Flex looking at her and then quickly tried to act like she didn't see him. "What was that?" Hunter asked as his eyes narrowed. "What was what, boo?" Danielle said . "Oh no," Hunter said as he stood back and shook his head. "Don't boo me." Perkins laughed out loud as she failed to keep her amusement controlled.

"You told her, didn't you?" Danielle hissed. Flex whistled casually. A clear indicator that he did, in fact, confide their secret with Perkins. "Guess who has a True Name picked out?" Flex said in a tone that sounded like a song.

"You're dead Ken Doll," Danielle said as a streak of darkness replaced her eyes for a moment. "You picked a True Name and told Flex before me?" Hunter said with mock disgust. "I swear it's always the girlfriend in the end that turns on you." Danielle balled up a fist. "It's not too late for that nut punch."

Quickly a force field surrounds Hunter for a second and then faded away. "Well let's have it," Hunter said as he propped on the table. "It better be good too, after all the crap you gave me for my name." "She teased me some for selecting Mystic, too," Jen added in.

Suddenly all of the jokes she had made about their names seemed to rush back to her. Danielle didn't put much stock or respect into the name until she had selected her own. Now, she felt like she would feel some type of way if they teased her half as much as she had teased them. She took a deep breath. "Obsidian. My True Name will be Obsidian."

Jen whistled as Danielle looked around the room. "Damn. That's pretty badass." "I second that," Power Prince said. "Where were you when I was selecting my True Name?" Danielle turned slightly to face Hunter. "Well, do you like it?"

"I mean it's no Paragon, but it'll work. I guess." Hunter said with a smile. As he pulled her in close. "No more villain in the sheets, since you went all hero on me now. True Names, doing what's right, saving cities.

You're not who I thought you were." She looked up at him. "I'm going to be taking the oath too, but it's always villain in the sheets," Danielle said as she kissed him.

Jen adjusted her ball cap and walked towards the door. "Alright, you two just made it weird, and I'm hungry. Cayden, double P wanna come with?" Both men nodded and followed her out the room leaving the two couples, and a frantically reading Mechanic, in the lab.

CHAPTER 39:
BEYOND SUPREME

Perkins was still a little groggy when she finally woke up. She didn't remember much in the last few hours, but she did remember how weak she was before she had gone under. As she sat up, the makeshift medical room was all but empty, except for Flex, The Mechanic, and another short, round man with red hair in a white lab coat.

A shiver rushed over her and the noise from her teeth chattering sounded louder that she expected. The sound alerted the room that she was awake. "So?" Flex said as he sat on her cot. "I feel fine," Perkins responded. "Better than fine actually. I feel, almost like a new person." She formed a fist and flexed her arms to add emphasis to her words.

"Good. That is what we wanted to hear," the man in the lab coat said as he made some notes on a pad. "With this success, Rondo and I can start spreading the word that we have a cure." The Mechanic said.

Perkins smiled as she could feel Flex squeeze her thigh, as he looked at the men in the room. "Thank Atlas." They had found Rondo pretty quickly in the last week. The second name on the paper from the lab belonged to a woman that died in the fall of the city. With Rondo's help the creation of the machines needed for the cure, and the research work included with it went by smoothly.

Flex had noticed that Rondo and The Mechanic got along very well. For the first time in a while, The Mechanic was working with a mind as sharp as his, giving him an equal and a little bit of a challenge.

He wasn't sure, but Flex thought he had seen a few glances exchanged between the two men while they worked. He didn't know much about The Mechanic's love life from the past. He seemed to always keep that, like the rest of his personal life, private. Flex was curious to see how their partnership would develop in the long road ahead of curing an entire world.

"So, what now?" Perkins asked. "I'm cured? Good to go? Varo Free?" The Mechanic looked at some formulas on the board in front of him, and then double checked a computer screen. "We will monitor your progress and run some follow-up tests in the next few days. If everything comes back well, which I have no doubt that they will, you will be given a clean bill of health."

"Sounds good," Perkins said as she got off of the cot and gave Flex a large smile. He looked at her and for a moment seemed like a statue. "What?" she asked him. He took a breath and shook his head. "You're beautiful, you know that?" She looked down at her baggy clothes, vest, and boots. "Is it because I don't have on my goggles?" she said with a smirk.

Flex shook his head. "I'm serious. When I first saw signs of the curse in you, I tried not to think about what I'd do if I lost you. I've fought a lot of things in my life. Grew up in a family that cared about their legacy more than their own child, and faced trials that many Icons my age never should. I've been afraid once or twice. Most recently when I had to catch a city, but nothing had made me feel as hollow as the thought of losing you."

"Wow, you really know how to make a woman that just defeated death by curse, feel special don't you?" Perkins said as her cheeks turned a shade of red. "Truly beautiful," Rondo said from across the room. While he remarked on Flex's words he missed the long glance that The Mechanic gave him.

"I love you," Flex said slowly. "And I love you more, pretty boy," Perkins said quickly. "Plus being involved with the strongest person on the planet, really makes me feel good inside. Danielle and Jen said I could pretty much pick a fight with anybody and be covered."

"Don't." Flex laughed. "Don't listen to them." Perkins laughed as she did a little spin towards the door. "That cure is something else. "Flex made his way to the door behind Perkins. "Well, now that you're up, we have to go see the others off," Flex said. "They should be almost ready." "Wait." The Mechanic said as he crossed the room and removed a drive from his pocket. "Give this to Paragon."

Flex looked at it and then to The Mechanic. "It's something he requested." Flex nodded his head and stored the drive in his pocket before leaving the medical room behind Perkins.

Inside the main area of the base, various tasks were being completed by the recruits. Each member of the team had a file in their hand as they worked. Some moved large carts with various parts in and out of the room. Others slowly set up large monitors, and a few just did the cleaning. While they worked Cayden and Hunter stood on a raised level and watched.

"They're like ants, almost aren't they?" Hunter said as he watched them quickly move around the base. One recruit walked by with a gun that looked like a blow torch, and then rose in the air by a flight band to begin working on the beams above them. "They are determined I'll say that. We didn't expect so many new people to want to join, but after word spread of what we did to Omega we transformed from a band of rebels to local heroes overnight. Although, some still curse our names. Mostly those that were once in favor with Omega," Cayden replied.

"Tell me about it," Jen said as she walked up and dropped a large duffel bag on the floor. She looked up and snapped her fingers and a recruit appeared out of nowhere and snatched the bag from her before trotting off. She adjusted her cap on her head and hefted her covered sword in her hand.

"Seriously, the base is crawling with people now. No wonder we had to relocate from that crappy backup base you all were in." Hunter nodded as he looked around. The new base was certainly larger. It had more rooms and space than both of the previous bases combined. "Say what you will about Omega, but the lady owned some damn nice buildings," Cayden said.

"She had the right idea," Hunter said slowly. "So did Perkins. Suggesting you all move here for a fresh start for Bravado was a good call." Power Prince and Danielle, both carrying bags similar to the one Jen had moments ago, walked up and gently placed them on the ground. Only this time, a recruit didn't come and take it from them.

"That it?" Hunter asked. Power Prince looked down at the bags and shrugged his shoulders. "I guess so. The Mechanic dropped it off at my room last night and said it was the stuff he talked to you about."

"What is it?" Danielle asked. "My dear Obsidian, that is a surprise for us all." Danielle raised a brow and then glanced down at the bags. "So, now that everything is up and running, what are you going to do, Cayden?" Hunter asked as he turned to look at the youth.

"I mean you're elite, so you have the right to, well rule I suppose." Cayden shook his head. "I don't think that's for me. I think it's better that the time of elites ruling the world has passed. I've spoken to Perkins about it, and I think I'm going to take my brother's spot as a leader of Bravado."

"Good call." Power Prince added in. "From one new leader to another, it will do your team good to have you around. You've got experience and, if I'm being honest, the power to really make a difference. Especially as you guys get this curse stuff handled. Being immune will greatly aid you."

"Well look who is up and running again," Jen said as Perkins and Flex walked through a sliding metal door. Over the next few minutes, greetings were made as they all talked to Perkins and got detailed information on how she felt after the cure was given to her. Among the chatter, Hunter saw Flex look at him and jerk his head to the side.

Flex quickly left the crowd and waited to the side. "What's up?" Hunter asked as he came over. "The Mechanic asked me to give you this. He didn't go into detail over it, though." Hunter looked at the drive in Flex's hand and smiled. "That fast-talking son of a bitch came through."

"I guess so," Flex said as he looked over to the crowd. "Hey what do we know about Danielle's parents? Anything." Hunter grimaced as he looked at Flex, and then looked to Danielle as she talked in the crowd. "I mean," Hunter said slowly. "The normal stuff. I suppose. She had a mom and dad, but wasn't raised by them. She never really knew her birth parents, and the people she ended up with weren't exactly model citizens. That's why she was a villain when I met her." His brow raised. "Why?"

Flex remained passive, but Hunter could see him clenching his jaw. "I don't know. It's just that while we were here, I've gotten a chance to see her use her powers more. Way more than back home, and she's stronger than we thought. I just can't test my theory here. We don't have the stuff we do back at the base. Not yet anyway."

Hunter shook his head. "It's likely the Two-Fold thing. She's stronger at night, and we don't see her use her powers much at night." Flex looked from the rest of the team talking and catching up, and back to Hunter. "I don't think that's it. I saw her control the night for a second, back when we were fighting. Like literally the darkness around us seemed to react to her."

Hunter didn't reply this time. Instead, he whistled and looked at Danielle. "Man, can I pick'em or can I pick'em. Supreme level darkness powers are rare." Flex shook his head. "You don't get it. Darkness is a fundamental force. It's part of the universe itself. When an Icon has darkness abilities it's normally just energy that is dark in color. True darkness control like what Danielle has puts her in a rare class already. That's why few can take her shadow form. But rare, doesn't always mean powerful."

Flex paused and looked at Danielle once more. "But if our Obsidian really did control the natural darkness around her, that puts her at a level far beyond Supreme. I wouldn't even know what to call it." Hunter let the words Flex just said sink in. What could be beyond supreme? He made a mental note not to make his lover angry anytime soon.

"My thought is that she doesn't know how powerful she really is, and until test are done or you find out about her history, you don't tell her," Flex said as he patted Hunter's shoulder. "Should I tell this to Power Prince? He's in charge now." "I already spoke to him about it, last night," Flex said. "You two will figure it out I'm sure."

"Hate to break this up boys, but we have to go," Danielle said as she walked over and wrapped her arm around Hunter's waist. He looked down at his longtime girlfriend and kissed her on the head. His previous conversation with Flex dancing around in his mind as he tried to understand the powershift in his relationship.

For as long as he could remember, Hunter was the powerful one. He had power, and unlike all other Icons, he had four. By definition, he was one of the most uniquely gifted Icons on the planet. Naturally, he would find the one person whose hidden potential was so great that there wasn't even a name for it. "Some guys get all the luck," he said under his breath as they walked to the rest of the team.

"Alright," Perkins said as she gave Power Prince something that looked like a cell phone made out of blue metal. "What's this?" he asked. "New version of a multibox," Perkins replied. It's already pre- set to the destination Hunter gave The Mechanic and Rondo. It also has a screen and connection to his counterpart." As she said this part, Flex held up a multibox that looked identical to it except it was red.

"Anytime you need anything, I'm a call away," Flex said. Jen frowned. "It can call across dimensions?" Perkins shrugged. "That's what I've been told and I don't ask questions. I wouldn't understand the answer if I did. They healed me, so I trust em."

Jen shook her head. "Point taken." Danielle and Hunter both lifted up the duffle bags of the floor. "Well Ken Doll, until next time," Hunter said with a smile as he extended his hand to Flex. "Don't worry. I'm still going to visit. Pretty often actually. We still have to keep our fights going. It's pretty much tradition now, and with your new power you might be a challenge and I won't have to hold back."

Hunter's smile shifted to a glare. "Bet on it, pretty boy," he said as he applied pressure to Flex's hand. The smile on Flex's face shifted into confusion as he looked down to his hand, and then back to Hunter. He didn't say it, but the strength he felt on his hand from his former intern was more than he expected. Possibly enough to really give him a challenge.

"I hate goodbyes, see you laters, and all that," Jen said. "If we drag it out, I'll cry." she leaned in and pressed a button on the multibox in Power Prince's hand. Instantly the green portal that they had all became familiar with burst into existence. Jen tipped her cap at them all and jumped into the portal.

"It's been fun," Power Prince said as he stepped into the portal. "Good luck," Flex said as Power Prince nodded to him, and then stepped into the portal. Danielle gave them all a hug and then was next to take the jump. As she hugged Flex, Hunter noticed that his former leader gave him a long glance. Hunter pursed his lips and nodded in return.

"Okay, I'm off," Hunter said as Cayden, Flex, and Perkins stood in front of him. "They likely already have questions about the landing space," he said as he hefted the bag over his shoulder. He turned towards the portal and then faced them again.

"If you need anything. Don't think twice about giving us a call." "Will do," Flex said. "I was talking to Cayden." Hunter said with a smirk. "I'm leaving him here with you two. The guy will never have any fun." Perkins, Cayden, and even Flex smiled.

"Don't you have too much fun your damn self," Flex replied. "Your internship will be over sooner than you think Training wheels come off, and you're a full- blown hero." "You know me," Hunter replied. "Fun. Gray zone. Bend the rules. That's pretty much my motto." He gave a final wave and then jumped into the portal.

In what seemed like seconds, Hunter landed on the ground. Feet first this time. He lifted his bag and it felt the same as it did before he went in the portal. "Nothing missing then," he said to himself as he looked around. The others were standing away from him, looking at a large building, that looked like a condemned warehouse of some sort. They could see water around them and in the distance, several barges passed by.

"Where in Atlas are, we?" Power Prince asked as he turned to Hunter. "This," Hunter said as he stretched his hand out and walked towards the building. "Is our new base." He turned to Danielle, Jen, and Power Prince. Each with confusion etched on their face as their brows raised. "Our what?" Danielle asked. "Our new base. If we are going to be the New Lords, then we need to shed everything that was the Imperial Lords."

"How can we-" Jen started, and then looked at a smiling Hunter. "You paid for all this?" Hunter nodded. "The entire lot." "How? When?" Jen asked as she took a few steps back to look at the warehouse.

It was large from what she could see. Easily four stories, large windows on the front that faced the water around then, and more graffiti that several subway cars could combine. "I purchased it before all this rescue mission stuff went down. It was to be a surprise after everything got finalized." Hunter said as he put a hand on his hip.

"This old girl has over ten thousand square feet. Best two mill I ever spent." "Two million dollars?" Jen and Power Prince said at once. Hunter shrugged his shoulders. "Give or take."

Jen adjusts her cap and gave him a side glance. "Dad know about this?" "Course he does," Hunter replied. "We had a talk and he felt it was time I handled the money my dad left me. I've got access to my entire fortune now."

Danielle raised a hand slowly. "How much of a fortune are we talking?" "Yeah man, how rich are you?" Power Prince added. "Rich enough that dropping two million on a single purchase didn't even scrape the surface."

Jen whistled. "Dad may have been a villain, but let's not forget he was the best at it. Now come on. Contractors should already be working on the inside. All we gotta do is get this place up and running in a few months, and then start on auditions for new members. But first," He dropped down beside the bag that Danielle had and unzipped both.

Inside of each bag was a large, sleek, tower-like device. One tower had a slot for a drive, and the other had a cord to connect the two. After he connected the machines in the bag, he gently inserted the drive. As he stood back the machines began to hum, as lights slowly blinked to life on the sides of the towers. "Hello, young Lords." A voice came from out of the air as a hologram appeared in front of them.

"Prism?" Danielle said in shock. "The one and only," the holographic butler said as he took a bow. "The Mechanic set all this up so he could be in the new base," Hunter said as he patted one of the sleek towers before he turned and looked at the shabby area in front of them all. "Now, our legacy as the New Lords begins."

"Unless you guys want a name change?" He asked out loud as he wrapped a force field around the equipment inside of the bags, and lifted it off the ground. "New Lords is fine with me," Power Prince said. "Same," Danielle muttered. "Well you know I'm not picky," Jen said as she stretched a fist out to Hunter.

He bumped it and smirked before turning to look at the building. "Then New Lords it is."

EPILOGUE
SIX MONTHS LATER

Sun shined through the glass and touched the back of Hunter's neck. He sat on a smooth bench made out of white polished stone and looked at the trees as the waterfall flowed gently near him. This was perhaps one of his favorite places in the new base.

Who knew having a fancy courtyard to visit every day would do so much for his soul? There were several stone benches like the one he sat on, but very few people, outside of approved visitors, even used them. The rest of his team would rather spend their time doing other things instead of sitting and listening to water flow around them.

Jen was usually in her room, or one of their luxury kitchens. Power Prince was either training with Danielle in the simulated arena or spending time in the movie theater. That was the only request that their leader had as the new base was being built and designed six months ago. A world-class movie theater. One that played movies of the highest quality, and streamed all of the companies he subscribed too, and there were a lot of those.

Hunter preferred the simplicity of their courtyard. If he wasn't there, then he would normally fly over to Ages Park, talk to his parent's statue, and then head back home. To be as popular as he was, he enjoyed keeping a low- profile life until the last few months of his internship were up. He glanced down at his watch and realized he had about fifteen minutes before he had to be at the arena.

All of his paperwork was in a folder beside him, and he made sure to bring a red pen. The last few weeks of auditions had been horrible. Various Icons with powers great and small wanted to be members of the New Lords.

Many didn't even know why. They just heard about the auditions and showed up. Others truly wanted to belong to a team, but none seemed to fit what they were looking for. The guy coming by today did seem promising.

Gleam, the teleporter that helped Power Prince transport to his showdown with Zeva, recommended him as a family friend. He looked good on paper, but then again, they all did.

"Figured we'd find you out here." Power Prince said as he strolled over with Jen. Power Prince had on his official black and orange uniform, while Jen had on pajamas and a baseball cap. She really did wear those with anything.

"Casual day?" Hunter asked as he glanced at Jen. "The world didn't need saving, so I'm relaxing as much as I can. Sasha is coming over later, though. So, I'll come out of these eventually." "Too much information," Hunter said as he laughed at his adopted sister. "Right. Don't forget we shared a wall in our younger years. The years when we didn't have as much of a selection process with our lovers," Jen said back.

"Point made," Hunter replied.

Power Prince looked around and nodded his head. "You know, even after six months I can't get over this place." "Why's that?" Hunter said as he stood up and stretched. "He was wearing a newer version of his Paragon outfit. He had to break it in before being seen out in town with it, and the line of toys associated with the outfit were set to be limited editions so he couldn't wear it much.

"Dude, the Imperial Lords' base was great. Like great, great. Top of the line tech, and never a dull moment. For Atlas' sake, I met you in a random hallway and look how all that turned out." Power Prince began to walk towards a large circular bubble near the end of the courtyard, with Jen and Hunter behind him.

He placed his hand on the surface, and the bubble opened slowly as they all stepped in. The door shut behind Jen and they began to move. Hunter hated these bubbles. He had requested they be a little larger, but they were unable to make it happen, despite the amount of money Hunter had spent on everything.

"I say all that because our new digs seem better to me. I didn't think it could be done, but you did it. You may be the best intern ever." Power Prince said with a laugh. "And the most paranoid," Jen added in.

"The security system, hidden weapons around the base, cameras, and defensive robots are part of the package I purchased. Plus, in my short time being an intern, I've clashed with some of the strongest people to walk the Earth. I know my luck and whatever comes next won't be a cake walk. The last thing I want is a base that is easily taken over, or taken down."

"Pussy," Jen said quickly. "While I have you both here," Power Prince said as the glass bubble slowed and opened again. "I want to touch base on the Danielle topic." they stepped out of the bubble and walked by several robots that were working on the landscaping.

They were an added perk by the company that did their security, and as chance would have it, were designed by The Mechanic while he was on the free market. The robots were responsible for doing all of the random chores around the base. Cleaning, landscaping, and random patrols. If the task were to arise, they were fully capable of putting up a good fight against lower level to average Icons.

Power Prince was the first to step into the glass elevator. The elevator was Hunter's design. While it was a closed space, the open glass made it feel large, and thus his phobia didn't hit him so hard. "What about it?" Hunter asked slowly. He had told Power Prince that he wanted to bring Jen in on what Flex had suspected.

"We can't seem to find her real parents. It's as if they don't exist." Jen groaned as they continued their descent to the lower levels. "She's a human right?" Jen asked. "Yes, she's a human, idiot," Hunter replied, but then glanced at Power Prince. "Right?" Power Prince nodded.

"She is. All of the blood work done on her when I decided we all need physicals, came back normal. Some things were elevated, but they were normal. I have Prism, and some brainy Icons looking into it, but for now, we have no clue of what her stock is, or why she may be as strong as Flex thought she was."

Jen adjusted her cap and crossed her arms. "Maybe we should just ask her?" Power Prince shook his head. "I don't want her to know anything until we do. Danielle is strong, but some things can still fuck up your day. Not knowing who you truly are or where you come from is one of them."

They all agreed to keep the secret to themselves as the elevator doors opened. As they walked down the long hall, Prism appeared. "Young Lords, your guest is waiting for you in the training arena." "Thank you, Prism," Power Prince said.

"I'm a state- of- the- art system, with functions that rival some of the most advanced computer interfaces in the world. I'm able to run various task with unmatched speed. Naturally, I enjoy playing the role of a humble butler. That is what my design is after all." Prism said as the hologram flickered in and out of view.

"And I feared you'd lose your smart mouth when we removed you completely from the old base," Jen said. "We could have left him there," Hunter said with a smile. "They destroyed the lower levels' but the museum is still up top. He could have been the best worker there."

The hologram took a slight bow. "Good day, Young Lords," and then he flickered out of existence. "You two keep teasing him and he is going to turn all these security measures on us in our sleep." Power Prince said as he entered some buttons on a keypad. Once he did so, the large metal door in front of them pulled away in various spots and allowed them entry into the training arena.

There was a round table that was floating about four feet off the ground with four chairs around it. Danielle sat in one chair and tapped her red pen loudly as she watched them walk over. "Took you two long enough," Danielle said. "I asked you to go get him, not take a casual stroll around the complex." Hunter leaned in to kiss her cheek and sat down beside her.

She was dressed in a white form-fitting outfit that showed off her figure more than Hunter liked. She thought it was funny to have darkness powers, be called Obsidian, yet have a full white outfit. Danielle was told the outfit was a part of her deal she worked out with the government.

All Icons that wanted to be heroes, had to intern. There was no way around that, and Power Prince technically had three now. Had Life-Line not still been tied to the team, the New Lords wouldn't be an official group and thus none of them would be able to intern. He kept his distance but on paper, he was still around. He had pulled some strings and called in a few favors, but he had worked things out in Danielle's favor.

She took the oath in front of the right people and was awarded time served for her time with the New Lords. Training, missions, otherworldly trips, everything counted towards her internship officially now. She would be rewarded with the title of hero the same time Jen and Hunter would.

Once they all got settled in, Hunter opened his folder and passed each of them a sheet of paper. Power Prince looked at the paper and then looked at the only other person in the room. Standing no less than ten feet away from their table was a casually dressed man with brown skin.

He had on some loose blue jeans, a gray shirt, and a black jacket. "Gregory Turner." Power Prince said casually. The young man nodded. "It's just Greg," he said in a relaxed voice. Hunter looked the man over and got a feeling already that he was different. All the previous auditions seemed to throw themselves at the New Lords.

They still had some fame around Atlas City after the Infinity incident, and many wanted to shake their hands, take selfies with them. A few even asked for autographs. Truthful, they didn't act like heroes. This Greg guy was different. He didn't even seem to care who they were.

"Alright Greg, give us the rundown. True Name, power, background, and why you want to join the New Lords." Greg smiled. "So, you want me to tell you everything that is on the application in front of you?"

"I like him already," Hunter said as he shifted in his seat. "Ditto," Jen said. Greg cleared his throat as he clasped his hands together. "My name is Greg Turner. Originally from Regalville, and the number one graduate from Celestial Institute in my year." Greg could see the smirk on Power Prince's face. "That's right, the rival school of the world-famous Paragon Academy. Don't worry, I won't judge you guys." Greg said with a grin.

"Moving on, where was I? Did my internship under the Justice Heralds but was told I had some temper issues. Decided to work alone after that because I didn't like the pack mentality of a supergroup. After what happened to my cousin, my mother suggested I join your team. That's when she reached out to Gleam."

Each member looked down at their applications in front of them. "I don't see that last part on here." Power Prince said. "What happened to your cousin?" Greg shook his head. "Wrong place at the wrong time. He was a target on Infinities hit list. You two were there when he died." Greg said as he pointed towards Jen and Hunter.

Power Prince and Danielle looked at them and raised a brow. Hunter thought to himself about what Greg had said and then his mouth dropped open. "Young Pyro was your cousin?" Hunter suddenly found himself the one who was in awe.

"Indeed, he was. My mom didn't want me running alone after that, and we decided the best place to be was with people that took down my cousin's killer." The room was silent for a moment before Power Prince gave Greg a nod.

"Right. Um, my True Name is Orbit Fury, and my power is that I'm a radial Elementalist." This was the part they all truly waited for. Elementalists weren't rare, in fact most supergroups had a few on staff.

A person controlling one element wasn't really great. Two was better, but a person that could master them all was rare. Very rare. "Define what that means," Jen said quickly. As Greg smirked, a bubble expanded from him. It wasn't like a force field that Hunter could create. It was more so a heat haze in the air around them that that could see.

The bubble expanded around forty feet with Greg being at its center. Then suddenly, it began to snow. Danielle looked around and stuck her hand out as snow touched it, and then melted. Instantly the snow stopped and then the wind began to pick up with such strength that Hunter had to create a force field to protect them.

Next came rain, raging fires that seemed to dance around, and even the ground began to crack and move. In an instant, everything stopped and the heat haze of a bubble vanished. "Once I create the haze field, anything inside becomes my elemental playground," Greg said.

"So, am I in?" Power Prince looked at his team and they all gave slight nods. "Welcome to the New Lords." Power Prince said as Greg walked over and shook his hand. "You'll have to complete some paperwork, and do a trial period, but in three months you're a full- blown member."

Greg did a slight bow and then began to shake their hands. The celebration was short lived as Prism blinked into existence again. The hologram made a fancy bow to Greg. "Welcome aboard, Young Lord." Greg smiled, but looked at the team and then back to Prism.

"You'll get used to it," Power Prince said as he expected the hologram to leave, but it didn't. "What's wrong, Prism?" In response, the hologram waived its hand, and a screen appeared in the air.

It showed a city in chaos with an aerial view of a city being surrounded by military staff at the border. "That's Regalville," Greg said as he stiffened. "My mom's there. What's going on?"

He looked at Prism. "Apparently there is an Icon by the name of Wraith that has created quite the fuss." "They're locking down the city for a single

Icon?" Hunter asked as he continued to watch the live feed. "It appears that this Icon is a necromancer."

Everybody in the room looked at Prism. "Of the supreme level," the hologram continued. "Necromancers don't exist," Danielle said slowly. "Do they?" "The people of Regalville seem to think so." Prism said. "Our assistance has been requested." The hologram continued. Power Prince took a deep breath and glanced at Greg, and then to Hunter. No words were exchanged as the white force field came into life around them. "I can get myself there. Thanks, though," Greg said as Hunter pulled the force field in some and allowed Greg to step out.

His heat haze formed around him, and with it came winds so loud that they could be heard by the rest of the team. He slowly raised off the ground. "Prism." Power Prince said. "On it, sir."

The roof of the training arena opened and exposed them all to the open sky. Greg was the first to take off, being propelled by his own wind control. "We ready?" Hunter asked as he looked at the rest of his team. "Are you?" Power Prince asked. "This will be the first mission where you get to use your new powers fully. You're our heavy hitter now that Flex is gone." "No pressure, boo," Danielle said with a smile.

Hunter smirked. "I was always the heavy hitter." With those words, he lifted them all through the air with little effort as he slowly began to unleash his new power. With a slight pop, they exploded through the air to face this new enemy. This supposed necromancer. This, Wraith.

THE END

The New Lords will return in: Wraith: An Icon Story

www.ingramcontent.com/pod-product-compliance
Lightning Source LLC
Chambersburg PA
CBHW020601310726
48979CB00008B/1291/J

* 9 7 8 1 6 4 5 7 0 3 4 5 7 *